Praise for
"DRINKING FROM THE STREAM"

"*Drinking from the Stream* was an absolute pleasure to read. The story is captivating, the description of Africa is so accurate, and it is all well written. It reminded me of Ernest Hemingway's stories set in East Africa! Probably because I live here and because I am an avid photographer, I could easily picture the scenes in my mind while reading. I wish I could do a trip like that! This book would be a great script for a Netflix series. *Drinking from the Stream* threads together the personal journeys of its two main characters with the chaotic postcolonial shifts of the 1970s in East Africa. The up and down emotions of Jake and Karl are very palpable as they navigate both their inner conflicts and their way through this part of the world reeling from dramatic changes. Through his many years in Africa, Richard Sacks has managed to capture vivid details creating a captivating atmosphere that immerses the reader in this African drama. And I mean it when I write that this would be a great film script."

—Philippe Demoulin, businessman, Dar es Salaam, Tanzania

"After finishing *Drinking from the Stream*, I was struck by its insights into a continent and history so unfamiliar to many of us in the contemporary Western world. Set during the early 1970s, the novel follows the intertwined lives of characters navigating personal growth and survival amidst political turmoil and revolutionary chaos. From the oil fields of Louisiana to the heart of postindependence Africa, Richard Scott Sacks paints a vivid picture of a generation caught between upheaval and discovery, constructing a gripping narrative that spans years, nations, and profound human truths."

—Anthony Horton, author of *Unpaved*

"With a Jack Kerouac–like writing style, Richard Sacks takes us on an odyssey across 1970s East Africa, at once breathtaking and backbreaking! The pace is fast and sustained. Adventures come in rapid fire, from the lighthearted ones to the imprisonments and death threats. The landscape, natural or human, is ever present and vibrant, the reader bouncing along on the top of trucks across East Africa's dirt roads, facing arbitrary custom officers, and meeting generous souls. In the middle of all of that, there is love (and pregnancies!), there is running away (as one character puts it to another on their very first encounter: 'What are you running away from?'), there is self-discovery, there is conceit, and there is heart-wrenching tragedy.
"The novel doubles as a textbook on postcolonial African politics and history, with in-depth and insightful discussions of events in Ethiopia, Kenya, Uganda, Tanzania, DR Congo, Rwanda, and Burundi. Characters offer different perspectives on trends and events in their casual conversations. It is a colorful bunch: Americans, Germans, Australians, a Frenchman, a South African, Ugandans, and more.

"*Drinking from the Stream* is both a compelling novel and an insightful essay. Highly recommended."

—Pierre Englebert, H. Russell Smith professor of international relations, professor of African politics, Pomona College

"Two young men fleeing early-1970s America for very different reasons are thrown together by happenstance on a hitchhiking tour of seething East Africa. What could possibly go wrong?

"*Drinking from the Stream* sweeps the reader along with them in a picaresque coming-of-age narrative that is always engaging and sometimes downright harrowing. Richard Sacks masterfully weaves colorful descriptions of a part of the world that for centuries was a blank spot on Western maps with clear explanations of the ethnic and political forces threatening to tear it apart. As Jake and Karl wrestle with issues like personal responsibility and racism—both in their own lives and playing out before their eyes—they accidentally stumble into one of the worst ethnic atrocities of the era. Their repeated near-death escapes will keep you spellbound. A great read."

—Thomas F. Daughton, former US ambassador to Namibia

"*Drinking from the Stream* is much more than the story of two surprising travel companions exploring Africa in a time of often violent change and the friends they meet on the way. I thoroughly enjoyed reading this book, especially the conversations the travelers strike up with locals and with the other travelers they meet. Their discussions of local politics and their reflections on their perspectives were genuinely insightful.

"As someone from Duesseldorf, I'd like to tell German readers that while this book touches on a variety of countries in Africa and their troublesome postcolonial power struggles, it is not oblivious to the general world political and post-World War II context. It was fascinating to me how one of the essential characters, Beatrice, a strong-willed, opinionated, and direct young woman from Essen in Germany, struggles to come to terms with Germany's Nazi past and how much the Nazi regime's ideas and people in power persisted within the Federal Republic even twenty-five years after the end of World War II."

—Johanna Brusa, German foreign service officer, New York

"In his debut novel *Drinking from the Steam*, Richard Scott Sacks captures the rise of East African dictatorships in the 1970s as seen through the eyes of a new generation keen to understand the world and themselves. A compelling story of despair wrought by prejudice, these sharp-witted young people travel through Uganda, Rwanda, and Burundi during waves of political violence, navigating the horrors of inhumane brutality against a backdrop of the beauty of African landscapes. Throughout their trials and adventures, Sacks's cast reaffirms the depths of human solidarity and affection.

"I respect this powerful narrative of bold adventure and personal discovery of a generation 'roughing it' through Africa and escaping death and captivity armed only with their wits, tenacity, and deep friendships."

—Andrew Robert Young,
former US ambassador to Burkina Faso

"Journey with Jake and Karl as their adventures lead them deep into the perilous, turbulent world of revolutionary East Africa.... Gripping."

—Bob Dorgan, USN veteran,
author of *Sea Pay: An Enlisted Man's Naval Adventure*

"A great story set in a fresh locale. Enjoy it!"

—R. M. Koster,
National Book Award nominee

"Richard Sacks's book *Drinking from the Stream* drew me in from the very first page. What a read! A group of young people, most of them Americans, travel around Africa Kerouac-style during the early 1970s, eating and drinking and making love and running out of money and lighting into political arguments and, often, almost getting themselves killed as revolution and war break out around them.

"The political upset and revolutions are history: Haile Selassie was indeed about to be overthrown at that time, Idi Amin had begun his massacres in Uganda, Hutus in Rwanda had been murdering Tutsis en masse for a decade, and Burundi was on a knife's edge. The group's conversations about antisemitism, the Holocaust, racism, and injustice take place just as new African holocausts are unfolding right in front of them. The book is gripping, absorbing, and the reader will want to join in the arguments with the benefit of historical hindsight. And then there's a backstory of murder on shipboard involving one of the characters that is purest Melville. In fact, *Drinking from the Stream* constantly reminds the reader of Melville: personal and immediate and more fatalist than not, as the travelers come to realize that their own survival is at stake.

"I read the book in one sitting, could not put it down, anxious to know if they'd get out of the turbulence alive. Sacks is a talented writer who knows how to spin a highly believable tale, and you'll come away not just entertained but also shaken by how such inhuman mass violence could take place in so many countries with the outside world paying so little attention. And the beautiful descriptions of Africa as the protagonists travel from here to there will make you want to get on the next flight to Nairobi. A must-read."

—Paul Berg, former US diplomat

"From the first pages of *Drinking from the Stream*, you are quickly engaged with the characters, Jake and Karl, as their personal journeys intertwine. You care about them as their paths take you through personal crises and growth against the backdrop of developing and revolutionary Africa in the early 1970s. Finally, you cheer for them as they survive the trials of beautifully depicted Africa travels and emerge with a truer, if sadder, understanding of themselves and the world.

"I highly recommend this wonderful, poignant story of life, love, exploration, adventure, and friendship."

—C. Silver

"A chance meeting turns two unlikely friends, Jake and Karl, into fast travel companions on an escapade across East Africa. As they seek new adventures and run from themselves, they land headlong in the middle of Burundi's 1972 genocide. From vibrant markets teeming with color and life, the adventurers are soon caught up in a violent race war, chronicling the terror of death squads and mass executions. Sacks takes you through gut-wrenching twists and turns with muscular prose that will keep you turning the pages to the end."

—Sara Gay Forden, author of *House of Gucci: A Sensational Story of Murder, Madness, Glamour and Greed*

"I just finished *Drinking from the Stream* by Richard Sacks. I am a big fan of historical novels. *Drinking from the Stream* reminds me of the works of Edward Rutherford and Ken Follett. What a wonderful way to learn about real history through the eyes of a set of interesting characters. Here, the richness of East African culture, geography, and turbulent social upheaval are described in brilliant detail as a handful of young Westerners travel throughout the region. Well done, Richard. You've created a page-turner in this, your first novel."

—Richard Hess, coauthor of *Night of the Bear*

Drinking From the Stream
by Richard Scott Sacks

© Copyright 2025 Richard Scott Sacks

ISBN 979-8-88824-643-6

All rights reserved. No part of this publication may be reproduced, stored in a retrieval system, or transmitted in any form or by any means—electronic, mechanical, photocopy, recording, or any other—except for brief quotations in printed reviews, without the prior written permission of the author.

This is a work of fiction. All the characters in this book are fictitious, and any resemblance to actual persons, living or dead, is purely coincidental. The names, incidents, dialogue, and opinions expressed are products of the author's imagination and are not to be construed as real.

Edited by Joe Coccaro
Cover Design by Catherine Herold

Published by

köehlerbooks™

3705 Shore Drive
Virginia Beach, VA 23455
800-435-4811
www.koehlerbooks.com

DRINKING FROM THE STREAM

A NOVEL

RICHARD SCOTT SACKS

VIRGINIA BEACH
CAPE CHARLES

DEDICATION

*This book is for my mother
Dorothy Tobin Sacks
who always wanted to hear Africa stories*

EPIGRAPH

"He will render judgment upon the nations, and they will be filled with corpses; He will crush heads over a vast land. He will drink from the stream on the way, and so will hold his head high."

— Psalm 110

"– for each of us going home must be like going to render an account – Say what you like – one must return with a clear consciousness."

— Joseph Conrad, *Lord Jim*

Table of Contents

1. GIANT KILLER 5
2. HEATHROW 16
3. THE GREAT ESCAPE 22
4. BLOOD RIVER 35
5. THE ITCH 44
6. TWO CONVERSATIONS 50
7. BALLIOL 54
8. DECISIONS 61
9. ADDIS 65
10. KEMBOLCHA 72
11. TURIYE FENTAW 81
12. THE EMPIRE'S HONORED GUESTS 96
13. HOW TO DO IT 107
14. BEFORE THE MAST 124
15. ABDULLAH'S 129
16. BEATRICE 142
17. LAMU BEACH 149

18. TONY 163

19. MOMENTS OF CLARITY 171

20. OUR MAN IN UGANDA 177

21. FORT PORTAL 190

22. DERELICT'S DELIGHT 199

23. MOUNTAINS OF THE MOON 213

24. BLOOD ON THE KNIFE 232

25. END OF THE ROAD 242

26. MAY DAY 256

27. SERGEANT MASINDA 268

28. BY THE LAKE 271

29. MAYI MULÉLÉ 282

30. HAROLD HIGGINS 287

31. TWO IF BY SEA 294

32. JOURNEY'S END 297

MAPS AND PHOTOS

Map 1 – East Africa, Late 1960s.................................. 4

Map 2 – Karl And Jake's Route, Ethiopia 1971 95

Map 3 – Karl And Jake's Route, Addis To Kampala .. 123

Map 4 – Fort Portal To Rwanda And Zaire 231

Map 5 – Jake And Karl's Route
To Burundi And Tanzania 241

Photo – *Ugandan President Idi Amin
And Former King Ntare V Of Burundi,
March 30, 1972*... 255

Foreword

Drinking from the Stream is a tale of modern Africa. The story takes place in 1971, 1972, and 1973, a time of violent upheaval when the Vietnam War and the Chinese Cultural Revolution marked a generation. The action spans ten countries, from Louisiana and the United States to Tanzania.

When *Stream*'s characters entered Uganda in 1972, a year after General Idi Amin overthrew President Milton Obote, mass killing was already in full swing. Yet Amin could not rule Uganda without the guns of his soldiers. Amin feared anyone, military or civilian, who might still be loyal to Obote. He opted to kill as many Obote supporters as he could. The killings started within the army and quickly grew to tens of thousands.

Post-independence Africa was unstable and very poor. Social change had been frozen for close to a century within nonsense colonial borders. Self-government was novel and untested. Political challengers—and there were many—incited armed uprisings, military coups, and merciless ethnic slaughter. In the years after 1960, the Great Lakes region—especially Uganda, Rwanda, Burundi, and the eastern parts of the Democratic Republic of the Congo (later renamed Zaïre), plus Ethiopia—experienced a level of mayhem that few Westerners understood or now remember.

Aside from Uganda, Rwanda and Burundi also were poorly equipped to cope with the rigors of independence. These two tiny former African kingdoms both counted a minority cattle-owning caste—Tutsis—and a majority agricultural caste of free peasants—the Hutus. In both countries, the traditional ruler, the king, was called the Mwami. But by introducing democratic politics the Belgians wrecked the centuries-old traditions that shored up stability. Free elections gave politicians in both countries the tools to mobilize Hutus as an oppressed underclass and a path to power. The first years of independence brought political assassinations, massacres, tides of refugees, and military coups. By 1972, Hutu soldiers ruled Rwanda and Tutsi soldiers ruled Burundi.

During the spring of 1972 bloody events overtook Burundi. They turned on a story so outlandish that no one could have invented it. Stewing in suspicion the ruling Tutsi military clique under President Michel Micombero was busy arresting rival Tutsis whom, they feared, were plotting to oust them from power and reinstate the Burundi monarchy. Then the unexpected struck. Not one, but two Black Swans occurred within a month of each other—an apparition followed by the Apocalypse.

First, the twenty-four-year-old ex-king Charles Ntare, the former Mwami Ntare V, arrived unannounced after six years in exile on a Ugandan helicopter, almost literally parachuting into Burundi. Charles was immediately arrested; the country was plunged into the deepest doubts about why he had returned. Conspiracy theories were rampant. Many imagined that Charles commanded an army of foreign mercenaries poised for invasion.

Meanwhile, as Burundi was freaking out about Charles, no one dreamed that Hutu revolutionaries, who for years had been patiently burrowing underground like Marx's Old Mole, were on the eve of launching an insurrection against Tutsi power. A month after Charles appeared the bloodstained Hutu revolt broke like a thunderclap. The timing was unfortunate—or perfect. Panic followed panic. Then confusion. Then savage vengeance.

When I first sat down to write this novel I wanted to capture in one fictional narrative the hardships of coming of age and making one's way in the world; to explore the unexpected, unpredictable consequences—good and bad—of personal decisions, the enduring blessings of friendship, and the joys of discovery; to illustrate the state of mind that propels adventurous youth to travel to strange and distant lands, and spend month after month on bad roads with little money.

Stream has several themes: Politics, of course, that endless contest for human allegiance; racism, that stupid plague; the lust for revenge and murder that infects the human species; the perennial lie or deluded dream that overthrowing the existing order—revolution, in other words—will right every wrong and resolve every social ill; and despite all, humankind's everlasting duty and will to resist injustice, oppression and tyranny.

I hope you enjoy reading *Stream* as much as I enjoyed writing it. And I'd love to hear your honest opinions as a review on Amazon. Or write to me via richardsacks.com.

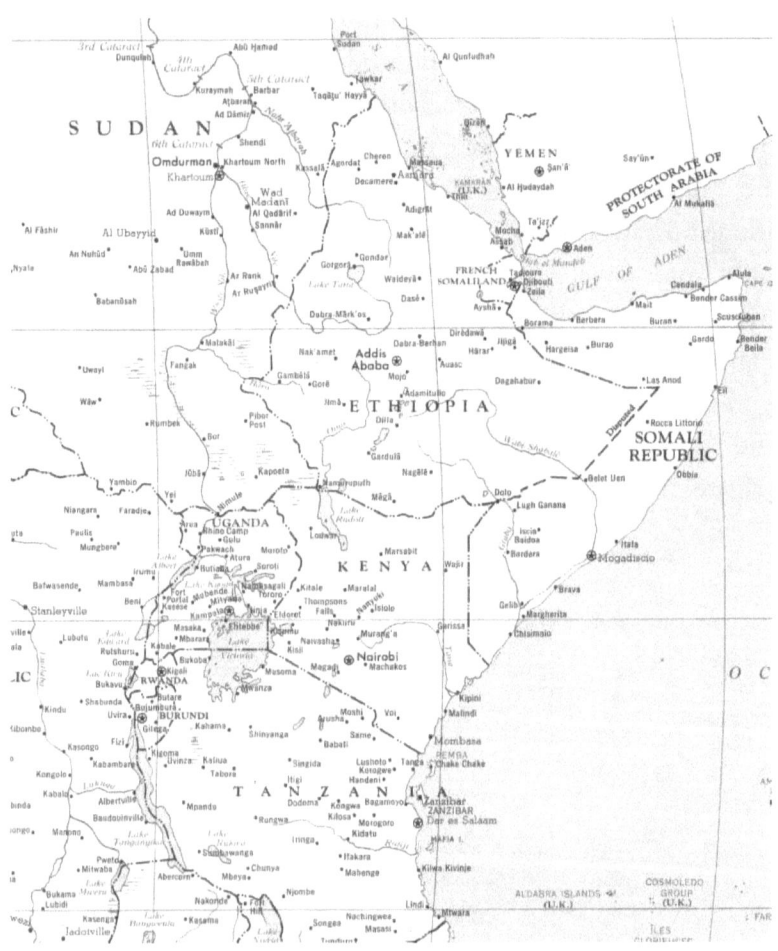

MAP 1 – EAST AFRICA, LATE 1960s

1. GIANT KILLER
(JAKE)

I didn't mean to kill Pudge. But I killed him, for sure. One minute he was standing there near me. The next minute he was gone. I was still alive; he wasn't. And I wasn't sorry he was gone, but I wasn't glad I killed him.

All right! He had his hands around my throat. It was an unprovoked attack clear as day. And I defended myself. But he died by my hand. So I was a murderer, that was plain. Maybe not a real, actual murderer. I hated Pudge but I had not planned to kill him. In a way, he had it coming. The whole thing was thrust on me. It was like an accident he inflicted on himself. Yet sure enough I ended him, which made me a killer. Now he was dead I didn't think better of him, though I didn't expect his death would move me like it did. I even started to feel a little sorry for this bastard who had tried to kill me. But mostly I felt guilty as hell. And plenty scared.

Toward the end of 1969 after I turned twenty, an oil company in Louisiana hired me to work on an offshore rig. I thought my luck had finally changed. I vagabonded after high school, taking the worst jobs available, scraping and scrimping to send money back home for my two kid sisters. Working as a roughneck was big money, some kind of miracle.

On a bright, sweltering day, three months before his death, Pudge showed up on my rig. He was the new cook, a company lifer. By then I'd been there over a year. Pudge was middling height, sparse blond hair, gray puffy face, short thick limbs and hands. He had a beer belly, which tugged at the lower buttons of his shirt, pushed his trouser waist almost down to his groin, hanging obscenely over his belt like a water bomb. Pudge took one look at me, got in my face and said straight out, "I don't like you, you son of a bitch. Stay out of my way and maybe we'll get along," his face turning dark, almost purple. I tried not to antagonize him, but he couldn't help messing with me. It was my nose.

Pudge thought I was Jewish, and Pudge hated Jews. He told anyone who would listen how the Jews were all rich moneygrubbers who secretly controlled everything through the so-called Christians they bought off, and that honest white Christians like himself couldn't get ahead. And the Jews were egging on the Blacks. Pudge liked to use that ugly word for the Blacks that I won't repeat. The Jews were giving them money and political support, encouraging them to riot. And there was a fair amount of rioting, like Harlem in '64, Watts in '65, Detroit and Newark in '67. The point was to create enough chaos so the Jews could step in and run everything openly, without having to hide it. But—and this was Pudge's favorite part of the story—when the mask slipped, the tables would turn. The country would erupt in a race war that would crush the Jews forever and shove the Blacks back down to their rightful place on the bottom.

My nose gave me away, according to Pudge. On the rig I was known as Beak. Here everybody had a nickname. My nose is kind of sharp, maybe like a beak, I guess. But who doesn't have a nose? I can't say I ever thought much about it. Before Pudge, no one ever gave me a second look. My mother's father and my three handsome uncles had the same nose. There was this picture that hung in the parlor for years of the three of them in their uniforms. We were all Germans, dammit, but they'd all gone to Europe to fight Hitler and never came back.

My hair does get a little frizzy in the humid air when I let it grow, another dead-giveaway for Pudge, and my name. I'm plain Jake Ries now but I was born Jacob Riesenschlaeger, which Ma and Dad had chopped to Ries. Word got out one day at school what Riesenschlaeger meant in German. From then on, I was "Jake the Giant Killer." I liked the old name. So did our pastor, who often quoted the fire-and-brimstone Old Testament prophets. Pudge claimed both the long and short versions of my surnames were Jewish, like Levi or Cohn.

I pointed out that German names could sound Jewish. But denying Pudge's stereotypes only cemented them in his brain. It infuriated him that I was posing as a White man. He'd caught me out and he wouldn't let me go, even if I hollered. It sure didn't help when I told him his theories stank. Hell, they wouldn't do justice to the mind of a four-year-old. Hatred flamed from his eyes. He swore he'd live to see my family frying in the ovens, the only fit place for people like me. He wasn't kidding. I saw the horror of his imagined murders in his glance. I tried to laugh it off. But I couldn't get his words out of my mind, the rows of ovens with open doors, ashes piling up, the residue of human bodies glowing orange waiting to be shoveled out to make room for more bodies.

It's not like I was a great friend of the Jews. I really didn't know much about them. My whole family was Lutheran. The only Jews I knew growing up were the Silvermans who ran the town drug store. Freddie Silverman was in the same class as my littlest sister, Margaret. And there was John Friedland, the company accountant in New Orleans, the guy you had to see to place a bet in the football pool, or on a horse race or a fight. That was it. But I loathed the man who boasted he'd kill my family. I hated him because of his designs on me and mine, if he ever got to where he could do something about it, not because of abstract feelings of racial equality or solidarity with the downtrodden. I was keen not to be one of the downtrodden. Pudge wanted to fry my flesh. He said so.

At first, nothing happened. I didn't do anything. Neither did he. We kind of avoided each other. I say "kind of" because it's not so easy to avoid someone on a small drilling platform. Mealtimes were tense, since he was the cook, and I never knew what he might say, though I didn't worry too much about being poisoned because we all ate from the same pot.

A month passed like that. Then a commissary man I hadn't seen before came out on the launch. Here was a guy as sloppy, as ugly, and as depraved looking as some comic book drawing. All his expressions looked like a leer. In fact, he was a double for Aqualung on the record album, like he had dressed for the role and was on his way to a Halloween party. He was authentic down to the drool, maybe because he chewed tobacco. He had long, greasy hair, walked with a stoop, and his smile revealed black, crooked teeth. His clothing looked filthy beyond belief. Though you could not pinpoint a stained or dirty place, yet the impression held.

I was working high up on the rig when I saw him, my eyes riveted on him as he mounted the lower steps. After a new pipe section was in place I had a few moments breather.

"Who's that?" I yelled.

"Who?" several voices responded. Then someone said, "That's Hink. That furry son of a bitch? Yeah." They all knew him, though he hadn't shown up at our rig since I'd been there. I heard he'd worked as a stevedore and a maritime seaman.

Hink. I have no idea where he got that nickname. Turned out he was Pudge's bosom pal. They'd known each other for years. Like Pudge, he was a company lifer. There were three or four lifers on the derrick. All hard cases, I was sure, with rap sheets as long as my arm. Which is why the company liked them. They were loyal. Where else could they find a job? The roughnecks mostly were young drifters like me, and they kept to themselves. No one much talked about where they were from, and no one asked. Like no one wanted to know that my dad and ma died when I was sixteen, and that me and my sisters were orphans. Which is why I had to go to work. Which is why I was on that oil platform with that bastard, Pudge.

With fifteen minutes off, I went down to one of the lower sections. Hearing voices just before I turned a corner, I stopped to have a look and a listen. They were leaning on a railing, Pudge and Hink, drooped shoulders touching conspiratorially, looking out to sea. I overheard Hink say, "You mean he denies it? The yellow-bellied bastard. You watch him. They're sneaky."

"I gave him a scare, you bet," said Pudge. "I'll get him. It burns me up to see one of them pretending to be a white man. Could be that little kike will have an accident. He's scared of me, for sure. They all get nervous when you remind them about the people who really got their number once and did something about it. They know there's no place to hide when the white race figures out the truth and does what it has to do. That son of a bitch. He better watch out."

I could have rushed them, pushed them off the platform then and there. My heart pounding, I turned back the way I came and closed my eyes. Flooded by the dark, I shook my arms, my legs, felt my muscles move beneath my work shirt. I knew I was ready if I had to be. I was sure I could handle him, or them. Then I got this idea. I'd get Pudge where it really hurt.

Pudge liked to play draw poker. He played at least two or three times a week, him and a few regulars. They were all older than me by a lot. Now, I've never been a big gambler or played cards to make money, though I always thought I might be good at poker. I have a steady hand, a steady lip, a steady gaze. I can look anyone deadpan in the eye. I can remember every card played. I can figure the odds.

So pretty quick, I asked them to deal me in. Everyone acted really surprised, of course. Pudge especially.

"You're going to let that damned Jew play with us?" Pudge pushed his chair back.

The others looked at me and back at Pudge.

"You sure?" asked one.

"I'm betting his money's as good as yours, Pudge," said a second, "and we don't mind taking yours."

I sat and Pudge was silent. Then he pulled his chair up and grinned at the cards he was shuffling, like he was waiting for the fun to start. In the early games I mostly watched, folding decent hands, or calling small bets when I had nothing. The truth is that Pudge was not a great card player. He was too easy to read. Like, he'd get all serious and quiet if he was bluffing, but with decent cards he'd smile and joke, all relaxed. Of course, his cronies had figured this out, too, and Pudge mostly lost. And so did I, honestly. I didn't want anyone to know I was gunning for Pudge. I never bet heavily, mostly lost small pots. But if I figured Pudge was bluffing, and no one else was betting, and if I had the cards, I went after him. By the time everyone went to sleep, he was down a hundred twenty-five to me. Two nights later, while he was blaming my earlier win on beginner's luck, I stung him for eighty dollars. Three nights after that, I took him for two hundred with a pair of aces after he folded. I kept at it. Luck's part of it, sure, but not mostly. It helped that Pudge and his pals drank. They liked their bourbon. Sometimes it seemed I was the only one sober at the table. At the end of the two-week shift I had lost hundreds, but I was up nearly eight hundred on Pudge. All I got from Pudge was IOUs, though he got razzed pretty good for it.

"Pudge, pay the kid for chrissake!"

And with a wink, "Whadda you, Pudge, some kinda tightwad Jew bastard?"

Losing money to me burned him more than even I imagined. To him, it was a Jew stopping a righteous Christian like himself from getting ahead. I knew my risks. If he continued to lose to me, though everything was on the up-and-up, he might come after me. I'd never seen him do anything violent; mostly I figured him for a blowhard and a coward. But If I got him crazy enough, I thought he just might snap. He might try something.

Work was going well. In fact, the geologist said we were about to strike oil. The company was so happy with us drillers that we were getting a bonus. But not the cooks. Pudge just glowered when he heard about it. I was getting rich but also restless. After twenty months on the rig I was tired of the two-weeks-on, two-weeks-off routine. I'd had it with that greasy platform and the grease-coated men, me included, who worked there. I didn't want to see Hink again, or Pudge. I was ready to quit. On the other hand the bastard owed me money. He would crow if I left without collecting from him. More than money, he owed me a psychic debt. I wanted payback. But waiting endlessly was not worth it. I figured to leave after the next two-week shift.

I told everyone I was quitting. I honestly couldn't wait for this part of my life to end. I was ready to go back to dry land, to try something else. When they asked where I was going, I said Mexico. Sit on some beach sipping margaritas. I don't know why I said it. How the hell did I know where I was going?

At the end of the two-week shift, when everyone was going ashore except Pudge, there was one last poker game. Before the cards were dealt, without saying a word, glaring down at the table, he slid me an envelope with four hundred-odd dollars in it, about half what he owed me. I opened the envelope in front of everybody, quickly counted the money, stuck the envelope in my shirt pocket.

"Thanks," I said, "but you're four hundred short." Though I figured I would never see the rest, this was unexpected. This was good. Pudge got really quiet. His silence was so noticeable someone joked that a young guy was making him look like a fool. He got up and stomped out, making a big racket on the steel plate. He returned a few minutes later and sat.

Hink was there that night, too, stranded by a nasty squall. He radioed in, told them he'd take us to shore early tomorrow in the launch, if the weather let up. Pudge was staying put, though, the platform being short a cook.

We had a game. For once, I was riding high with a pile of chips in front of me. Hink was idly shuffling cards when we changed decks between hands. Normally the dealer shuffles, but that night for some reason we dealt cards after Hink shuffled them. On my turn to deal, I took the cards from Hink and dealt myself a pat hand—three aces and two threes. Pudge immediately started to bet heavy and cracking jokes.

I didn't like it, so I folded. Pudge was called with three sevens. He won the pot. Then someone curiously found the seven of diamonds near my foot. How it got there I had no idea. I was sure I hadn't dropped it. I picked it up and placed it on the table.

"See," said Pudge, maybe a little too fast, "I can win on sevens with only three sevens in the deck."

Everyone laughed at that one. Since it was a misdeal we took the hand again, leaving the money in the pot. This time I shuffled the cards myself. As I dealt, I was thinking I had just missed getting set up. Pudge would have claimed I had cheated, dealing myself a full house and him three sevens, while holding the last seven out of the deck, even though Hink had shuffled. He'd claim I'd been cheating him all along. So he'd owe me nothing. He'd demand his four hundred dollars back and get in some cracks about the Jews while he was at it. There would have been a fight for sure.

On the next hand I folded early, took my winnings, and sat out the rest of the game. Pudge won some money while I sat there. He didn't look happy at the end of the table with his back to the wall, his puffy pink face scowling at his cards. I don't know what else he and Hink had cooked up, but now they couldn't try. I watched the game, trying to decide if my mind was playing tricks or if they really were messing with me.

The game ended. I went to my hooch to pack, feeling aimless. In a few hours I'd leave this job. I had no place to go. I didn't know what would become of me. I'd aimed to go to college, eventually. But now I'd gotten used to being independent and having money. I listened to the wind swirling around the rig. That night I had nightmares, like I'm drowning in the ocean and at my last gasp Pudge and Hink are running me down in a motorboat and laughing.

∽

I GOT UP EARLY. The wind had died. Everything outside looked strange that morning. Nothing soft was left in the world. Gray had disappeared. The sea was oil black. The drilling derrick was black, angular against the bright, electric sky. Bright green-brown crusty seaweed floated everywhere. Everything was brittle, sharp, threatening, even the swells.

After breakfast, I went up top to kill a few minutes. I was still wearing the shirt from last night with the envelope full of money sticking out. I folded it, stuck it in my back pocket. Just then, Pudge walked out from behind some machinery. He was holding an enormous monkey wrench, the one we used to change pipe sections while drilling. He must have followed me up the steps, edged past me somehow. That thing was so heavy it normally took two of us to handle it. And here he was trying to swing it over his head.

"I'll have that money back, you little kike. Give it back or I'll smash your skull. None of your Jew tricks. Hand it over."

It was a dangerous place to fight. We were high over the water. The platform edge was close, barely fenced. At first, I was too stunned to say anything. Then the adrenaline kicked in.

"You big idiot. No one's cheated you out of anything, except a brain. Plus you owe me another four hundred. You're not getting any money from me while I'm still alive."

He took two steps toward me, snarling in a low voice, "Hand it over, you cheat. Give it to me."

He swung, but it was easy to dodge. The wrench was so heavy he could barely hold onto it, which knocked him off balance. I jumped at him, gave him a big shove, hoping to make him drop the wrench. It worked. The big wrench fell over the side, hitting the water with a loud sucking plop.

He grabbed me around the throat and I kneed him, hard. That stopped him and I gave him a big push. He tripped over the foot-high railing near the edge, landing on his hands and knees, straddling the rail. The pain distracted him, I guess. His knee slipped over the edge taking his body with it. He grabbed the greasy platform awkwardly with his arms and elbows. He stared into my eyes for a long moment, his blue eyes looking tiny and pitiful, his pasty, jowly face speechless. I made a move to help him but stopped. He groaned, lost his grip, and fell. I saw his head strike a girder before he hit the water. He floated face down, then slowly sank out of sight.

He died so easily, so fast. I was shocked. It was all gone now, the plotting, the conspiracies, the twisted paranoia, his try at cheating at cards, his attempt to murder me or rob me, everything he had ever done or thought or had been or wished for. It was gone, all of it, except what still echoed of him in living minds. In my mind.

I pictured him again hanging there over the edge, looking at me. I might have grabbed his hand, called for help. Could I have saved his life? I didn't try. I just looked into his eyes. Then he fell. No one could say this was my fault. If he hadn't tried to kill me, he wouldn't be dead now. It was my last day on the job. I would never have seen him again. Yet it happened.

Now I had the overwhelming urge to flee, to put time and distance between me and where Pudge died and disappeared. There were no witnesses, no evidence. I didn't especially want to find out how a court would look at it. It might be ruled manslaughter or maybe self-defense. Sure, I knew running would look bad.

Then like I was in a dream I was walking downstairs, down to where everybody was gathering so they could exit this floating junk pile and return to some semblance of real life. They were waiting for me, wondering where I was, glad I turned up so they could leave. The day was overcast, sultry. The sea had turned gray. Brief squalls gusted in my face. Hink was ready to go but wanted to see Pudge. Had anyone seen Pudge? No one had. I didn't say a word. Someone said, "You know, I thought I saw him going above a few minutes ago."

"That's funny, I've been looking for him all over. The only place I didn't look was up top."

"I was up there," I said, "but I didn't see him."

"Maybe he locked himself in one of the coolers," someone joked.

"Pudge. Pudge," Hink cried, looking above us. "Come out, you no good cook. Pudge!"

The boys started to get restless. Everyone wanted to get started.

"Let's go already," several voices clamored. "You can talk with him on the radio when you're ashore," one said. "You get out here to the rig twice a week as it is. C'mon Hink, let's get moving."

Hink reluctantly moved his eyes away from the top of the derrick. "I wonder where he got to." He started down the stairs to where the launch was moored. We all got in. Hink sat in the stern and started her up. Before casting off, Hink tapped me on the shoulder. "You never saw him, did you? Hey kid?" Looking at his revolting face I shook my head slowly. "No." I turned forward and never looked back, though I could feel his eyes on me as the boat pulled away.

2. HEATHROW
(JAKE)

I stepped from the launch onto the fog-slicked pier, waved goodbye to my fellow workers, sprinted to the bus station and bought tickets to New Orleans and Chicago. Hour after hour on those buses I carried Pudge's last moments in my head. I was sure they would grab me at any moment. I had never been out of the country. Canada wasn't far enough. I needed to leave North America. England was the easiest far place to get to that spoke English.

Some hole-in-the-wall on the South Side of Chicago sold Louisiana newspapers. I read about the unexplained death of a cook, whose swollen body had washed up on a beach after a week in the water. The police had questioned the entire crew of the oil rig, except for one employee who reportedly was in Mexico. Though I figured eventually they'd circle back to me, the police speculated the death could have been accidental or even a suicide. By now I assumed they knew Pudge and me didn't exactly see eye-to-eye.

As the days passed, I learned the coroner had determined the cause of death was drowning, although a concussion, probably resulting from a fall from the platform, was the main contributing factor. There was no evidence of foul play. A large monkey wrench was reported missing, but the wound to the deceased's head was not consistent with a blow from that kind of blunt object.

No one was chasing me—yet. I was the only one who knew for sure what had happened. It was neat. A bit of unpleasant private business, then walk away. Still, the thought of what I did haunted me. I could have saved the man's life, or I could have tried. I could've grabbed Pudge, tried to pull him up, instead of staring at him and thinking how loathsome and pathetic he was. Of course, the bastard might have tried to pull me over the side. Maybe I wanted him to die, or maybe I didn't mind. I got to thinking I was as bad as Pudge, or worse. He was a fanatic, sure, an aspiring mass murderer, and maybe he'd kill people, if he had the chance. But he'd probably never killed anybody outside of his madman's dreams. Never once had I thought about killing anybody, but I actually had done it. If I ever spoke with the police, I feared my whole guilty story would spill out. I was looking at jail time, for sure. They might get me on manslaughter. Or maybe they'd trump up a real murder charge. That's as far as I liked to let my mind go.

No, I had to leave the country. All my actions since that morning on the oil platform would point to my guilt. I decided to get away and follow the plan. I had no family ties, except my sisters who I hadn't seen in a couple of years. They'd be fine without me and the few dollars I managed to send them.

I tried to convince myself that I'd forget about all this once I got to Europe. I was eager to travel, excited about starting something new and to meet exotic people even though the British weren't that exotic. I had twelve hundred dollars from my bank in New Orleans, though I was careful not to close the account, plus the four hundred from Pudge, and another five-six hundred from that last poker game. That and my pocket money made twenty-two hundred. If I was careful, I reckoned I could go for a year and then maybe find work someplace.

It took two slow, sweaty weeks in a cheap Chicago boarding house for my hometown to send me my birth certificate, then another two for the post office to hand me a passport. I took an overnight bus to New York, where I immediately bought a one-way ticket to London. I killed another week waiting for the charter. My hotel didn't cost much. I bought a backpack and a sleeping bag. I went to the zoo. Fed the pigeons. Museums. Went for walks. Rode out to Far Rockaway on the subway. I went to see a play in Central Park. Visited the public library. Counted pimps, whores, and fat cats in Times Square. I did everything I could think of that cost nothing, or next to nothing. For a week I spoke to no one, besides ordering a hamburger or paying the hotel. Except for one panhandler, a low-down bum who dogged me until I warned him off, until he looked me in the eye. And then he froze, retreated a few steps, turned heel, and fled as fast as his wasted body could move. He tripped, landed on his face, got back up, and lunged around the corner. Did he think I would kill him?

∼

SEEING A FAINT GLOW around the window edges, I pushed my shade up a crack. The sky was night-black fading to deep blue, with a bright line on the horizon. Looking down through the clear air the ground was indistinct, while in the east towered brilliant and gold silhouetted clouds as if they were a mass of jagged mountains. No, my mind was playing tricks, hoping I was farther from New York than I really was. No mountain ranges in sight. Just like flat Nebraska. The North Atlantic was below us, cold ocean, as black as the sky, like the bottom of a well. As black as the day when Ma and Dad disappeared.

My folks were last in a line of Nebraska livestock farmers. They were religious, conservative, and they brought us up strict. They gave us everything that could be bought or borrowed on farmers' pay. When I turned fourteen, my father took me aside. He said if anything happened to him and Ma, I'd become the man of the family. I'd have to look out for my sisters, Emily and Margaret, who were barely in grade school. I said of course I would, and never thought about it again.

On a Saturday morning when I was sixteen the sky went black as a pot bottom, sick green like some kid's greasy finger painting. I sent Emily and Margaret down cellar hoping Ma and Dad would get back from town quick. Tree branches snapped. The alfalfa shook like a raging sea. The rain rushed down crazy, the thunder made me fear the house would collapse. When it cleared, the radio said a tornado had zigzagged along the road that passed our farm. I was trying to cook dinner for my little sisters when the sheriff came to say they had found our car in the middle of a corn field with the doors open. My parents were gone.

Everybody was really nice about it. The neighbor women brought us food, though they lived miles away. I told my sisters that Dad and Ma would turn up sure enough. But I knew they were gone. After a few days they did turn up. My poor father rolled off the roof of a barn some farmers were trying to repair after the storm. Ma was found in a field close by rotting in the soybeans. She must have been carried away and tossed like a rag doll.

After the funeral Ma's brother, Uncle Paul, took us to Minneapolis. The family farm with the livestock fetched enough at auction to pay the loans and settle the mortgage, but not much more.

Uncle Paul lived alone. Luckily, he had a job and an old house big enough for him plus the three of us. There was no money for college. I stayed until I finished high school. On the day I left I was eighteen. I told Uncle Paul I'd work and send money home for my sisters as much as I could. But I didn't know what I was in for. After two years of practically begging to wash dishes, haul rocks in quarries, pick apples, pluck chickens, never sending back more than twenty-odd dollars a month, I wrote my uncle to say goodbye until my luck changed. I was wasting time slaving away for next to nothing. Then I got that job on the oil rig.

∼

THE PLANE TOUCHED DOWN at Heathrow and the passengers streamed out. All those people on holiday for one, two, three weeks, then back to their jobs, their schools, their families. I had nothing like that to come back to, which I wasn't sure I ever would. I waited nervously in line at passport control, sure someone would tap me on the shoulder. I recalled James Earl Ray was on the lam in London in 1968 after shooting Martin Luther King. Here I was on the lam for killing a White supremacist who probably liked James Earl Ray. But I feared I was cursed, and my life would be blighted for what I had done.

When my turn came a uniformed Brit looked me over carefully, asked how long I would be staying. My profession? "Mechanic," I answered. He was taking his time. Then he disappeared, returning with a tall policeman with a mustache who told me to follow him. He took me to a clean, white room with several chairs, had me sit, then walked out.

An hour later he came back, pulled his chair close and gave me a hard look. "We know who you are and what you did. We've got all the evidence. We expect a full confession." I just gaped at him, watching his mouth move. My heart drummed my ears so hard I couldn't hear. Just then a civilian came in, whispered something to the policeman. They both went out.

Trying to think, I figured clamming up was best. Then I'd ask for a lawyer. After fifteen minutes the civilian returned.

"You're free to go."

My mind was racing. "You mean?" I stammered.

"Yes, you can go." He showed me out. I was sweating. I was damn lucky. Or were they playing with me?

Again I was standing in front of the immigration man. "Have a pleasant stay," he said with a lilt as he stamped me in, then growling under his breath, "Seems they picked up the wrong bloke." I walked away fast but froze when that Brit called, "Young man. Young man. Please come back here." I turned back to his station. He looked at me steadily, waving something. It was my passport.

"You forgot this."

I was shaking. Who knows what might have spilled under questioning? I avoided the police. At any moment they might grab me again. A bobby directing traffic was all the reason I needed to look for another place to cross the street. I tried to think positively, but I was worried. With a fright, I kept seeing Hink in the crowd, his long, greasy hair. I even followed some guy gingerly for several blocks to get a look at his face. Not Hink. Maybe no one was on my trail. But there was no easy way back. I was in exile, like a man without a country. Who knew when I could see my sisters again?

I've always been a believer and tried hard to be a good person. But I know I'm not as pious as I was raised. I have a problem with forgiveness. Up to a point, I can forgive. But past that point, I will not turn my cheek. Am I to forgive murder? Or attempted murder? Someone who wants to harm my family? I can't be as good as my parents wanted me to be, not if I have murder in my heart for a man who tried to kill me. In their eyes I would be no better than him. Why didn't I try to grab Pudge in that moment before he fell over the edge? That was my failure to forgive.

I had grown up fast since losing my parents. You learn quick you're all there is. To me, being alone in Europe wasn't a big deal. I just worried I'd become some kind of hermit. Since the day my parents disappeared, I've assumed my death will be violent. Chances are I'll be run over by a truck, hung from a gibbet, shot by some cop, pushed out of a building. Honestly, it's my favorite dodge. If I'm not going to make it past thirty, then most things that can go wrong won't matter, like boredom, disease, injury, prison, divorce, poverty, senility, loneliness. I like the past. The past is safe and dead. The future can be anything. Except in my case, it's all too likely my number will be up next week. But the present, the annoying present, is a bitch.

3. THE GREAT ESCAPE
(KARL)

The train blurred past. As the cars clanged finally to a halt, time seemed to stop. Dazed, I saw a slim figure in blue light nimbly onto the platform. She was gazing in every direction but mine, bewildered.

"Helen!" She turned to me, grinning like a child caught doing something naughty. The problem with relationships is figuring out what your partner isn't telling you.

We'd had a nasty breakup just before I left the States. I had caught Helen in several lies, those times when she came home late or didn't come home at all. Still, I could have sworn she wasn't cheating on me. Or maybe she was. Nothing added up.

"Come," I said, in the way Helen liked me to decide things.

Right after the term began at Oxford, Helen wrote telling me she was pregnant. She didn't know what to do. Like I knew? Wasn't she on the pill? Without warning, this very morning, in fact, she called from London saying she was arriving by train in the afternoon. "This is all my fault, it's all my fault," she cried, blaming herself on the phone, though she didn't say what exactly was her fault.

We walked silently through town to the university. We got to my room. I embraced her. She looked about the same, maybe a little puffy in the cheeks. The same sparkling gray eyes, clear white skin. It was quiet. She was taking everything in with wonder. She wheeled around. "This is quite a place you've got." She put her hands on my shoulders, flashing that imbecilic smile again. "Karl? Karl?" I didn't speak. "Karl," she repeated with mild insistence. "It's good to see you. I'm glad I'm here." She rested her head on my chest. I stroked her hair.

Our last night together before I went off to Europe I had blurted out, "Do you think we're right for each other? Should we quit?" She agreed. I guess she agreed. She said she did, while she was sobbing under the sheets. Then she sat up and screamed, "I don't need you anyway. Get out!" That was the last time I saw her in the States. Now here we were in Oxford. Pregnant.

I could guess what Dad would say about this mess. He'd shake his head whenever he thought I was acting green or gullible. "I always think the worst of people," he'd say. "They seldom let me down." He really drilled it in that the world is a dangerous place, that you trust people at your peril. And he was always right. About everything. You could not argue with him. His rants and his judgments made me rebel, but they also filled me with doubt.

A war hero with a raging case of combat fatigue and a lifetime of bad luck and betrayals behind him, Dad expected no help from anyone. His war story was seared into my consciousness, repeated so often I imagined it had happened to me.

In April 1944 while parachuting from a burning B-17, within sight of ditching in the cold Adriatic and almost certain rescue, he watched the plane crash on a Bosnian hilltop and explode in flames, killing the entire crew. Captured by German troops, he was brought to the old Turkish fort at Mostar with a hunk of shrapnel in his thigh, kept naked in solitary in a freezing cell during weeks of interrogation, then sent north by train under guard to a prison camp on the Baltic coast, until Konstantin Rokossovsky's Second Belorussian Front—the Soviet army—liberated them all on May 1, 1945.

Dad prized self-preservation above all, but he also prized his grievances. Permanently enraged, he never forgave the US Army for damaging his life. Getting shot down was bad enough. But thanks to the army's dog tags, stamped with the letter *H* for Hebrew or *J* for Jew, identifying and segregating the Jewish prisoners of war was child's play for the Gestapo. And though Dad hated talking about life in the camp, I managed to pry a few things from him. Like how in the winter of '45 they twice lined up the Jewish POWs for mock executions, these American *Untermenschen*.

Not everyone survived. Take Fritz, for example. A day after the liberation, while strolling through the town of Barth in uniform, Dad and his POW buddy, Mel, both second lieutenants, bumped into a burp-gun-toting Soviet infantryman named Pavel Andreievich. The three of them palled around, slapping each other's backs, swapping cigarettes and chocolate, until Mel poked Dad with his elbow.

"Say, isn't that Fritz? From the camp? In civvies?" The German surrender was one week away; Fritz was still a German soldier and a combatant. Pavel Andreievich perked up.

"*Wehrmacht?*" he growled, pointing the black barrel of his weapon at Fritz's receding back.

Mel shook his head. "*Luftwaffe.*" The German Air Force ran the camp, not the German army.

Pavel Andreievich nodded quickly and followed Fritz around the corner. A pause. Then *BRRAP-PAP-PAP-PAP-PAP-PAP-PAP-PAP-PAP* at nine hundred rounds a minute.

I'm sure Dad resented how easy I had it. I'd never been shot at or jumped from burning airplanes or been thrown into the tender care of Nazis. I'd never had to run from Irish gangs or find a job during the Depression at age fifteen, or been forced to raise a kid brother so my mother could go to work. And how could I match his war record? The more he was right about everything, the more I was wrong. He'd just say, "Karl, what were you thinking?"

Growing up I'd do crazy stuff just to impress him, to show him I was capable, resourceful, and brave like him. It never worked. Like the time, at age eleven, I set out to ride a hundred miles on my bike. I got a flat and had to call home from a farmhouse. That forced Dad to drop everything to rescue me, and he seethed silently, angry all the way back. And I knew I still was ten million miles away from getting a warm wink of his approval.

Okay, I was naïve. What kid isn't? But I was careful. If you never gave anyone enough rope, I figured they couldn't hang you with it. I liked to think my naïveté ended with Vietnam. That was the big eye-opener. Growing up in the '60s, I believed Americans were always the good guys. Not so in Vietnam. We took over France's colonial war after the French lost it. We said it was about Communism. We were strangers, intruders, invaders, occupiers. We napalmed villages. Defoliated forests. Killed babies and women. Carpet-bombed crowded cities. We were the only foreigners there, trampling a country we knew less about than the dark side of the moon.

At the university one day, I overheard two soldiers on furlough joking about throwing Vietcong suspects out of helicopters as a routine interrogation tactic, something the Germans would have done if they had helicopters. But never us.

"You throw the first one out of the 'copter—Ha! The next one in line is always ready to talk."

Something snapped. "Bastards!" I shouted. "The nation applauds your bravery, you killers!" They jumped me, cursing, after I poked one of them in the eye, and we traded punches and rolled around in the dirt kicking each other until the campus police broke it up.

Oh, it's hard to be on the losing side. We forced the Vietnamese into a war of attrition, all right, a meat grinder war. We'd kill twenty Vietcong for every one of us, maybe more. We gloated as their bodies piled up by the thousands. The trouble was thousands of Vietnamese were willing to die for the cause. But not many Americans wanted to die.

The '60s were about confusion if they were about anything. With Vietnam and all the assassinations and riots, no one I knew was sure what they were doing or why, or what to believe. Some said the '60s were about experimentation. Right. If you're confused about how things are, you're going to try something new.

At that point, when absolutely nothing made sense, I met Helen. She was from Cincinnati, like me. Helen was a breath of fresh air, smart, capable, good-natured, unlike the malcontents I normally hung out with. And she was gorgeous. Helen and I became inseparable. We made no plans. The future seemed as senseless as the present. She was my goddess.

No surprise that Dad didn't like her. He shook his head. "Flighty," he pronounced. "Unreliable."

But me and Helen had this massive optimism. We thought we could make a difference. We marched to the Pentagon in October '67. At the end of January 1968, the Tet Offensive ripped a hole in the war for all to see. For a breathless week it seemed that power was lying on the streets in Saigon waiting for someone to pick it up. In August '68 thousands of us so-called radicals drove to Chicago for the Democratic National Convention, where the police pushed us around like rabble, chased us, gassed us, and beat us up. We ran, leaving bleeding bodies and pools of blood on the pavement. Enormous street cleaning machines were sent out to wipe them up.

In mid-November '69 half a million people came to Washington to protest the war. A few hundred of us radicals marched to the Department of Justice in that frigid dusk to protest the arrests of the Chicago Seven, who were on trial for the Chicago riots. We later heard they had put machine gun emplacements in the first-floor corridors with orders to fire if anyone broke in. We had no plan to storm the building. No matter. We didn't get within four hundred yards. The police attacked and we fled through the dark streets, retching and blinded by tear gas. Watching this mayhem from the roof, Martha Mitchell, the US attorney general's wife, told reporters it was just like the Russian Revolution. As if she knew. A few weeks later Chicago police murdered Fred Hampton, Mark Clark, and other Black Panthers. We marched to protest the invasion and bombing of Cambodia and the murder of four Kent State students by the National Guard. Everyone was slightly deranged. We leafletted, lost sleep talking and arguing, organizing meetings, giving speeches, signing petitions, writing articles. Some fell for Chairman Mao and *The Little Red Book*. Nothing did any good.

After 1970, I despaired. With graduation nearing, the anti-war movement broke down. Activism lost its mass allure. Helen and I were drifting apart. The women's movement was rising, and Helen was all in. She was constantly at meetings where no men were allowed and coming home late or not until the next day. Something was off. My desire for her didn't change, but our interactions were brittle. The emotion was dying. We no longer fit.

"Look," I told her, "you say we're equals but you always want me to lead."

She ignored that. "Why do you need to go to Oxford?" She crossed her arms on her chest, asking me for the twentieth time.

"They accepted me. It's an interesting program. What else am I going to do next year? And it doesn't cost much." I hesitated, looking at her. "You could come."

She frowned. "Me? What would I do in Oxford? Why not stay here?"

"I don't want to. I've had it."

"You've had it with me, you mean."

In the fall of 1971 I arrived at Balliol College, Oxford, and plunged into the study of revolution. The topic fascinated me, but I guess the whole thing was doomed from the start. Of course my father told me I was wasting my time. "Get a job," he said, and I was glad to put distance between me and Cincinnati. Maybe my father was right. The program only made sense if I stayed at least two years—one year to earn an English bachelor's degree, one more to start on an advanced degree. I already had an American BA and had dabbled in African Studies. Did I really need another degree? I'd pace up and down in my room asking myself, "Become a professor of revolution? Why would I do that?"

Oxford was awfully pretentious. I hated it. A big show right down to my put-on Queen's English, one of my preposterous talents.

I wondered why, after fooling people who took me for the son of a British peer, I'd go back to my room in a total rage. No one suspected I was a phony, playing a part. But why would they? Everyone at Oxford was playing a part.

My tutor was Harold Higgins, a brilliant scholar, yet totally at sea outside the university. He studied revolutions, social upheavals, ethnic turmoil. Africa was his specialty. But I doubted whether Harold could imagine the searing sting of teargas, that stop-action moment when a club is lifted near your head. He was a theoretician. He reveled in abstractions. For him, revolution was something argued in books.

Don't get me wrong, Harold was no dummy. Quite the contrary. He understood current events much better than me. But had he seen blood on the knife? Were peasants and kings merely pieces on a chess board? Could he conjure the actual peasant, wallowing in ignorance, crushed by a brutal system, beating his wife out of grief and self-loathing because he could not feed her, finally risking his life in revolt because every avenue was closed off? With Harold, revolution was something almost arranged in advance, neat, logical, inevitable, preordained. No messy, unforeseen, on-the-fly outcomes created helter-skelter by desperate actors struggling in the moment, grasping for power amid a whirl of happenstance. I soon tired of seeing everything though Harold's clairvoyant hindsight. What about the actual messy outcomes, and the motivations, illusions, bravery, cowardice, brilliance, incompetence, will to power, greed, or outright bloodlust of the revolutionaries?

It wasn't Harold's fault that I was frustrated. He was not boring. Far from it. Harold probably was the smartest man I ever met. Briefly I worked harder for him than I have ever worked in school. My topic was "When is revolution justified?" Harold suggested focusing on the Rwandan Revolution leading up to independence in 1962: Hutu demagogues on a mission to overthrow what they saw as Tutsi oppression. A vindictive ideology. A ruthless campaign, egged on by the Belgians, who believed Hutus were oppressed. A murderous mass uprising. Revolution was the gecko on a wall. Trifling at first, seemingly immobile, yet with secret, rapid steps the sinuous Hutu marauder closed on a jittery, distracted, unwary Tutsi fly. The Hutu victors called it the "Wind of Destruction," toppling the four-century-old Tutsi monarchy and bringing Hutus to power in a majority-ruled Rwandan republic. Meanwhile, amid sporadic outbreaks of savage violence, 400,000 Tutsis, nearly 15 percent of Rwanda's population, fled for their lives. That was as many people as lived in Cincinnati.

To me, revolution in Rwanda meant eliminating the old overlords and replacing them with new ones. Tutsis had run the place for hundreds of years. Now Hutus were running it and killing Tutsis. But Tutsis had not been murdering Hutus under the old monarchy. Watching me flounder, Harold encouraged me to press on with this tiny speck on the map, a poor new nation that was only good at producing corpses, in my view. *When is revolution justified?* I hated the topic because there was no good answer. But maybe that was Harold's point.

LATER THAT NIGHT IN my room Helen woke up. She had dozed off on the bed. I was sleeping on the floor. "Karl, aren't you coming to sleep?" She patted a spot next to herself on my mattress.

I was silent for a moment. "I'll sleep here," I said tentatively, pointing to my cushions.

She insisted. "Karl, come to me."

Sleeping together didn't feel right. The lovemaking was normal. But Helen turned from me afterwards, like she never had done before, and asked, "You didn't want to sleep with me, did you?" Then she wouldn't let me touch her. I jumped up and got back on the floor. Helen and I were going to raise a child together?

Decisions can illuminate things or make them muddy. Deal with things as they are; don't moon about why things aren't different. Then decide what to do. But what the hell did I want? I was going with muddy. Next morning, I woke up early and went out for a walk. When I got back Helen was getting dressed. Though she felt nauseous, we went to breakfast.

She sipped her tea, looking at me. "I'm sorry I bothered you, Karl. But you know why I came."

"Well, Helen." She avoided my hand reaching for hers.

"Well, what?" She glared at me over her tea and toast. "You're the father. That's what you were going to ask, isn't it? It's definitely yours."

I took a deep breath. There seemed to be only one choice. "Helen, why don't you stay here? With me. If you want to. I'll support us."

"Really?" She continued sipping her tea.

"Sure." I took her hand. I began thinking about this out loud. "They'll kick us out of my room when they figure out you're living there."

"Then what?"

"Then we'll have to get a place in town. It'll be more money. I'll have to get some kind of job."

"But what about us?"

"We'll figure it out. I . . . I don't know. It's been kind of rough, don't you think? We'll need to talk."

She put down her cup. "That's just what Ernestine told me you'd say."

"Ernestine? Who's that?"

"You know her."

I thought a minute. "That girl—"

"Woman!"

"Ah, that activist from Free Fems Forever? But who's Ernestine to you? Or you to Ernestine?"

"Karl, you never had time for the women's movement, did you?"

Now she was taunting me.

"I always thought the women's movement had no time for me."

"You have no idea what's going on, do you?" She pushed her cup aside and stared at me with pity—or was it ridicule? "I'm going to have this baby. I think I'm going to have it. But I'm not going to have it with you."

"When did you decide that?"

"When? Why, just now! I'm here because I thought I needed you. I had to see you, hear what you would say. But I see you really don't care. Suddenly it's all up to me."

"Helen, I asked you to stay with me."

"But you don't care about me anymore, do you, Karl?"

I insisted I cared about her. I insisted repeatedly. "I do care about you, Helen. Helen, what will you do alone with a baby?"

"Oh, I'll be fine," she spat. "Who says I'll be alone? I want this baby, not because it's yours, which is how I was thinking about it, but because it's mine."

It hit me like a wave. "What do you mean? Helen, you're being absurd."

"I'm being absurd! No, I don't think so. There's someone who cares about me. It's just not you." Frowning, her mouth twisted the words. "Only women understand women."

"You mean Ernestine?" She stared away. "You could stay here," I pleaded.

Helen left that afternoon. The next days were terrible. Oxford was terrible. The world was terrible. I was terrible. I hadn't helped Helen. And what about her? Was coming to see me some sort of expedition to weigh her options? Decide between me and Ernestine? Figure out her sexual identity? Did Helen really prefer Ernestine to me? That stung. Did I want Helen back? I was relieved there would be no abortion, but I was angry at myself. Shouldn't I have been more welcoming, more ardent? Why hadn't I seen this coming? Not the baby, but Ernestine. And I was angry at Helen. She'd rather raise our baby with Ernestine? I tried hard to remember when I had seen Helen with Ernestine but came up with nothing.

Whatever I was doing at Oxford now seemed totally pointless. I couldn't stand staying in my room. I needed a change, someplace where nobody knew me. My head swirling, I bugged out. I figured I'd go to France, the closest place I could think of that was different from England. After briefly consulting Harold, I took an early morning train to Paris via the Calais ferry and watched the white cliffs slowly sink into the Channel, like my academic career, taking my spirits with them.

I WANDERED AROUND PARIS. The city reeks history from every sewer and storm drain. Paris is practically a museum; almost every stone has been written about or painted or photographed. But Paris is for the rich. The shops cater to the managers, the professional classes, who seem fond of blatantly phony opulence, aping the style of long-defunct French royalty. Paris is not a place for casual conversation with strangers. I pretended to admire the ghosts of famous Parisians—Victor Hugo, Baudelaire, stray communards. The actual people treading the streets I ignored.

I wound up in a nondescript bar with a dark interior full of empty tables. I flung my bag on a chair. Smoke from a thousand cigarettes slanted from the windows to the bar's dark recesses. The only clients, two drunks, got up to leave. I ordered absinthe, what the French call *pastis*.

Someone in baggy army-issue fatigues bustled in carrying a bundle of newspapers under one arm. He was grinning imperceptibly, nodding at the empty chairs and at the sagging, dusty, bottle-choked shelves behind the bar.

He threw down his beat Mao cap on my table, dropped his newspapers thump on the floor, and addressed me politely in French. "You are sitting alone. Looks like you want company." His feral face—prominent nose, small forehead, receding chin, alert brown eyes—was clean of marks or whiskers. *Baguettes et vin ordinaire*, I thought. He lives on bread and cheap wine.

"I don't. *Pas de tout*," I said. I had studied German for years; my French was not as good.

He shrugged. The barman took his order for a small beer. My French-speaking Maoist friend bit his thumb. He leaned forward, conspiratorially. "I know him, he owns this café. He's a despicable cheat, a petit bourgeois bastard. His wife owns a pawn shop." His guileless eyes wondered aloud why a man like that should be allowed to live.

"Why do you come here," I asked, "if he is so rotten?"

I was pondering my half-full glass, wondering how to escape before the pitch began. It was coming, as sure as the fall rains. I didn't want to argue or buy his paper. I could walk out. I could tell him to go to hell. But I sat there, feeling cross for speaking with a stranger.

He began. "Have you seen the buses parked on the side streets at night filled with riot police? How they swagger on the sidewalks with their truncheons, their automatics. We gave the bourgeoisie a big fright in sixty-eight. They still haven't got over it."

"I'm a tourist."

He continued. "The people have to breathe but that scum," he swept his arm to include invisible enemies and the bartender, "is blocking our throats. One cough and we'll spit them out." His eyes were quite mad. "Do you know this?" He clutched a newspaper and began reading out loud.

Then someone else entered the bar. He came right up to the newspaper reader, told him his time was up just as a proctor instructs a class to put down its pencils when the examination is over.

"You're making an ass of yourself," the stranger added.

"Who are you to order me around?"

Listening with studied nonchalance, polishing glasses behind the bar, the café owner was getting ready to throw us out. I stood. Startled, the Maoist news hawker gawked at us, gathered his papers, his cap, threw some coins on the table, stamped out the door. Through the window we watched him hurry down the sidewalk.

The stranger held out his hand. "Howard Chapman."

"Karl Appel." We shook.

"You really shouldn't do that."

"Do what?"

"Talk to idiots, of course." Howard pursed his lips. "I know him. He doesn't like me. Owes me money. Long story. Funny, I like embarrassing him. It seems fair. He's flogging that wretched rag. And his murderous ideology." Howard frowned. "Maoists, I hate them."

The barman began bustling about, cleaning up the glasses. "*Messieurs?*"

"I'm sure they have lists of people to kill." He stood. "I'm off."

I paid and strode after him out the door into the breezy October sunlight as he started down the sidewalk.

"Wait," he turned to me.

Howard had a pleasant face, brown beard, broad forehead. His neatly combed hair fell over his eyes. They were deep brown, almost piercing.

"Are you into politics? An activist? A radical?"

I looked at him blankly.

"Sorry to keep you." He smiled cheerfully, walked away. After about ten paces he turned back. "Are you a student?"

"Oxford."

"Oxford. Oxford? But you're in Paris."

"Yes, well—"

"I usually eat at the Mensa. Do you know where it is?"

"The Sorbonne?"

"See you around." Then he turned the corner.

4. BLOOD RIVER
(KARL)

Howard Chapman is why Jake and I went to Africa. While we were on the road, waiting for trucks, riding on trucks, hitchhiking who knows where, I had plenty of time to mull my chance meeting with Howard on that odd day in Paris.

The problem, as Howard saw it, was this: Change the world? Or stay alone in a small room? The commissar or the yogi. Save the world one soul at a time, starting with yourself, or convert the masses to the cause. For those in a hurry, for those without scruple or qualm of morality, massacre is a whole lot quicker than conversion. But what if the cause is no good? And where do you put the bodies?

If you crave solitude, try tramping through the Ethiopian interior ignorant of the customs and languages, while preachers, lepers, and police swarm the streets, and the masses whirl and twist with all their charm and fury. That was still in the future. But it began with Howard.

~

I FOUND HOWARD IN line at the Mensa.

"That was fun yesterday in the café," Howard said. "Did you see how fast our Maoist friend cleared out when you stood up? How tall are you, anyway? Six-three?"

"It doesn't always keep me out of fights," I laughed.

We were in a large hall. At least a thousand people were eating lunch. Maybe this was the largest daily assemblage of intellectuals, professors, academics, students, ex-students, professional students, phonies, bohemians, political agitators, ne'er-do-wells, hangers-on, and hippies on the continent. It hit me that in another day or two I'd have to return to Oxford.

"It doesn't cost much to eat here," Howard said. "You'll pay about a dollar. Though that's five times what we French students pay."

The line lurched forward.

"Ah, so you're French?"

"Not exactly. I'm not exactly a student, either. But the difference is this." He flourished an official-looking paper. "*Une carte d'immatriculation*,[1] a prerequisite to success at the Sorbonne. It says I'm enrolled and paid up." He held it up to the light. "Not a bad forgery, either."

"So you're not French, not a student. And you don't work?"

We shuffled forward a few paces.

"I work. The sociology professors hire me to give lectures. I was a student, and everyone thinks I'm still a student. So there's no problem. I'm studying, too, I assure you, except I don't pay. Instead, they pay me." Howard arched his eyebrows. "It's very satisfactory."

"Why France?"

"Can't stand England. And I'm finished with South Africa."

We reached the front of the line, got our food, and found a place to sit down.

"You're American, aren't you?"

I nodded. "And you're South African, right?"

"Well, I'm English, mostly. I have a British passport. But I've barely lived there. I spent a year in the South African army. Does that surprise you? After high school, it's the army or jail."

"You hated it, I suppose?"

Howard shrugged. "We English are not popular in the army. I take it you never served?"

---

1   Enrollment certificate

"Nixon's draft lottery saved me."

"I see. We were considered substandard material," he continued.

"What do you mean?"

Howard grinned. "In the army the Rocks didn't like us. They knew we'd never fight to keep South Africa white. As far as they were concerned, none of us were real South Africans."

"The Rocks?"

"The big Dutchmen, you know, the Afrikaners who run the show in the army. Tough rock spiders, you see, guarding our peace and tranquility on the border, protecting us from the African National Congress and nasty communists." He swirled the wine in his glass. "They think someday a communist Kaffir army will appear on the border." Howard saw my confusion. "Kaffirs. That's our pet name for the blacks. Arabic for infidel. Not a polite word. No, not at all. But then, few Afrikaners worry about being polite to blacks." Howard took a drink of his wine. "And they'll have to defeat that army. Like at Blood River. There won't be a second chance."

"Blood River?"

Howard winked.

"Well, I know why you left South Africa," I said.

"Oh, yeah? Why?"

"It's a minority-ruled, white-supremacist police state."

"You might say that." Howard sat back in his chair. "It's rather like the American South. It's a white man's democracy if you don't mind one-party rule. The National Party runs the place like Democrats ran the old Confederacy. Look," he said, putting his hands behind his head, "it's a thoroughly racialist undertaking. I'm not planning to go back."

"I don't blame you. How could you stand being there?"

"That's the hard thing," he said. "For some of us South Africa is home. But I do get rather sick of hearing you Yanks bang on about all your so-called freedoms."

"But there's no comparing America to South Africa, is there?"

"Is that what you think? Let's talk about America. You managed to kill off the Indians, I mean at least ninety-five percent of the Indigenous population. Impossible to perform that trick in Africa. Too many blacks and not enough whites."

"That was a long time ago."

"And they're conveniently still dead. Are we forgetting two hundred fifty years of African slavery? The Civil War?"

"We abolished slavery."

He paused. "What followed slavery was not much better. The freed slaves didn't get the vote for another century—until 1965. Your Jim Crow is not so different from Apartheid."

"Jim Crow is on the way out."

"A bit late! The 1935 Nuremberg Laws that stripped Jews of German citizenship? I'm sure you know the Nazis used Jim Crow as a model for Nuremberg.

Yeah, I knew that. Hell! We sent a segregated army to fight Hitler. "We're making progress," I said. "We defeated the Nazis, you know."

"With a little help from the Russians and us Brits. Good show! Well, what do you say about Hitler's plan to kill off the Russians, push them far to the east and give their land to German settlers? You know, for *Lebensraum?*"[2]

"What about it?"

"Well, didn't Andrew Jackson do the same to those Cherokee and Chickasaw sub-humans, the ones he couldn't kill?"

"What? That's crap!" Honestly, I didn't know a thing about Andrew Jackson.

"Crap, eh? Cleared them out. Chased them across the Mississippi. Trail of Tears. Manifest Destiny and all that. White slave owners took their land."

"What's your point, Howard?"

"Don't you see? If Jackson could do it, why couldn't Hitler?"

"Please."

But Howard was on a roll. "The Nazis claimed the Urals were their Mississippi. You're a pack of racists, you Americans. You banned

---

2   living space

Chinese immigration for eighty years."

"Maybe they were overrunning the place." I nodded impatiently.

"But you didn't mind them building your railroads, did you? You interned Japanese American citizens during the war and stole their property. And you've probably killed several million Vietnamese by now, not to mention Laotians and Cambodians. You're dropping jellied gasoline on them. What's it called? Napalm? Just like you did in Japan. And Korea."

I was speechless. I might have said something like this myself, but I hated hearing it from a foreigner. I got up to leave.

"Going so soon?"

"Sorry Howard." I grabbed my bag.

"Don't you like arguments?" Howard smiled. "Can't stand debate? Defend yourself! Refute what I said!"

I clenched my teeth and sat.

"Not everybody, Howard. We're not all racists. Vietnam, well, there's the reason I left the States. America has its agonies. The war's still on. But we have a Bill of Rights. We have free speech. Don't tell me that America is as bad as South Africa."

"As bad?" Howard smiled. "Maybe not. But your America is so damned influential. We're a bad lot. But so are you. You have 'All men are created equal,' even if it was proclaimed by a slave owner. You have 'We the People,' but you can't figure out exactly who the *people* are. And your famous constitution counted a slave as three-fifths of a person."

"We are the world's first elective, representative democracy, and you know it."

"True, you're mankind's brightest hope. You can march your feet off anytime you like. And the courts protect you. But America doesn't live up to its ideals. The country is racist. When will you Americans admit you're no better than the rest of us?"

"In the end Americans do the right thing."

"After first trying everything else? Let's hope you keep getting second chances."

"Shut up, Howard."

"Hey, I can be truthful about South Africa. What about you?"

Things got a bit better after that. My urge to strangle Howard faded. We ate. We drank wine. We talked. Or mostly Howard talked, veering wildly all over the map. His stories were electrifying. In the '60s he'd dropped out of the Sorbonne and crossed Europe, Turkey, Iran, Afghanistan, Pakistan by road to get to India. Disguising himself as a beggar, he lived for months on handouts, not quite starving himself to death. When he'd proved his point, he returned to find France on the brink of revolution. Money from Dad had stopped, of course. Howard listened intently to my accounts of street fighting in Chicago and Washington. On the other hand, Howard had lived through those near-insurrectionary Paris days in May 1968, when the future of France hung by a thread. Then he'd landed on his feet at the Sorbonne. Or was he hanging by his fingernails?

Howard leaned forward. "So, you're a student?"

"I'm at Oxford. I'm studying Rwanda," I said.

"Rwanda? Tell me about Rwanda."

"It's just one massacre after another, Hutus overthrowing the Tutsi power structure and murdering their Tutsi neighbors."

"If massacres interest you, we've got plenty back home in South Africa. Like Sharpeville in '61, when I was off at school in England. But then, you've got plenty of your own."

"Massacres? The Boston Massacre? I can't think of any others."

"Really?" Howard hooted. "Sand Creek? Colorado Territory? Hundreds of Native Americans shot to death. 1864."

"There you go again. That was a hundred years ago."

"Wounded Knee, South Dakota?" Howard continued. "That was 1890. At least the Zulus had a fighting chance at Blood River. But the three hundred ghost dancers shot dead at Wounded Knee were unarmed. And what about 1921? That anti-black pogrom in Tulsa, Oklahoma? Several hundred dead. The richest parts of Tulsa burned to the ground."

"Do shut up."

Howard looked at me, shaking his head. "And all those lynchings? And My Lai in '68? There's plenty more."

"We've had mob violence in Cincinnati," I nodded. "But wait a minute. What's Blood River?"

Howard sighed. "The Day God Whipped the Kaffirs. December 16, 1838. It's the founding myth of the Afrikaner nation. On a hill in Pretoria stands the Voortrekker monument like the Dark Tower of Sauron. Every year on December 16, a shaft of sunlight falls directly on the memorial cenotaph." Howard placed his hand over his heart in mock reverence.

"My God."

Howard took another sip of wine. "Blood River was a battle that became a massacre. At first it seemed the Zulus would do the massacring. That was the idea. They outnumbered the Boers[3] fifty-to-one. But the Afrikaner farmers knew how to shoot."

"I don't follow."

Howard spread his hands on the table. "In Cape Town, the British had just abolished slavery and plenty of Boers were having none of it. They were getting away from the British as fast as they could and taking their so-called servants with them. But they had to cross Zulu territory."

"Sounds like cowboys and Indians."

"Maybe." Howard sipped some wine. "A column of Boer wagons trekking into the interior ran into the Zulu army. Dingaan, the Zulu king, invited seventy Boers to his *kraal*, his encampment, to watch a war dance. Supposedly in their honor." Howard paused. "They surrendered their muskets at the door. To show respect for the king. But at a prearranged signal the Zulus fell on them. Not a single Boer escaped."

"Pretty tricky."

"Next, Dingaan's *impis*, his regiments, thousands of armed men, headed for the Boer camp some distance away. There were five hundred women and children there. They murdered them all."

---

3   Dutch-speaking farmers. pron. "bores."

I whistled. "Zulus two. Boers zero."

"The next year," Howard continued, "in 1838, Dingaan attacked another Boer wagon train camped near a stream. A few hundred Afrikaners, armed with muskets, faced twenty thousand Zulus armed with *assegais*—metal-tipped stabbing spears. The Zulus charged. The Boers shot them down while the women and children furiously reloaded. The Boers kept firing. Soon thousands of dead or dying Zulus piled up in the grass. The stream ran red with their blood. That's why they called it Blood River. Not a single Boer was killed."

"Howard, I still can't figure out what you're up to," I said, gesturing at the vast dining hall. "I get that you like it here in France. But you don't seem, um, completely anchored."

"You know," Howard leaned back in his chair, "British South Africans are not entirely British, but we're not completely South African, either. We're orphaned outcasts of a tattered, decrepit empire. I'm not sure where I belong."

"How did you end up in South Africa?"

"We moved to Johannesburg after the war in 1948, right after I was born. That's when the National Party brought in Apartheid. My dad became a big shot in finance. All he seemed to care about was money."

"And the invincibility of the white race," I added.

"Which is the same thing. I dreaded whenever my mother took me to his office downtown. I had just started grammar school, but I'd stand on the sidewalk glaring at his building, wishing I didn't have to go inside. Even children understand that status and race are connected." He looked into the distance. "I love Dad and Mum, but I don't like them much. Or maybe I pity them."

What bothered Howard were the immense privileges enjoyed by South African whites at everyone else's expense. After all, where did the money come from that paid for the lush suburban house, the swimming pool, the cars, the servants, his mother's clothing and jewels, Howard's education?

"Anyone could see the ragged hovels out the window on the train to Cape Town, or the miserable crowds that filled the streets at the pass office," Howard said. As most British South Africans did, his parents stood back, indifferent to the seething humanity that was everywhere Howard looked. They reveled in their lifestyle and gladly let the Afrikaans-speaking whites do the heavy lifting on politics and race.

"Mum and Dad were almost never home, except evenings," Howard continued, "so I grew up with the servants. In a way they were my real family. By the age of six I was fluent in Sesotho.[4]"

"The local language?"

"I picked up Zulu, too. All of this horrified my mother. She'd say"—and here he switched to falsetto—"'I really can't understand your attraction to that conniving, lazy, low-class breed.' They both complained about the servants, blamed them for everything, fired them at the drop of a hat. My mother didn't have a lot to do at home. So she drank to fill her time. Then they sent me to middle school in England, hoping to set me straight."

"Shipped you off to boarding school?"

"I hated it. I didn't last a year. I couldn't stand England. I made friends with the other colonials—Aussies, you Yanks, Indians, Pakistanis, Arabs, Nigerians, Jamaicans."

"Now you're at the Sorbonne. What do you lecture about?"

"India, mostly. What else? I spent almost a year there. No one wants to hear about South Africa."

"Going back to India?"

"I . . . I don't know. My French friend, Bertrand Lefèvre, is in Burundi. I'd like to visit him."

"Burundi?"

---

[4] pron. seh-SU-tu. One of South Africa's major languages.

5. THE ITCH
(KARL)

Howard and I spent the rest of the day arguing while walking all over Paris. I rolled my eyes as Howard adopted personas as they suited him—mystic, radical, world traveler, outcast, professor, free thinker, Africa expert—discarding them at his whim. He exaggerated a bit but never bragged, described only what he saw and felt, his mind oscillating between politics, history, travel, and spirituality. He was practical and steady—except when he wasn't. He was a functional dreamer. His travel stories infected me. He'd been everywhere.

Howard went off the grid in India. One day he was meditating by the Ganges. He got up, bought a bowl for begging and some Indian kit, shalwar kameez, and baggy trousers; he sold his backpack, handed his money and clothing for safekeeping to a friend he wasn't sure he'd ever see again, sewed his passport into a pouch around his neck, and wandered the streets, penniless, for half a year. No one knew he was not Indian. No one cared if he lived or died. He went anywhere he liked—Kashmir, Rajastan, Bombay, Calcutta; the railways let holy men travel for free. There were weeks when he spoke with no one, and often he could not beg enough to eat. Somehow he survived.

And here I was worried about getting a leave of absence. I began to dread returning to Oxford. Howard's idea was to head for Kenya, specifically Lamu, a Swahili-speaking island on the Indian Ocean north of Mombasa. You could rent a house and live there for almost nothing. If Oxford was so hollow, so contrived, I told myself, maybe it made sense to go to Africa and get closer to the action. But leaving Oxford seemed crazy. I'd have to put everything on the line— my money, my chances, my future. On the plus side if I skipped out, I'd be done with Helen, at least for a while.

I wound up crashing at Howard's flat, a tiny place with scant room to stretch out on the floor. But first I steered us to my dismal hotel to retrieve my things and try to reclaim my nineteen francs for that night. The hotel keeper, a short old man with a large hairy mole in the center of his forehead, ignored my arguments, pointing to a sign reminding guests to check out before one o'clock. We tried to talk him down to half-price. He wouldn't return a centime. He still had my passport.

He shook his head unsympathetically. "No, monsieur, please read the sign. All guests must be out by one. It is the same to me whether you use the room tonight or not. But you must pay." I cursed him. He calmly put my passport on the desk and said if he saw me again, he would call the police. Howard hustled me out, telling me to take it easy.

We landed in a big, well-lighted, noisy, crowded café near Howard's apartment, found a table next to a wall, and ordered two beers. Howard sat silently pondering his glass as I scanned the room.

"That scared me at the hotel."

"Oh, pooh. That guy was jerk."

"You could have been arrested. He might have had a knife."

I ignored him. The bohemian crowd drifted over toward a lively clarinet player in the corner.

"Karl?" said Howard, above the din. "Did I ask what are you doing in Paris? Aren't you in the middle of a semester?"

"It's a long story," I said, practically shouting. "My old girlfriend Helen came to Oxford. Just sort of popped up. It didn't work out."

"Sorry. But maybe you should feel relieved. At least it's over and done with."

Helen, over and done with? "It was messy. I could have handled it better."

"Guilt? Well, you may be a louse, after all."

"Hey!"

"But get over it. Relationships are iffy. No one bats a thousand. Isn't that how you Yanks put it?"

"She expected something from me, something I couldn't give her."

"But why are you in Paris? Because of Helen?"

"The main thing is I don't know why I'm at Oxford. It's interesting as hell. It's also phony, pretentious. My tutor is driving me crazy. So far, this year is a total blank, an enormous weight hanging over my head. I can't get going, can't concentrate. I feel itchy. Like I should do something else."

Howard poured another. "Traditionally, when people stop studying, they go to work. To pay the bills?"

"Yes, the bills must be paid. But what if there are no bills? Like when you were in India? No family to feed. No meaningless job to pay the rent."

"Who says a job must be meaningless? Is your life too precious to rent for a bag of silver? Or maybe no one could possibly pay you enough?"

"Mock on, mock on," I grinned. "I'm not against working. I could have worked back home, had an apartment, a car, stereo, black lights, lava lamp. Being in Europe is like a long vacation. I can ignore politics. In the States I get tense every time I look at a newspaper."

"So you're hiding out, too? I feel like that about South Africa. Though I like France."

"I don't want to settle down to any grind. I want to do things."

"What things?"

"Something gutsy. Anything not boring, ordinary, expected, forced, or messed up. Flip over the game board. Strike out on my own. Disappear off the edge of the map."

Howard arched his eyebrows. "Really? You're ready to chuck everything for a backpack?"

"Do whatever the hell I want. Apologize to no one." I took a sip of beer. I knew I was ranting. "Student life is pathetic. It's so cushy, safe, predictable. My biggest risk is pissing off my tutor. I want to see the world. I've never been on my own or away from the safely familiar. I want something different. I want to shatter expectations, including my own. I need something gripping."

"That sounds like me."

"Another thing. My father thinks I'm an idiot."

Howard frowned. "Seriously? Your father won't think you're nuts for quitting Oxford?"

"He thinks everything I do is crazy, including going to Oxford. Maybe vanishing unexpectedly will get his attention."

"Even so, you must live somewhere," Howard said. "I can see both sides of this. You do get to the end of adventures, at last. You can go do your thing, however crazy, but later you pick up the pieces. There's always a bill to pay at the end."

"Didn't you sort of write the book on doing your own thing? You've been at this longer than me."

"So maybe I'm not the ideal person to pontificate. But in a way I am."

"Part of me is deathly afraid of taking such a big gamble. I may never get back to Oxford."

Howard bit his lip. "Okay, I've been there and back again, and here I am in Northern Europe where I started. Those amazing things I saw and experienced in India? Unforgettable. But coming back to Paris from India in 1968 was disastrous. Apart from being broke and unable to work, nobody could understand what I was talking about or had time to listen. Everybody was pursuing their lives the same as when I left. A lot had changed. But nothing had changed."

"Nothing had changed? With France close to revolution or civil war?"

"True, society was staring into the abyss. That was exciting. That's not what I mean." Howard thought a moment. "Here's the thing. I had changed forever. It was shattering, as you put it. But I was on the exact same square as when I left, except I had dropped out of school and was unemployed. But life went on without me. Whatever I had seen, done, or learned in India hadn't affected anything here. Everyone was pursuing their lives, just the same as before. Talk about naïve. What did I expect? The fact was, I went to see the world and put my life on hold. No one stopped me. No one cared. The worst part was I had no partner to talk to when it was over."

Howard ran a hand through his hair. "I was left alone with my visions. What difference did it all make? I'd had my great adventure, but I still had to put food on the table. People heard me out about India, politely at first, but later they wanted to change the subject. It was too big, too rapturous. I probably sounded like a madman. They excused my ravings as chit-chat, just another story. People like talking about themselves. After all, wasn't that what I was doing? So they'd tell me about a movie they'd seen last week. I had been places, lived things that they didn't know a thing about, had never dreamed, would never see. But they could only talk about the last film they'd seen at the bioscope."

"Bioscope?"

"Sorry. That's what we called movie theaters in South Africa." He finished his glass and looked around the bar. It was noisier than ever. The clarinetist was playing Django Reinhardt, "Avalon," it sounded like. The crowd pressed toward his corner.

"Where was I?"

"At the bioscope."

"Ah. I realized I was tired of Europe. I couldn't get used to it. India was still in my mind. I half-expected to see some broken-down cow meandering down the street. Paris is so clean, so lifeless, dead, superficial, snobby. So new."

"To Americans it seems old."

"India is ancient, its philosophies dismiss the world as a mere heartbeat in an endless succession of creations and destructions. Proud Europe thinks it's the pinnacle of human achievement and holds the rest of mankind in contempt. I admit I'm European, and always will be. That is sad, because somehow I thought I'd acquired a new identity in India. I remember watching the rivers." Howard looked intensely at me. "Man, I sat on the banks of the Ganges, watching it flow into the ages, eternal, unmoved by the pious hordes washing at its banks, carrying away all their sorrows into timelessness."

Howard was right about one thing. Like his French friends I had no idea what he was talking about. "You should write a book."

"Yeah. I tried." Howard stared at me, his eyes focused on the infinite like some ascetic wandering down a road removed from time. "The queer thing is, I'd like to go again."

"You want to head off again?"

"Isn't that strange? East Africa this time. I'm already lecturing about India," Howard said, "so in the end I've forced some people to listen to me. Maybe I can lecture about Africa when I get back."

I was watching a small, blonde girl heading directly toward us. Nineteen or twenty, fashionable, wearing a fur-fringed knock-off Afghani sheepskin coat with multicolored embroidery.

"Do you know that girl, Howard?"

"Which girl?"

But she had already reached the table.

6. TWO CONVERSATIONS
(KARL)

My mailbox was stuffed with messages when I got back to Oxford. Helen called twice. And Harold wanted to see me. I trudged up the stairs to my floor. The hallway telephone was ringing. It was Helen.

"Hi Karl. I've been trying to call you."

"Helen?"

"Where were you?"

"I've been away," I sighed. "Just got back."

"Is everything all right?"

"Peachy. Couldn't be better."

"Oh. Good."

Dead silence.

"Helen, where are you?"

More silence.

"Helen?"

"Ernestine and I are moving to a women's commune in Michigan."

"Swell," I said. "Michigan? That's swell. Where in Michigan?"

"I don't have to tell you that. I just thought you might want to know."

"Thanks for telling me."

"Karl, I want to ask you something. When you said I could stay with you in Oxford, did you mean it?"

I hesitated.

"Karl?"

"Why are you asking this, Helen? You just said you're going to Michigan. Are you coming back here?"

"Karl? Did you really mean it?"

"Yes, Helen. I meant it."

"Okay. Just checking."

"Well?"

"Well what?"

"Are you coming back?"

"No, I'm not coming back. Um, I have to go."

"Wait! When will I hear from you again?"

Some muffled conversation at the other end, a clang as the receiver fell on the floor. The line went dead. My hand held the wall. So Helen, who was pregnant with my child, was going to live in a women's commune somewhere in Michigan with her lover, Ernestine. As for me, I didn't care to talk with Helen again. I couldn't figure out why she had called me.

Next day I went to see Harold. He had this plum, multi-room fourth-floor office with big windows and a great view, stuffed with books, carpets, African carvings, tea sets, and comfortable chairs. On the wall beside diplomas and antique maps of Africa were framed pen and ink drawings of Danton, Robespierre, and Lenin. Given his focus on revolution, that didn't surprise me. What did were Harold's conservative political views. On one wall was a large painting of a British man-of-war in full sail. Seen from the stern, its starboard cannons flamed a brutal, unanswered broadside at a frigate flying the colors of revolutionary France.

Motioning me to sit, Harold greeted me warmly, as he always did, and handed me a cup of tea. He reminded me about a paper—biographical sketches, he'd assigned before Helen's visit.

"Karl, I wonder if you're taking this program as seriously as you should. It's demanding, and it can get away from you quickly if you don't keep on top of it."

"I know."

Harold leaned back in his chair. He got busy with his tea. Then he stared at me, pursing his lips.

"Is everything all right with you?"

"Not really. I'm having personal problems." The words came out faster than I wanted them to. "I'm beginning to wonder whether I should continue. Maybe I should come back next year."

Harold looked at me askance. "Are you seriously thinking of quitting? What comes next?"

"The truth is, I'm thinking about going to Africa."

"Africa? Where in Africa?"

"East Africa."

"And why?"

"I'd like to get closer to the action. I figure I can learn more about Africa and revolution in Africa than reading books about it in England."

Harold considered this. "Idi Amin in Uganda might well do something rash to destabilize the entire region. He's hardly a revolutionary. But he's one to watch."

I knew nothing about Uganda, and Harold knew it. I knew it was next to Kenya on the map.

"My friend Howard wants to visit Burundi. So, it's possible—"

"Burundi?" For a moment Harold looked off into the distance, a finger on his chin. "Now, that would be interesting." But then he frowned, leaning forward in his chair, rubbing his hands while looking straight at me. "Leaves of absences at Oxford are hard to come by, Karl, especially for a new student who has not even completed a semester. In fact, you haven't been here a month. I'd say it's out of the question."

"Maybe it would be better if I dropped out entirely, then reapply."

Harold shook his head. "There's no guarantee that Balliol would take you back." Harold watched to see what impression this made on me. "Though we might if you could show a level of achievement during your absence. It's a gray area."

I asked Harold whether he would support my decision to take time off, if that's what I decided. All he said was, "You show a lot of promise, Karl. But many students would be happy to have your spot." He patted me on the back as I left, reminding me about the reading we were to discuss in two days.

The days passed. I went through my academic motions, trying not to think about Helen. But inside I was seething with ideas of exploring Africa and extracting myself from Oxford.

7. BALLIOL
(JAKE)

Two days in crowded, expensive London were enough. Someone suggested Oxford, an easy sixty miles away. Next day I rode the tube as far as it went, then started hitching. England is the ideal country for hitchhikers, I was sure. As soon as one car dropped me off, another would stop. I could not believe my luck. All kinds of people picked me up—businessmen in three-piece suits, plumbers in overalls, grandmothers with granddaughters, shop owners, five miles here, seven miles there. Finally, a trucker brought me to Oxford. I ditched my pack at Left Luggage at the train station.

Oxford is not a university town like you might think. It's really a big industrial city with lots of bicycles, bookshops, and students milling about. The university is a green sprawl of colleges and ancient buildings. A woman in a shop suggested looking at Balliol College.

I gawked at the architecture, trying to picture myself studying there. Since high school I was always broke. Any extra money I had went to my sisters. But I always was good at school, and I spent my time in my hooch on the oil platform reading, novels mostly—Dostoyevsky, Tolstoy, Faulkner, Melville, Tolkien—on the off chance I might get to college someday. College was impossible now, though I had money. I chitchatted with a female librarian about Oxford admissions. Where was I from? The Midwest?

"We have a student at Balliol from the American Midwest, I think. Is Ohio in the Midwest?" She pointed toward a sea of desks.

"He's sitting right over there. Shall I call him?" Before I could stop her, she did.

This serious-looking, tall guy with a trimmed brown beard walked up, his hair combed straight back from his forehead.

"I'm glad I could introduce you two Yanks," the librarian said, while turning to leave. "Karl, we're having a small party on Friday night. Why don't you bring Jake?"

I introduced myself, stammering it was all a mistake; this kind woman was trying to help me; I wasn't applying to Oxford; I just got off a plane. Karl said don't worry. We got to talking about things back home, like politics and football. He seemed glad to meet me. We were both twenty-two. I figured Karl for a real intellectual. Karl said I was the only person he knew who worked with his hands. That's all I knew how to do, working on harvesters, milking machines, trucks, tractors back on the farm, then the oil business. I heard plenty about Helen, Howard Chapman, Oxford, Africa, Harold Higgins, and an island called Lamu.

Karl did most of the talking. He needed to talk. I guess not knowing me made it easier for him. Helen had left him. He was upset about it, but he wasn't about to chase Helen back to the States. It seemed like he had it made but he was dropping out of Oxford. Now he was headed for Africa and needed a partner. I had a hard time following all of this. It sounded interesting, especially Africa, which was farther from the States than Europe. That was good for me. Probably a lot cheaper. Adventurous. Karl admitted he had no clue about Africa travel. Why not check the library, I said? We spent the entire afternoon there.

That evening, after signing up for the youth hostel, I came back to Balliol to meet Karl for dinner.

"Howard got me thinking about Lamu, that island I had mentioned?" Karl pushed his hair back from his face and attacked his steak. "But we never nailed anything down."

"Sounds like paradise."

"Here's the thing. It's a small town on a small island. I'd like to see a bit of Africa before landing there."

"What about it?"

"Frankly, Jake, I'd rather not go by myself."

"I can see that. I wouldn't go by myself, either. Europe is one thing. Africa is whole different kettle of fish."

Karl leaned closer. "It's true Africa is my field, but I actually don't know much about it. I know a few things about Rwanda. Otherwise, I'm hopeless."

Now I attacked my steak. *They eat good here at Oxford,* I thought, looking up at the ornate vaulted windows, the twenty-foot ceilings.

"What I don't get is why you'd ever want to leave this place. Looks like you have it made."

"You could say that. It's magnificent. I just need some time off."

"What else would you do? I mean, you seem cut out for academia."

To me, all this to-and-fro sounded nutty, like people with too many choices. Maybe it hadn't been that hard for Karl to get to Balliol College in the first place. Maybe he wasn't worried about coming back.

"So what about you, Jake?"

"Me? I grew up on a farm in Nebraska. Worked in the Gulf of Mexico on an oil rig."

"Why'd you head to Europe?"

I had rehearsed this. "Figured I'd give it a try. I had money saved up. I was tired of working. Plus, my uncles were in Europe during the war."

"Oh?"

"They never came home."

I pushed the plates away. We got up to leave.

"That's tough. My dad was a flier. Got shot down. Spent a year in a German prison camp."

"Really?"

"By the way, Jake, library parties are famous. Don't miss it."

Karl suggested we meet for breakfast in town. So the next morning I showed up early.

"Hi, Jake. Look at this." Karl unfolded a large-scale map and spread it out on the table. It was a Michelin road map of northeast Africa about four feet square. A professional traveler's tool, it clearly showed every road, every border, every mountain, every river in detail, and marked every distance.

"What would you say to Ethiopia? It's not super expensive to get there. Living is dirt cheap. We can hitchhike around the country, then head down to Kenya. How does that sound?"

"Sure, I'll think about it. When do you want to go?"

"Maybe in a few weeks. I'll see what I can do about finishing the semester early. I'm also curious about what Howard is going to do. He's been sending postcards from Paris almost every day. But I'm nervous about finances. How much money do you have?"

I lowballed, cutting a thousand from what I actually had. "Twelve hundred, more or less."

"I'll be lucky to scrape together a thousand," Karl sighed. "It's whatever's left from mowing lawns and shoveling snow in Cincinnati when I was a kid. It comes down to how much of my expense money to take. Probably makes sense to take it all, leave the tuition money in the bank, worry about making more later."

"You think?"

"Place one big bet on red, spin the wheel."

I liked the idea of getting even farther away from Louisiana. My money would last longer in Africa. And now I had a partner. Funny going to Africa, with Pudge's phobias about the Blacks. At least they wouldn't be racists like him and his friends. To me, Ethiopia sounded exciting, like heading back in time. The country was crumbling, apparently. Its emperor, Haile Selassie, was almost eighty. He'd defied Mussolini, but the Italians overran the place in no time and stayed six years, until 1941, when the British kicked them out. The threadbare monarchy had been in charge ever since. That was thirty years ago. I wondered what they had to show for it.

Friday came around. We showed up for the party around nine. The place was jumping. Someone stuck beers in our hands, then loudly introduced us as Oxford's Africa explorers. This caused a sensation.

"I might have mentioned something about it," Karl exhaled.

One female student walked up to me. Said her name was Kim. "Are you going to write a book?" she asked.

"Jake," I said pointing at myself. "I haven't decided whether to write a book. I'll wait and see how things turn out."

"That's a wonderful answer." Kim smiled. "I love your accent." She kissed me on the cheek.

I didn't realize I had an accent. I lost focus on the party. God she was pretty. Brunette, shapely.

She took my hand. "You've got some fantastic eyes," she said, coming closer.

A tall boisterous drunk pointed at me. "So this is the new John Hanning Speke? Mr. Speke, sir. Please speak to us."

"Who is this Speke guy?" I asked Kim, practically shouting to be heard over the general din.

"Speke? Let me see. Um, explorer of the sources of the Nile?"

"That Speke. Of course."

"You know us Balliol students," she said, curtsying in her tattered jeans. "Tranquil assurance of effortless superiority."

"Wait," the drunk roared at Karl. "And who are you? Sir Richard Francis Burton?"

Karl pointed at me. "No, he's Burton."

"Burton?" the drunk repeated. "Who risked instant death if discovered as an infidel while traveling to Mecca disguised as an Arab?"

"Precisely. You might want to try it yourself. After one more vodka and tonic." Karl gave him a gentle shove.

Kim sidled up to me. The scent of her hair made me dizzy.

"How long are you here for?"

"I don't know. I just arrived. Maybe a few weeks?"

"They're impossibly blue, those eyes," Kim said. "They're piercing, radiant." She was looking right at me now. "They glint like the eyes of a fanatic," she grinned. "Are you a fanatic?"

"Not sure," I said, waving my empty beer bottle. Kim grabbed it, reappeared with a refill.

It was horrible meeting Kim. She might have been the best thing that happened to me in months, but I wanted to flee. I had nothing for her. Before Louisiana and between jobs, I hitchhiked out West for a couple of months. I was maybe nineteen. Wound up in a stunning Arizona box canyon. That's where I met Lorraine. We fell in love—at least I thought we were in love. She made me laugh. I got used to being on my own after my folks died. Since leaving home, I never had close friends or romance. I was always alone with my thoughts, my plans, my dreams, my problems. But being with Lorraine was like walking through a door to a new world. We imagined traveling together, picking fruit in California and the Pacific Northwest. She insisted I meant everything to her. I sketched her like she was this gorgeous model. After two weeks one morning she was gone. *Had to leave,* the note said. I never found out where she was from. I couldn't get over the way Lorraine ditched me. It still hurt. Better to treasure nothing. Better to love no one. But after I killed Pudge on the oil derrick, my isolation got much worse. How could I explain murder to anyone? I panicked when women got close to me. What right did a killer have for such enjoyments?

∼

KIM WAS RUBBING MY shoulder and my neck. I looked her over again. She sure was pretty. Hadn't been drinking much, at least compared with everyone in that room.

"You're at Balliol? What are you studying?"

"Classics. Dead Greek and Roman lit."

"You know I'm from Nebraska?" I wanted to get that out in the open before anyone assumed I was at Oxford. "I grew up on a farm."

"Fascinating. My cousins are farmers. Where is Nebraska? Is that near Illinois?"

"One state over. Not far."

Karl approached. "Look, Jake, I've got some business to do. Can we meet here tomorrow for dinner?" He rushed off.

"I think I should be leaving, too."

Kim put her hand to my cheek. "Want to meet me for lunch?" She wrote down an address. It was set for noon the next day. But I forgot to show up. I never saw her again.

8. DECISIONS
(KARL)

I desperately wanted out. To escape? To make my mark? I had never been farther from home than Paris. So far, my alleged plan was to dump Oxford and lose my first semester tuition money and my savings and maybe any hope for a career in order to hang out with Howard at the equator for a few months. I kept telling myself this was not madness, but it was hard to keep a straight face. On the other hand, the freedom of the road was seductive. I had enough money, barely. When would I have this chance again? But what if Balliol would not readmit me, what then? How would I ever reach Harold's level of achievement? I hemmed and hawed. This was a patently insane idea. But it excited me, too, excited me more by the minute. *Nothing ventured, nothing gained,* I kept repeating. But I knew it would be like jumping off a cliff.

A postcard from Howard arrived with his scribble on the back. It was a photo of Mont-Saint-Michel, a soaring medieval hilltop abbey looming above a walled town on the tidal flats in northern France.

October 29, 1971
Dear Karl,

Hope you got back to Oxford OK. Guess what? Linda moved in with me after you left. No surprise? When I mentioned that you and I might be going to Africa she immediately wanted to go. Claims she's tired of art school. I tried to talk her out of it—she's barely an undergraduate, after all—but she is adamant. Has the travel bug. And money is not a problem. Seems her old man has pots of it. I know this complicates things a bit. I thought it'd be just us two academics. How would you feel about having Linda along? She's a great travel partner. We sneaked off to Normandy on a day trip and she was fabulous. This crazy thing called love. It's sort of like being electrocuted: Sudden, shocking. But mostly not fatal. We'll be up in London in no time for the flight to Nairobi. I'll let you know.

Yours, Howard

Linda. That was her name. The American tourist who had rushed our table that night in the Paris bar, supposedly to ask directions, but within minutes things between her and Howard got hot and heavy. I wrote back something bland and non-committal. I wanted to go to Africa. I wanted to see Howard again. But a threesome? The quest began to deflate. That's when Jake showed up, free as a bird and ready for anything. True, I didn't really know him. But within a few days we decided to team up.

I was a mess, worried about a million things, running this way and that, selling whatever I didn't need, getting signatures, withdrawing money from the bank. I luckily got out of paying most of my room rent, and the residence allowed me to store my stuff in the basement for a year. The cheapest one-way ticket to Addis Ababa cost $420, but a half-price deal for students brought the price down to $210. An afternoon's work got Jake an international student ID card, which Ethiopian Airlines accepted without question. I bought a backpack, a sleeping bag, and boots. Together we bought mess kits, anti-malaria pills, a waterproof tarp, and a tiny tent.

I'm sure Harold Higgins thought I was nuts. But despite that dismal, depressing meeting in his office, somehow he arranged matters for me with Oxford. He made clear I'd have no formal institutional linkage. My justification to do research on revolution in Africa was beyond flimsy. "Just keep your finger on the pulse of the revolutionary artery," he told me in his jaunty way. In the end, it was all done with a handshake. The truth is, every time I offered to resign from Balliol, Harold would say, "Let me handle that, Karl." I never saw any official paper. I was not convinced the administration even knew what I was doing. The deal was this: I would mail Harold periodic reports "gauging the susceptibility of African societies to revolution," or anything else that I found interesting. It was beyond seat of the pants. I guessed Harold was sticking out his neck for me, managing my absence out of his back pocket, so to speak. Harold was my only ticket back—if I was coming back.

Before leaving for Africa, Harold had me write one last, crash essay about how Rwandan independence had destabilized the region, especially Burundi, starting with the 1959 peasant uprising that overthrew the Tutsi monarchy in Rwanda. Hutus, under the new republic, had murdered Tutsis by the thousands, while Tutsi refugees flooded into the Congo, Uganda, and Burundi. So I knew that little bit about Africa.

As the day of our departure approached, my mind swirled with unknown futures. What Helen might do next plainly scared me. Yet for the present I was more anxious about how Jake and I would get along. Thrown together into long-distance travel was like a marriage. No, it was worse. Suddenly we were together all the time, but minus the intimate moments you might enjoy with a wife or girlfriend. The same guy at night, in the morning, and every minute in between. It's an extreme roommate situation. It's like being locked together in a room, or say in a spaceship, where people can visit you anytime as you cruise on, but neither of you can leave. You must do everything together—eating, sleeping, sitting on the bus, waiting by the road, discussing, negotiating every detail amid constant bickering. The committee of two must convene each time you want to drink coffee or run to the bathroom. Ha! I know how Jake felt about it. He'd say flat out he was sick of me. It gradually dawned on me that Jake was the only person in the world besides me who'd know anything about this period in my life, who'd remember what happened and what was said, even if I forgot. And I was that person for him. Even so, I wondered if this partnership would turn out to be a terrible mistake. It seemed like the height of stupidity at some moments, genius at others, like quitting Oxford.

I had no such qualms about Howard. I knew all about Howard, opinionated, fearless, and easily smitten. But I had barely met Jake, didn't know him from Adam, really, didn't know anything about his background, like whether he had a price on his head, never mind how he might react in situations we might face. But I needed a partner. There was no other plan, and it was too late to change it.

Late afternoon on November 5, Guy Fawkes Day, Jake, and I met with Howard and Linda at St. Pancras station in London. Smoke hung in the streets. I introduced Jake, hugs all around. We helped carry their baggage to a pub.

Surprised to see Jake, Howard said, "So who's going on the plane?"

"Howard, there's been a change of plans. Jake and I will meet you guys in Lamu," I said. "But we're going to Ethiopia first."

"Ethiopia? Ethiopia?" Howard was at a loss. "So you're not coming to Kenya?"

"Ethiopia makes sense to us. We'll see the country, then hitchhike down to Kenya."

"How long will that take?"

"Dunno." I looked at Jake. "Two months, max."

"We thought," Howard said, glancing at Linda and patting her knee, "we'd all rent a house in Lamu."

"Lamu does sound exciting," Linda said, "from what Howard tells me."

"This way you guys get some private time before we barge in," I said. "Makes more sense to me."

Howard looked at Linda again, who squeezed his hand. They conferred quietly. "All right. If that's how things are. January then?"

Two days later, all waves and well wishes, we watched them get on the plane at Heathrow. A week later it was our turn. We flew to Ethiopia on November 14, 1971.

9. ADDIS
(JAKE)

Addis Ababa is eight thousand feet above sea level with high ridges on every horizon. The sun warmed me in the dry mountain air. Being outside felt good, unlike cold, wet England. I was in a different world.

In the terminal Karl spotted people from the plane talking with an American Peace Corps volunteer named Mike. He led everyone outside to his Land Rover.

"We always come to the airport to meet the flights," Mike said. "We like company."

Karl and I got in with two other Americans and one tall Canadian. Frank, the Canadian, had a big red maple leaf flag sewn on his pack with "Canada" written above it in black block letters, and he sported a maple leaf pin on his T-shirt. Who would dream of harming a Canadian? Those maple leaves would hold off hate-filled mobs of anti-American rioters, who'd line up to shake Frank's hand after cutting our throats. Funny how he looked down at his pin when I asked where he was from.

Frank's partners were Wayne from Michigan, and Sarah from California. The three of them never stopped griping. Walking from the airport, waiting by the car, in the car, they kept at it.

We roared off. I was glued to the window. We bounced on the ruts and potholes, dodging donkeys, dogs, taxis, horses, camels, push carts, cars, buses, loud trucks. People carried bags on their heads, boxes, books, melons, machetes, and shoes. Mike mentioned breezily that the light poles lining the airport road had been used to display for weeks the bodies of rebel soldiers, two on a pole, after a failed coup in 1960.

We blazed through downtown, veered off the main road, climbed a hill, swerved around a big curve, and squealed to a stop outside a slapdash fence of wooden poles and corrugated steel. Mike beeped, the gate opened, and Ethiopians greeted us at a sprawling one-story structure with a rusty steel roof. Mike led us to a room with four bunk beds.

"Anyone want to get high?" someone called in the door. Karl stayed in the bunk room. I walked into the main room. Mike sat with Sarah and Frank behind a large pile of weed. Sarah passed a joint to Frank, who wasn't giving it back.

"Give me back the damn joint, Frank," Sarah said.

"Ah, don't fight about it. We've got plenty," Mike said.

A map of Africa, six-feet square, hung on a wall—three separate Michelin maps joined together.

"Here's Addis Ababa," Mike pointed somewhere above us. "The main road goes through Dessie and Makale[5] up north to Asmara, Ethiopia's second biggest city. You're hitchhiking, aren't you?"

I nodded.

"Not a speck of pavement anywhere in this country. Just so you know. Then coming back from Asmara to Addis you can take the other north-south road." I followed his pointing finger. "There's Adua, where King Menelek crushed an Italian army in 1896. And Axum, the Queen of Sheba's capital. That road goes through Gondar. The Falashas live there, the Ethiopian Jews. That blue spot is Lake Tana, the source of the Blue Nile. And there's Bahar Dar at the bottom of Lake Tana, near Blue Nile Falls."

I gaped at him. All this was straight out of Tolkien. Bahar Dar was Barad-dur, the Dark Tower of Mordor from *The Lord of the Rings*.

---

5   Meh-KEH-lay

Gondar, well that was Gondor, the great kingdom and white-walled city of Middle Earth.

"Right in the middle of the two roads, here," Mike continued, "is Lalibela. Churches carved from solid rock. You need a donkey to get there. Now, east of Addis you can take a train through the desert to Dire Dawa and Harrar."

Mike was talking about the Hyena Man of Harrar, but this was pure Tolkien again. Harrar: The Haradrim, the southern Corsairs from Umbar. And Dire Dawa—all those *Ds* like Dimrill Dale—the valley below the gates of Khazad-dum, the dwarves' great fortress in the Mountains of Moria.

"From Asmara you can go down to Massawa on the Red Sea, and you can hop over to Yemen, if you like."

Karl emerged from the bunkroom. "There's a war on in Yemen," he said. "We're not going there."

Then it hit me. We were in a fabled African kingdom. All the vague lines on that huge map, the obscure names, oddly shaped boundaries, the lakes, rivers, mountains; we were minutes from a road that would take us to any of them. This was no fantasy. What was Africa? To find out, all we had to do was go outside.

Mike gave me the list of Peace Corps volunteers in Ethiopia and where they worked.

"They all love visitors," he said. And with that, Karl and I went out the door.

The city was green with mimosa, jacaranda, eucalyptus. A modern high-rise loomed above an endless traffic jam of carts, enraged drivers, thousands of pedestrians, dusty, gritty, cacophonous, a throwback to an earlier age. I blinked my eyes in bare belief. The smells were indescribable. Cows and braying donkeys were everywhere, chickens underfoot, herds of goats, screaming naked children chased oxen, beating them with long canes. I saw many tall, trim, graceful, striking people in white homespun, fine-featured faces, high cheekbones, and serious, stern, dignified expressions.

Men held staffs or rode burros. Women walked together, balancing bundles on their heads.

I had been on this continent, in this town, only two hours and I already was stoned, adrift, open-eyed amazed, in a front-row seat at a movie set with thousands of extras. Vendors, con men, school kids, market women, mothers with children, wedding parties, crones, priests, cripples, beggars, hunchbacks, polio victims with shriveled limbs, and lepers missing limbs poured through the streets. Herdsmen, travelers, merchants, police, soldiers, prostitutes, hawkers of every imaginable good selling fresh fruit, spices, grain, rice, and meat. Workers hauling heavy bags on their heads or driving overloaded animals. There were families, ambulant pharmacists, holy men, preachers, blind men, jesters, jugglers, fools, drooling crazy men. Everything was for sale. Coffee shops, restaurants, gas stations, auto repair garages lined the sidewalks, while tinkers, tailors, book vendors, gold merchants, souvenir sellers, antique dealers, dry-goods men hounded the numberless horde. We passed some men drinking, smoking, sitting around a small table beneath a faded beach umbrella. All drunk as hell, they kept falling off their plastic chairs. Salesmen staked out sidewalks flogging religious articles, animal feed, used auto parts, radios, records, soap. It was staggering. It was biblical. I half-expected to see a knight in armor ride by.

"What do you make of it, Karl?"

"It's not Ohio."

Everyone was Black. Everyone but us. In Nebraska practically everyone was White. Though once, when Ma took me to visit relatives in Chicago, we cut through the South Side. I saw more Black people on that day than I'd ever seen in my life.

"Where are we?" I asked Ma.

"We're on the South Side."

"Ma, how come so many colored people live here?"

"Hush up."

"But Ma—"

"You hush," was all she said.

We got back to the homey Peace Corps house before dark. The Peace Corps guys looked just like us—long hair, beards, dusty jeans.

"You're planning to visit James Murphy in Dessie?" Mike asked.

"If he's on the list," Karl said.

"He's on the list all right. How was your walk?"

"It's crazy out there," I said.

"You know what they say about Ethiopia? Leaping headlong into the thirteenth century."

Great crashes of pots, shrill voices, and spitting fat. The treacherous trio were cooking dinner.

"Looks like we did it right this time," said Frank, cutting onions.

"Oh boy oh boy, this is gonna be great," said Wayne.

Sarah waltzed a slab of red steak into view. "We bought this in a butcher shop," she crooned, holding it with two hands up to Karl's nose like it was a rare woodcarving. "Paid one-fifty Ethie a kilo."

"Sixty US cents a kilo? That's, uh, less than thirty cents a pound?"

Sarah was so happy she clucked. "What are you guys eating?"

We had sardines, but I didn't mention it. My Ethiopian visions vanished. I watched them huddle over the stove.

"Time to eat?" Karl asked me.

"Let's wait."

"What for? Aren't you hungry?"

"In a little while."

"Look, I'm hungry. I'll save you half."

Nothing for it. I dug the cans and the bread out of my pack. Immediately Frank spied them.

"What's that you've got there? Sardines?"

Sarah's face shined. "Sardines?"

"That's fine with us. We like sardines," I said.

"I like sardines, too," Wayne laughed. "But I do like steak better."

I opened the sardine cans while Karl cut the bread. You take your hunk of bread, put your little Portagee fish two-across, mash them, spread them fine. Don't forget a jot of the precious oil. They're tasty, if you can curb your imagination.

"Steak's done," Sarah chirped, holding a steaming pan. Frank immediately moved on it.

"Hold on there, Frank, that's my piece," Wayne said.

"Aw, what's the difference, Wayne? They're all the same. Anyway, that's the piece I want."

"I'll flip you for it."

"No you don't," Sarah scolded. "You're not leaving me out. I flip, too."

They all flipped coins.

"Looks like I win." Frank reached for the meat.

"No, you didn't," Sarah said right away. "You were odd and out. Now I flip with Wayne."

"I was odd hell. I won!"

After a high-pitched squabble they flipped again using Frank's rules.

"Looks like I won after all, Frank," Sarah crowed.

"All right. But when do I get my money?"

"What money?" Wayne said. "For the steak? It was $2.10 Ethie. You'll get it."

"I want it now." Frank held out his hand.

"After we eat," Wayne said.

"For heaven's sake, Frank, we owe you eighty-five US cents." Sarah smiled at us. "We call Frank our Jewish banker."

"What's that supposed to mean?" Karl said.

"He's always after us for money. Isn't that right Frank?"

"So, Jews are always looking for money?" Karl said. "Every Jew is a banker? And every banker is a Jew?"

"It's just a joke," Sarah said.

"A pretty bad one."

"Hey Sarah," I said, getting up. "If I was Jewish, would you try to kill me?"

"What?"

I looked her straight in the eye. "Would you try to kill me? Because I was Jewish?"

"Are you crazy?"

"I've known people like that," I said.

"It was a joke," Wayne said. "Just a dumb joke."

"I don't like being called a Jew," Frank said. "It's no joke to me."

"You people make me sick," I said. "People died because of talk like that. Millions died."

"Oh, shut up," Sarah said.

They sat stone-faced to eat. Karl finished eating, pushed his plate away and left. I cleaned up, watching them chew, dead silent, staring straight ahead. Chewing hard. Chewing, chewing. Except for Frank; he was hacking at his meat with a Swiss Army knife. He finally grabbed the meat in his hands trying to rip off a chunk with his teeth. Then he spit it out. One by one they gave up and walked away, leaving the unfinished steak on the plates. Then Sarah came back and threw it all in the trash.

10. KEMBOLCHA
(JAKE)

It was a bright, new, perfect day, nothing but blue sky and a tan road ahead.

"The hills really are green. So green you could cut them up and put them in a salad bowl," Karl said.

"What's that?" I looked around. "Yeah, what I like is how the trees grow at an angle, straight out of the hillside, like a kindergarten kid drew them."

It is November 18, 1971. Two hours of hitchhiking had brought us about ten miles north of Addis Ababa. We walked down the road in the cool morning air carrying our packs, the sun already impossibly strong. Villages and farmland printed a gay pattern on the wrinkled hills, stretching higher and higher into the clouds. Children played their games on the road secure from traffic since there was no traffic. Cotton-clad men shuffled past holding long staves. Women carried bundles of thornwood on their heads. As they passed, they turned back to gawk at us. We were bedraggled apparitions, unkempt prospectors separated from their mule. An old man stood on the road mumbling toothless questions in Amharic. His elbows and knees were splintered from dryness more than from age. Calloused and deeply cracked at the heels, his feet had seldom walked in shoes. He pointed at us good-naturedly. We stopped a minute to laugh with him. A crowd gathered, pushing us to move on.

"Where are you going?" students asked us, proud of their rough English. The answer is some town to the north. It may only be the next town of any size, but it's very far on a dirt road. Many have never been there. We tried explaining that we were going to Asmara, then back to Addis on the Gondar Road. From there to Nairobi. It made no sense to them.

"Ah, tourist," they smile. We're as strange to the students as we are to the peasants.

I put my pack down. "Let's wait here."

"I'd rather keep going."

"What for? Karl, this place is as good as any to find a truck."

"I want to get away from these people."

A dozen kids ran up to gape at us.

"There are people wherever we go. We might as well wait here."

More kids swarmed. Soon they swamped us, ten, twenty or thirty of them. They inched closer, pushed by the ones in back, sucking their grimy fingers, the older ones carrying infants, their eyes wide. Everything we did was wondrous, worthy of comment. They stared until our eyes locked on theirs, and they saw that we saw them. Then everything we did was fearful. Adults arrived, scolding, serious, pushing the children to the rear, smiling at us apologetically, but then they forgot to leave. We were a vision of the future. Full-blown prodigies. Men who fell to earth.

"Wonder when a truck's going to come," I said. "Wouldn't want to wait all day." I opened my pack to get a book to read, drawing oohs and ahs from our observers.

"Now who's impatient? We could hardly see a truck pass with this big crowd. Two trucks might have gone by already. You wouldn't even know it."

I stood trying to glimpse the road over the enveloping throng. "I see what you mean. The drivers will never see us."

"This is death for the ride business," Karl said. "We may be here for a year. We'll become a permanent tourist attraction."

"We'll charge people for pictures."

"We must look weird to them."

"About as weird as they look to us," I said.

"They're not giving us much space. We're tightly packed," Karl said. "It's like being in a demonstration." Then he said, "I hear a truck coming."

"You do?" I cocked my head. "That's no truck."

"I'm sure I heard it. Let's get to the middle of the road."

"I'll stay here with our stuff. You're taller. You'll stand out better than me."

I could see a dust cloud at the bend in the road. A low rumble riled the crowd as the truck climbed a small incline. Everyone turned to watch the truck. The truck blasted its horn, and they reluctantly gave way. I waved my arms. The truck passed in a whirl of dust.

Karl walked back. "Damn. I told you this was no place to wait. That driver didn't even see me." Turning to the spectators, he said, "You people go home. What do you want?" They stared at him.

"Karl, they are home."

"I know. I know. It's annoying."

"We'll get a ride. That was only the first truck."

"This is so slow. How will we get to Asmara? It's so far. Maybe we should take a bus."

"What bus?" I kicked the dust with the toe of my boot.

"If one comes."

"Aw, calm down a little. Enjoy the day. This is our first week in Africa. What's the rush? You see the people here?" I swept my hand over the road. "Are they in a hurry?"

"Aren't we supposed to meet Howard in Lamu?" Karl pouted. "We don't have all kinds of time."

"Man, you could walk back to Addis and get on a plane, if that's your hurry. I want to see Ethiopia. We'll get to Kenya. It's not going anywhere."

"You're right, Jake."

Howard could wait. The spectators could wait. I started reading a few pages in *Light in August*, trying to figure out what Faulkner meant by the title. Then I heard a truck and stood. "That's a truck. You run up the road. I'll run down the road to thin out this crowd."

Karl ran, got in the clear. The crowd wandered after me. The truck arrived like an earthquake, all dust and metallic squeals. It was a huge red Fiat pulling a trailer. I ran up to Karl, breathless.

"Debre Berhan?" Karl asked the driver. The driver nodded. "Dessie?" The driver waved a finger. Dessie was about four hundred kilometers north.

"What's he say?"

"He's going to Debre Berhan," Karl said.

"Where's that?"

"We're going. It's the next town."

The driver waved his thumb over his shoulder to the load in back, indicating to climb on. He revved the engine. People in the crowd were already handing our packs to passengers above us. We climbed into position. The driver sounded the horn. Everyone cheered. The truck surged forward. The trees rushed by; the hills floated past like waves. I lay on the canvas in the sunlight. The road slowly wove through mountains with distant ridges all around.

"This is great," Karl said.

"Told you we'd get a ride." The scenery was magnificent. "Hey Karl, I was just thinking."

"What's that?"

"How poor everybody is."

"Yeah."

"Is the whole continent is like this?"

"You mean, poor?"

"Isn't that because we have so much?"

"Don't be ridiculous. You think their government had nothing to do with it? Or the emperor?"

It was past noon when we got to Debre Berhan. We thanked the driver. Market day was at its height. The streets were full of people. I jumped back from several lepers who thrust their bleeding stumps at us.

"They don't mean to shock you," Karl said. "They're just trying to get a coin."

"You know so much about lepers? I wouldn't even know how to give them a coin."

"You ever seen a leper before?"

"Not close up."

"Me neither. Man, I could get used to this climate."

Before long, a truck on its way to Kembolcha stopped. That was almost all the way to Dessie. We jumped on. A couple of peasants with their goats were on the tarp. We found a place forward, right above the cab. You always want to sit higher than the goats.

The truck roared off. I lit a joint, took a poke, handed it to Karl. The Peace Corps people in Addis had thoughtfully packed a mailing tube full of weed for us before we left.

"What are you doing?" Karl asked.

"Don't worry. They don't care. No one's paying any attention." The passengers, most of them, were staring down at the tarp. They ignored us. We spaced out for a few hours.

The truck stopped before dark in a high village. It was cold. Mist hung in the treetops below us. The driver and his passengers in the cab left for the restaurant. I climbed over the side, jumped down to the road. I brushed myself off. The dust nearly covered the tops of my boots.

I walked over to where a bored policeman was sitting by a pole across the road. He seemed glad to see me. "We pass?" I made a sweeping motion with my arm. The policeman sternly wagged his finger. He got up from the chair to show me the padlock on the barrier; the padlock was rusty, broken. With two fingers he repeatedly brought an imaginary cigarette to his mouth.

"Sorry, don't smoke."

He raised his eyebrows, pointing to Karl.

"Naw, no luck." I walked back to the truck. "Karl, let's get something to eat."

The restaurant was a white-washed mudbrick building with a tin roof. Inside were wooden tables and chairs, a hard dirt floor, rough brown walls. And a bar.

The waitress brought a basin of water, a scrap of soap, and a small, dingy, damp rag, then she took away the thin mud we left in the basin. I ordered kai wat, a fiery beef stew served with injera, a bluish-gray pancake riddled with air pockets. It was made from tef, a grain smaller than mustard seed. In Debre Berhan, we'd seen them scalding the sour, fermented batter in big pans cut from the bottoms of fifty-five-gallon drums. That made a huge pancake nearly three feet across, which they folded twice. You pulled off pieces of injera to wipe up the wat. If you did it right, you kept your fingers clean. Karl stuck with spaghetti. For a US dime we bought a big bottle of bubbly Ambo spring water, complete with mineral assay signed by an Italian chemist with his photo on the label. Mineral water was something the Italians gave Ethiopia, besides roads and spaghetti.

Karl motioned with his head. "What do you think of the waitress?"

"What do you mean?" She was standing by the driver's table.

"Isn't she beautiful?"

"She's way too thin, like she's about to starve to death."

The waitress was trying to get away from the driver who held her by the wrist. She was wriggling, hitting ineffectually at his fist with her free hand. The driver was talking to her and to his friends. When she struggled too much, he squeezed her wrist harder till she stopped. Something the driver said made her laugh. He let her go. She ran laughing through a doorway behind the bar.

"Don't tell me she's not pretty," Karl said.

"Hello. Hello you." The truck driver was calling us.

"Go see what he wants," Karl said. "After all, he's not charging us."

Karl walked out the door, looking for the bathroom in back. I went over to the driver's table. The mechanic was there, a guy in a sport coat who was on the truck, a student, plus several bar flies.

"Hello, American," the driver said. "How you like Ethiopia?"

"I like it."

Everyone smiled. "How you like Ethiopian people?"

"We're all God's children." That puzzled the driver, so I added, "You speak good English."

"Only a little. It is difficult, but I like to try. You drink tej?"

That was the murky, straw-colored liquid everyone was drinking. Everyone leaned forward.

"No thanks."

Everyone frowned.

"But you must try a little, anyway. This is tej." He held up a bottle over his head.

"What is it?"

"Tej."

"But how is it made?"

"From, from." The driver consulted the student. "Ah, from honey, you know." He made buzzing noises, darting his fingers about like a symphony conductor. Mead. I was curious. They poured me a glass. It looked terrible, smelled terrible. What were those little floating brown specks? I almost put the glass down. I swallowed hard to get past the first few gulps. It was warm and sour. I clenched my teeth hard so I wouldn't retch. I was sweating.

"You like it?" asked the student.

"I'll tell you later," I said, trying to smile. "Do you like it?"

"I like to get drunk."

The waitress brought another bottle. The driver grabbed her wrist again, talking to her. The waitress looked away, smiling, shaking her head slowly. The driver kept at it, the waitress kept shaking her head and laughing. The driver let her go for a moment to take a sip from his glass. She took off for the door behind the bar, bumped into a chair, and lost her balance. The driver tried to catch her. She got away, ducked behind a table. The driver chased her around the table a few times. Then he had her by the wrist again. They both were laughing hard. After a few moments they disappeared behind the bar. A door slammed.

The mechanic filled my glass. I was getting drunk. The tej was still terrible, but it went down easier than before.

"What was that?" I asked the student, motioning behind the bar.

He shrugged. "She's a bargirl. Anyone can have her."

"Does the driver know her?"

"I don't know."

I walked outside. It was freezing cold. Karl was standing in the middle of the road, looking up. The sky was a foam of stars.

"See all the stars? See the Southern Cross? There it is." Karl pointed.

I couldn't believe the stars.

"What's going on inside? Sounded lively."

"Everyone's drunk on tej. The driver made off with the waitress." I was silent a beat, thinking about the waitress. "Funny system they have here. See a girl you like, drag her off to the back room. No one interferes, no one complains."

"From what I saw, it seemed like they knew each other."

"Don't tell me that wasn't a rape. Even a whore can choose her customers."

"What was really going on? Do you know? You don't speak the language, right?"

"Maybe she was afraid of being beaten or losing her job."

"Maybe she figured she might as well enjoy it. Don't be naïve. She meets lots of men working in that bar. No respectable woman goes into a place like that alone. Only bargirls."

"I hate to see anyone treated like that."

"That's her life. Weren't they both laughing? Like it was a game? She wasn't scared and screaming."

"It's not right."

"So what?" Karl said. "She has no choice."

"Even bargirls have rights."

"She puts up with it because she needs money. Isn't it obvious? And bargirls have no rights."

"What's that supposed to mean?"

"I mean no one has to respect her. She's an outcast."

"An outcast? Dammit! Who are you to call her an outcast? Or say she has no rights?"

"Hey, I didn't invent this system. She has no family to protect her. Maybe she pissed off her father."

"Pissed off her father?"

"Yeah, like maybe she ran away or got pregnant. If you want to get married around here you have to pay bride price to the father. That makes the groom's family extra picky."

"Oh, I get it. Her dad couldn't marry her off, so he threw her out."

"Men make all the decisions here." Karl yawned. "You want to get some sleep?"

"Not yet."

"There's nothing doing now except getting drunk."

I walked back to the bar. Well, I was an outcast, wasn't I? I couldn't go home. And where was my family? My parents were dead. That bargirl and I had a lot in common.

11. TURIYE FENTAW
(KARL)

The passengers and their goats were bedded down when I climbed onto the truck. The air was frosty, but the sleeping bag was warm. Dogs howled in the distance. Dark trees waved in the wind across the star-struck night. I lay up there on the tarp thinking about Helen and her so-called plans for motherhood. Was she in love with Ernestine? Who would raise our child? And then I was struck by my boastfulness with Harold, telling him I could learn more in Africa than at Oxford. That was pretty rash. What had I learned? People were laughing in the restaurant. I was sure I heard Jake's voice in the din.

With the sun in my eyes and the sky lurching dizzy above me, I started up on my elbows, the truck already dozens of miles from the barricade. Jake, to my relief, was huddled in his sleeping bag beside me, asleep. Eyelids and nostrils caked with hardened dust, his face streaked, smeared with dirt, his beard was road brown. In every fold, every crease of his sleeping bag lay a deposit of dust. Dried streams of mud ran over it. His head, like a Rasta man, was all clots. The truck was rumbling through a flat stretch, about to start a big climb. I could see the hills coming up.

Jake woke up. His profile kind of struck me. "Hey," I said. "You look a little like Bob Dylan."

"What? You're crazy. How do I look like Bob Dylan?"

"You've got the same dark frizzy hair. The same nose."

"Shut up. I don't look like Bob Dylan."

"Without the beard you do. You're better looking than Dylan. And not as skinny."

"I told you don't say that. He's Jewish, isn't he?"

"Dylan? Maybe. I don't know. His name was Zimmerman."

Jake and I arrived in Kembolcha before dusk. The driver was going on to Asab on the Red Sea, 460 kilometers to the northeast according to Michelin. We got off. Dessie was not far now. We found something to eat and a room for two Ethiopian dollars. It was that or try our luck outside with the hyenas. It was a big room with one bed and two chairs. We flipped for the bed. I lost. We cleaned up and sat on the chairs with the landlady's kerosene lantern.

"Hey Jake. I wanted to ask you. Why'd you get so upset back in Addis at Sarah's joke about Frank being their Jewish banker? I mean, I didn't like that joke, either. But you really let them have it. You're not Jewish, as far as I know."

"What's not being Jewish got to do with it? You mean, only Jews should get upset about that?"

"You seem sensitive about it."

"Let's say I have a special relationship with the Jews. Maybe someone tried to kill me once because they thought I was a Jew."

"Someone tried to kill you? Is that what you told Sarah?"

"You're part Jewish, right? Don't you know how the Nazis painted Jews in the worst possible light? Who stood up for them? Who objected when they murdered them? And if they could kill Jews, they could kill anyone."

"But you say someone tried to kill you?"

"Talk like that gets me, that's all. I don't like those people."

"So I noticed. But you didn't answer my question."

NEXT MORNING WE WERE waiting on the road for a ride to Dessie when two kids came by. Jake took a baseball from his pack. He threw it to one of the boys, who threw it back to Jake. Jake threw it to his friend, who threw it to me. We had a nice game of catch. The boys were excited. They were not used to catching or throwing a ball. The ball rolled between the legs of one of the boys. A policeman picked it up. There were two policemen. The boys were frightened; one policeman put the ball in my hand, the other one standing with the boys. They began beating the boys with long sticks, driving them down the road.

"What was that? What the hell was that?"

"Damn the police," Jake said.

"Did we make that happen?" I said to Jake. "Was that our fault?"

"We have to stop this. Hey," he shouted. "Stop that. Hey!"

The police ignored him. They were moving farther away, hitting the boys with their thin sticks.

"Hey! Cut it out." One of the policemen looked at Jake for a moment, then went back to his stick, ignoring Jake. Jake made a move toward them.

"Whoa Kemosabe." I held my arm out to stop him.

"This is wrong. We have to stop them. Let me go."

"I know it's wrong. How do you propose to stop them? And do you really know what's going on? I don't. I can't speak their language. Can you?"

"Well—"

"Want to spend today at the police station?"

"I hate them, I really do." Jake backed off. The police and the boys continued down the road until we couldn't see them.

Almost as soon as they had gone a Peugeot station wagon stopped for us. We sat in the back seat. I gave Jake back his ball. The road climbed and climbed. Dessie was up on the escarpment, thousands of feet higher than Kembolcha. About twenty minutes passed when the driver, an excitable little man with sparse, black hair slicked back, started talking rapidly. It sounded like English, but neither of us could make heads or tails of it. He slowed down to let a bus pass. The bus was crammed with people. The driver stopped the car abruptly when we reached a big curve in the road. We were far above Kembolcha now. The view was outstanding.

The driver fetched a rifle from the trunk. The driver's helper ran down the road with a round piece of flat metal. The driver waited for his helper to set up the target against a tree on the far side of the road. Then he began firing. He took about ten shots, kept reloading, but missed the target every time. He handed the rifle to me. I took five shots. I hit the target once. The helper ran down the road to set up the target again.

"This is a great place for target practice. We're firing directly across the road." I handed Jake the rifle. "You want to have a go?"

"No, I don't believe in it."

"Don't believe in what?"

"Guns. They're only good for killing things."

"We're not killing anything," I said. "We're shooting at a piece of metal. And what about our dinner last night? That beef on your plate was once a cow."

"I don't want any part of guns, even if I'm not vegetarian."

"What if somebody was shooting at you? Would you shoot back?"

"If someone shot at me? Of course I'd shoot back."

"Learning to shoot may come in handy," I said.

The driver approached. "You want to shoot?" He took the rifle from me, offering it to Jake.

"No thanks."

"All right. I shoot." The driver shot a few rounds, stopping once to let a bus pass. The helper ran down the road to reposition the target. When he got back, the driver took more shots. The helper took some shots. Then he ran to retrieve the target. The driver took it and was about to put it back in the truck with the rifle, when he turned to us and said in clear English, "We pretend this is the emperor."

Jake and I looked at each other. "You mean, you were taking pot shots at Haile Selassie?" he said.

By late morning we were in Dessie. It was like a garden. The cacti were luxuriant. The escarpment and even the mountainsides were filled with crops growing under the dry, warm sky. After two long days on the road, it was time for a breather.

"Do you know where James Murphy lives? The American teacher?" I asked the first student we met. Without hesitation the boy led us down rutted dirt roads hemmed by cactus fences to a rambling house on the edge of a grassy expanse.

"He lives here."

We knocked. An Ethiopian opened the door. Then a strapping guy in his mid-twenties with a red beard came out.

"Everyone calls me Murph. It's a little crowded right now. There's room, if you don't mind sleeping on the floor."

"Damn." Jake slapped his leg. "Damn. They beat us."

Wayne was standing over his pack. "Ah, they made it."

Sarah sat on a couch, smirking. "What took you so long?" Frank pretended to read a book.

"When did you leave Addis?" I asked Wayne.

"The afternoon of the day you left. We thought it would be hard for the three of us to hitchhike, so we took a bus. The bus got in late last night. Lucky Murph was still awake."

"We had a hard trip," Jake said. "We didn't pay for rides, though."

"I like sitting in a seat," Sarah said. "I'd never get on a truck, unless it's the cab."

"Seat?" sneered Wayne. "You did have a seat most of the way, but you didn't like who was sitting next to you. What was the matter with him? Did he smell?"

"Yes, he did. He smelled like he'd just made love with a goat."

"Nonsense! They all smell like that. No sense being stuffy."

Murph turned to Jake and me. "Maybe you two would be interested in this. We're all going to the Danakil market in a little while, so I thought we might get something to eat now. Normally I would be working, but it so happens I don't have to teach today. If you want to come along with us to Kembolcha? Now I realize you just came from there. If you want to stay here, no one will bother you."

Frank got up from his corner. He threw a funny look at Sarah, who followed him with her eyes out the door.

"Where's he going?" I asked.

Murph stood. "He knows the way to the restaurant. He was there last night. Are you all ready? I want to get moving."

"What's the story with Frank?" I asked Wayne on the way to the restaurant. "Are you two going to kill him?"

"The other way around, most likely. He's mad at Sarah for stealing his seat on the bus. He had to stand the whole way."

THE RESTAURANT WAS A big open place with a wooden floor. Jake caught me as I was coming out of the bathroom.

"Look, I really can't stand this crowd."

"They're not my favorites, but how can they ruin a market?"

"I'm not going."

"Nonsense."

I walked back to the table. The food was great. Beef tibs were a specialty.

"Everybody set?" said Murph. "Let's get down to the bus."

"What's the big deal about this market, anyway?" I asked.

"The Danakils hold this market every few weeks when they come off the desert," Murph said.

"We're going to see some bare breasts today, oh boy," Wayne said.

Sarah threw him a dirty look. "Is that all you think about?"

"It's not all I think about. But it's one of the things. What do you think about?"

"Whatever it is, it's not you," Frank said.

"You're right about that," Sarah said.

"I want to buy a whole lot of things for my apartment back home," Frank said.

"Where are you from?" Murph asked.

"Winnipeg."

The bus left almost as soon as we bought our tickets. It bumped all the way to Kembolcha back down the same road we'd just come up. We waited an hour at the station for the bus to drive the remaining stretch to the market, scrambling back on with some townspeople and a bunch of Danakil women. The women wore beads but little clothing. Their hair was done up with dried reddish mud. They had that peculiar smoky funk of people who cook inside huts without chimneys or running water to bathe. They were in high spirits, laughing, joking with each other. One young woman couldn't keep her eyes off Jake. Watching her, Wayne said, "I hear those Danakil maidens make good wives." When the girl saw Jake blush, she smiled a broad smile and clapped her hands, staring even harder at him.

In the distance were a caravan of camels and some wooden stalls. Merchants squatted in the dust. The Danakils got off the bus first. Murph hopped out. Sarah, Wayne, and Frank pushed their way to the front of the bus. We stayed in the back.

"I shouldn't have come today," Jake said.

"Why the hell not?"

"I don't like those people. They're shallow, money-grubbing, prejudiced, like people I knew back home. They're quick to judge, slow to learn. Selfish. I wanted to get away from all that."

"Just ignore them. Go explore the market."

We joined the others. "Where are those monkey skin rugs, Murph?" Frank asked. "You said they'd have them."

"They always have them," Murph said.

"Look at this," Wayne said, holding up what looked like an old Italian officer's sword.

"Junk," Sarah said. "How come you always go for the junk?"

"I like those painted calabashes," said Jake, pointing in a different direction.

"I like them, too," said Murph.

"There are the rugs," cried Sarah, pointing at a stall. When we caught up with her, a bearded man in black trousers and white shirt was spreading four or five round rugs on the ground.

"How much does he want?" asked Wayne. He rubbed his thumb and his fingers together. The man wrote *$250* on a piece of cardboard.

"Two hundred and fifty dollars?" shouted Frank. "Where does he think he is? That's a hundred US."

"Maybe he means for all of them?" Sarah spread her arms in a circle over the merchandise. "All? All?" The man thought for a while, went back to where more rugs were piled. He brought out a larger one.

"No, no, I don't want a bigger one."

"Wait a minute, let's have a look at it." Wayne held it up. "See, it's nicer than the first one. How much for this one, bud?"

The man wrote *$350* on the cardboard.

"Too much for me. I see more over there." Frank walked away, scowling.

"What do they do with the monkeys?" I asked.

"Probably eat them." Wayne laughed. "How'd you like to eat a monkey? It must look terrific on the plate."

The merchant looked at Sarah, crossed out $350. He wrote $300.

"I'll give you forty for that rug." Sarah wrote on the cardboard. The man smiled. She turned to us. "Forty Ethie is how much? About thirteen-fourteen US? Okay, I'll go up to fifty, but no more." She crossed out $40, writing $50 on the cardboard.

The rug merchant pointed at the rug, squatted beside it, showing her how nice the fur was, how well it was stitched.

"No, thanks." Sarah started walking away, but the merchant tapped her shoulder. Crossing out *$300*, he wrote *$250* on the cardboard. Sarah took it from him, underlining *$50*.

Jake walked away. I followed him. "Where are you guys going?" Wayne called. "Wait."

"Don't you want a rug?" Jake asked. "I thought you wanted one."

"I do, but I'll find another dealer."

"Why's that?"

"I didn't like his stuff that much. I have to see more before I make up my mind. Now, maybe I'd like one of those masks." Wayne pointed to a woman holding up a carved wooden mask. It was elongated, colored red and black, with ridges signifying facial scars running laterally in parallel rows.

"What are you going to do with that thing?" Jake asked.

"I don't know. I didn't even decide to buy it yet."

"If you buy it, how are you going to carry it? What's the point of getting loaded down with a lot of useless junk?"

"I see you've been talking with Sarah. I wouldn't carry it farther than Asmara anyhow. I'll mail it home from there. I think it would look good on my wall."

"On your wall? On your wall?" Jake was incensed. "That's all this is, an extended shopping trip? Is that all you think about, your wall at home? Did you come all the way to Kembolcha just to decorate your walls?"

"What's he talking about?" Wayne said, looking at me. "What's wrong with putting something on your wall? No, that's not the only reason I came here, but as long as I'm here I'm going to get a few nice things to take back with me. Providing they're not too expensive, of course."

"You asses are playing rich Americans." Jake was gesturing with his hands. "What's the point of carrying home around with you wherever you go, as if you never left?"

"I suppose you're not as American as me? I suppose you're not going back home?"

"No, I'm not going back home." Jake was almost shouting. "I'm certainly not thinking of redecorating my house."

"Do you have a house?"

"It's none of your damn business about my house. I'm tired of you and your friends. Why can't you be more sensitive about this place instead of pretending you're still in Grand Rapids?" Jake turned to me. "I'll meet you back at the bus."

"What's with him? Who does he think he is?" Wayne huffed.

"He got a little excited," I said. "I'll see you back at the bus." I went to find Jake. He was standing at a stall eating skewered beef. I ordered one.

"Watch out, they're really hot," Jake said. He pointed to a chipped enamel dish. "There's sauce if you want it hotter."

"Are you nuts? Who could eat something hotter than this?" I took another bite before changing the subject. "I can't understand why those guys bother you so much. They're tourists, pretty average ones at that."

"They make me ashamed to be American."

"Frank's Canadian. Look, the merchants have goods to sell. The buyers haggle about the price. That's the market. It's as old as the first buyer and the first seller. I don't get it, Jake. What's eating you? Why'd you say you're not going back home?"

At that moment Frank arrived. "What's that you're eating? How much do they cost?"

"Don't worry. You can afford it," Jake said, without looking at him.

"The little kebabs cost fifteen cents Ethie," I said. "The big ones are thirty."

Frank got a big one and a little one. He was wearing his maple leaf lapel pin again.

"Try this sauce," said Jake. "It makes it better."

"It does?"

"It brings out the flavor of the meat."

Frank looked at the red sauce. Jake held out the dish with the spoon in it.

"It's good."

"No, thanks." Frank turned to me. "Where did Wayne go? He owes me money. Do you see him?"

I scanned the market. "There he is. See?"

Frank had that special excellence that made you want to lock him in a closet.

"That stupid lapel pin makes me mad," Jake said after Frank left.

"Maybe he's patriotic."
"My ass."

~

We got back to Dessie after dark. Jake and I went out, strolling among the *bunabeits,* the coffee huts, a girl and her mother inside each one. An older woman, maybe not exactly her mother. But that was the idea. Outside, the air bracing cold, braziers filled with roasting meat on sizzling charcoal. We chose one and sat down. Inside, the girl passive, bored. The older woman, bustling, hurrying with coffee or beer, pulling out chairs, moving tables, struggling to hide many emotions with one smile: suspicious, curious, lewd, maternal, worried, worn out, respectful, resentful, avaricious. We ignored them. The girl dropped herself into Jake's lap, her face expressionless. We were in a better mood than her. We weren't working, after all. But we had the money. Language was a huge problem, of course. Jake pushed her off gently. She came to me, but my legs were stretched out under the table, blocking her. She glided out of the room, disappearing behind a beaded curtain. It wasn't much of an evening.

Jake insisted on leaving Dessie when he heard Wayne, Frank, and Sarah were staying on. He wanted to put as much distance between us and them as possible. Murph recommended taking a bus because hitchhiking was difficult. In the morning, Jake and I got up early to walk with Murph to the edge of the escarpment. Rocky hills above us, deep ravine below. Far below that was Kembolcha in a valley, barely visible in the brilliant sand-colored haze. Baboons played in the rocks, rolling stones down from time to time, as if warning us not to get closer. We threw rocks back, but they fell short, clattering uselessly. They were laughing at us, if baboons could laugh.

"Say, where are you boys from?" Murph asked.
"I'm from Nebraska," said Jake.
"Ohio," I said.

"I'm from Ohio, too. Cleveland."

"I'm from Cincinnati. Hey, we wanted to ask you something."

"What's that?" Murph said.

"Two days ago, in Debre Berhan, we were playing catch with some boys when the police arrived. They began beating them with their sticks."

"We shouted for them to stop, but they ignored us," Jake said.

"Street kids," Murph said. "Orphans, maybe. Delinquents. The police don't like them." He smiled. "You boys have a good trip."

The bus ride was tough. The seats left no room for our knees. We were squeezed between the windows and metal walls, the low ceiling, and people in the aisle with their animals, bundles, and boxes. We desperately tried to stay on the seats while the bus lunged and lurched. Men carried guns of all kinds—ancient flintlocks, breech loaders, shotguns, muskets, Italian castoffs, old hunting rifles. They brought them right onto the bus, placing the butts on the seats or on the metal floor. Every plunge, bump, and swing of the bus hammered them. I kept pushing muzzles away that were pointed directly under my chin. *Don't worry,* I told myself. *Probably the riflemen can't afford ammunition. Probably ammunition is no longer manufactured for that weapon. Probably the ammunition is faulty.*

At a rest stop that afternoon in Weldiya we spotted a tourist we had met at the Peace Corps house in Addis waiting at the trailhead to Lalibela to see the monolithic churches. Four days in and four days out on the back of a donkey. We wished him luck.

There was a Christian holiday happening. The bus stopped to pick up a group of two dozen white-robed men, carrying rifles or staves. *Pilgrims,* I imagined. They were rhythmically shuffling down the road in a long file, chanting, seemingly in a trance. The bus was already packed, but they boarded anyway without breaking stride, marking time with their feet in the aisle. After a few minutes, the bus stopped at a deserted place. They all got off, formed ranks again, stepping down the road chanting into the distance.

∼

THE NEXT STOP WAS Kobbo, then Maichew. Makale and Asmara were farther on. Makale was the capital of Tigre province. The bus was going as far as Maichew. Then it was back to hitchhiking for us. The driver announced the bus would stop in Kobbo while they worked on the engine. We were wandering around when one of the locals, a man named Abebe, invited us for coffee. He led us to a barely furnished small house under construction, though it had no roof. It was a few hundred yards off the road within sight of the bus on top of a small hill. We drank the coffee that Abebe gave us. He refilled our cups. In came a girl, about seventeen or eighteen, wearing a blouse, skirt, head wrap, all cut from the same bright blue cloth. She evidently knew Abebe. Seeing us, she went right back out but stopped to say something. She looked at us through a square hole in the wall.

"She likes you," Abebe laughed, looking at Jake. "Wants to know your name."

Jake looked at the girl. "My name is Jake." The girl tried several times to pronounce it.

"She says you are very handsome."

Jake drank his coffee. He looked at the girl who did not leave. She kept staring at Jake through the square hole in the thick plaster. The builders hadn't gotten around to putting the window in. We passed her a cup of coffee. Abebe had no problem. The girl stayed outside. She looked at us, at Jake.

"Where are you from?" Abebe said. "The girl wants to know."

"We are from America," Jake said.

"What is your job? Where are you going? How long will you spend in Kobbo?"

"Tell her we're going to Maichew this afternoon," I said. "Then to Makale and Asmara."

Abebe smiled. She says, "I want to go to Asmara. I want to go someday."

"She's pretty, don't you think?" Jake asked. Abebe translated that. The girl smiled and looked at Jake.

At that moment, the bus driver blew the horn. I looked out and saw passengers heading back. "Looks like the bus is leaving," I said.

We finished the coffee, thanked Abebe again, and stood to leave. Abebe followed us outside. The girl walked up to Jake, put her arms around him. She hugged him, hard, for a few moments. She let him go and stared at Jake's face, saying something to Abebe.

"She wants to sleep with you," Abebe explained. "She says, 'I watched him walk up the hill. I said to myself, 'Who is that man?' You can sleep with her," Abebe said. "She says you don't need to pay her."

"Who is she?" Jake asked.

"She's a bargirl."

Jake looked at her carefully. The girl got closer to Jake, gently touching his face with her hand. She touched his hair and his beard and ran her fingers slowly down his nose and lips to his throat. She held his face with both palms, stared in his eyes, then stepped back again. The driver blew the horn again.

"Please tell her she is beautiful, but I'm sorry I can't stay longer." Jake looked searchingly at me.

The girl smiled at first but frowned after Abebe finished translating. We lifted our packs to go back to the bus. The girl hugged Jake again. She said something to him. Then she spoke to Abebe. Abebe went back into the house. He came back with a pencil and a piece of paper.

"She wants you to write to her."

The girl took the paper, held it on the white-washed wall of the house with one hand, slowly signing her name with the other. She handed the paper to Jake, who read it aloud. "Turiye Fentaw, Kobbo Town."

"I wish I could stay longer." Jake looked at me again. "Can't we stay longer?" he asked me. Abebe didn't translate. I said nothing. This was Jake's deal to figure out. He looked at her for a long time and kissed her on the cheek. Then he turned, and we left.

She stood waving while we walked back down the hill to the bus.

MAP 2 – KARL AND JAKE'S ROUTE, ETHIOPIA 1971

12. THE EMPIRE'S HONORED GUESTS
(JAKE)

The way north went through wild mountains dotted with scruffy towns. Bargirls harassed us wherever we stopped. Crawling up unimproved mountain roads left by the Italians, the truckers knew to grind low gear up steep grades, slower than you could walk, and sometimes for hours. We clung to the tops of trucks, drifted through stoned, crystal clear days and starry nights. The weather was just like the Southwest when I was nineteen and on the loose. Life on the road drove me deeper within myself. An orphan, my protectors gone, I relived the deep emptiness of losing my parents, of leaving my sisters, of Lorraine abandoning me, my fear and loathing on the oil rig. Maybe Pudge had sensed I was ripe for the slaughter. My head was split. The present was a dream. The future anyone's guess. Only the past was real. And now Turiye. Already just a memory.

We continued on to Asmara. No one knew us. No one spoke to us, and we spoke no local tongue. We were strangers in a strange land. If the emperor were overthrown, we'd be the last to know. We were interlopers, jesters, harmless idiots, not loved or reviled or even remembered. My urges marked time—time to eat, time to piss, time to sleep. Despite the daily kaleidoscope before us, we were only skimming the surface of life here. Except, except that girl, Turiye, Turiye Fentaw, who had touched me, offered me things undeniably real, sincere. Her affection. And her body. The only things that belonged to her, the only things she had to give.

Karl and I got along, more or less, but there were tensions. Like more than once I almost blurted out that I killed Pudge. Saying anything at all about Pudge was the last thing I wanted to do. But I kept almost doing it. Like hinting that someone tried to kill me. It was always on my mind and close to the surface. I kept brooding about it. *I never planned to kill Pudge,* I told myself. *So that means I'm not really a murderer.* But wasn't I thinking about pushing him and his friend Hink over the railing that day I heard them plotting about me? I tried another tack. *Maybe I did the world a favor by getting rid of the guy.* But that was exactly how murderers rationalized killing, like that student who killed the pawnbroker lady in Dostoyevsky's novel. Maybe Pudge deserved to die. But who said he deserved death? And why was I the one to kill him? At times I wanted to confess, to share my secret, though for sure I could never do that. But I almost blurted it out, that a guy tried to kill me because he thought I was Jewish. And the way I covered it up made Karl angry.

Both of us were moody. Karl moped about Helen. "Isn't it clear you two are finished?" I admonished. But honestly, if my girlfriend was having a baby in the wild, so to speak, I'd worry, too. I also realized too late that I'd reacted badly when Karl said I looked like Bob Dylan. I knew Dylan was Jewish. Hearing someone tell me I looked Jewish irritated me no end. Luckily, Karl and I didn't have much time for heart-to-hearts, neither on top of roaring trucks, nor while surrounded by staring crowds on the road. Mealtimes were irregular, rushed. I wondered how long we'd be together.

I didn't take my own advice about not moping. I couldn't stop thinking about Turiye, wondering about her, dreaming about getting to know her better. She haunted me. A million things rolled around my brain. *What if she collects men like beads on a string?* I figured I'd forget her fast like I always forgot women. I never wanted anyone close to me after Lorraine, and Pudge's death only made it worse. I had needed to protect myself and liked being alone. Now I wasn't sure. What if I had stayed longer in Kobbo? What then? All right, so what if she was a bargirl? I imagined having dinner with Turiye, holding hands with her, walking down the road, sleeping together, waking up together. I said nothing to Karl about this at first. He was mad enough after I told him to forget Helen. He'd call me a hypocrite. But I could not get Turiye out of my mind.

We got to Asmara, showered at the hotel of some German expat who let us crash on his floor, then went straight to an Italian restaurant. We were starving. The food was great. Far better service and prices than anywhere in New York. All the waiters were Black, of course. People on the street were agile and handsome. They spoke Tigrinya, Arabic, Amharic, and Italian. But Italy it's not.

A few days later we met Hans Dieter Genffler, if I remember the spelling right. Hans was probably the reason Karl and I stayed together as long as we did; he had this way of getting between our disagreements. Difficult to pick out at any distance, Hans tended to fade into the background. But he kept popping up. I had spied him rounding Asmara parading on the back seat of a red MG sports car with the top down. Next morning, he was loping along on the sidewalk, thin and grizzled, clutching an odd scrap of cowhide that held his blanket roll and all his possessions. Passing swiftly, hot on some errand in flipflops and a stained sweater holed at the elbows, he vanished around a corner. At dusk, sunset blazing above gray streets, we spotted him sitting on a curb playing his flute, facing a metallic crescent moon, a shard of silver nailed to a vermilion and turquoise horizon.

We finally cornered Hans on the roadside heading to Massawa. Within minutes we were on the back of a truck bouncing down to the Red Sea. Sharp cheekbones, spotty beard, straw-colored short-cropped hair, skin peppered with dark blotches from years of tropical suns, average height, slightly stooped, his head thrust forward like some weight pressed on his back. He grinned at the world and its inhabitants as if asking a question he already knew the answer to, like he'd seen it all. And he pretty much had.

Speaking English to me, he switched to German with Karl. Ethiopians loved to guess our ages. Karl they pegged at twenty-five, me at thirty on account of my beard was longer than Karl's. But they always put Hans over seventy. That cracked him up, his watery blue eyes laughing while his face dissolved into wrinkles of delight. He may have been forty.

Karl and I lived on a shoestring of maybe four Ethie dollars a day each, but Hans needed even less. "Do you have too much money and not enough to spend it on?" he'd chide Karl for buying some tourist trinket, like it was a lavish outlay. He worked to live, traveled to avoid being in thrall to any system. His West German architecture degree landed him a few weeks of work in Addis and five hundred Ethiopian dollars, a fortune that saw him through at least three months. Money plus a passport equaled freedom. He ridiculed anyplace he sniffed hypocrisy, not just the East German workers' paradise he'd left as a teenager. He scorned every class, every nationality and government, anyone who loved money, or fame, or status, or power. For him they were all in the same pot—craven West German capitalists, arrogant American imperialists, bumbling East European and Soviet apparatchiks, corrupt imperial Ethiopian stooges, and he didn't leave out the Beatles, the US dollar, NATO, or Disneyland. Having no hope for the world, the world could not disillusion him. He simply had opted out.

He was a genuine prophet of the road. He'd been everywhere: the Sahara, West Africa, South America, Mexico, India, Thailand, Nepal, Afghanistan, Australia, Bali. And he'd been all around Ethiopia, too. He'd even got as far as distant Gambela, near the Sudanese border in Ethiopia's far southwest. Took him a whole week by road. "You can't imagine," he'd chuckle. "So backward."

With Hans around, Karl and I had a break from each other. Before Hans showed up, decisions often boiled down to either-or and someone had to give in. Now I could ignore Karl, or I could ignore both of them. But that pushed me deeper into my head. Always, always I was thinking about that last day on the oil rig, the day I watched Pudge slip over the edge. Some nights in a shudder I heard Heaven crying out for my blood.

∼

WE BUMPED DOWN FROM the cool highlands to Massawa, just seventy miles from Asmara but an eight-thousand-foot drop in altitude, passing burned-out black hulks of tanks and military trucks bombed by Eritrean guerrillas that lined the road.

Massawa was so hot it nearly killed us. "Excrementitious," Karl called it. *Scheisslich*, according to Hans. Dead-dog miasma of tropical bogs. Nights were oppressive, the air motionless. Daytime was worse. Even the crud thrown up on the beaches rotted in black piles, attracting flies. Unswimmable, the sea was a stew of brown flotsam. Somewhat warmer than water hot dogs floated in at the ball game, somewhat cooler than a cup of coffee left standing, the sea was saltier than the salt water your mother forced you to gargle with when you stayed home from school with a sore throat. I stumbled from the waves spitting and kicking, peeling seaweed from my scalp, my arm pits, my eyes, looking futilely for somewhere to wash. I rubbed myself dry with sand.

We pitched our little tent on the beach, and I monopolized it. I pretended I was in the desert. I strained to glimpse Arabia. Through the haze, ships sailed north to Suez, south to the Indian Ocean. It was like being in my old hooch on the oil platform. I sat at the tent flap studying our Michelin map. Or reading the *Bhagavad Gita*, which was all about Krishna and Arjuna going to war, and the three *Gunas* or qualities—*Tamas* (ignorance, inertia), that was definitely Pudge and Hink. *Rajas* (action, longing), I figured I was mostly *Rajas*. Like, there were so many things that I wanted that I wasn't getting. And I knew to a penny how many months of money I had left. That was Rajas. Last was *Sattva* (harmony, joy). How to achieve Sattva? Hans claimed India was even cheaper than Ethiopia. Could that be right? Our life in Africa weighed lightly on us; no obligations, no timetables. We were young, healthy. We spoke English, had American passports, enjoyed the aid and comfort of gracious, informed, intelligent, well-provisioned, hip Peace Corps volunteers, who were not a little jealous of what we were doing. In effect, we were the empire's honored guests. At least they tolerated us.

There was a weak breeze by the sea, and I could sleep in the afternoons. With Hans and Karl chatting outside, I'd stay in the tent dreaming about Turiye. Just me alone in the tent for hours with a hard-on. From the way she hugged me I knew Turiye was strong. I daydreamed about showing up in Kobbo, walking up to her unexpectedly, watching the expression on her face when she saw me, kissing her at first on the cheek. We'd find some shack to live in.

THE NEXT DAY WE ventured into town. It was a mistake. We passed low, crumbling buildings, deep into salt-assisted decay, along garbage-strewn, reeking, rutted, cur-slinking streets. Here it almost never rained. We ate in a two-hands restaurant; one hand shoveled food in your mouth, the other fanned away the flies. Outside nothing moved except us and the small boys following us twenty steps behind. The heat was intense, choking. It was the start of cool season.

At the port, a few ships were tied up, mostly Greek. Loitering by the water was a ferengee[6] couple. The guy stuck out his hand. "I'm Robert. This is my wife, Christine." Christine stared out to sea.

"I'm Jake. This is Karl. Hans. Welcome to Massawa."

Robert wiped his brow. "It's a shocker coming out of the cool cabin when the ship is stopped. There's no breeze. We came down here to see what was going on."

---

6   foreigner

"Not much," Hans said.

"How long you've been out of the States?" Karl asked.

"About eight months. We caught the ship in Iran. Bandar Abbas. Lucky, because we were dead broke. We thought traveling would be easier than it turned out to be. The captain's been great. We eat at his table, drink his wine. He's letting us work off our passage. Right, hon?" Christine turned away.

"What do you do on the ship?"

"Christine cooks for the captain. I'm usually at the other end of the boat all day in the laundry, right hon? I wonder why the captain has me doing the laundry?"

"I haven't a clue," Christine murmured.

"Isn't it hard to find work on a ship?" I asked. "Don't you need a seaman's card, credentials?"

"Normally. By myself, forget it. Being with Christine made all the difference. She seems to hit it off with the captain. It's the only way to travel. You get regular meals, peace and quiet, privacy."

"What happens when you get to Athens?"

"We're not sure. There might be some money waiting for us. Or we'll look for work. Picking grapes or olives or tomatoes. I'm not too worried about it. What about you guys? You must be seeing some country!"

"Right," said Karl. "Traveling by road is the exact opposite of the ship. No regular meals, no air conditioning, no privacy. We're a couple of weeks out of Addis, heading back there soon, then down to Nairobi."

Christine walked away. "Hon? Christine? Excuse me." Robert ran off after his wife and some furious conversation followed. Then she walked away again, turned to him and said sharply, "He's a better man than you." She walked off. Robert caught her again. Breaking free, she shouted over her shoulder, "In every way."

Karl exchanged looks with Hans. From the sound of it, Robert might soon be picking grapes by himself. I wandered away to gawk at the ships towering above us like Manhattan buildings. The sky was hazy, the horizons fuzzy, indistinct. Massawa seemed like the end of the earth.

We got up early next day and hiked out of town. It took us ages to get out of Massawa. We sang "Marching to Pretoria" to pass the time. The sky was dull overcast. Not hot, just extremely warm. There was no traffic. After about an hour we came across a long line of tanker trucks parked one after the other by the side of the road. The tankers were nearly identical. I went from truck to truck asking for rides. The drivers shrugged, pointing up the road. It was another long walk to get near the head of the line. When we saw soldiers and army vehicles, we figured it for a convoy. A soldier asked for our passes. Lucky we had them to show. After a giant run-around, the Imperial Ethiopian Army division headquarters in Asmara had given Karl and me passes for the Massawa road. Hans also had a pass. We asked the soldier for a lift. The soldier found an officer, who was most cordial. We would have to ride in the back of the armored personnel carriers. Impossible for us to ride in the cabs. That made no difference to us. We had to split up. Karl and Hans walked back downhill to the far end of the convoy.

I was in the lead car. It was almost noon when the convoy got underway. But it immediately stopped. There was a long delay. Then we started but stopped again. My watch was showing nearly two o'clock. We got going at last, but at a crawl. I was beginning to worry about the ELF.[7] The road wound through plenty of curves that forced the trucks to stop, then creep slowly up the long hills. There were huge boulders everywhere. Perfect for an ambush. This very weekend the foreign press was in Asmara covering an international exposition. What a great moment to splash headlines of a rebel attack worldwide! Soon I was seeing guerrillas behind every rock. The troops, on the other hand, seemed unconcerned, laughing and joking, never glancing at the road. Their high spirits annoyed me.

---

7   ELF-Eritrean Liberation Front

The convoy halted and we sat. One soldier walked a few paces off the road with his assault rifle, taking aim at a dead tree. A few short bursts shattered it, leaving everyone in no doubt about his marksmanship and fighting prowess. We got going again. Now the men were eyeing the sides of the road intently, nervously flipping their safeties on and off. I prepared to dive onto the floor at the first sign of trouble. The personnel carrier was nothing more than a small, open truck. Anyone could toss a grenade in it. I was sure the front of the convoy was the worst place to be. They'd probably go for the lead car. Then again, when the firing began, the lead vehicle might get through. On the other hand, if the road was mined, the lead vehicle might strike the first mine. Or maybe not.

The driver stopped on the steep, winding grade, waiting for the heavy tankers to catch up. If hit, they would burn for days. We all got off, watching them inch up the incline. When we climbed back in, two soldiers tossed their weapons onto the metal truck bed. I could see the safety catches were off. The Imperial Ethiopian Army was disenchanting me. I thought our odds of survival were better with the guerrillas.

When we reached a town about halfway up the escarpment, the convoy ended. Karl found me as he came up the hill with Hans.

"What was that firing we heard?"

"A little target practice. Some guy blasted a dead tree to bits."

"Really?" said Hans. "Where we were they began handing out clips."

"It was indecent how scared we were, Jake. At last, something came over their radios. We had no idea what was said but it calmed everyone down."

"I wondered what it would sound like at the end of the convoy," I said.

"You can bet we all thought the ELF was striking pay dirt," Karl said.

We sat by the road watching the army disengage from the convoy. The day was blistering. I found a shady spot to sit. Hans asked if I was all right. The next thing I remember was waking up in the cab of a tanker truck, the three of us crammed into the passenger seat, the Danakil driver singing some wild desert song, Karl coaxing me to drink water from his canteen. It was already dark. Karl had the window. I was more or less lying on top of him. Hans, sitting by the driver, said I had heat stroke. I drank some water and began to feel better. I vomited when we left the truck, dizzily following Hans and Karl back to our Asmara hotel.

We had a big fight, Karl and I, the next morning when I announced I was going back to Kobbo. This had been building for days. I just had to see Turiye. Karl gave me a ton of crap about it. This is how it went:

"That bargirl? I'll bet she sleeps with a dozen men a week."

"How many men was your girlfriend sleeping with?"

"What about her family? Her employer? You might need to pay them off, you know. You're going to drop in by parachute to straighten everything out?"

"I can handle it."

"We might not be here when you get back."

"Suit yourselves."

It was perfect. This was a turning point, a whole new chapter in my life. With Turiye, I could bury myself in Ethiopia and no one would ever find me. I'd never have to face the music back home. I decided not to explain anything to her about Pudge. But then I saw it was wrong to use Turiye for my own convenience. I decided to explain everything to her and why I came to Ethiopia and let her be the judge.

I WALKED OUT TO the road and got a lift right away. The truck was going to Makale, about halfway to Kobbo, which was still five hundred kilometers south. Two days later we arrived in Makale early in the morning. I got something to eat in town, then walked out to the road. I stood out there all day, until nightfall. Then I walked back into town. I found a bar to get something to eat. I was lonely, full of doubts. I had to admit I missed Karl and Hans.

A girl came and sat next to me. She was pretty. She watched as I ate. She spoke to me, laughing, though I could not understand what she said. She wore a beautiful colored dress. Her skin was dark. Her voice was like music. She smiled at me, kept trying to brush my hair with her hand. When I finished eating, she asked me to buy her a beer. *Okay,* I thought, *I'll buy her a beer then find somewhere to sleep.* We drank a couple of beers. Time passed slowly. It was starting to get late. I got up, motioning that I had to go. She just smiled, asked me to follow her.

We walked into a room without windows. She closed the door. I sat on the chair. She spoke to me in her musical voice, sitting on the bed, waiting for something to happen. She looked at me, I supposed, wondering what I was like. Curious how it would feel, I touched her arm. It didn't bother her. Her arm was soft, not the arm of someone who worked all day scrubbing pots. She sat watching me, talking and laughing. Her voice was like a song. Time passed. We sat. She asked for money. I gave her a couple of Ethie dollars. She was happy with the money, glancing up expectantly. I realized I had not thought about Turiye for hours.

I stood, bowed politely, and moved toward the door. She sat on the bed, quietly watching me. I walked out into the cold night, found a cheap hotel. Hitching back to Asmara the next day, I wondered if Karl and Hans were still there. It felt like the end of something.

13. HOW TO DO IT
(KARL)

Asmara is an odd, African copy of Florence oozing Italian charm. There's even a Duomo, Italian restaurants, and a market where you can pick up any size bust of Mussolini. Hans, with *Ossi* irony, claimed Asmara was better, less corrupt than the original, and a whole lot cheaper.

"How do you know it's less corrupt here than Italy?" Jake asked him.

"Italians have been perfecting their skills for centuries. They're professionals. The Eritreans are novices."

But Jake wasn't sold. "I think you're underestimating the locals."

Three hitchhikers created a different dynamic. We had to wait longer for rides. No more committee of two. Often it was two-against-one, with Jake and Hans against me. But Hans's droll East German pessimism was steadying. For one thing, I could observe Jake more objectively. I liked Jake. He brought real energy, freshness to whatever we did, an appreciation of the practical side of life. But he was stingy, considering how much more money he had than Hans or me. He conserved money like it was his blood. If I spoke German with Hans, he'd accuse me of badmouthing him. He made me deny it so often I wasn't sure I hadn't done it.

Jake was increasingly erratic. Jumpy. What I had taken in England for a self-indulgent but mostly healthy dislike for authority was trending toward paranoia. His long brooding silences got on my nerves. For one thing, he was conflicted about the police and confused them with the military. To him they were all pigs. Uniforms unnerved him, even ragged uniforms. I couldn't figure it out. He acted like he was on the run from something. When I asked him if the police were after him, he'd say "not yet." But if he felt provoked, he'd rebel with insolence, belligerence even. And that was a problem. Doing anything administrative with him risked disaster.

Like that day in Asmara before we met Hans. We applied for passes at Imperial Ethiopian Army division headquarters for permission to travel to Massawa. Jake froze when he saw the sentries.

"I'll wait outside. Take my passport."

I told him it was no good, but he just shoved his passport at me. Naturally, the officer I spoke with inside, a relaxed major, asked why my friend hadn't come. I explained that he felt sick. But he insisted on seeing Jake. I went to get him.

Jake walked rigidly past the sentries, up to the officer. He was sweating.

The soldier sat smiling at his desk. "So this is your friend? All right. Are either of you carrying guns or ammunition?"

"No," I said.

Jake didn't answer. The officer looked at him, expectantly. Jake's fingers were quivering.

"Are you?" The officer stood. "Well?"

Jake placed his fingers on the desk. "Would we tell you if we were?"

The officer knitted his eyebrows. Then he understood Jake was taunting him. He ordered a corporal to take us back to the hotel to search our room. After retrieving our packs the corporal escorted us back to headquarters.

"It was a joke," I told the officer when we arrived for the second time. "We don't have any guns."

"You had better not." He was not smiling. He watched the corporal search every item in our packs. We finally got the passes, but what should have taken fifteen minutes became a five-hour ordeal. We were lucky not to get thrown in jail.

Outside Jake leaned against the brick wall of the headquarters building. "I can't even remember why we wanted to go to Massawa. I'd rather not go."

"The Red Sea was your idea, remember? Soldiers like straight answers. And who's being pigheaded?"

With Hans things were much more straightforward, though he'd grown up under Hitler and lived through the Second World War. I imagined him stepping over bodies in the street on his way to school. In 1945, he found himself in East Berlin, in the Soviet zone. He spent his teens plotting to escape communists. When he turned twenty, he left his parents, rode the subway, the U-Bahn, west before the Berlin Wall put a stop to it. He was not going back. He was less jaded than blasé. He prized the absurd. Aimlessness was his goal. Far too bleak for me. I needed a purpose. I just didn't know what that was.

AFTER ALL THAT DRAMA at Imperial Army Headquarters, Jake was fine with the military that day we rode back up the escarpment with the Massawa convoy. He'd seen the soldiers took no particular interest in him. But when we got back to Asmara there was something new. All he could talk about was that bargirl we'd met in Kobbo. Turiye this, he'd say. Turiye that, like they were old friends. Don't get me wrong. I had nothing against Ms. Fentaw. He acted as if Turiye were a lump of potter's clay he could mold to fit any situation. Arthur Rimbaud, the great French poet, got stuck for years in Harrar, I told him, married local, exported Ethiopian coffee to France, tutored Haile Selassie's father, Ras Makonnen. I didn't see Jake as Rimbaud, and neither did Jake. But then he disappeared for five days.

Hans talked me out of dropping Jake.

"He's looking at trouble and expense," Hans told me. "Give him a few days to figure it out."

Yup, several days later Jake showed up early one morning at our favorite bunabeit.

"Are you back now or what are you doing?"

"I'm back. I never got to Kobbo. I hitched as far as Makale. Let's not talk about it."

I was glad to see Jake. But I was getting fed up.

Jake acted like his head was wrapped around something he didn't want to talk about, but sometimes something would slip out.

One day, the two of us alone, Jake says to me, "You're Jewish, or half Jewish, aren't you?"

"My father is Jewish. So what?"

He looked off into the distance. "Some guy I knew once asked me at a card game whether Jews were buried standing up. Smaller plots, you see. To save on funeral expenses."

"Why do you repeat such trash?"

"I told him to shove it." He was quiet a moment. "The thing is, he was baiting me because he thought I was Jewish. He was trying to get a laugh from the others to make me look bad."

"What about it? Was this the guy who tried to kill you?"

"No, that was someone else."

"What about this guy?"

"He had an accident and died."

"What do you mean, he had an accident?"

"He had an accident, that's all. Hit his head. I read about it in the newspapers."

"But wasn't he on the job with you?"

"He died after I left."

"So, one guy tried to kill you because he thought you were Jewish. Another guy who made anti-Semitic jokes at your expense died after you left when he hit his head. Is that right? Sounds like that place you worked was a hotbed of anti-Semites and fatal accidents."

"Naw, you idiot. I made it all up." Jake laughed out loud. "Don't tell me you believed that crap?"

"Now you're saying you never meant a word of it? Who's the idiot, asshole?"

We didn't talk for days after that. Had someone really tried to kill Jake? That would explain a lot.

We had our diversions. Like that afternoon after we got our Ethiopian army passes for Massawa, a red MG sports car with the top down pulled over. In it were two American soldiers in civvies. It was the same car we'd seen Hans riding in before we met him.

"I'm Greg, this here's Sandy." Greg was tall. We shook hands all around and stuffed ourselves into the back seat while they drove us to our hotel.

"Damn," Greg said. "You hitched up here from Addis? I didn't know you could do that!" They invited us to their apartment.

"You have an apartment?" Jake asked Sandy, the short, skinny one. "What do you guys do?"

"You mean, besides getting ripped?"

We found their place after dark, a stone-faced building with a liveried doorman. Upstairs four soldiers shared seven rooms. Rock albums, hundreds of them in shelves, covered half a wall. On the floor were two waist-high bags of weed. Sandy passed us a joint.

"We're soldiers at Kagnew Station. It's just out of town." The bigger, chunky one, Greg, his black hair slicked back, pronounced it *"Can-you."* They had rare permission to live off base.

"But what do you do? You're soldiers?"

"We run the TV station."

"TV station?"

I'll be honest, I was not enthusiastic about visiting Kagnew Air Station. With the Vietnam war still on I was not high on the American military, though I was curious to see where Greg and Sandy worked. Jake kept insisting we could get a hamburger at the commissary. Hamburgers decided it. Our US passports were enough to get us past the gate. A muscular Army captain interviewed us in his office. His hair was short, shorter than Helen's eyelashes. His razor-creased khakis made me uneasy. A framed citation for bravery in Vietnam hung on the wall behind his desk. It was dated August 17, 1968. About a week, I calculated, before the police riots at the Chicago Democratic National Convention.

"Americans think anyone can come on this base." He sat on his desk hands gripping the edge with one foot on the floor, his face averted, a surly reserve in his speech. "If you just want to look, I guess it's none of my business. But," he glared at us, "it's demoralizing for the men to see all that hair. I'll be damned if you're going to the commissary looking like that. I'll give you passes if you get haircuts."

All right. Fine. Haircuts were fifty cents. We scraped together a greenback. The Eritrean barbers on base chopped away gamely. The barber shop was cozy like back home with bottles of Wildroot under the wide mirror and real leather American barber chairs. We had come all this distance to be back in America.

"Now that's what I call haircuts," the captain laughed when we re-entered his office. He happily signed our passes. While we ate our hamburgers, a soldier at the next table bellowed, "I don't care what he thinks of Nixon. He's the fuckin' president. You don't talk like that about the fuckin' president."

Maybe a thousand American souls lived and worked on this leased bit of small-town America, plus twice as many Eritreans. The supermarket looked straight out of Cincinnati, it was stocked to the ceiling with every product you could buy back home. It turned out Americans took easily to colonialism. They gruffly ordered their workers about, with endless complaints about their mental abilities, their laziness, their thievery, their blackness.

Jake asked a military wife in curlers if she ever got off base. Lips pursed, like she smelled something unpleasant, she said, leaning on her shopping cart, "It's not safe. Besides, what is there to do? I'd be afraid to eat the food." She took fright when we guffawed that we'd been eating the local food for weeks and fled to another aisle.

Around four in the afternoon we met Sandy and Greg on base. They ran a regular TV studio full of expensive equipment, large TV cameras, mikes on booms. They wrote, directed, produced, and presented fifteen minutes of daily news and weather completely stoned. No one noticed. Soldiers they may have been, but they weren't so different from us, though they were employed and we were not. They had a great gig far from Southeast Asia. As Sandy put it, "They told us Asmara was a town of mud huts, that Kagnew Station was thirty miles away. Ya-hoo! This just ain't what I expected."

AFTER JAKE FINALLY TURNED up again the three of us headed south to Addis by the Gondar Road. Two hours back on the road a hand slapped on my pack already raised a dust cloud. We were looking at fourteen hundred unpaved miles to the Kenya border, nearly two thousand miles to Nairobi. The countryside was glorious. South of Addis the highlands gradually gave way to verdant farmland amid the Rift Valley lakes, part of the deep diagonal slash bisecting the country that lunged landward toward Lake Turkana in Kenya. For us it meant rugged mountains, a few days of pleasant lakes and valleys, then mountains again, which got progressively drier. Past Shashamane,[8] two hundred fifty kilometers south of Addis, our bus turned onto the Dilla road. Traffic was scarce.

A hundred kilometers more, somewhere past Dilla three students got on. You could tell they were students by their Western-style clothing. I judged they were around fourteen or fifteen. It was late afternoon, the sun slanting through the windows. Hans and Jake were huddled in conversation. I was alone on the backseat. They piled in beside me.

This gang had one great subject—Chairman Mao and the Great Proletarian Cultural Revolution. Just a whiff of sedition could get you

---

8   Sha-sha-MAH-nay

shot in this country, but here they were talking their heads off about the glories of Communism. Their mastery of the Maoist catechism was astonishing. The Chinese masses were meting out class justice. The Capitalist Roaders had been defeated. The Soviet Revisionists were next.

Would Americans help Ethiopians overthrow Haile Selassie and his feudal oligarchy? Not likely, I told them.

They had that calm, slightly mad look—like that newspaper hawker in the Paris bar—as they set out to patiently expound their sanctified beliefs about the rightness of which there could not be the slightest doubt, to raise the revolutionary consciousness of the unenlightened masses. In this case, me.

When they finished their harangue, I interviewed them. They studied government and sociology in a school near the capital. Their fathers were minor officials. They "certainly never" breathed a word about politics to their families. "Of course" all their friends agreed with them. "Our professors, too." Though not openly.

"What will you do with your enemies if you win?"

"We will kill them. We only need weapons and ammunition."

If Maoism had seeped down to provincial high schools, when would it get to the army? Or was it there already? But they looked at each other and clammed up when I asked if they knew any soldiers.

Then something happened that I did not expect. The bus stopped abruptly. Two men got on, a policeman with a holstered pistol and a civilian in a white shirt. Scanning the passengers, they swiftly walked to the backseat. The pair ignored us *ferengees,* though I saw Jake's back stiffen as they passed him in the aisle. The students' faces went ashen as they saw them approach. In an instant, the civilian's angular features—ink-black eyes, small, hooked nose—loomed over them. In a few sharp words he demanded ID, then singled out the tallest one sitting next to me with a barrage of questions. Stammering, pale as death, the student jumped to his feet, whacking his head on the low steel roof at the end of the bus. Grabbing his wrist the policeman marched him out the door. They pushed the boy into a car and drove away.

Without speaking another word the two remaining students got off an hour later on a forlorn stretch of highway, as the sun was setting on bare jagged mountains. Not a single house was in sight. After they left, I told them Jake and Hans about our conversation.

The bus lumbered on. Thirty minutes later the driver stopped in some hamlet; the bus was almost empty anyhow. He announced he was going no farther that night. *Shiftas*, he said. Bandits. We stood in the dust as darkness gathered, looking around for someplace that sold food. We found bread and a few cans of sardines.

Without warning an army Jeep stopped. The passenger, an officer, told us to get in, saying we were not safe on the road at night. We all squeezed in back. They drove through a forsaken wilderness, at last reaching an army camp. It was pitch dark. The sentries waved us through. A sergeant led us to a small concrete-block house with windows but no roof. Latrines were not far away. He gave us two lanterns before he walked off, leaving us alone. We washed, placed our sleeping bags on the frigid, bare concrete, and ate our meager dinner.

The Maoist students reminded me of something, a German poem my Oxford tutor had given me, knowing I had studied German. It was Harold, of course, who introduced me to the "revolution business," as he liked to call it, and Heine's poem aptly summed it up. I got out the folded paper where I had added my translation.

"Hey, look at this, Hans. Do you know Heinrich Heine[9]?" Harold had joked as he handed me the poem. "Here are the implementing instructions for the revolution in three stanzas."

"Heine?" Hans said. "I'm no literature major. I'm an architect, sort of an engineer. But I know Heine, of course." Hans studied the poem by our flickering lanterns. "Heine uses fancy words. I think Karl's translation is close, if not always so artful." He rubbed his chin. "'How To Do It' might be a better title."

Jake took the sheet from Hans and read it carefully.

"You want to change the world? You have to kill people. The

---

9 German poet, writer, literary critic. b. Düsseldorf 1797, d. Paris 1856.

revolution requires certain people to die. You can't succeed unless you get rid of them," Jake said. "But I don't get it. Is this guy Heine praising revolutionaries? Or mocking them?"

"It's hard to tell," Hans admitted. "But I like it. Heine strips away the gloss. It reads like a manual. This is what you need, Heine says, if you want to make a revolution: guns, bullets, troops, and training."

"You better like killing," Jake said.

"Those Maoists we met?" I smiled. "They'd have firing squads working around the clock."

"Ya," said Hans. "Killing brings power. A revolutionary who can't kill should join a debating society. But battles need careful planning. You're going up against professionals. The stakes are high. You must be serious. Calm. And sober."

"Fanatics aren't sober," Jake said. "And enthusiasm doesn't win revolutions. You need clear thinking and naked force. That's the point.

HEINRICH HEINE

VERMITTLUNG

Du bist begeistert, du hast Mut –
Auch das is gut!
Doch kann man mit
Begeisterungsschätzen
Nicht die Besonnenheit ersetzen.

Der Feind, ich weiss es, kämpft nicht
Für Recht und Licht –
Doch hat er Flinten und nicht minder
Kanonen, viele Hundertpfünder.

Nimm ruhig dein Gewehr zur
Hand –
Den Hahn gespannt –
Und ziele gut –wenn Leute fallen
Mag auch dein Herz vor Freude
knallen.

*(Heinrich Heines Werke, Letzte Gedichte
Die Bergland-Buch-Klassiker, p. 506
Verlag „Das Bergland Buch" Salzburg)*

MAKING IT HAPPEN

You're inspired, you're brave and true
Ready and willing through and
through!
Zeal is precious, in its season,
But zeal will never defeat cold reason.

Our foe, we all know, does not fight
For justice and light –
But he is armed to the teeth. You agree?
With all the most modern weaponry.

Take your firearm calmly in hand
Chamber a round, make your stand –
Nothing quite compares with the thrill
Of aiming well and shooting to kill.

(Translation: Richard S. Sacks)

Revolutions are won by merciless, cunning, cold-blooded killers. To win, you must become exactly like the people you hate. It's what those Maoists on the bus told Karl, that political power grows out of the barrel of a gun."

We spent an uneasy night in sleeping bags on the cold concrete. When it was light, we ate the stale bread, returned the lanterns, and got back on the road. It took two more days to traverse a hundred miles of rocky tracks to the border over extremely rugged terrain through the town of Mega, deep in Sidamo province. There were crowds of Galla women dressed in bangles, beads, rawhide, and not much else. After almost six weeks in Ethiopia we crossed to Moyale,[10] Kenya, on December 22. It looked like we'd spend Near Year's in Nairobi.

MOYALE WAS DESERT. THE Somali men wore European-style clothing with white head cloths that unraveled and trailed by their sides. The women wore head-to-toe dun-colored robes. It was hot, a lot hotter than Massawa, easily the hottest place I had ever been. Moyale was like being in an oven. You just hoped the heat didn't get turned up one single notch higher or you might start smoldering. We spent several days there. The heat and food were a shock. We assumed the tough meat we were eating was camel, though the waiters claimed it was goat.

A total surprise at Poste Restante in Addis; while looking through the pile for a Kenya-stamped letter from Howard I was stunned to see one from Helen. My parents must have told her I was in Ethiopia. I had not written to them since England, or to anyone else. I got it out and looked at it again. Of course, Helen had no idea if I would ever read her letter, and she said as much.

---

10   Moy-AH-lay

November 20, 1971
Dear Karl,

I bet you thought you'd never hear from me again. I was surprised to hear from your parents that you dropped out of school. I hope it had nothing to do with me!

Well, you might get this if you pass by the post office in Addis Ababa to look for mail. I don't know how fast the mail gets to Addis Ababa or even where you are. Or where Addis Ababa is, exactly.

It's hard for me to figure out what you are doing over there in Africa. I wonder what the country is like, the food, the climate, how the people live. I picture Ethiopia in my mind as a place as exotic as the name, inhabited by a noble race, perhaps poor, but sure of where they have come from and where they are going. I don't think I have ever met a single person from Africa.

Are you traveling around or just staying in one place? What things have you seen? Who have you met? What stories can you tell? Mostly I wonder how long you're going to stay over there, whether you'll get back to Oxford in one piece. Or if I'll ever see you again.

As for me, that thing with Ernestine didn't work out. So now I'm back home. My parents have been great. I'm staying with them. I found a job at a grocery store downtown which is not too strenuous. I'm in my fourth month now, just beginning to show. My breasts are getting bigger. I can't fit into any of my clothes but at least I have not been sick much.

I'm lonely, Karl. It's not your fault. I'm not blaming you. You may laugh but I miss you. I do. I'm starting to think about this child, how to raise it, what I will do after the delivery (sometime in April, I think), where I will work. I don't think we ever spoke about children. I can't remember if you like them. I was never a big fan, but my situation changes the way I think about kids, if you know what I mean. It won't be just any kid. It will be my kid. And your kid, of course.

Write me when you have a chance. Send me a picture of you riding a camel. Or if there aren't any camels, a horse will do.
Fondly, Helen

All my confusion came flooding back. Helen sounded so reasonable. Or at least stable. Whereas before she seemed deranged. But what did she want? "That thing" with Ernestine didn't work out. Not a word about that relationship, or how Helen felt about it, or how it changed her, or how it ended. Nothing about our old disagreements. Was she clear now about her sexuality? Or had that been some meaningless "blip?" Maybe I expected too much from a letter, but it was skimpy, considering.

Thinking about Helen all alone and pregnant made me miserable. We'd end up married, that was sure. It was not a great idea. But maybe it was the only one. Who had great ideas, anyway? Certainly not me. My conundrum was though we seemed headed for marriage, I couldn't imagine us married. I couldn't see us together for fifty or sixty years. Or five. Or even two. I told myself the problem wasn't about *commitment*, that awful word, but *compatibility*. Was I making excuses? Even so, Helen was not pushing for commitment, not even now, post-Ernestine. In fact, she had done her best to ditch me. But what would she do next? Helen and I were on different tracks, not just different continents. We were moving in opposing directions, at varying speeds. We were like binary stars averting catastrophe by remaining in our separate orbits. The worst part was I still desired her. That bit about her breasts set me off for days. I pictured her back home on the outskirts of town running shirtless in the rain, that day when a thunderhead boiled overhead:

∽

RAIN WAS PELTING DOWN. People dashed in all directions. "Hey, Karl, let's race to that fence." A smudge by the distant woods. "Without shirts."

"Huh?"

She was already sprinting, naked from the waist up. It was hard to catch her. Alone at the edge of the field, we hugged, laughing. We made love in the woods, shivering in the downpour.

There was no way to mail anything until Nairobi, but that didn't stop me writing a letter:

Dear Helen,

You surprised the hell out of me. First, the pregnancy. Then the visit to Oxford. But you left Oxford in anger the day after you arrived. That "thing" with Ernestine? Weren't you seeing her when we were still together? Now you broke up. I'd say your rather warm note is quite a U-turn, don't you agree?

But I added that I still loved her, still dreamed about her. Hell, I still had the hots for her. Could we live together? I doubted it. She was totally confused, I told her; me too. I promised to come to her after she gave birth. I promised to support her and the baby.

I wrote it all down, signed it, put it in an envelope, addressed it, and never mailed it. But I did mail this one:

Dear Helen,

I got your note in Addis. I'm sorry you're lonely. We'll figure things out together after the baby is born. If that is what you want.

Fondly, Karl.

∾

WE FOUND A DRIVER in a small Bedford flatbed going to Sololo, the next watering hole in Kenya. Gone were the giant Fiat tractors in Ethiopia. And now we had to pay. From Sololo the route went through the great game park at Marsabit down to Archer's Post and

Isiolo, where pavement began, then a long jog around Mount Kenya to Nairobi.

Our threesome was breaking up. Hans was headed south, and he and Jake talked about climbing Kilimanjaro. After much argument, Hans reluctantly agreed to take our tent. We argued it would keep the hyenas at bay if he had to sleep in the bush. I wouldn't need it in Lamu. And Jake didn't want it. I figured I'd reach Lamu by mid-January. I wasn't sure I'd see Jake again, though he promised to get to Lamu by March.

I was itching to get off the road, sit at a desk so I could write something serious for Harold back at Oxford. My topics were dark and piling up: Inflamed ethnic hatreds. The crumbling Ethiopian state. Guerrilla war in Eritrea. Target practice on the road to Dessie. The arrest of the Maoist student on the bus. Whatever Helen thought about Ethiopia, I doubted any Ethiopian knew where the country was headed. The empire seemed to be nearing the abyss. Polio victims and lepers were everywhere. Smallpox, measles, venereal disease, were rife, not to mention famine and ignorance. Ethiopians faced beatings, hangings, and oppression at the hands of a ravenous rural oligarchy. A peasant sharecropper might keep a quarter of his harvest. I was seeing things up close, all right. But who knew what Harold would make of them?

I made Jake suffer through my checklist. The country was a prison house of nations. Christian highlanders, Amharas especially, oppressed everyone else, including Muslims. Muslims scorned tribal animists. Highland Tigrinyas oppressed Eritreans, or sometimes the other way around. Provinces were in revolt. The Tigrinya Liberation Front wanted an independent Tigre. Eritreans despised Ethiopians but also hated each other, their guerrilla movement split between the ELF[11] and the explicitly Marxist EPLF.[12] The emperor was respected, even revered. But national cohesion? With over a hundred ethnic groups and languages? The ramshackle imperial dynasty was all that held the place together.

---

11   ELF-Eritrean Liberation Front
12   EPLF-Eritrean Peoples Liberation Front

∼

IN SOLOLO WE QUICKLY found a truck going south crammed with piles of carefully tied leafy bundles, but there was a bit of space on the truck bed in the rear. The canvas tarp was high enough for standing. The driver and the passengers were busy chewing the cargo, leaves they called *qat*. They passed around sugar to cut the bitter taste. We declined to buy any. It took a knee-high stack of qat, two pounds of sugar, and half a day of chewing to get high. We stood in the back of the truck taking in the view. The other passengers sat on the truck bed chewing qat, their feet dangling over the road.

The scenery was brown desert plains sprinkled with green grass. After two hours we were in genuine park country with wide sweeps of empty grassland interspersed with acacia trees. You could see for miles. We'd seen nothing like this in Ethiopia. In Paris I had told Howard I wanted to see the world. I was seeing it. I had been on the road not two months. I'd covered thousands of miles already. I kidded myself that all this was improving my prospects. Mostly I didn't know what to do with my mind. My prolonged unemployment made me antsy. I constantly second-guessed myself. Maybe I'd go back to Oxford. I felt no urge to go back, or for domestic bliss with Helen and our child. I was fixating about my future, worried, much too late, about making the right decisions, certain I already was not employable, when in the distance I could see giraffes nibbling the top leaves of the increasingly tall trees.

They were hard to make out. Giraffes were standing behind solitary trees that seemed miles from the road, one giraffe per tree. Then nothing, nothing. Nothing. Then a herd of zebras running full tilt away from the truck. Jake and Hans were watching intently; the passengers concentrated on chewing qat. The road spun on behind the truck, a brown torrent rushing beneath us. There were herds of antelopes, zebras, giraffes everywhere we looked, endlessly to every horizon.

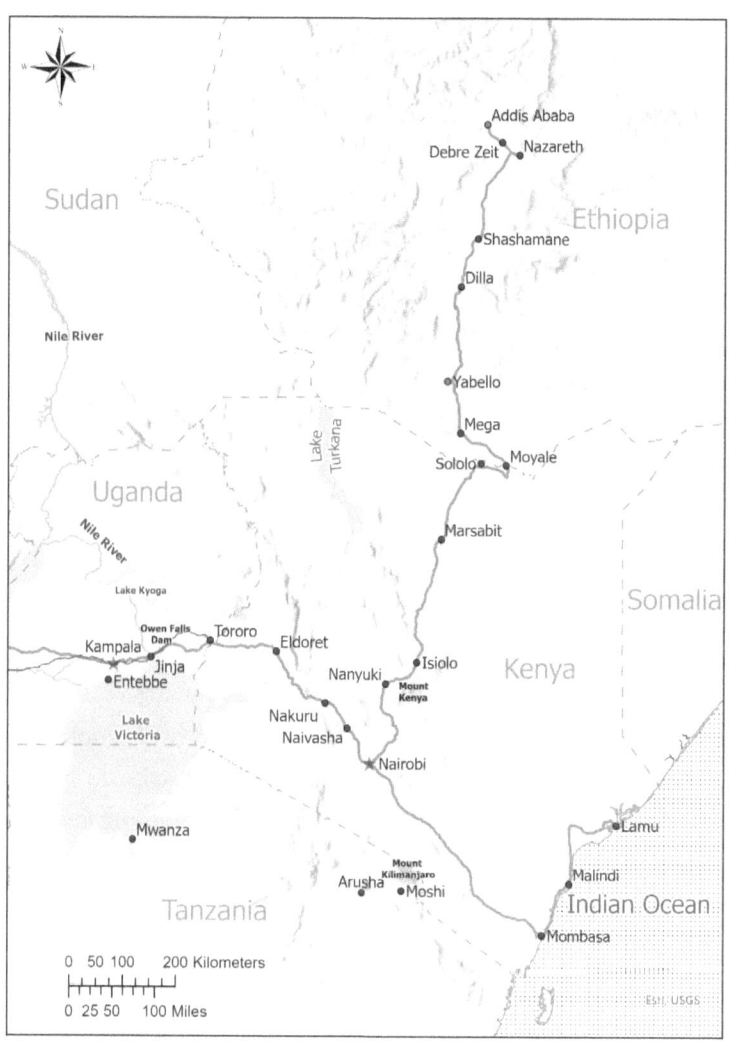

MAP 3 – KARL AND JAKE'S ROUTE, ADDIS TO KAMPALA

14. BEFORE THE MAST
(JAKE)

I wanted to climb Kilimanjaro. Hans didn't.

"Every tourist wants to climb Kilimanjaro. What's the point? It's cold up there, hard to breathe. Do you have warm clothing? Neither do I. We'll freeze to death. The view from the top is flat savanna in all directions. It's an old volcano, you know? It's like walking uphill at the beach."

I assumed he didn't want to go because of the physical strain. The harder I tried to convince him, the harder he pushed back.

"It'll be expensive, you know? We'll have to stay a few days at least in the Moshi YMCA at the base of the mountain, which isn't cheap. We'll have to buy camping supplies, food, pots, plates we'll never use again. Unless you want to hire a porter? You can't really cook up there anyway because the air is too thin. It's a six-day trip up and back. What are we going to eat? Sardines? We can't carry bread for six days. I don't mind looking at the mountain. But climbing it?" He shook his head. "It's one of those crazy things the tourists do."

I could have left him and his stubborn engineer's mind, but I decided not to. I kind of liked the guy, though now that it was back to being a twosome instead of a threesome with Karl, everything was either-or again, with a tendency to long silences.

After Karl went on to Lamu, Hans and I spent several days in Nairobi trying to decide what to do. Nairobi was the first big African city I saw after Addis. In Nairobi everyone was on the make. Money talked. In fact, it screamed. Scads of backpacking Westerners fresh off cheap flights from Europe or Johannesburg were keen to experience "the real Africa." For each tourist, three con men were pushing you to change money or buy dope, both illegal. The police paid the dope dealers to bait the tourists so they could sweep in for the arrest and the shakedown. Or, if you weren't careful, polite young money changers would take your dollars and hand you a sealed envelope full of crumpled newspaper. There were bargirls by the hundred. By the time you opened the envelope to look for your wad of shillings, they were long gone.

If you had cash and avoided dealing with strangers on the street, Nairobi was a small urban paradise. Western food was plentiful. All-you-can-eat deals were offered at ritzy hotels for a dollar. After weeks of slow starvation riding on trucks in Ethiopia, this was a welcome change. Unlike Addis, the streets were paved. Like Addis, the weather was perfect.

Hans spent a day or two following up job leads in Nairobi but got no offers. After the first of the year, Hans and I headed south. We crossed the border into Tanzania. This was wide open savanna, big-game country. Kilimanjaro dominated the landscape. You could see it easily from thirty miles away. I convinced Hans to walk a few miles up the mountain trail from Moshi. The Kilimanjaro trail starts as a road, winding through neatly cultivated farmland and pasture with wooden fences. If you squinted, it looked like Wisconsin. The road quickly becomes a track, then a path. We sat down on a grassy knoll.

"The farmers here work hard. The soil is rich. Volcanic, I guess."

"It is beautiful," Hans admitted. "I know nothing about farming, never been near a farm, besides Africa. I spent all my life in cities. Berlin, mostly."

"I grew up on a farm."

"Really? I never met a farmer before."

"Ever been to the States, Hans?"

"Ya, once, only for a few days. New Orleans, Houston, then Mexico."

"New Orleans?" That surprised me. "I spent almost two years on an oil rig in the Gulf of Mexico."

"Really? Tell me about it."

"It was hard work, but we made good money, and unless you went crazy on shore-leave, there wasn't much to spend it on."

"That sounds hard," Hans said. "Not the work. I mean being thrown together in a small place with people you don't know and no way to escape."

"You're right about that," I said. "There were some real characters on the rig. You had to know how to play them." I didn't say much on the walk back to Moshi.

Hans wanted to see Dar es Salaam on the chance of finding work, maybe for an international aid organization. I took the long bus ride with him. Dar was the opposite of Nairobi—hotter than hell, run down beyond belief, zero for tourists, no buzz, no oompf, no excitement. After three or four days, Hans found nothing.

"There's no way I'm going to find work here. I'll have to go south."

"You mean, South Africa? Rhodesia? I would never go there," I said.

"Why?"

"They're police states run for the whites. You'll just be exploiting the Africans if you work there."

"What choice do I have if I want a job? No jobs around here. And to me South Africa doesn't seem much different from Louisiana. How many blacks worked on that oil rig of yours?"

I had to think about that. "I guess we had one or two black cooks. Maybe a few maintenance guys."

"I bet they had the lowest-paying jobs."

"I still wouldn't go to South Africa. A man's a man, Hans. But over there, you're not a man unless you're white."

"I think you have the same problem in America."

Hans was right more than I let on. I dropped the subject. We had to say goodbye. He was heading south. I was heading back north to Mombasa, then to Lamu to meet up with Karl.

"Are you ever going home again?" I asked.

"No, probably not. Where is home? Berlin? I don't think I have a home anymore. What about you? When are you going home?"

"Not for a while. I'm in no rush to get back. I'd like to get a job here in Africa, like you." The truth is I missed my sisters. They were far away. I tried not to think about it.

Hans and I split. I headed to Mombasa the next morning. Mombasa was a step up from Dar. Livelier. More attractive. Less trash lying around. People were better dressed. The food was great, especially if you liked Pakistani samosas, tandoori chicken, chapatis. It was still hot, no getting away from that. I checked into a cheap hotel, strolled down to the port. I immediately ran into platoons of young men eager to sell me lottery tickets, ivory carvings, elephant hair bracelets, marijuana, or to change money. Squads of young women, too, trying to sell something else. I shooed them away. I passed a guard ten shillings to get into the port. I walked around aimlessly looking up at the giant ships in the brilliant sunshine, like we had done on the Red Sea in Massawa, but Mombasa had a lot more ships.

A tall guy with a well-groomed beard, dressed in a blue jacket and brown slacks, was standing by the railing at the water. He was maybe in his early forties, serious looking, passing time in the heat, apparently.

I offered my hand. "Hi, my name is Jake."

"I'm Sven. Sven Torvalson," he said, surprised. He looked me over. "What are you doing here?" That put me on my guard because I had bribed my way in. "Sorry," he said, "sometimes I'm too abrupt. Are you working? Are you a tourist?"

"I'm a tourist. Last time I worked was last summer."

"What brings you to Mombasa, then?"

I told him I had just hitchhiked around Ethiopia.

"No kidding?" He seemed genuinely surprised. "That must have been interesting. Where are you from?" I mentioned Nebraska, the Gulf of Mexico, oil drilling.

The oil business seemed to impress him. "Can I buy you a beer?" I looked around. There were no stores or bars anywhere. "Let's go to that ship there. I'm working on that ship." He indicated one of the larger cargo ships two berths down.

"That's nice of you. But will they let me onboard?"

"I think it will be all right. You see, I'm the captain."

The ship was named *Scylla*. We walked up the gangplank, then up two flights of stairs. We reached a spacious, well-furnished cabin. We sat at the captain's table drinking Carlsberg.

"Jake, you may be able to help me. Here's my situation. We've been in Mombasa longer than I like, waiting for a replacement for one of our assistant engineers. This fellow is taking his time. I'm not waiting any longer. We're sailing tomorrow. Now, I was thinking with your background working with farm machinery, and oil drilling, you would be well placed to do this job. If you're interested, of course."

I was dumbstruck. "You, you're offering me a job? What does an assistant engineer do?"

"Yes, I'm offering you a job," he laughed. "Basically, the assistant engineer is a chap we send to troubleshoot and fix machinery. Not the big ship engines, we have specialists for that. But a ship has lots of other machines that we depend on. I'm going to tell my company to cancel that replacement for now, at least until we get to Lagos. I'm through waiting for him. I'm not going to tell them I hired you. I'll keep you off the books for now. I have a way to do that. We'll pay you well, give you a cabin, all your meals, traveling expenses."

My head was spinning. I was inclined to accept. We talked about salary. It was much more than the oil company. I was sure I could handle most of the jobs Sven mentioned. The gig probably would last two months at most. That was fine with me. I'd have time to get back to East Africa. Relatively speaking, I would also be rich.

Sven introduced me to the paymaster, the quartermaster, the first mate. He showed me to my cabin, a big step up from my old hooch. After they gave me an ID card and a pass to get into the port, I went back to town, had dinner, checked out of my hotel. Then I walked back to the port with my backpack, passed the gate, and climbed on board.

15. ABDULLAH'S
(KARL)

I met Beatrice Bergmann at Abdullah's Tea House one morning shortly after I arrived at Lamu. She was sitting alone. Slim, medium height, short brown hair, quick brown eyes, a bit older than Howard and me, Beatrice stood up and waved when I came in, mistaking me for someone else, then invited me to sit. Abdullah took our order for *mandazis*, East African fried coconut dough balls, and tea. *Chai*, as Kenyans called it, is poured boiling hot from a huge kettle with milk and sugar already added in.

Beatrice, I soon discovered, was always ready for an argument, but we got through the preliminaries. I practiced my German, joked about Lamu, where men dressed in white and women dressed in black, and Western tourists who were overrunning the place.

"I suppose you think you're not one of them?" she asked. She was smart, vivacious, intense. Talking with Beatrice was like talking with a shrink. She was always thinking and wanted to know everything, while she ruthlessly analyzed you, herself, and everyone else.

"From what you say, your travels with Jake are sliding into ruin, but now you say you're rooming with a South African yogi named Howard?" When I mentioned that the anti-war movement in the States had collapsed after Nixon abolished the draft, she said, "Do you want sympathy or congratulations? And by the way what are you running from?" Beatrice had a way of getting to the point no matter how uncomfortable it might be. I fessed up immediately.

"I'm an academic refugee. I fled academia betting that I could learn a whole lot more in Africa than at Oxford."

"So, you're a writer? A journalist?"

"Not exactly. Though I send essays to Harold Higgins, my tutor."

"Your ex-tutor, you mean? Didn't you say you dropped out?"

"Yes," I admitted.

"So you're on an unpaid, non-sabbatical from a non-academic, non-position," Beatrice snorted.

The more I spoke, the more she wanted to hear, and the more I told her. Mostly I talked about Helen. I admitted I had no way to solve it. Beatrice accused me of being weak and selfish with Helen. Arguing was pointless. I didn't ask what strong and generous would have looked like. I didn't let on that Helen had left me for Ernestine. Was this an interrogation? To her credit, Beatrice never hesitated to put herself on the witness stand. It was more like a mutual confession.

What we called Abdullah's was ground zero for Lamu tourists. A restaurant it was. The actual name was Lamu Restaurant, a wooden, mudbrick and thatch affair with two sides open to the street. But everyone called it Abdullah's Tea House. Stuck in the straw above the door lintel was always a small sign, a tourist prank, variously scrawled: *Abdullah's Fun House, Abdullah's Friendly Loan Association, Abdullah's Poker Parlor, Abdullah's Funny Farm, Abdullah's Bait and Switch, Abdullah's Last Stand, Abdullah's "Quick Fix" Laxative and Emetic.* To the owner, Hamid, a quiet man who spoke little English, *Poker Parlor* sounded irreligious, so the name disappeared after a day.

Abdullah, the famous, though much-maligned, half-crazed waiter, was alternately pleasant or rude, fluent or stuttering, all smiles or all frowns, placid or in a funk. He had a slight limp, perhaps a touch of polio. He was entirely subservient to his master, Hamid, and obeyed his command instantly without a word, though Hamid was mild as masters go. But Abdullah grew restive under the incessant orders, questions, complaints, slurs, and taunts from tourists who wouldn't accept that this was Africa, after all, not some burger drive-through in Skokie. The cook cooked what he wanted or what Hamid asked him to prepare, or what was on hand that could be got. When it was gone, it was gone, despite what the menu said, no use insisting. Maybe tomorrow, *inch'Allah*. A short walk from Abdullah's were two or three other restaurants, but Abdullah's was Lamu's default favorite. Despite constant disappointments from the kitchen, the place was usually packed, even in the heat of the day.

Abdullah was moody. At times nasty, at times ingratiating, he could be inscrutable, irascible, and recalcitrant, or full of jokes. Select diners got the silent treatment. When confronted he would roll his eyes and shrug, all the while muttering in Swahili or Arabic, which was anyone's guess what he was saying or whether he understood what you told him or whether he was even listening. His English was sketchy. Some customers saw or imagined they saw Abdullah serve other people the exact thing they had ordered that Abdullah had told them was not available. Inevitably that started a ruckus. It was no use because Abdullah never lied, as far as I could tell. Often, he would disappear in the kitchen, come back with food no one had ordered, repeat that two or three times, saying whatever had been ordered was finished, until the frazzled, hungry customers took what was put in front of them, though an almighty row usually broke out about the bill.

Beatrice took it all in. She didn't say how she had landed in Lamu, but she was clear about why she left Germany. "Anger. Anger more than anything. But also resentment. Or maybe it was bitterness. And guilt." I had to listen closely because she spoke so fast. She seemed too young for so much guilt and bitterness. "I bet this all sounds like too much. Like, what is this woman talking about? Why these neuroses? Why these compulsions?" She picked up the teacup. "Germans are obsessive, that's our failing and our charm, I suppose. Does it take a genius to guess why Germans are stuck on the twentieth century?"

She gave me no chance to reply. Instead she blurted, "What were you doing in 1968?" Beatrice smiled mischievously but carried right on without waiting for me. "In Germany we students were demanding de-Nazification, demonstrating for democracy. Life was wild. But you have to understand," she lowered her voice, "this was about our parents. I grew up in Essen, in the Ruhr. You know where that is?" She looked up at me. "The Royal Air Force, and you Americans flattened Essen. Because of the Krupp Works."

"Krupp?"

"Yes, Krupp. Guns, tanks, munitions. Essen was destroyed. Payback for the death and misery that Krupp spread during two world wars. We were practically homeless when I was a baby." She frowned. "As I said, 1968 was about our parents. My mother, Ursula, is a housewife. My father, Ulrich, heads a Siemens corporate finance division. During the war he was on the Eastern Front. He took part in Barbarossa, the Nazi invasion of the Soviet Union. He demobilized in 1945, the year after I was born. He was a Wehrmacht major in military intelligence. The Wehrmacht, that's what they called the Nazi army."

She contemplated her cup as she held it with both hands. "Perhaps he was not a party member. As a Wehrmacht major, he didn't need to be. But he never liked to tell me exactly what he did in the war, though I always asked him. And, you know, Hitler decreed Barbarossa as a war of extermination." Beatrice told me that ever since she was a teenager she had hunted for bits of evidence around the house; she rifled drawers and closets for photographs, souvenirs, notes, memorabilia. She collected eavesdropped snippets of her parents' conversations, like when Ulrich's war buddies came to visit.

"My father talked a lot about his duty to the nation, to the *Vaterland*." She looked me in the eye. "I'm convinced my father actively took part in Nazi atrocities in Russia. I'm certain he's a war criminal. Have you heard of Babi Yar? No? It's a deep ravine near Kiev. In two days in September 1941, we Germans murdered thirty or forty thousand people, Jews mostly. Shot them all to death. I think my father had a direct hand in it."

"Is there proof?"

"He once admitted he was present in Kiev during that time. You know, a Wehrmacht intelligence officer would have been no idle bystander. The German army was not exactly clean. German soldiers were killing Jews every day. I'm sure my father with countless others was working hand in glove with the German killing units trailing behind the army, the *Einsatzgruppen*, who massacred every Jew they could find. They emptied the villages, the *shtetls*, entire cities, like Kiev. Herded them into forests. Made them dig their own graves. Stripped them naked and shot them to death."

"Where's your mother in all this?"

"My mother always defends my father to the nth degree, accuses me of belittling Germany's sacrifices defending European civilization against the, get this, the Bolshevized Asiatic hordes. Typical Nazi-speak." She nibbled another *mandazi*. "Hardly anyone from their generation paid any price for their atrocious crimes."

"You mean, besides the millions of Germans who died at the front or by bombing?"

"We started the war, didn't we?" She leaned forward, tapping the table with her index finger. "We deserved to die. I mean the survivors paid no penalty after the war." She stroked her hair with both hands before saying, in a level voice, "They're criminals, many of them. But they're prosperous now. Respected hypocrites, like my parents. Older Germans don't want to dig deeply into the war years. Those people with big jobs in the bureaucracy, the universities, big business? Like my father? They're all Nazis. Where is the reckoning? We demonstrated, we fought the police, demanded that the Nazis be thrown out on the street. They should be punished, imprisoned, humiliated, ruined. If my father and thousands like him are guilty, why should they be rewarded? I care nothing for my family's status, or its wealth. Germany is corrupt, illegitimate, shameful, criminal."

Abdullah came to refill our cups. The place was filling up fast.

Beatrice sipped the hot, milky tea. "But it's even worse than that. Our intelligence service is full of Nazis. Many politicians were party members. Even our prosecutors are mostly Nazis." She squeezed her cheeks with both hands. "How many former Nazis do you think they'll lock up?"

"You left out of disgust?"

"Partly." She stared off into the distance. "Anger. Bitterness. Disgust. The other part was fear. The entire German left is unhinged. You say *unhinged?*"

I nodded.

"My friends are all radicals. They hate capitalism, which they equate with Naziism. They're making bombs. They want to blow things up, kill people. We had this place deep in the woods where we trained. We had guns, explosives, and ammunition. Lots of it." She shook her head. "I knew I had to leave. If I was still in Germany, I'd probably be caught up in that by now." She shifted in her seat. "I believe we Germans need radical change. I want to put people in prison. But I don't want to kill anyone."

"Well, I see why you left. But you also can't go back if that's how things are."

"I can't," she admitted. "I couldn't take a serious job, not yet. I want justice. But killing people will not solve the problem. We need to change how Germans think. It's possible that my generation can do it. Maybe I can prosecute those bastards."

"Including your father?"

"Maybe even him."

Here were three people, Beatrice, Howard, and me, all politicals, all exiles by conviction, all with serious family issues.

The conversation drifted back to my bare month at Oxford, the so-called research on Africa I was doing for Harold Higgins. Speaking of the Maoists on the bus in Ethiopia I recalled Heinrich Heine's poem about revolutionaries. I recited it for Beatrice in German. *"Du bist begeistert, du hast mut . . ."*

She looked at me wide-eyed. "I've never read that poem. What's your translation?"

"You're inspired. You're brave and true . . ."

"You know," she said after I had finished, "this poem reminds me of my former friends. They would like the part about aiming well and shooting to kill."

At that moment Howard walked in. He sat next to me and the conversation went off the rails.

Beatrice was quick off the mark. "Howard, what are white students in South Africa doing to end Apartheid? Please tell me."

"Not a lot," Howard smirked.

"Actually, he was in the army," I said.

"What? You were in the South African army?"

Howard gave me a quick glance. "I'm not ashamed of it. It was something I had to do."

"You boast about it?"

But it appalled Beatrice nearly as much to learn that he'd wandered around India with a begging bowl and, even worse, had been an unemployed spectator in Paris during the May 1968 events.

"You're a counterrevolutionary," she told him. "First you do nothing to fight Apartheid. To make matters worse you join the Apartheid army. Then you imagine Apartheid will disappear by your navel-gazing. And you sit on your hands in Paris instead of helping French workers and students tear down the capitalist-imperialist state?"

"I don't think you understand South Africa," Howard said in a level tone. "The number of white students is tiny. Most of them support the system. By the way, the army isn't optional, if you're white. It's either the army or jail. And it's not like I killed anybody. In Paris I was practically homeless."

"To me it sounds like you have all the excuses." Beatrice got up to leave.

"I don't need excuses."

They both walked out, leaving me alone at the table. I wondered when I'd see Beatrice again.

∼

I WANDERED THROUGH TOWN, sat by the water to watch the harbor. When I stood, I ran into Tony. Here's a guy who'd been out of Australia for five years but never lost his deep Outback accent. A former merchant seaman in his early thirties, he hadn't had much formal schooling, but he was well read and wildly opinionated. He was a fixture on Lamu.

"Karl, come along. I've been waiting for you to take back your bloody sleeping bag."

"It's at your place?"

I followed Tony through the sweltering streets to his hotel room. "Blast! I know it's here somewhere." He rummaged around, finally tossing it to me.

Then he said, nodding into space, "Two days, yeah, day after tomorrow."

"Day after tomorrow what?"

"I'll be gone."

"Really?"

"My brother says to come home quick if I want the job he's got lined up for me. Me back is to the wall. I'm off to Sydney. First visiting me mates in London, then to Aussie. What about you? Sticking around the equator?" Tony pronounced it *ee-quay-tah*.

"Not sure."

"Karl, you're the explorer type. You haven't had a proper African adventure yet."

"What about the two months in Ethiopia? Doesn't that count?"

"That's just a warmup. What if I come by tomorrow night? I'll tell you what to see. That'll be my sendoff."

I headed home, slogging through the dust in the street, moving right to let a herd of goats pass. The herder, a young girl in a faded shift, softly sang to herself. Completely absorbed, she tripped over a board, landed on her knees with a sharp yelp, her features tightening with the pain. I started to help her up. When she saw me, she panicked, jumped to her feet, hobbled after the goats, looking over her shoulder to make sure I wasn't chasing her.

I turned back to the road. *What do their parents tell them about us?* I wondered. The shops gradually left off. The palm trees went down to the water on the right. The path veered left into the coconut forest. Now the sand was cool enough to walk barefoot. I waved at some people passing. They said "*Jambo,*" turning to look at me after I had passed, surprised to see a White man this far out of town, a *muzungu*,[13] as they called us.

It was hot. I kept to the sparse shade speckling the wayside. Sensing movement in front of me, I saw Howard, sitting off the path, looking down at something in the sand.

"What are you up to, Howard?"

"I'm sitting here meditating." He stood and shook off the sand. "They're dung beetles, you see? They walk backwards, rolling tiny balls of shit with their rear legs."

"You mean they spend their lives rolling little balls of shit down the road?"

"They're a gas to watch. They're an allegory for the human condition. For me, they sum up the meaning of life."

Tucked in a grove, our rented, one-story brick house was square and squat, plastered with fine, white-washed grout. The sandy courtyard was full of palms and rotting coconut husks. We had no electricity, but there was a well nearby and we had a charcoal stove and a few pots and pans. It was quiet, shady, secluded. Exactly why Linda and Howard took the place.

Just after I had arrived, Linda and Howard were on the rocks. She left two days later. I took it that Linda had been one of Howard's projects. He had meant to save Linda from her father. A year in India had filled him, as Howard put it, with overwhelming love, a love he could focus only on one person at a time. That person, his current

---

13   mu-ZOON-gu. A European; white person.

girlfriend, got the full glare of his indulgence. He let Linda tread on him like a mother dog. He was generous to a fault. You'd think that might make for smooth relationships. Howard admitted that women baffled him. Maybe they did not love him as much as he loved them. Maybe they did things he would never do. But he always blamed himself when things didn't work out.

"I made a mess of things," Howard frowned. "From the moment we got here I knew I was in trouble, the way she spoke of her father. I miscalculated. She was so strongly attached to him. You know, her mother died when she was little, and her father brought her up alone. I wanted her to declare independence. He really knew how to crack the emotional whip. I thought coming here, a little freedom, a little distance, would be good for her."

"Wasn't she the one pushing for Lamu?"

"In Paris she was keen to think for herself and cut the cord. In the end neither of them could do it. They need each other too much."

"She left you and went back to Europe, didn't she? Nothing wrong with art school. But wasn't that Daddy's dream?"

Howard seemed not to hear me. He covered his mouth with his fingers, staring out the window, then, "She got several letters from him every week and lectured me from the contents. 'I can't keep wasting my time at the ends of the earth with savages and hippies,' she announced, quoting Dad. Can you believe it? We had some pretty scenes. Like the time she slapped me at Abdullah's and threw a plate of beans at me? I couldn't stand it anymore. I told her in my most caring tone of voice, 'You're a big girl now, big enough to decide for yourself what you want to do without feeling ashamed.' That was the slap. Then I slipped something in about the old man. That was the beans. What a mess. Me chasing her down the darkening streets, plucking beans out of my beard and my pockets."

The day was blazing. A breeze stirred the palms outside. Howard was rationality personified. If reason could cure all ills, he'd live to be two hundred. He dissected his emotions so utterly I wondered where he got the courage to act. Yet he could be decisive. Like heading to East Africa or to India on next to nothing. But one moment of resolve usually saddled him with weeks of introspection and doubt.

It was still. We each flopped on a bed, dozed off. A sudden thump on the gate. Howard went out to open the door. McMurdock strode in, followed by Rogers, two famous troublemakers.

"Ah, the Australian contingent," Howard said mockingly. "Are you here to brag you were up by noon? Or maybe Shiftas[14] have invaded your part of town and you're on the run?"

"Naw," said McMurdock. "We're back from the beach. We couldn't stay any longer. The sun's too strong."

"The beach?" Howard fairly screamed. "You're back from the beach already? Ah, I have it. You spent the night there. Must have."

"That's right. It's hot as blazes. How about some tea?"

"Ho ho ho, by all means. Sit down you Tasmanian devils. Karl's pouring."

Prior to our nap I had started the charcoal and put a pot on to boil. I found the last clean cups.

"By the way Howard, what are your travel plans?"

"That's a bit up in the air."

McMurdock sipped his tea. "Beatrice did her free magic show again," he chuckled.

"She does magic shows?"

"Not funny, Rick." Rogers glared at McMurdock. "A man was killed. There was nearly a riot."

"We thought you two might know her. She never mentioned she was a street performer?"

"For God's sake, tell us what happened," Howard said.

McMurdock put down his cup. "Like Ned says, there was a small riot. Out by the market this morning. Never seen the act?"

"What act?"

"We were both there. Maybe an hour ago. We were coming back

---

14   A bandit or brigand.

from the beach. She does magic tricks, makes an egg go through a plate. People wanted to see the plate up close. She passed it around. Everybody was pawing at it. To find the secret hole, you know?"

"It's worked brass. From Morocco or some such place," Rogers continued. "Looks like gold. Anyway, some beggar tried to steal it. Ran off with it, he did. Nearly got away. People chased him. They would have beat him to death. You know how they are about thieves."

"Ned and I followed behind," McMurdock said. "The devil was outrunning them. He cut down a side street. We were about to give up and turn around. Then the guy tripped over a cow sitting in the dust just as the cow was getting up. He fell hard. Something strange happened. One of the cow's horns caught him in the stomach, impaled him, stuck clear out his back. The cow walked a bit with him draped over her head."

"That's how they found him?" Howard said.

"They pulled him off the horn, but it was all up. Bled to death."

"Hard to believe, eh?" Rogers grimaced wryly. "He lay there for a while, his blood running into the sand."

"He couldn't have gotten away on this island." Howard sighed. "Where would he go?"

"Beats us."

"She's going to blame herself. I know Beatrice will blame herself."

"That's why we've come, Howard," Rogers said. "For poor Beatrice. In case you knew her."

"Last we saw her, she looked like a ghost." McMurdock looked around. "Come to think of it, I left my pipe hereabouts somewhere. Did you see it?"

"Yep. Where you left it. On the table over there." Howard pointed.

McMurdock put the pipe in his pocket. "Well, mate, time to shove off. We'll probably get sunstroke." At that they ventured into the blinding afternoon.

"Ahhrgh. Those guys," Howard muttered, "they're full of it. They wouldn't go out of their way for their mother. That's why we've come.

For poor Beatrice.' Who are they kidding?"

"At least they told us about Beatrice."

"You know, I rather like her."

"You two didn't exactly hit it off."

"She has spirit." Howard rolled over on the bed, face to the wall. "I'm going to sleep."

16. BEATRICE
(KARL)

It was night. I got a fire going. Listened to the breeze in the palms. The window frames were open to the outside, no screens, no glass. I imagined the dark dhows in the harbor on the other side of the island, anchor lines taut, bows toward the wind, a line of surf beating the beaches. The charcoal crackled, spraying sparks around my feet. The water in the pot was growling.

Just then, Howard came in.

"Where'd you go off to?"

"I went for a walk. Looked for coconuts. Sat by the water counting meteorites."

"Want to go into town?"

I took the pot off the stove, and we went out. Soon I could hear the water lapping against the shore. The moon was getting high, the trail hardened, lights became distinct. Shopkeepers sat behind counters, double doors opened wide, kerosene lamps hanging on nails in the shelves behind them. Street vendors stood by their carts. We stopped to eat samosas, the first food we'd had since morning.

"Say, Howard, isn't that Beatrice sitting on the quay?"

It was indeed. Howard turned to me and whispered, "Be bloody careful what you say to her." Beatrice spotted us.

"Hello, hello, queen of the night. Two errant elves, at your service." Howard nearly lost his balance making a swooping, flamboyant bow. I giggled, hopped forward, trying my best to imitate a leprechaun.

"An wot may a pretty lass like yerself be doin' alone un such a night with dodgy bein's circulatin' around?"

Howard piped up, on hands and knees, stuck his head through my legs. "That's right. You never know when some troll or, or, or Balrog might take a fancy to you. Then where'd we be?" Cocking his head to look up, he pushed my knee. I fell over on top of him.

"Look out, you horse's arse," Howard shouted. "Get up. Get up."

"I can't. You're on my leg."

We sprawled in the dust, our legs tangled. Beatrice stood watching this foolery. She walked slowly away. Howard ran up to her, took her gently by the arm.

Beatrice winced slightly. "Please don't try to cheer me up."

"You okay, Beatrice?" I asked. Her eyes looked vacant. That morning at Abdullah's Beatrice was busy, nervous, almost frantic. Now she looked tired, miserable. Howard was a few steps ahead.

"After what happened today I feel like nothing matters. I feel empty. Do you ever feel like that, Karl?"

"Empty?"

"I feel full as a bladder after six rounds of beer," Howard said, over his shoulder.

"Don't mock me." Her voice was sharp. We kept walking. "You know, things don't always work out for the best. They tell us they do when we're young but it's not true."

"We heard what happened today," I said. "Sounds ghastly."

"Yes. A man was killed because of me."

Howard slowed to get even with us. "Oh, it wasn't entirely because of you. He did try to steal something, am I right? Then there was that cow."

"Do you ever feel like nothing matters?"

"At times, I suppose," Howard conceded. "But at the moment I feel full of purpose."

"What purpose fills you that's so important?" Beatrice's combativeness was returning.

"I never said important." Howard took a step toward Beatrice. "At the moment I must praise the magic of the night, with memories of splendid nights past, and the beauty of a woman who is standing close to me."

"*Scheisse!*" Beatrice angrily crossed her arms. "Don't you realize? All these memories, dreams, illusions? What are they worth? To you or anyone else? We are utterly insignificant." She swept her arm at the dim stars. "Where's our place in all of this?"

People were slowing to watch us. We arrived at Abdullah's and sat at a small table by a window. Several minutes passed. Howard launched into a monologue on South African wildflowers.

"Howard, do you know you're a bloody bore? Howard, do stop."

"I thought no one was listening."

"I am. It's boring me," Beatrice complained.

"They are beautiful, you know. The Cape wildflowers are famous."

"Simply not in the mood right now." She threw up her hands in mock surrender.

"Very well. You talk about something."

"I don't want to talk."

"And you don't want to listen."

"No." Beatrice frowned. "Not tonight. I want to go home." She started crying. "You didn't see it. The cow, I mean. Covered with blood, bellowing, scared out of its wits, the crowd chasing it." Howard offered her a napkin. She blew her nose.

Abdullah came with the order, staring off into space, making no sign anything was out of the ordinary.

Howard and I looked at each other. We couldn't do anything about the golden plate, about the cow, about the dead thief, about the blood, about death, about existence, about the universe. There wasn't a thing we could do, except to try to cheer Beatrice up. Howard stroked her head. Eventually she calmed down. We walked her to her hotel. The night was soft. Hardly anyone was in the streets.

Outside her hotel I said, "Beatrice, why don't you come to the beach with us tomorrow? About eight?"

Beatrice looked grateful. "Come pick me up when you're ready." She kissed us both on the cheek before going inside. Then we started walking home.

"Beatrice likes you."

"Do you think so?" Howard said. "How can you tell? She certainly didn't like me this morning. You know, we had another talk on the street after we left you. She shouted at me again. But we made up. We went back to Abdullah's. I bought her *samosas*."

"You convinced her you're not some self-indulgent sellout?"

"I talk a good revolution. I was more active in Paris in '68 than I let on. That seemed to soothe her."

"She forgave you for joining the army?"

"When she understood how much I hated it."

"And for India?"

"When she saw how much I suffered."

"No kidding?"

"But it's true."

"Beatrice hardly seemed the steely revolutionary just now."

"She's no killer," Howard agreed. He placed both hands behind his neck, stretching. "Actually, you know, I was thinking about Linda. I wish she was here. I miss her."

"Isn't it better this way? One less woman to worry about?"

"She can be difficult." I was not sure whether Howard meant Linda or Beatrice, then he added, "I don't like being alone."

"Don't worry, Howard. You've got me."

"Huh. Big joke."

We kicked sand in the street. "We should be thankful," Howard said. "We can do exactly what we want to do. And for now we've abandoned the capitalist-imperialist state."

"Abandoned it? For what? Post-independence African dictatorships?"

"Good point."

"Where tea is penny a cup. Grass is a dollar a pound. I didn't spend fifty shillings[15] this week." We stopped at the last store in town, now dark, where the path led through the moonlit palm forest back to our house.

"What ever happened to that friend of yours, what's his name? The guy you hitchhiked through Ethiopia with?"

"Jake?" I had no idea what Jake and Hans were up to.

"What's the plan if he comes?"

"We'll play it by ear. Maybe stay on here another month or two. Or leave immediately. Didn't you say you wanted to travel to the interior?"

Howard pondered this. "It's that or India."

"We could go to Zaïre. Or Malawi. Jake might have an idea."

"Africa fascinates you, doesn't it?"

"It seems unreal. I've never felt more completely an outsider. And the languages change every fifty miles. I have no idea what's going on in people's heads."

"You don't understand what's going on, therefore it's not real?"

"It's real all right. Something is happening. I just don't know what it is. I can't see Africans clearly. I have no idea about their reality. Sometimes I feel like I'm not real, either. Like I'm invisible."

"All too visible, you mean."

"For them I'm some random offspring of former colonialists, just another white face, without personality or social significance. No one knows me. My presence here is equal to my absence. My only power is to increase the tea business. If I disappeared, no one would care, or even know."

"Because you're a stranger? A traveler?"

"Africa has this cinematic quality. But often I feel like I'm the movie."

"I don't quite—"

"I've come all this distance to check the place out, right? Instead,

---

15 Around five dollars.

I'm as strange as can be. Everyone wants to check me out. Don't you feel like you're the main attraction wherever you go?"

"Sometimes. In South Africa, walking in the African reserves, like Zululand, where there aren't many whites. People look at you."

"Lamu is used to tourists. But in Ethiopia crowds lined up to see us. Wouldn't leave us alone. They'd come up close when we were waiting at the side of the road, watched our every motion, commented on every move we made. I'm the movie. I'm the man from Mars."

"You should have sold tickets," Howard laughed.

"We joked about that. The stranger they look to you, the stranger you look to them. Some women would gawk at us and practically fall over laughing. They couldn't get over our beards and long hair. Only old men wear beards. Only women have long hair. They're barefoot, balancing jugs on their heads, barely dressed at all, with outlandish beads, big earrings, tattoos, scars, wild braided hairdos baked with mud. They couldn't get over how peculiar we looked and acted."

"You must have looked like bums after weeks on the road."

"It wasn't just that. We struck them as hysterically funny. Don't you see? Our only possessions on our backs. Like two bugs in the bloodstream, circulating on the road, no aim at all, nothing to gain, no reason in the world to be there except we felt like it. No comforts. No friends, food, families, or warm beds. No roof over our heads. No water to wash with or to drink. No mirrors, razors, or music."

"Ah, I see. Riding on the tops of trucks over unpaved roads in the rain, floating from place to place like flotsam, your main amusement watching the scenery and smoking weed, each day a new adventure." Howard had been there.

"They're right, too," I said. "It's almost incomprehensible, even to me, what we were doing, how we looked to those women who probably were born only a few miles from the spot where we met them. They may have been poor, illiterate. But they knew what they were about, where they fit in, what they had to do for their families. We, on the other hand, were performing no discernible function, did no work, had no fixed address, no home. We weren't like anyone they'd ever seen."

Howard was quiet a moment. Then he muttered, "That place is going to end badly."

"Ethiopia?"

"Haile Selassie, that doddering antique. If he's overthrown, and it's only a matter of time, unless he dies first, the army will do it. No peasant uprising, mind. They'll shoot the courtiers and any opposition inside or outside the military, the Maoists first of all. It will quickly descend to dictatorship. That or the empire will fly apart. You talk about killing? Plenty of people will die."

"We're here on Lamu. No need to get worked up."

"Quite so." Howard reached down, picked up a coconut husk lying at his feet, flung it into the blackness. We listened as it crashed through the undergrowth. "If we're taking Beatrice to the beach, we must get some sleep."

17. LAMU BEACH
(KARL)

First light always woke me up. The doorways had no doors, the windows had no curtains. Outside was still. The hour before sunrise was the coolest time of day. No sun, no heat, no flies. You could work without sweating. A few cocks crowed. The sky was deep blue without a streak of cloud.

I got out of bed, started the charcoal stove, put the water to boil, and walked outside through the courtyard gate. Nothing moved. Behind the house was a tiny village on a slight rise. My eye caught the red gleam of fire in one hut, blue wisp of smoke curling above the doorway. I walked up the hill.

"*Habari yetu,*" The hello to all of you greeting got no response. I tried again. A woman who had sold me eggs before opened the door, tucking her *kikwembe*[16] under her arm. Up here at the village she put aside the usual full-length *niqab*, which was compulsory in town. My fractured Swahili came from several urgent afternoons with a grammar book. I had this routine down pat.

"Hello madam."

"Hello sir."

"What's the news?" Meaning, how are you?

"The news is good." Meaning, I'm fine. "What would you like?"

"To buy eggs, if you have any."

"Yes, there are eggs, sir. How many would you like?"

---

16 ki-KWEM-bay. A skirt-like wrap made of colorful cloth.

"Six?"

"I have five."

"Fine. I'll take five."

Five eggs, forty cents an egg. I gave her two shillings. She said to come back if I needed more eggs. A small child shyly tottered past her feet and plopped on the dirt. I couldn't get over being called *bwana*.

Back in the house the water was boiling. I cleaned our mangy fry pan, took the kettle off the fire, began cooking the eggs, cut some bread, placing it near the coals to toast it.

"Wake up, you no good Pommie[17] bastard," I yelled.

Howard grunted. "Karl, you could have the decency to wait until I've brushed my teeth to insult me in the Australian dialect."

"Breakfast's almost ready. Time to get out of the sack."

"So self-righteous." He sat up and rubbed his face.

"Now be a good boy. Wash up. Get dressed."

"Listen to him. Quite the mother hen."

Howard ate silently. What a fine place we had for maybe six bucks a month. Everything was simple. People were friendly. Pineapple, coconut, mango, papaya were almost free for the taking. If you were discreet, there were no hassles about weed. The ten-mile-long beach was empty. Paradise.

I had reached life's common denominator. For the present I was bound only by what I might decide at the spur of the moment. I knew it couldn't last but Lamu let you take your time. I had no plans, no obligations, no problems. All right, maybe I had one or two. Helen's penumbra floated above everything I did and thought. I had told Howard about Helen's pregnancy the day before. Besides a stern look, Howard's only comment was, "You know, women do get pregnant." Howard's idea was simple: You should always assume that any woman you sleep with might end up bearing your children.

By now I had sent several analytical essays to Harold. Had they

---

17   Also "Pommy." Derisive term for an Englishman.

reached him? Was he reading them? I had no idea, still less what he thought of them. Eventually I would run out of money. What then?

As I calmly beheld my own shipwreck of a life, Howard was a mass of worries. With Howard nothing was decided. He fretted. Second-guessed himself. Couldn't leave things alone. Despite what he said about crazy Linda's crazy daddy, in his mind he kept fighting with the guy. He'd call him a cliché, a caricature of a caricature, a boorish Texas millionaire. And Linda he feared he'd driven away. But then he wondered if he'd got it all wrong, that everything was all to the good and no regrets. Then he'd flip again, blaming himself. I feared Howard might go chasing Linda back to Europe. But now Beatrice attracted him. The scene with Beatrice last night weighed on him. Maybe he should have been more sympathetic, or maybe he should have made more jokes, or better ones. But he hadn't grasped that Beatrice's mood had nothing to do with him.

"Where did you get the eggs, Karl?" Howard mumbled with his mouth full.

"The village on the hill." Howard looked uncomprehending. "They sometimes have eggs."

"They should eat the eggs themselves."

"It's their cash crop. Anyhow, better than trekking into town and breaking half of them getting back here. More tea?"

"Naw, best to get going. The sun gets high awfully quick. Maybe I will have another cup."

The sun was peeking over our eastern wall, throwing brilliant light on the compound. The beach was almost two hours away. From noon to three o'clock it was impossible out there. You came back before eleven o'clock or risked sunstroke and second-degree burns. The only shelter was a grove of trees on a hill at the corner of the island where the beach began. That spot was currently colonized by two amiable West Virginians, Paul and Jackie. Paul was a large, quiet man with an enormous beard and the patient, affable disposition of a pony. Jackie was a vivacious, attractive blond, well proportioned, gregarious, intelligent, but totally down home. Howard and I had visited them once or twice. There was no rain during this season, no cold, no mosquitos. They had built a rough shelter, sleeping on the soft sand on their hill overlooking the sea.

I got the towels, put on my sandals, my hat, walked out into the shade-dappled sunlight under the palm trees. We started off through the sand. It was a mile into town, plus another three miles along the rocky shoreline to the beach. The sun was already hot. We stopped to get Beatrice. She was still in bed when we arrived. We waited while she dressed, waited while she ate at Abdullah's. The whole time she didn't speak or look up.

The three of us got on the rough trail over the rocks that followed an old sea wall. It was a much cooler route than walking through the palm forest. A fresh breeze blew on our faces, as the path stuck to the channel to the southeast. Below us dhows were tied up in the harbor. To the east across the water was the airport, a mile or two away on the neighboring island, glaring brightly in the morning sun. The whitecap-flecked tide was going out fast, flowing down the channel. A dhow was making for the ocean, sails taut and close-hauled, riding the current, bound either north for Arabia and Iran or south for Zanzibar and Dar es Salaam. A couple of lateen-rigged harbor dinghies chased behind as the dhow bore down the channel, tacking against the wind.

We took our time on the path. We often paused to behold the foaming water, the blue sky, the baking continent behind us, and glimpses of open ocean ahead. Beatrice, now full of chatter, said she was glad we had come for her, adding she feared we'd dump her after last night. Howard patted her arm.

Soon we pulled even with the island's only real tourist hotel. Through the wooden fence slats we could make out a few tourists lolling by the pool. The hotel guests came in by air, then over the water by private ferry. They were never seen in town. What is there to Lamu if you're at the bloody hotel pool all day drinking cocktails? Besides the weather, what is the point? They irked me. They spent more money in a day than I spent in three months. I had come overland thousands of miles to get here. Howard and I were roughing it with a well, candles and a charcoal stove in our rented house outside of town. We felt virtuous and authentic. They didn't seem to care a bit.

We were almost at the beach. Above I could see people on the bluff. Jackie waved to us amid uproarious laughter as we walked up the sandy path. It sounded like those two Australians, Rogers and McMurdock. Beatrice had lagged behind on the trail. Howard went back to look for her. Jackie waved to us again; Paul was playing a recorder. Rogers and McMurdock were sitting in the sand.

"I hated Nairobi." McMurdock half-rose with his elbow in the sand to make this pronouncement.

"Aw, it wasn't half-bad, Rick," Rogers said.

"It's a stinking hole, I tell you, nothing but pickpockets and con men." McMurdock was warming to the subject. "You sit down on a bench. Presto, a student sits next to you with a hard-luck story. 'Excuse me, sir, could I discuss with you a matter of some importance?' Family broke, quit school, came to Nairobi, fired because he couldn't hack off-loading pallets at the market. And he paid two weeks' salary to buy the job in the first place."

"Rick, that probably was the most genuine hard-luck case we heard all week. That bloke looked desperate."

"Who cares? What do I look like? A social worker? A philanthropist? What've I got to do with their bleeding country, anyway? I didn't make any of their stinking jealousies. They'd like me to leave my money here and go away. They don't give the slightest damn about me. Listen, Teddy boy, you know how far we'd get if we were starving and asking them for handouts? I'm here to have a good time for myself, not for doing good deeds."

While the two Australians bickered, Paul looked out to sea from his palm-frond lean-to like an ocean deity, complete with pink chubby cheeks and sparkling eyes. Jackie flashed me a warm smile. Ah, she was pretty. Far out to sea a passing schooner was pasted on the horizon.

Down at the beach three black-draped females were approaching the base of the sand dune. I walked a few steps down the path to sit and watch them. Women in Lamu all wore the same loose black cloth that covered everything but the eyes, making it hard to judge their age, let alone see who they were. Which was the point. But these three dropped their niqabs, and they were transformed into high school girls in bright African prints. They had a radio, and they practiced dance steps, swinging their hips to the African tunes. All along the coast you never saw a woman's face. But out here on the beach, they were dancing. We muzungus might watch, but we didn't count.

Howard and Beatrice were trudging up the path, staring at me quizzically because I was blocking it. I got up to greet them. Beatrice was smiling, her brown hair pulled back under a wide hat. She was holding Howard's hand.

"Ah, the tables have turned." She cocked her head, gave me a sly smile.

"What do you mean?"

"This time it's you who is lost in thought," she giggled.

"Meditating?" said Howard sarcastically. "Or," he said, inclining his head toward the beach, "is it lust?" Howard hesitated when he caught sight of the Australians. But Rogers saw him.

"Howard. Beatrice? Come join our party. Delighted, delighted. Sit down here. I saved a place. I always like to talk with Howard. No, I mean it. I like to talk with someone intelligent for a change, instead of this oaf," he said, poking McMurdock with his elbow. Howard sat some distance away.

There was a lull in the conversation. Tinny guitar music wafted up from the beach. Big waves crashed on the sand. The wind rustled the palms.

"Hey, would anyone like some mango?" Jackie asked. Several hands reached for the plastic serving plate. More silence, broken by spasmodic slurps, as people sucked the juicy mangos.

"Ah, this is one of the best things about Africa," said McMurdock. "It's one of the few enjoyable things you can really do here."

"Then why do you stay?" Howard asked.

"That's a question I keep asking myself," McMurdock grinned. Mango juice was running down his chin all over his shirt. "Take that movie the other night. Karl was there, I think. What a bloody waste that was."

"What was wrong with it?"

"The trouble, Howard, was the film was in English. No one but the foreigners could understand it. The Africans were jabbering up a storm, laughing, shouting. Drowned out what the actors were saying. Forget following the plot. For us, like for them, it was just wordless visuals."

"Everyone was in the same boat, then. What theater is that, anyway?"

"It's outside of town," I said. "Open air. Everyone sits on mats. Costs a shilling or two."

"And it does no good asking them to keep quiet," Rogers piped. "They act like it's their natural right to talk as loud as they want during a movie."

"They're in their country, after all," Beatrice said, standing by the lean-to.

McMurdock ignored her. "Sometimes the chatter will die down when there's no action. But let anything happen on the screen—this was a Western, remember—like if someone gets shot or falls off his horse or gets hit over the head with a chair, they go crazy. Right away, everybody starts talking, laughing, arguing, or running around aping the stunt. First one will pretend to hit a guy with a chair, he'll slap his leg a few times, then the other will do the same, then they're both howling. Multiply this by a hundred. It's insane. No one is even watching the film, they're all babbling at top speed. I tried to get our money back. Forget that. An African will always take your money, but he'll never willingly part with it."

Howard laughed. "I'm glad I wasn't there. Now, Rick. Imagine the roles reversed. Imagine the film's playing in Sydney. It's in Mandarin. And no subtitles. The plot is a puzzle. It's set in some mysterious Chinese time and place. You can't grasp a thing about the characters or the action. It's the only movie theater in town. All your mates are there. You paid a dollar. Wouldn't you at least try to have a good time? Even if you made noise?"

"No. We have manners in Sydney."

"Throw in that this imaginary Sydney crowd of yours is really poor, a lot poorer than the odd Chinese in the audience who can understand the dialogue. You could hardly afford the price of a ticket. How does that change things?"

"But that's not the way things are," McMurdock frowned. "The Africans are the poor ones. Isn't it the world's poorest continent? Now the British have gone, nothing works," McMurdock continued. "The buses break down. The banks barely function. Look at the farms upcountry. They were beautiful. Now all the fences are down. There's squatters every which-way hoeing half-acre subsistence plots."

"Try to gain a little perspective," Beatrice said. "This is 1972. Independence was only nine years ago. The entire continent is in transition."

"Transition to what? Give me a break. The problem is they don't work. They work enough so's they can eat, but not one lick more. Kenya exported grain when whites ran the farms. Look at them now. Africans ruin everything they touch."

"And where are your Sydney manners? Or are you all racists?" Beatrice put her hands on her hips.

"You're forgetting," I said. "Kenya was a British creation. They drew the lines on the map where no country ever was. They invested practically nothing. They left it in its present condition."

McMurdock laughed. "I'll grant that the British were low on altruism. But I haven't met one Kenyan, black or white, who says things are better now than they were before. It's shameful the way Kenyans treat Kenyans. Rich Kenyans are first in line for the spoils. VIPs get the nicest chunks of land. They're all driving Mercedes, or building expensive homes, or sending their children to study in Europe."

"What's so damned special about VIPs, anyway?" Rogers asked. "They all grew up in mud huts, ate cornmeal mush like everyone else."

"It's politics," McMurdock spat. "To make it big in Nairobi, you need connections. You must be Kikuyu. Nairobi's where the money is, most of it supplied by Western donors, of course. If you're Luo or, God forbid, Turkana or Masai, forget it."

"You can't or you won't see that this is a period of great change in Africa," Beatrice insisted. "We're living through it. Yes, there is ethnic discrimination. Aren't you Australians also guilty of it? You Americans?" she said, looking at me. "My own country, Germany, was the worst of all. In Africa citizenship, nationhood, is a completely new concept. What ordinary people understand is family and clan. Not national identity."

"So what's keeping the bloody place from flying apart? Political parties are tribal based. Kenyatta holds it together, somehow. When he goes, all bloody hell's going to break loose. There'll be killing galore."

"We've had plenty of killing in Europe, I can tell you that," Beatrice said.

"Africans are good at it. Look at the Congo."

"What about Sharpeville?" Beatrice said. "Hundreds of unarmed Africans shot down in 1960 peacefully demonstrating for political rights, many shot in the back as they fled. Sixty-nine died."

"South Africa gets blamed for Sharpeville. That was regrettable," McMurdock said. "But I don't think the solution was to turn the country over to the blacks. After one short convulsion, order was reestablished. People kept their jobs. Not even close to the mayhem we've seen from African independence."

"Aren't South Africans civilized?" Beatrice said. "Look how they treat protesters."

"The South Africans aim to keep their civilized government. They had to do it, Beatrice. Looking north South Africans saw killings, massacres, monstrous cruelty, not just in the Congo. Tens of thousands of Tutsis were hacked to death in Rwanda in a few days in 1963, maybe a million refugees. Try comparing South Africa to that."

"South Africa should be setting an example for the rest of Africa," Howard said.

"You're British, aren't you? That's just what a Brit would say."

"No, I'm South African by adoption. I served a year in the army."

"You take the viewpoint of the colonizers," Beatrice continued, "as if they were neutral parties."

McMurdock ignored her. "Africa? It's the most backward place on earth. There's no civilization, nothing old. There's no writing, no literature, except maybe here along the coast where they know Arabic. There's no history, no collective consciousness of the past. All African history is foreign, European, or Arab."

"No writing? No literature? No history? You go too far, I think," Beatrice said.

"I tell you, without the white man, half of Africa would starve. All these countries make a big show of despising South Africa and Rhodesia. But where do you think their food comes from?"

"Black labor is producing that food," Howard said,

"Would blacks know what to do without a white man telling them?" McMurdock said. "Why, the blacks themselves in so-called racist South Africa have a higher standard of living than anywhere else on the continent."

"Don't imagine South Africa won't change," Howard shouted. "I know it looks invincible now. But look around you. White rule is on borrowed time. Apartheid will disappear. You'll live to see it, McMurdock. I give it twenty, thirty years."

"You're mad," McMurdock scoffed. "It'll never happen. I know South African blacks get pushed around plenty. But you know they'd be worse off under a black government. Look around you. Do you see any African government trying to help its own people?"

"There are some good things," Beatrice said. "Tanzanians are pulling themselves up by their bootstraps. It's slow but they're making progress."

"I know about all the great news from Tanzania," McMurdock said. "Julius Nyerere, another bloody dictator who thinks he's the Messiah."

"You mean President Nyerere?" Beatrice said. "He's a good guy. I rather like him."

"Yeah? Well, he's forcing Tanzanians onto collective farms. Nyerere sold out to China. The country can barely feed itself. Now they're feeding tens of thousands of Chinese laborers building Nyerere's socialist railway to Zambia. Why? All to avoid routing Zambian copper through ports in South Africa, Portuguese Angola, or Mozambique. Tanzania's already got a good road to Zambia the Americans built. Why don't they use it? It makes me sick." McMurdock scowled. "They can have their bloody continent. They're making a dung heap of it anyway. The only countries on the continent worth anything are South Africa and Rhodesia, and Mozambique and Angola. They're on the right track. You know why? They're not run by Africans."

Howard shook his head. "South Africa is racist, corrupt. It's damned. It's a vast prison, where body and spirit are kept under lock and key. It's no shining city on a hill."

"At least South Africa has no use for this bleeding-heart bullshit of letting Africans run things. You can't trust a Kaffir further than you can throw him."

"I don't like that word." Howard was shouting again. "I hate that word. It reeks of hatred and blood. It shows that your arguments are false, pure cynicism. You think you're more civilized than the blacks? Sure, five blacks living in misery so one white can have a car and a swank apartment in Hillbrow. That's civilization? We're for progress all right, as long as we keep the profits. That's what our civilized system is all about. It's close to slavery."

McMurdock glared at Howard, who glared back.

"All I know is South Africa is the one place on the continent where I didn't have to wallow in filth and disease. Look at the way people live here. Why, they're no better than animals."

"You think British crofters or Russian peasants lived differently?" Howard shot back. "It wasn't that long ago."

McMurdock powered ahead. "Talk about slavery? Why, Africans themselves sold their black-skinned brothers to the white man. The slave traders couldn't have bought slaves if Africans weren't running the business for them, rounding up the slaves, bringing them down to the coast."

"That's so," said Rogers. "He's right there."

"They're lazy, thieving, ignorant. They're good for scrubbing floors, carrying water. Some of the women are good for a whirl in the sack but only if you're randy, desperate, and don't mind the smell. They're a joke, Kaffirs." he said, chuckling to himself. "A bad, bloody joke."

Howard, who had been sitting with his back against a tree, jumped up. "I told you, I don't like that word," he said slowly, his teeth clenched, his eyes slits.

"What's the matter?" McMurdock jeered. "You talk like you have a Kaffir for a brother-in-law."

"You're scum," Howard barely whispered. He rushed McMurdock. Fast on his feet, Rogers got between them. He held Howard off, a good thing because McMurdock was scrappy. I got there a moment later. I'd never seen Howard so angry, so ready for a fight. Pleased with himself, McMurdock remained sitting the whole time, unperturbed. Slowly, Howard regained his composure.

Paul stirred himself, walking calmly over to McMurdock. "I think you'd better clear out."

Stung, surprised, McMurdock glanced up at Paul, a giant with clenched fists. "Glad to. It's a pleasure." His face turned deep crimson.

"You coming Ned?" Quickly, Rogers looked around, nodded goodbye, and hurried down the sandy path after his friend.

Jackie watched them walk down to the beach. "They are so unpleasant. I can't stand them."

"Scum. He's scum." Howard muttered, kicking the sand.

Beatrice embraced him. "McMurdock has a point."

Howard flinched. "You're defending him?"

"I'm not, Howard. He's a disgusting racist. But there are plenty of African racists."

"He's not wrong about Rwanda," I said.

We stood in the sand, listening to Beatrice.

"Howard, Africans are stoking ethnic hatreds all over the continent. Racial cleansing is the next step. I'm talking about mass killings. Rwanda is one such place. Uganda is another."

"The solution can't be white minority rule," Howard said.

"Of course not." Beatrice folded her arms tightly across her chest. "It's . . . it's this intoxicating idea of killing with nothing to stop you. Look at Europe. Just thirty years ago. Africans are catching on. Stalin killed ten million, or was it twenty million, of his own citizens in the thirties and forties. Mao's Great Leap Forward starved thirty, maybe forty million Chinese farmers to death in '60, '61. And that was in peacetime. During the war we Germans tried hard to exterminate the Jews. We shot as many as we could. The rest we killed in death camps. We murdered almost six million. And we killed another fifteen million civilians and Russian prisoners of war. This doesn't include thirty million more who died in military operations in the war we unleashed."

"But those were dictatorships," Jackie said.

Beatrice frowned. "Oh, and what about the million or so dead in the Irish potato famine in the 1840s? And the two million forced to emigrate? And another million dead when India was partitioned? Britain was no dictatorship. But Africa has many dictatorships. Mass killing is about political power. Go ahead, blame Hitler, Mao, or

Stalin. They all had armies of eager accomplices. But so does Africa." Beatrice exhaled. "Here's another thing McMurdock had right, the continent is unstable. Its tectonic political plates are starting to slip after the long freeze of colonial rule. They're rubbing against each other now. We should expect earthquakes."

Out to sea the schooner had vanished. The music had stopped. The dancing girls had gone.

18. TONY
(KARL)

Tony arrived around seven. I had lit our three lanterns. Howard was asleep. We were wiped out after the long walk from the beach through the heat. Beatrice had stayed behind with Jackie and Paul.

"My God, look at you," I said, as Tony came in the door. His face was beaming, almost cherubic. "You'd think you're on your way to a wedding." I clapped him on the shoulder.

Tony looked down critically at his shirt. "A sad state of affairs it is when someone with my reputation has only clean clothes to wear."

Tony normally wore the same clothes for days on end. Today he was shiny. His shoulder-length dark hair was washed and neatly combed. He wore a clean khaki shirt. Even his jeans looked new.

"A week from now I'll be on my way home. By the way, where's your buddy? Sleeping, is he?"

Without a pause, Tony sat and launched into his pep talk for African explorers.

"Now, from Nairobi I'd say you could thumb all the way to Kampala. But you'll need luck getting past Naivasha, that hot scummy town at the bottom of the Rift. What a letdown that place is. From the rim of the escarpment Lake Naivasha looks all shimmering pink from the flamingos. Once you're past the Rift it's a piece of cake. Plenty of farmers will pick you up. You can stay at the Sikh temples at Nakuru and Eldoret. At Jinja you reach the Nile and the Owen Falls dam. It's a great place to have a look. Anyhow, for us tourists Uganda's cheap. It's cheap enough in Kenya. Uganda is half-price."

"Why's that?"

"Well, the Indians and Pakistanis who run all the shops and businesses are worried Idi Amin will kick them out. They're selling Uganda shillings fast as they can. That pushes down the exchange rate."

"Sounds right."

"I'd say go north directly to Murchison Falls. It's the best thing to see in Uganda. You can take a boat ride beneath the falls. Hundreds of hippos and crocodiles are on the banks and in the water. Herds of elephants graze on the shore. It's a sight, I'm telling you, like the day God created Adam and Eve."

"What else?"

"Depends what you like. You can go way down southwest to Kigezi.[18] It's rollin' hills, terraced mountainsides, lakes, everythin' green, banana groves like forests. Them big-horned Ankole cattle are everywhere. Lots of volcanoes, too. Heard there was one over the border in Zaïre that's eruptin'."

"Erupting volcanoes?"

"I ducked into Rwanda. Tiny country. Pretty. Villages sit on top of hills like bird nests. But it's a nothin' country for tourists. There's no diversion, no entertainment, no shops or restaurants, nowhere to stay, neither. Nothing to see. Just a lot of hills and cows. Completely rural. No towns of any size. Even Kigali has barely twenty thousand people and two paved streets. The rest of the country is unpaved. And it ain't so cheap as what we're used to. They speak only French. Actually, they speak their own local language. They've got tea, coffee, pyrethrum. Bananas and plantains grow like weeds. That's it. They're all poor farmers."

"Sounds like Ethiopia. What about Zaïre?"

"Big, big country. Never been there. Heard it's devilishly difficult to get around. Roads are bad. Not just bad; they're past believin'."

---

18   Kee-GAY-zee

Tony lit a cigarette. The match flared, casting garish shadows into the recesses of the room. Howard stirred lightly.

"It was wild in the Congo up to '68, '69, first ten years after independence. Nobody knew who was in charge. Rebellion and war can wreck any country, I reckon. President Mobutu[19] changed the name to Zaïre in '71. You hear all kinds of stories about the Congo."

"Tell us one," said Howard from the bed.

"Hi Howard. 'Course I can't vouch for anythin' firsthand. Most of it seems funny now, in a way, since the killin' is done. At least for now."

"Funny?"

"Funny 'cause it's so crazy, like a bad dream. You know the kind of dream when you wake in the morning, you're runnin' it over in your mind, it just don' make no sense no way. You can't figure out why things happened the way they did. That's what I mean by funny."

A lantern spluttered. I turned to it, adjusted the wick.

"For some reason, the Belgians forgot to educate the Congolese and tell them how to run the place without them, an' when independence came in '60, the whole country had only three or four African college *gre-ju-wits*, and one African doctor. The Belgians left two weeks after independence. All of 'em. There'd been some shootin,' an army mutiny. But nothin' serious, mind." He chuckled. "So the Belgians cleared out as quick as the planes could take off. They took all their airplanes with them, too, and they took the blueprints and the plans for all the public works projects in the country, all the economic data, all written records. They figured they'd done and paid for everything, so why leave it for the Africans, who were actin' real ungrateful by wantin' independence?"

Tony paused to crush out his cigarette. "The truth was no African man had been promoted higher than secretary or sergeant. Mobutu was one of them sergeants. He's now the president."

"Just like Idi Amin," I said. "He was a sergeant in the Ugandan army at independence."

19 Pron.: Mo-BU-tu

Tony nodded. "'Course, the secretaries and the sergeants wanted to start where the Belgians left off. They wanted to drive the white man's car, sleep with his wife, have lots of money, be the boss. Work was another story. They'd always done all the work. They saw the white man didn't work but had all the money. So, the last now bein' first, why should they work? And even if they did work, who would pay them? The common people felt the same way. They grabbed and looted all they could carry, whatever wasn't nailed down. Now the white man was gone, who could tell them what to do?"

Tony lit another cigarette. "How am I doin', Howard?"

"Intriguing." Howard was resting on one elbow. "Please go on."

"The politics are a bit much. I don't have the heads or tails of it. First the southern part of the country seceded with all the minerals. Then two more provinces seceded. In '61, Lumumba, the first prime minister, was murdered. Then in '64 those Maoist Simbas came in and the eastern Congo seceded. There was mayhem for years. *Can-ni-bal-ism*, too." He slowed, separating the syllables for dramatic effect. Tony looked at Howard with the barest trace of a grin.

"Do you want us to faint or something?" Howard asked. "Tony, you claim the darkies won't work the plantation anymore. But where's the bloody interesting side of things? Humor? Romance? You know, what makes people tick?"

"Don't get steamed up, Howard. I'll tell you a murder mystery."

"Does it involve poison darts? Pardon me, Tony. I think I need to get some air." Howard grabbed one of the lanterns and walked out.

"What's eatin' him?"

"Don't worry," I said.

Tony crushed his cigarette and lit another. The door opened. Beatrice walked in. Her movements were graceful, relaxed. She was smiling. She looked good.

"Hi Karl. I decided to come back to town before it got too dark. The outside gate was open. Have you seen Howard?"

"Howard just left," I said.

"I saw someone with a lantern going up the hill."

"That was him."

"Were you two talking? Don't let me interrupt you. I'll just listen."

"Hi Beatrice," Tony said. "There's one other thing," he said, turning to me. "Stay away from Burundi."

"What's wrong with Burundi?" I asked.

"Politics are tense. Hutus and Tutsis killin' each other first chance they get. Just like Rwanda. Then there's that murder mystery. An Arab shop owner I met in Rwanda told me."

"What'd he say?"

"It was more the way he acted. Like it was such a tremendous relief he'd left Burundi. Poor beggar was on his way out to stay with some relative. He was shattered. His wife had died from a mysterious illness. His young boy, too. I suppose there's nothin' in it that couldn't happen in a score of countries. Still, his words made me shiver."

"What words?"

"He said, 'Stay away from Burundi.' Pretty clear, ain't it? He must have felt like somethin' was goin' on there more than bad luck."

Beatrice stared intently at Tony. "One foreigner has a problem and the whole country is bad?"

"Mind you, I've heard lots of horror stories. Never thought a thing about them. But something about his story made me stop. You see, both his wife and kid died of this strange wasting illness. No doctor could find a thing wrong with them. They didn't have any pep, kept losin' weight until they couldn't get out of bed. Then they died. The guy himself looked like a wreck, like he hadn't slept in weeks. Because of the nightmares. I asked him, 'What nightmares?' He sort of collapsed, wailin', moanin', whimperin', cryin'. I wasn't much impressed. Then he said something that scared me. He said, 'They're devils, devils and witches.' He had to board up all the windows of his house for fear of the evil eye. He found weird fetishes hangin' in his garden."

"Fetishes?" Beatrice asked.

"Who was mad at him?" I asked.

"Seems he had an argument with one of the locals. The Arab ran a store. A local guy owed him money, lots of money. This guy had done a big favor for the Arab. Never stopped askin' for credit, though. Finally one day the Arab stopped giving him credit. They had an argument over a basin."

"A basin?"

"The Burundi guy wanted a basin for his old grandmother who lived in a solitary hut apart from the rest of the villagers. Somethin' odd about this ol' bird. Seems she took up with a sorcerer when her husband died. Everyone was afraid of him. He would disappear for days in the forest. Each time he was gone, several villagers fell ill and died. The Arab told me that."

Beatrice had grown quiet.

"The guy pleaded with the Arab for the basin, practically begged him. He threatened him with the wildest things. His house was gonna burn down, even though it was made of brick. He'd be run out of the country. Like that. Finally, he left, telling the Arab he was sorry for him because his grandmother was goin' to be really angry. The Arab never saw him again. Then all sorts of things began going wrong. His wife died. All the plants in the garden died. He began having trouble with his visa. Finally, he lost his business to the state, had to leave the country. Then his son died. It's kind of strange and scary, is all."

Tony stopped talking and stared off into space. He lit his last cigarette and crushed the empty pack. "Maybe there's nothin' to it." Tony shrugged. "Say, I've got to be gettin' back." He stood up and looked at me. "Good luck to you, greenhorn. Write me if you make it to India. If I don' hear nuthin' from you, I'll assume you went to Burundi."

"Good luck, Tony," said Beatrice. "Please let us know what happens with you."

Tony paused on his way out the door. "It's quite clear what happens next. I'm goin' to settle down to a job. In two years I'll have a wife. In ten years five kids. Can't stay on the road forever. No, no, you get tired of it. You start to want to sleep in the same bed night after night. As long as you're sleepin' there, you might as well not be alone." He winked as he left.

"Helluva good guy," I told Beatrice. "On his last night on Lamu he came out here to give Howard and me some travel tips."

"When are you guys leaving?"

"Anyone's guess. You?"

"I don't know. Until yesterday I thought I'd stay with Paul and Jackie out on the beach."

"What happened with the police?"

"Everyone was quite pleasant," Beatrice sighed. "I showed them the trick I performed. They only asked me to write a report. But at this point I feel like hiding. I don't want people pointing at me when I go out."

"You could come with us if you like."

She brightened. "Except you don't know where you're going, or when."

Howard came in holding the lantern. "Hi Beatrice." He touched her shoulder.

"We're talking about where to go next," I said.

"I'm up for anything," Howard said. "Except India's definitely out."

"This sounds a little better," said Beatrice.

"Why don't you come with us?"

"Your partner already invited me."

"Yes, I did. Wasn't it a good idea?"

Howard smiled at me. "Oh, quite."

"I'm happy to leave Lamu anytime," said Beatrice. "I've been here fourteen weeks as it is."

"It's all settled. We'll go together."

"Go where?" I asked.

"I'd go straight to Tanzania," Beatrice said. "I want to see the game parks. I want to see Kilimanjaro. I want to see the Masai. India's supposed to be cheap. But could it get much cheaper than this?"

"Do we have any word from Jake?" Howard asked.

"He'll turn up," I said.

Howard sat on the bed next to Beatrice.

"Tony liked Uganda," I said.

"That place makes me tremble," Beatrice said.

"Bloody Amin," Howard said.

"But he told us to avoid Burundi."

"My friend Bertrand is in Burundi. I'd rather like to see him."

19. MOMENTS OF CLARITY
(JAKE)

The Scylla got underway in the dead of night. We were already beyond sight of land at six when I woke up and rushed out to the railing to look at the dark sea. We had stops at Dar es Salaam, Beira, Lourenço Marques,[20] East London, Port Elizabeth, Cape Town, before heading to West Africa. The crew was Portuguese, Greek, Filipino, Chinese, and one or two Americans. I was up to my ears in work repairing auxiliary diesel generators, pumps, electric motors, winches, pulleys, clothes dryers, dishwashers. I worked alone. Luckily, the chief engineer, who was from Singapore, was patient with me. The crew segregated itself by language. Though they were not unfriendly, Chinese stuck with Chinese, Portuguese with Portuguese. I was a short timer. The Swedish officers were welcoming but kept to themselves. No one wanted to get to know me. And that was fine with me.

I borrowed piles of books from the ship's library, spent my hours off holed up in my room reading novels, history, newspapers, biographies. I didn't talk to anybody much. I avoided card games or socializing. We crawled down the east coast of Africa, rounded the Cape of Good Hope, made quick stops in Walvisbaai, Lobito, Pointe Noire, Libreville, Douala. The time went fast.

Two crewmen, Americans I heard, had gotten on the ship in Libreville. They were in the bar that evening when I went to drink

---

20 Now Maputo.

a beer. It was my last night on the *Scylla*. We were a few hours from Lagos, my last stop. It was just me alone at a table, the two of them at the bar facing the bartender, ignoring everything but their gab and their whiskey. By the time I got there they were both sloshed. I sipped my beer.

One of them said, "Terrible thing. He was a fine man, too. He had his issues, ya' know what I mean? But a great guy. I knew him since we began working in the Gulf together years ago."

"Why'd you leave?" the other one asked.

"You kiddin'? This is a better job than supplying those floating junk piles," the first one said, downing another slug of bourbon and wiping his mouth on his sleeve. "The police didn't really know what to make of it at first. They had a body that had washed ashore. No evidence or witnesses. Then it sorta dawned on them. The one crew member who had skipped out to Mexico probably was the last one to see him alive. He's the one they want to talk to. Issued a warrant last month for the sonofabitch."

I was panicking. *And who was that guy doing the talking?*

"But he's in Mexico? How'd you find all this out?"

"I was on the rig the day Pudge disappeared. I knew the sonofabitch who killed him. Name of Jake Ries. I'm looking for him."

"How're you gonna find him?"

"Dunno. But he better see me first. Hope he hangs."

It was Hink. My mind flashed that he'd worked as a seaman off and on. I had to get out of the bar without him noticing me. With the dim lights and my beard, and his back to me, I had a chance. I calmly finished my beer while keeping my eyes on them, left the bar, and walked quickly away.

So Hink was on board. I was thinking rapidly. The bartender didn't know my name, though the beer was charged to me. *I could be murdered in my cabin. Tonight.* And there was a warrant out for me. *Never can go back to the States now.* All those tense weeks after Pudge fell to his death came flooding back to me. My final ride to the mainland on Hink's launch, the buses and hotels in between New Orleans and Chicago and New York before I finally cleared out and flew to London. I had to get off the *Scylla* before Hink saw me.

Next morning after we docked in Lagos. I watched carefully who was on deck before I claimed my last pay. Then I went to say goodbye to the captain. I'd been planning all along to leave the ship in Lagos.

"Sure you don't want to stay?" Sven asked. "We could use you. We could up your salary a bit."

"No, unfortunately I've got promises to keep."

As I started to walk away, he said, "I almost forgot. You did a great job for us. I wrote this recommendation letter for you, in case you want to work on a ship again. It may come in handy."

I went down the gangplank into Lagos. I was sure Hink hadn't seen me. Anyway, I had promised Karl to pitch up in Lamu by March. I only hoped Karl was still there when I arrived. That evening I was on a plane to Nairobi. I was rich by my lights. I had thousands of dollars, which I converted to traveler's checks. I treated myself to a room at the New Stanley Hotel for two nights.

Before long I was on a bus up the coast to Malindi, a pretty town. North of Malindi the road deteriorated by the hour through rough, empty country. A ferry crossing at a river. It was already getting dark when we finally stopped by the sea in the middle of nowhere. An island was close offshore; Lamu. Presently a ferry arrived. I'd heard about Lamu for months, but it was nothing like I expected. Dirt roads. No cars at all. Crowds, shops filled with goods. Plenty of restaurants. Lots of Westerners. Hippies. Women covered in night-black sheets. With their black skin you could maybe see their eyes, a hand, but nothing else. The men wore Western dress or robes and white skull caps.

Figuring I'd find Karl later, I started looking for a hotel, but I saw a procession starting. Dense throngs lined the main street. At first, I couldn't make it out. Files of somber, earnest men in black pants and white shirts paced slowly forward, then took a few paces backward. With a quick sidestep maneuver, they paced forward again. A hundred male voices chanted, while a drummer beat a solemn cadence. The air was reverent, almost worshipful. In the center of this company, left to march by themselves, were three men in formal black dress, two older men on either side of one who clearly was the groom, each holding an arm, each precisely stepping the same tattoo, practically carrying him along. He was maybe twenty. He tottered like he was about to collapse, his eyes fixed on infinity. His face was ashen. Hell, his skin may have been black, but he was white as a sheet. The two older men paced proudly beside him to the pulsing percussion. They gripped his arms to steady him. He could not simply run away. His number was up, and he knew it.

Finally, all the men passed, opening a big space. Far behind followed a noisy, jumbled crowd of women in their black dresses but showing their faces. They were joyous, exultant, flagrant, indecent, in complete disorder, ululations, screams, flashing eyes, clapping, gestures, laughter, total mayhem. A marching band blared with drums beating madly. They shrieked and shouted. In the center of it all was the bride. She was allowed a little color in her dress and gold jewelry. Close to her was an outrageously flamboyant youth, a gaudily made-up young man, perhaps the town transvestite, beating a tambourine. He was singing, laughing, dancing, screaming, ululating just like the other young ladies. It seemed like the women were mocking the ultra-serious men and he was mocking the groom. They all passed. I was slack jawed, completely forgetting what I was doing when someone grabbed me by the shoulder. It was Karl.

"Jake! You made it."

"I just got off the ferry. That was some parade."

"Crazy. Glad you're back. It's been, what? Two months? Let's go to Abdullah's to talk."

"Abdullah's?"

Abdullah took the order and brought plates of curry. "There've been some changes for Howard," Karl said. "Linda left. Beatrice is the new Linda. I'll introduce you. But what about you?"

Karl was impressed, maybe a little jealous, about my job on the *Scylla*. "Well, we know who to ask for a loan," he said. Karl wasn't surprised to hear that Hans had headed south. "Where else could he find work? But your timing is good. We're all eager to get off Lamu. It's now March-something and Howard has been here since mid-November. But we weren't sure when you'd show up. It looks like we're going to Uganda, then to Burundi to meet Howard's friend, Bertrand."

"After that?"

"Who knows? Tanzania? Malawi? Wherever."

I wondered about Uganda. I had heard about Idi Amin, but I figured he probably wasn't murdering tourists. Maybe it would be okay. I could not have found Burundi on a map.

"So this is Jake?" Howard said when we got back to Karl's place. "I was sure you'd never turn up," he said, slapping me on the back.

Beatrice shook my hand firmly in that German way. She was curious about me, especially when she heard about my jobs on the oil platform and the *Scylla*. She called me the group's sole proletarian.

She wanted to know more about being raised Lutheran. "Well, we know the Bible," I told her. And she pumped me about Ethiopia. "How did the locals treat you white men?" she asked. "Is Ethiopia poorer than here? How long will the emperor last? Did you like the food? How do they treat Ethiopian women?" I started telling her about the bargirls, but Beatrice insisted things were not really so different in Hamburg, where every year hundreds of small-town girls become streetwalkers on the Reeperbahn.

Sleeping arrangements were cramped. A sheet hung from the ceiling with Beatrice and Howard's bed on one side, and Karl's on the other. I found a spot on the kitchen floor for my sleeping bag. The next days were a jumble of maps, discussions about routes, equipment sorting, smoking weed, getting sunburn at the beach, and eating at Abdullah's while Howard, Beatrice and me got to know each other. The plan seemed good; we were turning away from the coast and plunging into the heart of Africa. But I worried. I was sure seeing Hink on the *Scylla* was one in a million, but it would not leave my mind.

20. OUR MAN IN UGANDA
(JAKE)

Beatrice put her arm over the bus seat to talk to me and Karl. "You know, I really surprise myself that I agreed to go to Uganda. Idi Amin, that murderer! Howard convinced me somehow. I don't know how he did it." She affectionately brushed Howard's hair with her other hand.

"Hush now," Howard said. He was seated next to Beatrice and shouted over the engine rumble and the bus wheels grinding the gravel road from the Lamu ferry. "What about Rwanda? What about Zaïre? Or Ethiopia? If you get too picky, you can't visit any country. They all have their problems."

"Tell me Amin isn't soaked in blood up to his elbows?" Beatrice turned back to Howard. "You know he's a bloody torturer and dictator."

"We won't be there too long. We discussed this before. The fastest, most scenic route to Burundi goes north around Lake Victoria."

"Why are we going to Burundi? Oh, that's right. Your friend, Bertrand. Do you like him better than me?" She winked at me. "I do hope he's a good cook."

"We can go to Tanzania later, if you still want to."

"I want to visit the socialists. Maybe they're better than these capitalist goons."

"*Goons?* Do Germans know that word?"

"You English did not invent the world."

For most of the way to Malindi, Beatrice, and Howard huddled forehead to forehead, exchanging seething but affectionate diatribes. Then they abruptly stopped, looked out the window, held hands, hugged each other, rubbed noses. No kissing. This was, after all, a public bus in prudish Kenya. Soon they were back to fierce whispering.

I liked Beatrice, though she was extremely direct. Was that because she was German? For example, the evening I arrived in Lamu she cornered me. "So what are *you* running from?" Stressing the you in her know-it-all air. I froze, at first not realizing she assumed every one of us was running from something, herself included, as she was running from her radical friends and from money-grubbing, corrupt, decadent Germany, still full of Nazis, like her parents.

"Yes. They were Nazis. They're still Nazis," she told me. Europe was complacent, fat, cruel. Capitalism was on the way out. The Cold War was unbearable. "But Jake," she repeated, looking at me slyly, "you never said what you were running from." She was impish, she was gay, she was funny, she was moody, she was sly. Africa's problems she mostly placed at the feet of colonialism. Except for Uganda, which she blamed on Amin. She had a soft spot for Milton Obote, the socialist ex-president Idi Amin had overthrown. Now Amin was looting the place, killing anyone in his way.

WE FINALLY GOT TO Mombasa. It sank in that we might not meet again for weeks. Karl and I were hitchhiking. Howard and Beatrice were taking the railroad to Nairobi and beyond, to Kampala and Kasese[21] in western Uganda. A train, Karl and I agreed, was no way to see a country. On the road you see things close up. Maybe that was a bit too rough for Beatrice and Howard after months on sleepy Lamu Island. Everyone was ready for a change. On our last night in Mombasa we ate at an Indian restaurant, drank beer, gave toasts.

"To the tortured intellectual, who is not sure whether he is coming

---

21   Ka-SAY-say

or going, whose home is wherever he hangs his hat," Beatrice said, raising her glass to Howard, who blushed.

"I don't have a hat," Howard said. But he returned the compliment. "To the next Rosa Luxemburg. May she hold the red banner high."

"Let's not get carried away," Beatrice said. "No one's standing me against a wall."

"Remember to hunt in the morning, criticize after dinner," Howard said.

"And fish in the afternoon." Beatrice stuck out her tongue at Howard.[22]

"This one's on me." I ordered more beer, filled everyone's glass. "To Howard, who at least knows something about Africa."

"But still he insists on going to Uganda. Explain that?" Beatrice complained.

"To Jake," Karl said, "the only one we know who can still get a job."

"To Africa," Howard said, amid cheers. "To Africa, the land of surprises."

At breakfast Howard proposed to meet in Kigali on April 15, at 6 p.m. under the big Primus beer sign in the center of town. We knew about the Primus sign in Kigali because Howard's friend Bertrand had proposed meeting us there, but then changed his mind. Instead, he invited us all to his lakeside bungalow in southern Burundi, close to the Tanzanian border.

---

22 Beatrice and Howard were joking about this passage from *The German Ideology*: "For as soon as the distribution of labor comes into being, each man has a particular, exclusive field of activity, which is forced upon him and from which he cannot escape. He is a hunter, a fisherman, a shepherd, or a critical critic, and must remain so if he does not wish to lose his livelihood; while in communist society, where nobody has one exclusive sphere of activity but each can become accomplished in any branch he wishes, society regulates the general production and thus makes it possible for me to do one thing today and another tomorrow, to hunt in the morning, fish in the afternoon, rear cattle in the evening, criticize after dinner, just as I have a mind, without ever becoming hunter, fisherman, shepherd, or critic." Karl Marx and Frederick Engels, *The German Ideology*, Progress Publishers, Moscow, 1964, pp. 44-45.

"What happens if we miss our date, Howard?" Karl asked.

"We'll wait until you show up."

It was real trouble at first to find lifts, as Tony had predicted. Days later, after we passed Naivasha and crossed the Rift Valley, things got easier. One shivering night we were outside Eldoret at seven thousand feet in western Kenya. We bought two hooded sweatshirts in a store run by an Asian couple. The owner said, "Would you fellows be interested in buying a tent?" We weren't interested. "It's only four hundred shillings. It's quite a good camping tent. I bought it from a Norwegian chap who was leaving Africa. Looks like he never used it." The tent was Swedish, had a rain fly, could sleep three in a pinch.

I offered two hundred shillings. He immediately agreed. I put the tent in my almost empty pack. The collapsible poles I tied to the outside of the pack. We found a cheap hotel that night, reaching Tororo at the Uganda border before eleven o'clock next morning.

We had trouble as soon as we reached the border. At first, the customs officer refused to let us enter Uganda. We had no Ugandan visas. We hadn't needed visas in Ethiopia or Kenya. Finally, he said he'd let us in, but we'd need to apply for visas in Kampala. I thought we got off lucky. No way I was going back to Nairobi. He stamped the date, March 29, 1972. It was Wednesday.

That was the day we met Lonnie McIntyre. After walking through Tororo we got out onto the road. Karl was sitting by the trunk of a big tree reading in the shade. It was a calm, pleasant day. I was standing by the road, watching sunlight filter though the leaves. Then a crashing sound. *Thunder? Muffled reverberation?* I strained my eyes down the way we came, where the road dropped out of sight to the east. Over the hump shot a white streak. I stuck out my thumb. The driver blurred past me and slammed on the brakes, squealing and smoking rubber across the pavement for at least a hundred yards. He stopped dead, brake lights glowing through the blue haze.

Karl stood quickly. "What was that?"

"BMW, I think. Diplomatic plates."

A full minute passed. While Karl and I looked on quizzically, the car abruptly backed up until it was level with me. Like Kenya but unlike Ethiopia, Uganda drives on the left side of the road. I walked around to the right side of the car, the driver's side in this formerly British part of the world. The driver immediately offered his hand. He was British, about thirty-five, with a carefully trimmed mustache, sideburns, longish wavy brown hair that fell over his gray eyes. Despite the heat he wore a wool blazer. The shift knob sported a Union Jack.

He clung to my hand, looked me over, turned his head to take a long look at Karl and our backpacks by the tree, back to me. He was sweating. He obviously had been drinking. Gin, I guessed. The smell of alcohol poured through the window, like a bottle had overturned in the car.

"Lonnie McIntyre."

"Jacob Ries. That's my buddy Karl Appel."

He stared at me curiously, then released my hand. I returned his stare.

"Say, do you fellows need a lift?"

While Lonnie revved the engine, Karl shot me a look over the roof as we stood on opposite sides of the car. Sure, the guy was drunk as a skunk, but he'd steered straight as an arrow at speed when he passed us and his reflexes were intact, the way he'd stomped on the brakes. Maybe this was his normal mode. He'd also just passed Tororo customs. Plus, there wasn't a ding or a scratch on the car. I gave a thumbs up.

I got in back, moved the empty gin bottles out of the way, arranged the packs. We barreled off.

"Cool car," I said. "Is it stock?"

"We made some mods," Lonnie smiled. "Fuel injection is factory BMW but the camshaft, compression, suspension, wheels and tires, transmission, differential, are custom." He shifted into fifth gear when the speedometer hit 130. I did a quick calculation. Eighty miles an hour.

"You know, we don't see many Westerners around here. Where are you boys coming from?" Over the road noise Karl walked him through our fabled, complex, yet inevitable tale of where we had started our travels and where we were going.

"I see." Lonnie kept his eyes on the road. "My grandfather was one of the first advisers to the Uganda colonial government. My father came out to Kenya in the twenties, after the Great War. As for me? British embassy. In Uganda it's called the High Commission. I'm in charge of press. What you Yanks call public affairs. Shameful what we've done here. Just shameful."

"What do you mean?"

The speedo hit 140. Up ahead the two-lane road curved to the left. A big truck started pulling off the gravel apron into our lane, blocking our view. We couldn't pass. There was no way to stop. I braced myself. Lonnie slid the car left, jammed the shifter into third, steered hard right, stomped on the gas. The tachometer redlined. Our rear wheels drifted left, our front wheels drifted right, just like four-wheel drifts I'd read about in the car magazines, spinning on gravel at eighty-five miles an hour while flinging stones at women frantically grabbing children to their breasts. A horn blasted. Maybe we could squeeze by if the truck kept moving right. I held my breath. The huge rear of the truck filled the windshield. We floated past it and the wooded embankment on our left and popped out onto the asphalt. Lonnie slotted the lane, accelerated, and shifted into fourth.

"I'm sorry, what did you say?"

Karl and I looked at each other.

"That was fancy driving," I said.

"Thanks."

"Ever kill anyone?"

"Not so far."

"You're a professional?"

"Not now. Placed fourth in the Circuit of Ireland, 1970."

Lonnie shifted into fifth. The landscape fled past.

"Umm, I was wondering what you meant by *shameful?*" Karl asked.

"What do I mean by our shameful conduct?" He glanced over at Karl. "Do I mean the way Whitehall fell all over itself to recognize Amin's government last year? Within ten days of overthrowing Obote, that wicked socialist? When the killing had already begun? When a word from us might have made Amin stop or think twice? 'But he's only killing soldiers,' they whined. And what if it *was* just soldiers? *Oh*, but clearly it wasn't *just* soldiers they were killing. With tens of thousands of Ugandan civilians now missing? All of us know what *missing* means, don't we?"

"Worse than we thought. Sounds like your foreign ministry wasn't sad to see Obote go."

"The Israelis weren't sad to see Obote go, either. They helped Amin overthrow him. But it's not going well for them now. Amin booted them out last Friday."

That was news to us. "Who's getting killed?" I asked.

"Whoever Amin doesn't like. Lots of soldiers, starting with the top brass. Soldiers from northern Uganda, Langi, that's Obote's tribe, and Acholi. They're almost all dead now. Officers, privates, sergeants, all of 'em. Anyone not from his West Nile province is dead meat. He's got his Nubians from Sudan. But the others? Dynamite them. Shoot them. Cut their throats. Bash their skulls with sledgehammers. Bayonet them. Decapitate them. Place their severed heads in the fridge overnight for breakfast tomorrow. Burn them alive. Ex-ministers, anyone from Obote's family, anyone from the opposition, anyone he gets his hands on who liked Obote. Anyone he's afraid of. Anyone who has something he wants. Anyone who looks at him crosswise. Religious figures. Businesspeople. Asians. Even the odd American journalist. If they flee abroad, he entices them back with guarantees of safe conduct. Then he murders them. Feeds their bodies to the crocodiles."

"Really? Crocodiles?" Karl asked.

Lonnie looked at Karl. "I'll show you."

We flew down the road. All the while Lonnie sipped from his silver flask. Didn't seem to affect his driving. He screeched to a stop by a nondescript shop. We got out to stretch. Lonnie came back straightaway with a bottle in a bag. He filled his flask. Off we went.

"You boys want some?" We declined. If Lonnie didn't kill us all, I figured we'd get to Kampala by afternoon. It took us under an hour to cover the eighty miles to Jinja, at the source of the Nile, about fifty miles from Kampala. Lonnie swerved off before crossing the Nile bridge. It had rained like mad the night before. He drove too fast through a rather deep brown puddle, splashing muddy water on two tall soldiers on foot. Their skin was noticeably darker than Kenyans. And their eyes followed us with a look of hatred that was hard to shrug off.

I figured Lonnie never noticed. But then he laughed, "Those two chaps? They may be wearing Ugandan army uniforms but they're not Ugandans."

"Who are they?" Karl asked.

"They're Sudanese. Here to help Amin with his killing."

"They didn't look too happy about being splashed," I said.

"They can't touch us," he scowled, though I doubted whether they couldn't touch Karl or me. "They can go to hell. Let's go see the Owen Falls Dam." The dam was not far away. Two or three army vehicles were in the parking area, but Lonnie headed for a dirt track. "Downstream the view is better," he said, navigating the muddy ruts that led away from the dam. "These wide wheels are good in the mud," Lonnie said. After about a mile the road was high above the Nile. We parked and got out, gingerly avoiding the mire until we reached the trees lining a steep drop into the pool below us. Lonnie squinted. "If we hit this right, look over there at the far shore."

It was hard to make out anything because of the spray and the mist that hung over the water. Also because the bodies were the same color as the banks. They were there all right, twenty or thirty of them, maybe more, swept to the side by the current. Dozens of crocodiles were in the water or walking or dozing along the bank. They apparently had eaten their fill. We could see more bodies floating around in the water.

"See what I mean?"

Lonnie sat next to a tree resting his head against his knees. Just then we heard the sound of a grinding gearbox as a vehicle approached, a Ugandan army Jeep. Lonnie huddled with the lieutenant in the passenger seat. The Jeep reversed, turned around, drove away.

"We'll have to go." We followed Lonnie back to the BMW.

"Is it dangerous for us here?" I asked.

"Naw. They don't bother us. They saw my plates." He spat, looking at the retreating soldiers. "They're not much good for anything."

"You mean the Ugandan army?" Karl said.

"They're quite good at killing unarmed prisoners." Lonnie stopped short, leaning on the car. "They like to dismember people. Alive. You can't believe what's going on here. They'll chop off your arms and legs while you watch. They might start your interrogation by slicing off your dick and handing it to you." He searched our faces for the impression this made. "Corporals can make lieutenant colonel overnight by murdering someone Amin wants dead. Amin promotes them to the rank of their victim. But if they got shot at? They'd run."

"So they pose no danger to neighboring countries?" Karl asked.

"With corporals in command? Not much. They're only dangerous to Ugandans."

WE DROVE INTO KAMPALA around four in the afternoon. It was a big, busy town with lots of traffic, big buildings, plenty of shops and pedestrian hawkers. But that scene at the dam was starting to sink in. Deep. There was mass killing going on. We'd just seen it. Yet on the surface everything seemed to be functioning normally. I tried to remember why we had come. Howard had said it was easier to get to Burundi by this route. Something about the roads being better on the north side of Lake Victoria, the Uganda side.

"Say, would you chaps like to go to a party?"

"Great!" Karl said.

"We don't have party clothes," I said.

"Doesn't matter. Come as you are. It's at the deputy chief's house. You might find it amusing."

"Wait," Karl said. "Isn't Wednesday an odd day for a party."

"It's a pre-Easter thing. Easter's this Sunday, April 2nd, you know. Something to relieve the pressure."

Lonnie dropped us off at the YMCA. We cleaned up a bit. At seven he was outside waiting for us. The party was opulent. About a hundred people were there, half of them Ugandan. Lots to eat and drink, especially drink. A Ugandan band played dance music. There was roast beef. Chicken. Lamb chops. All kinds of salads and tropical fruits. Lonnie introduced us around while gulping martinis.

"These gentlemen have hitchhiked across Africa," he announced to a group that included Mr. Watson, the deputy chief of mission. Drink in hand, Lonnie sat down on a couch.

"Is that right? When did you get to Uganda?" Watson asked.

"Today," Karl said.

"We hitchhiked from Ethiopia," I said.

"I didn't know you could do that!" said a voice behind me, a young woman. "I'm the commercial and economic officer." She offered her hand and her card. *Molly Graham, British High Commission*, the card said.

"I'm Jake. This is Karl." We really stood out with our beards and our traveling clothes.

"What's going on in Ethiopia?"

"It's really poor," Karl said.

She turned to me. "Was it dangerous?"

"I don't know. Isn't it dangerous here?"

"Only if you're Ugandan."

"Or Israeli," Watson said. "Amin ordered all Israelis out two days ago, on Monday. He's about to break diplomatic relations. He's accusing the Israelis of organizing a secret army to overthrow him."

"A secret army?" Karl said.

"Yes. A secret army with seven hundred men. Amin is quite daft. At this point there aren't half that number of Israelis left in country, and they're getting out fast." Watson stepped back, sizing us up. "By the way, how did you meet Lonnie?"

"He picked us up hitchhiking outside Tororo," Karl said. "He's quite an amazing driver."

"He's a great officer, Lonnie is. Especially when he's not drinking."

"How often does he drink?" I asked.

"Lonnie?" The deputy chief looked over at Lonnie sitting on the couch. "He drinks all the time."

My new friend drew closer. "How long are you staying in Kampala, Jake?"

"Can't tell. Might leave tomorrow. We're meeting some friends in Kigali."

"Do you like the music?" She shouted over the band's throbbing African pitch. Her greenish-blue eyes were large, luminous. "Want to dance?"

"Maybe in a bit."

She stepped back, studying me. "If you stay in town, give me a ring," she smiled, before disappearing into the crowd. I knew I'd never see Molly again.

After the party Lonnie drove us back to the Y. He couldn't speak intelligibly at that point, but he still drove like a champ. We arrived after curfew. We talked our way in.

Next morning we headed to immigration. A soldier with stripes on his sleeve was standing at a high desk.

We handed him our passports. He scowled while he looked through them. "You don't have Ugandan visas. Why?"

"The official at the border told us we should apply in Kampala," Karl said.

"We don't have visas here. You can't get visas here."

"What do you mean?" I asked. "Your official in Tororo told us to go to Kampala to get visas. That's why we're here."

"We don't give visas here." The sergeant started to walk away. "You'll have to go back to Nairobi."

"We're tourists. You have to give us visas."

The sergeant turned around laughing. "I don't have to do anything."

"This hardly seems fair," Karl said. "We've been several days getting here from Nairobi."

The sergeant looked thoughtful. "All right. I'll give you visas. If you pay the fine."

"The fine? How big is the fine?" Karl asked. "How much does a tourist visa cost in the first place?"

"The visa is a hundred shillings. The fine is a thousand."

"A thousand shillings?" I gasped. "A thousand shillings?

"So that's," the sergeant calculated, "eleven hundred shillings. Each."

"You're trying to rob us," I said.

"Rob you? Rob you? You can go back to Nairobi if you don't like it."

"There's no way we're going to pay eleven hundred shillings for a visa. We won't do it."

"So you won't pay? All right." He grabbed our passports, made some quick stamps and notations. Then he gave them back to us. I looked at mine. A bold blue stamp said *No Facilities*.

"What's this? No facilities?" Karl asked.

"You have no visa. You are here illegally. You refused to pay the fine."

"What does this mean? Can we leave Uganda with this stamp in our passports?" I asked.

"Yes, but you must do so quickly." The sergeant left the room.

Karl looked at his passport. "Christ, what do we do now?"

"Let's get out of here." We walked out to the crowded street.

"What should we do? Maybe we should go back to Nairobi," Karl said.

"I'm not going back. The hell with it."

"It's dangerous. We could be picked up."

"They can get stuffed."

"Didn't you hear what Lonnie told us? How many people he's killed? You saw the bodies."

"Look, they can arrest us anytime we try to leave the country. Even if we go back to Tororo."

"You just want to keep going? I don't agree." We were standing on the sidewalk, arguing.

"I'm not going back to Nairobi."

"Well, Jake, I may have to go by myself."

"You do that. But what's the point?"

"Aren't you risking a lot?"

"We're all right. We're tourists. No one will bother us." No one was bullying me back to Nairobi.

I didn't know if no one would bother us, but that definitely wasn't true for the Israelis. Watson was right. The Ugandans had broken relations and closed Israel's embassy that morning. It was all over the newspapers. That and frenzied reports of a secret Israeli army in Uganda plotting to overthrow Amin. The Israeli embassy was across the street from immigration. We watched from the sidewalk as soldiers carried out telephones, office chairs, file cabinets, framed pictures, lamps, carpets, typewriters, televisions, chandeliers, refrigerators, potted plants, desks, bookcases. All of it went down the stairs into army trucks. They were looting the place. We stood there gaping until a soldier told us to leave.

Karl finally gave in about going back to Nairobi. Instead, we headed west via overnight train to Kasese, figuring we'd run into fewer soldiers. But Kasese was full of soldiers. In a restaurant we managed to find a truck driver going to Fort Portal, about a hundred kilometers north, which we hoped was quiet. But we'd have to come right back to Kasese on our way south to Rwanda.

21. FORT PORTAL
(JAKE)

It was April Fools' Day when Karl and I met a pretty Ugandan girl at the Fort Portal market. She was leaning on a fruit stand wearing a bright yellow sarong-style skirt with a sleeveless blouse cut from the same material and a matching head scarf. She sent us an inviting glance. Was she curious? She definitely looked us over.

We wanted peanuts, for some reason. We asked everybody all around for peanuts but all we could find was peanut butter. The market ladies brought out little round globs of peanut butter arranged neatly on large green leaves, half-a-penny a glob. What we wanted was a bag of roasted peanuts. Soon a score of eager hawkers with maybe twenty pounds of peanut butter between them was pursuing us. With the heat and the market noise I did not notice a gentle tugging at my sleeve. When I turned to look, I saw only Karl's back amid the uproar. I looked down. There was a little girl with her hair in braids clutching a plastic bag bulging with peanuts.

"How much is it?" I started to put my hand in my pocket. At this she shook her head violently, pointing at a row of shabby huts.

"She wants us to follow her, Karl."

"Why?"

I indicated the bag of peanuts.

"My God! The bag is almost as big as her head."

We followed her to one of the huts, leaving the disappointed mob to jeer us. She brought us to the doorway of one of the larger huts, then turned still clutching the bag, smiled playfully, disappearing behind the corner. Bewildered, I started after her.

"Let's see who's waiting for us," Karl said, a bit impatiently.

We stepped into the room. It was dark. I could not see anything at first, the glare outside had been so intense. Gradually my eyes adjusted. I saw the walls of the hut were baked mud; the roof was thatch. One long table and four chairs were the only furniture. At the table on a bench sat the girl in the yellow dress, gazing intently at us. She kept staring for maybe half a minute. Karl began to leave.

Abruptly she spoke. "Hello. I've been watching you. I wanted to ask you a question. Come in. Sit down. I'm not a lion. I'm not going to bite you." It was the first time I had heard English spoken so well by an African woman. We sat across the table from her. There was no one else in the room.

She looked sideways down at the table, considering something. She had taken off her head cloth. She was pretty. Her hair was cut short. Her skin was smooth and glossy. She had long eyelashes, short broad nose, graceful neck, graceful arms, large intelligent eyes. She was radiant, self-possessed, though cautious.

"I'm not sure how to say this," she began slowly with a soft, confidential air. Looking up at us directly for the first time, her confidence faded. Fear replaced it. "I want to leave Uganda. But I can't do it by myself." She sounded regretful. "Maybe you can help me?" She looked first at me, then at Karl, then back to me.

"How?" I asked.

"Do you have a car?"

"No. We're on foot."

"Where are you staying?"

"At the Ismaili Temple."

She sat there, considering. "Would you go with me to Kabale[23] and the Rwandan border? I can pay."

---

23 Ka-BA-lay

Kabale was around four hundred kilometers from Fort Portal over bad roads.

"Look," Karl said. "This is too mysterious. Who are you? What are you running from?"

"Yes, I should tell you," she said slowly, but deliberately. "My name is Swepani Arungowe. I will tell you my family history, or at least the things you need to know." Here she stopped, searching our eyes warily, first me, then Karl, then me, before continuing. "You must know I have chosen you because you are foreigners. I could not have trusted Ugandans with my story." Karl looked at me briefly. "I am a student in Kampala at Makerere University," she continued, "though now I have left it. My mother died when I was small. My father remarried but I have not seen him or my stepmother since Amin's coup. He was a subminister of health under President Obote, but now they are hiding in Kenya. He can't come back here. They would have arrested him if he stayed. My three younger brothers are in the village with my mother's family. We are Baganda. That's our tribe."

She paused. With one hand she played idly with her yellow head cloth on the table. "Maybe you have heard of the Baganda? We live in central Uganda around Kampala, down to Lake Victoria. Since last year, since the coup, I have been living in Kampala with my Uncle Nelson, my father's younger brother. He has been paying my costs since my father left. He is one of the few Baganda in the army."

"That's it? Why are you running away?"

She shifted on the bench, looked down at the table, then raised her eyes to meet ours. "That is the difficult part. My uncle changed after Amin came in. He became ambitious. Nelson was a sergeant one year ago. Now he is lieutenant colonel. I don't know how many men Nelson has tortured or murdered for Amin to get that promotion." She paused. "That, and something he did, tried to do, to me.

"You're afraid he'll kill you?"

"Not exactly." She looked at Karl. "I'm afraid he will rape me. He has already tried once. That's why I'm running away." She bit her lower lip and cried for a few moments, then composed herself. "I am staying with my classmate's mother. When Nelson figures out where I am, he will send his soldiers to find me. He does not know I have a passport. I need to disappear."

"Why don't you go to Kenya to see your father?"

"I could do that. But my stepmother and I never got along. Besides, crossing at Tororo is too risky. The best bet for me is Tanzania. Nyerere and Amin hate each other. I would be safe there. And I think my mother's brother is in Dar es Salaam. He is an agronomist. He also fled Uganda."

"I can see why you're afraid of Nelson," I said.

She wiped her eyes with her long fingers.

"What do you want from us?" Karl asked.

"I want to leave this town. I don't want anyone to know where I've gone. I want to get out of Uganda."

Why she thought we could help her, God only knows. With all that was going on in Uganda and our visa problems, Karl and I were in no shape to escort a runaway girl whose uncle might have us shot for helping her. She offered us one hundred shillings to take her south to Rwanda. We both said no. She was clearly desperate and frightened. But it was hard to gauge her story. It was believable, but what was she leaving out?

She said simply, "If you tell me when you will leave Fort Portal, I will leave town the night before and wait on the road about four miles out. I can't have anybody seeing me leave. You tell the driver to stop when you see me on the road. Will you do it?"

"We'll think about it," I said.

"What?" Karl looked at me, annoyed.

"I told you I'd pay," the girl said.

"Why don't you leave early one morning on some old truck? No one will see you," Karl said.

She was slow to answer, her eyes gleaming as they caught a ray of sunlight. Then I saw her bare arms were shaking.

"I'm afraid," she said softly. "I can't go by myself. A young girl? Alone? There are lots of soldiers around. You have no idea what they're like. If they see I am alone they will want to take me. They think they are gods. I can stop them only by mentioning my uncle. So, you are right to think I may bring complications. I need cover. Traveling with you will help me."

We got up to leave.

"Wait," she pleaded, holding up an arm, then scribbling a note on a scrap of paper. She handed it to me with a soulful look. "This is how to find me. In case you change your mind."

We walked into the white heat outside. I had killed a man. I had enough on the negative side of the ledger already. I wanted to put something on the positive side. I wanted to help her.

"Why did you say we would talk about it?" Karl said, obviously annoyed.

"We should try to help her," I said, handing Karl the paper Swee'Pea had given me. He stuffed it in his pocket. I had decided Swepani sounded like "Swee'Pea," and I guess it stuck.

"Are you crazy? We can't do a thing for her without risking our lives. I can't imagine what trying to travel with her would be like."

"It would be risky as hell," I agreed. "Though she might help us to leave Uganda."

"That's a thought. But remember how hard it was for us to hitchhike with Hans? How exactly are the three of us supposed to travel without being seen?"

"Maybe she could hide in the bushes while we stand on the road?"

Karl was quiet, considering. "She was feisty, though."

"Pretty hard edged," I agreed.

"Yeah, but also pretty needy."

I liked her searching eyes, her athletic arms, her smile, her wit.

The bright yellow dress she wore set off her dark skin perfectly. I'm sure Karl noticed, too, though he wouldn't say it.

We never got the peanuts.

~

That evening we ate dinner in the small house the Ismailis lent us. The moon came up. Manjo knocked on the door, pushed it aside. He strode into the room. A Ugandan hipster, Manjo wore a red headband, wireframe sunglasses, an unbuttoned multi-color dungaree jacket with the sleeves ripped off, no T-shirt, flipflops, khaki shorts. His hair needed a trim. Manjo was doing Jimi Hendrix. We had met Manjo as we got off the truck yesterday in Fort Portal. We'd smoked grass with him, arranged to buy some more.

"Hey, Manjo, what's going on? You're late," said Karl.

Manjo sneered. He looked around the room. Then he patted something in his ragged tan shorts, a large object in his back pocket. He laboriously extracted it, which took him several minutes. The opening it had to fit through was small.

"It better be good, Manjo."

Manjo waved his hand. "Manjo always bring good stuff. It no good, you no pay Manjo." Moving his left hand over to the pocket to help his right hand, he tilted his body at a crazy angle. "Wait. Oh, no. Comes." At last he pulled out a big wad packed in a tough brown leaf, tied with a bark cord. He grinned ear to ear, showing a full complement of extraordinarily large white teeth. He stood holding it in his hand like some bizarre statue. "Manjo take back? You no want?" He moved toward the door.

Karl jumped up, grabbed the packed wad, flipped it to me. I brought it into the light, opened the covering. The stuff was pungent, dark brown, sticky, minty. My head reeled. That smell that smells like no other smell. I nodded to Karl.

Manjo was hovering, hands behind his back, the merest shadow of a grin on his face, watching me. "You like? You like?"

"Not bad."

"No' bad? That stuff good," Manjo was shouting his sales pitch. "It 'da best! You smoke now, you see."

"All right, we'll give 'er a shot." Karl closed the door. I got out some papers, began to roll, but Manjo was too impatient for that. With thick brown paper from his pocket he quickly rolled a fat cigar.

"Humf. Now you see." He whispered to the cigar, widening his eyes, then knitting his brow. "This difficult business. Customer give trouble, farmer give trouble, police give trouble. Nobody happy in this business. Only when smoking, then everybody happy." He lit the cigar, took great puffs, like a locomotive belching steam and flame he filled the room with smoke. Sucking one last great puff, the end of the cigar turning bright red-orange like a log in a fireplace, he thrust it at me like a punch. The cigar was smoking furiously, soggy with Manjo's saliva on the other end. I handled it gingerly, puffed once or twice, passed it to Karl, who attacked it with little more gusto than me, giving it back to Manjo.

"That all you smoke? Pfff." He ignored us while puffing up a bonfire, again thrusting it at me. He looked at me intently. "Now you smoke like Manjo."

Smoke like Manjo? That weed had killer potency for all I knew. I was in no mood for passing out on the floor. To placate Manjo I took two discreet puffs, more than I wanted, gave it to Karl, who handed it back to Manjo. We let him finish it off.

"How much do you want, Manjo?" Karl asked.

He had his answer ready. "Fifty-five shillings," he said, smacking his lips.

"We couldn't possibly go over twenty for that small amount."

"But this really good shit. No silly farmer's weed. Fifty-five shillings." Manjo leaned his back against the wall, cupping his chin in his hands, smiling cherubically.

"Manjo, we talked about this before. We expected something for twenty shillings. Remember?"

"Manjo knows. You want silly green stuff? Manjo gets you for ten shillings, but this stuff special." He was still smiling.

"I don't feel anything special. Manjo, we'll give you twenty-two shillings, but not more."

"Twenty-two shillings?"

"Twenty-two shillings. That's all."

We were offering a little over two dollars for a big double handful of weed. Manjo stopped smiling. He poked the pile, muttering to himself. He divided the pile roughly, pointing to one of the halves. "This much for twenty-two shillings."

"Manjo, forget it. Take it back." Karl sat and got his book out.

"Okay, okay! Give twenty-two shillings. Manjo friend. Manjo no mad. You get good deal. Twenty-two shillings." He pushed the piles together.

By this time I was high as a kite. Everything around me was interesting. Manjo's movements were machine-like. Every movement he made was absurdly exaggerated. I watched his black body ratchet silently, unselfconsciously from pose to pose, like he was acting. I blurted out, "Manjo, you big actor."

He followed me like a dog when I ran out the door, saying, "What you say, what you say? No, no, no, no. No act. This really good shit. A-number-one good fucking shit." The faster I walked away, the faster he followed. It was funny. I couldn't stop laughing. Everything was funny. The little huts below us down the hill? A scream! The moon in the gum trees? Hilarious! I laughed uproariously. Karl stuck his head out the door, bellowing at the stars. Manjo was down on all fours, hopping after me, while I rolled and howled.

Everything was funny because it was just the way it was. The huts were just the way they were. Round. African. Kind of cute. Looking just the way they should look. The moon's face was exactly like itself. Manjo was, well, Manjo. Now I became suspicious, and nothing was funny. Manjo's clown act was masking his contempt. Out to get our money. A real money grubber. And me? I was a person so important in his own country that he couldn't return. A runaway, a murderer. Now losing his mind slightly north of the equator.

Karl made a sharp whistle. I walked back to the house. Karl was sitting on the stoop.

"What happened to Manjo?"

"Manjo's gone."

"What a crazy dude."

"Your camera's gone, too," Karl said.

"What?"

"And I think he got my sandals."

I saw clothing scattered on the floor, our shrunken packs tossed aside. That was a pre-war Leica Manjo stole. Didn't cost me much in London. No way to buy another camera, not in Africa. The original store sticker still stuck inside said *Foto Feldmann, Adolph Hitlerplatz 11, Hamburg*. Would have done Pudge proud. But I had to admit. That thing took damned good pictures. Like the one Karl snapped of me and that Danakil girl at the Kembolcha market.

"When did he do this?" I asked.

"I went out to take a piss. When I returned, he was gone."

"You left him here alone with our stuff?"

"I thought he was with you outside, rolling around in the dark somewhere."

"That's right. I remember. He wasn't fifty yards from me." I sat next to Karl. "What are we going to do?"

"What can we do now? We'll look for Manjo tomorrow."

"He better see me first. I'm so mad I feel like breaking him in two."

"Sure. I'm not happy about it, either. Before you break him in two, remember he's pretty well built."

22. DERELICT'S DELIGHT
(JAKE)

We woke up early Sunday morning. Roosters cried thinly in the distance, their silly songs popping like corks all around us. Mist blew outside the window. It was our fifth day in Uganda, Easter Sunday, the second of April 1972. Fort Portal is five thousand feet above sea level. It was cold. We boiled water on the gas stove. Breakfast was not satisfactory. The instant coffee would not dissolve completely. Brown chunks floated among Styrofoam-like lumps of powdered milk. There was no sugar. I nibbled at day-old bread, sipping coffee by turns. The bread was like soft wood, crunchy but tasteless. Mixed with saliva it had the consistency of plaster.

I stood. "Let's go."

"Go? Where?" Karl asked.

"Into town. To find Manjo?"

"What time is it? Quarter to seven? The shops aren't even open."

"So? Maybe he's an early riser."

"Wait a bit. I'll come with you."

"I want to go now." I started for the door. "Are you coming or not?"

"Don't be like that. Wait a bit. I'm coming."

I walked outside. The road was deserted. I walked slowly, taking a stroll. After a while I noticed I was headed to town. Maybe Karl would catch up with me later. The mist was rising above the trees. A sudden blasting noise from behind. I leaped off the road as a pickup sped by. It was loaded past the cab roof with empty chicken cages swaying and teetering as it veered from side to side. The driver drove like a drunk. I picked myself up off the ground. My mood was not improved when I saw my torn pant leg, a bloody scrape on my knee. I dusted myself off and walked stiffly on.

As I approached the market, which was almost empty, a rock came floating out of the shadows, crossing my path, clattering into a pothole. A tremendous grin stuck out from behind a tree. It was Moru, a crippled boy who walked with a staff taller than he was, wore a dirt-colored sheet with a hole cut for his head. He had large, inquisitive eyes, a mouthful of buck teeth. Karl and I met him at the temple, one of his hangouts. Moru could hear but he could not speak, a faculty he lost, we were told, after seeing his mother die in a gruesome road accident. He never spoke again. His leg was shriveled by polio when he was a baby.

Moru, always cheerful, loved to follow us around. But I was not feeling cheerful. I made signs not to follow me. He stopped, still grinning. I walked on a hundred feet. He was still behind me. I threw a rock at him. He took it as a game, dodged behind trees, showing his mischievous face.

"Quit following me." I went into a restaurant not far away, sat, and ordered chai and mandazis. I skimmed yesterday's Kampala rag dated April 1. Headlines screamed Israeli spies and mercenaries were sneaking into Uganda on sabotage missions.

But they'd just been expelled. In Kampala I had bought peanuts wrapped in a page of an Israeli phone book. As we had watched Israel's embassy being looted, dozens of Sudanese refugees were camping out on the exterior staircases, waiting for travel papers from the Sudan embassy in the same building. They wanted to go home after the Sudanese rebels had signed a peace agreement with the government in Khartoum. The Israelis had been helping Amin to arm the rebels, the better to fight their enemies in the Sudanese government. But now the two sides had made up. Maybe Amin didn't need the Israelis for now.

As Karl explained, Idi Amin owed Israel a lot. Israelis had been training the army, paving roads, supplying technicians, medical people, builders, engineers, trainers. Even the tanks Amin used to stage his January 1971 coup came from Israel, weapons captured from Egypt in '67 in the Six Day War. Some said Israelis had driven the tanks. But when Amin asked for Phantom jets and a large loan the Israelis balked. Soon after that, in Libya, Muamar Ghadaffi reminded Amin he was a Muslim with a big check. That was the end for the Israelis.

Seeing Moru hanging around outside, I motioned him in. The Asian owner, carrying a huge kettle, poured ropes of hot milky tea into large enameled metal cups. I left Moru happily eating two of the grease balls I was calling breakfast. His teeth protruded so much that his lips could not close properly when he chewed.

I took a side street that petered out into an alley leading around the side of a building. Our drug dealer, Manjo, was leaning against a post, dressed in an old charcoal raincoat, wearing Karl's sandals, squinting while trying to focus my camera on the sky. I yelled his name, walked up to him, and hit him hard in the face. He dropped the camera. I grabbed him, ripping his coat, but he got away. Two seconds later he had vanished. People were watching me from across the street. They didn't look friendly. I picked up the camera. The lens had broken.

At the end of the alley, across the main street near the market, next to a dilapidated hotel was that pickup, loaded to the trees with chickens. I ducked into the hotel. It was still early but already a fair-sized crowd was at the bar. They all turned as I ordered a Coke. For all I knew one of them might have been that driver who ran me off the road. My knee was sore, though the blood had stopped. My knuckles hurt from punching Manjo. *I shouldn't have hit him,* I told myself. At that moment I panicked because if the police raided our house, they'd find the big pile of weed Manjo sold us before he ripped us off.

A thin man in a natty business suit approached. It seemed too early for wearing suits.

"Friend, hallo." He offered his cold hand. "I am Ephraim. Come and sit down here. My friend and myself will enjoy your company."

"I—"

"We want to buy you a drink."

"I have a drink." I held up the Coke bottle.

"Perhaps you would like another? You have had a hard journey." He glanced at my knee. "We are happy, indeed, pleased to invite you. You must have come many miles. It is hard, indeed, difficult, to come so far a distance. Difficult. That is to say, troublesome." He was nervous and spoke fast.

His friend wore a shapeless white shirt and tattered black pants. He waved to me listlessly from a table cluttered with beer bottles. I didn't crave company, but neither did I want to be rude. I also wanted to figure out how to leave the bar while avoiding the people who had seen me slug Manjo.

"Did you want a beer?" asked Ephraim. I agreed to a beer as we sat.

"What are you doing? What are you?" Ephraim's friend demanded, coming to life.

"How do you do?" Ephraim corrected hastily. "How are you?"

"Yes, yes. How are you? Where are you coming from?"

"You mean before Fort Portal? I was in Kampala."

"Kampala, of course. And before Kampala?"

"Before that I was in Kenya."

"Ah, Kenya, ah, ah. Before Kenya? Your nationality?"

"I'm American."

"Ah. American. But—"

"But what?"

"You're not Israeli?"

"No. Never been there."

"You're American. Not Israeli. Hmm."

"Where are you staying?" Ephraim asked.

"At the Ismaili Temple. Say, what's this about?"

"My friend thinks you might be Israeli. You're not Israeli, are you?"

"I told you. No! Is this about those crazy newspaper stories? The secret Israeli army in Uganda? What's your friend's name?"

"His name is Daniel," Ephraim said.

"Daniel, I don't know about the secret Israeli army. I'm American."

"And you have American passport?" Daniel asked.

"Of course."

"I may see it?"

"It's not here." I wasn't about to show my passport to anyone. I turned to Ephraim. "You wanted to buy me a drink? Instead, your friend—"

"Yes, my friend, Daniel."

"Why does he want to ask me questions. I have done nothing wrong. I'm not Israeli."

Daniel pressed on. "What kind of work do you do?"

I had a good look at him for the first time. He was heavyset, jowly, small intense eyes.

"I'm a tourist."

Ephraim became more serious. "Daniel works for the police."

"How long now have you been a tourist?" Daniel asked.

"A few months. Half a year."

"How much are you paid?"

"Paid?"

"Yes. How much?"

"I don't understand the question."

Ephraim said, "My friend wants to know how much you are paid."

"Paid for what?"

"For being a tourist."

"Who would pay me?"

"Surely your government pays you?" Ephraim asked.

"No, they don't. Why should they pay me?"

"For being a tourist."

"Nobody pays me. Being a tourist isn't a job."

"But how do you travel?" Ephraim asked. "You must pay for hotels. You pay for food. You pay for your passport. You must have a ticket. Buses, airplanes. Visas. Where does the money come from? Someone must pay."

"I pay, but no one pays me. I don't get money for being a tourist."

Ephraim was confused. "Then you must be rich. You don't work but you have money to leave your home and come to Africa."

"Not so rich."

"But you spend your own money? No Ugandan would spend his own money to go to America if the government didn't pay. This is impossible for us. Where did you get so much money?"

"I worked in America. I saved my money to come here."

"We work here, also, but we have no money to do such things. How much were you paid?"

Converted to Uganda shillings it was a big number. Ephraim gasped.

"I had a good job," I admitted.

Ephraim translated for Daniel who took the news calmly.

"What happens when you run out of money?" Ephraim asked.

"Then I have to work."

"What kind of work would you do?" Daniel asked.

I explained my job in Louisiana on the oil rig.

"Hmm. Very difficult in Uganda. To get the proper papers. Difficult. Besides, we have no oil here," Ephraim pointed out.

"I'd have to leave Uganda to get that kind of job again," I explained.

"Your life sounds hard, even though you are rich. But you Americans are brave."

"Are we?"

"I think so," Ephraim said. "You come here alone, far from your parents, your friends, no wife to cook for you, no one knows you, you are lonely, you must spend money every day, you must travel constantly. That is a difficult thing. Uncomfortable. You are surrounded by strangers with many languages, not to mention diseases. Strange food. What if you get sick? How can you communicate? Who will help you when you need help?"

"That's a point." Ephraim had concisely summed up my life on the road.

"We pity you. You are young, far from home. But you are brave. Do you agree the Americans are brave, Daniel?" Ephraim asked.

"Ugandans are brave, too," Daniel replied.

"Yes, it is true. But these Americans. Ah-ah-ah-ah. They went to the moon, Daniel. They walked around up there." Ephraim pointed at the ceiling. "That's a brave thing to do, walking on the moon. Why do it? It's dangerous. There's no money in it. Where's the gain?"

Daniel was matter of fact. "They put a military base up there. They can hit anyplace on earth."

That alarmed Ephraim. "Did you do that?" he asked me.

"Of course not," I said.

"Of course they did. Of course," Daniel insisted. "They didn't go all that way just for the parade. Just for a photo."

They make a fine pair, I was thinking, Ephraim and Daniel.

"What do you think of our Fort Portal?" asked Daniel, smiling.

"Beautiful."

"What about Kampala?"

"Very modern."

Daniel was scrutinizing me. He had maybe eight empty beer bottles in front of him. He squinted, giving his face a shrewd, tough cast. "Do you know you look like an Israeli?"

"We are afraid of spies," Ephraim said.

"I told you I'm American. I'm not Israeli."

"But you look like one," Daniel said.

"Why do you say that? That's impossible," I objected. Daniel talked like Pudge before I killed him.

"You look like one. Your nose. Many Israelis have noses like that. And your hair," Daniel said.

"My mom and dad, may their souls rest in peace, were both born in Nebraska, in America. And their parents were born in America. So you see—"

"But where is the proof? Do you have a passport?" Daniel interjected.

I couldn't show my passport because of the visa problem. There was an awkward silence.

"To me you look Nigerian," I said, turning the tables on these two.

Daniel jumped. "No no no no. I'm Ugandan. I couldn't be Nigerian."

"What do Nigerians look like?" asked Ephraim.

"Exactly like Daniel," I said.

"Ho," said Daniel. "Ho, ho."

I drank my Coke, then started on the beer. A few sips made me heady. Outside a largish crowd gathered across the street. Two men were shouting, pointing at the bar. I supposed they figured they'd cornered the guy who had punched Manjo.

"The Israelis are leaving Uganda as fast as they can," I said. "Didn't President Amin just expel them? Last Thursday I watched soldiers pillage the Israeli embassy in Kampala. Now they're ordered out. Why would they stick around? Not everything in the newspapers is true."

Daniel peered at me. "This is what our government tells us. Are you saying that our government is, is—" Daniel searched for the word. "Is untrue?"

"Is lying," Ephraim corrected him.

"Yes. Our government is lying?" Daniel leaned forward. "Is that what you say?"

"No. I'm saying the newspapers might exaggerate."

Daniel considered this. "What if, what if foreigners were making problems in America?"

"Problems?" I asked.

"Yes, trying to invade you?"

"Israelis can't invade you," I said. "Israel is far away. It is a small country. They were your friends until last Monday."

"You see?" Daniel turned to Ephraim. "He talks like an Israeli."

Ephraim pondered. "Yes, but Daniel, they were our friends. That is true, Daniel. They gave us many things, sent people to help us. They built roads, houses, trained our soldiers."

"Don't forget the schools they built. And the airports," I said. At least that's what Karl had told me.

"We can't be sure. They are smart. But they are sneaky. Maybe some Israelis are organizing secretly. It might be a plot," Daniel said.

"A conspiracy," Ephraim added.

"Yes, a conspiracy."

"You know, your president has spent time in Israel. He has Israeli paratrooper wings. The Israelis were his friends. Were they acting like enemies?" I asked.

"We must be careful. We don't have a long independence like you Americans. The British left only ten years ago, in 1962. We are minding our independence," Daniel said.

"We are jealous of it," Ephraim said.

"Yes, jealous. Slavery is finished here," Daniel said. "We will kill anyone who tries to take our independence."

Daniel grabbed my camera, which was lying on the table. He opened the case. "What kind of camera is that? How does it work?" He held it up, looked through the eyepiece.

"It's an old German camera."

"How old?" He held the eyepiece to his eye.

"Almost forty years."

"How does it work?"

"You look through here. You focus by turning the lens."

"Take my picture," Daniel insisted.

"Unfortunately, the lens is broken. See?" I showed them the broken lens.

"I still do not understand how to focus it."

"You look through here."

"Show me outside. It's too dark in here." Daniel got up from the table holding the camera. He went out the front door. Out front was the last place I wanted to go. The crowd outside would see me. I excused myself, asking for the toilet. Perhaps I could find the back door, get to the temple, maybe leave town before anyone came for us. The stink off the back corridor led me to the toilet. I took a deep breath, opened the door.

It was a windowless room about three feet square with a hole in the floor. The door was visible from Ephraim's chair. I left the door open a crack to watch Ephraim. Luckily, he was distracted by the commotion outside. He moved closer to the window, turning his back to me. I went out fast, closing the door behind me. I moved quietly down the corridor, out into the sun, ran down the stairs but almost tripped on a woman in a nightgown peeling vegetables.

I worked my way through the back paths, got to the market, then I walked to the Ismaili temple. Karl was not there. I cursed myself for going off by myself and leaving without him. Nothing to do but write a note saying to meet me in Kasese, though I was afraid the police might see it first. I could not locate the weed. I threw my stuff into my pack. Within five minutes I was walking south on the road out of town.

∽

AFTER ABOUT A MILE I saw a policeman walking toward me. I almost broke for the bushes. Instead, I satisfied myself with stolen glances at his face, which was impassive. He drew up to me and tried to strike up a conversation. He was wearing a fresh gray police shirt. He had a baseball cap with the logo *B & O Railroad*. To my relief he spoke no English. We waved, smiled. I watched him walk away toward a bend in the road which would separate us visually, when his body stiffened. He threw himself off the road. I stood there stupidly until that damned chicken truck blasted around the corner blaring its horn. It swerved to miss me, then slammed to a stop. One of the chicken cages toppled to the ground.

The driver hopped out, calling to the policeman. Then he walked over to me. He was cordial. We had a short chat in English. His name was Harry. He owned the bar where I met Daniel and Ephraim. He had seen me running down the stairs where his wife was preparing food. He saw me leave the back way. Harry had bumped into Daniel after I had left the bar.

There was nowhere to run. The policeman was coming up. Harry plowed on with his roundabout courteous accusation. It was the merest luck he had come across me now. He had promised Daniel to bring me back if he saw me. The policeman walked up at that moment, spoke a few words with Harry. His expression changed from placid to fiendish. He firmly grabbed my arm and pushed me into the cab. Then he went to help Harry load the fallen cage.

Despair. Being arrested is bad enough anywhere, but in western Uganda? Many foreigners were being arrested for making unguarded comments about Amin. My mind raced to recall everything I had said to Daniel. What would they do with a white man who punched a Ugandan? Especially one who might be Israeli?

Harry and the policeman got into the cab on either side of me. We drove back to town, stopping at a rundown two-story building some distance from the main road. Nine or ten soldiers and police were hanging around. The policeman ordered me to get out. They jumped me with a shout when Harry drove away. Twenty hands grabbed my boots and my belt, emptied my pockets, a fist or a rifle butt caught me on my left side. They threw me in a cell, a pit about five by five. The roof was too low to stand. The floor was indescribable. My ribs felt like they were broken.

Dim electric light filtered through the sagging carpentry and bars of the cell. I could see them going through my pack. I figured they were looking for money. Since Kampala, I had hid my passport in my underpants. The putrid sludge I sat in squeezed through my toes. I cried. How little my paltry life was worth. My possessions were strewn in the dust. I prayed they wouldn't kill me.

Nothing happened. Misery passes slowly. The stink made it hard to breathe. My sore ribs made it hard to breathe. I couldn't move. They hurt like hell. Hideous fields of time stretched before me. I got hold of myself. There was no point thinking what was next. *Take it as it comes,* I thought, endurance is key. *Show no weakness.* Then it got dark.

I woke with a start. Cold air flooded over me as hands grabbed my shoulders. The air was so sweet I almost fainted. They brought me to an enclosure under a building open to the night on two sides. No one said a word. A guard was posted by the gate. Above his head the waning moon brought greetings from the universe.

I heard a tiny sound close by. I turned quickly. Karl was standing behind me, his finger raised to his lips. He brought his mouth close to my ear. "We're not supposed to talk. They're letting you out, I think." He waved off my questions.

When morning came, an energetic, stiffly starched adjutant appeared and ordered our release. We saw him motioning to the guard.

Daniel popped up out of nowhere, scowling, arguing loudly. "I have reason to believe this man is an Israeli spy." The adjutant told him in English he could complain to the captain if he wanted. Daniel shut up. He sat sullenly in a sagging beach chair as they gave me back my boots, belt, pack, all my belongings, even my money. Then we walked through the gate to the road.

"What now?" I asked Karl.

"We go back to the temple."

"I have to get out of these stinking clothes."

"Back to the temple. You'll ditch the clothing and take a bath."

"Let's get out of town."

"We'll see about that."

We were walking in the narrow side streets. People edged along as close to the buildings and as far from me as they could, holding their noses as I passed. I was free. I felt taller. I had screwed up but all that was behind me. I was so happy. I didn't care about the camera.

"Would you mind telling me what is going on?" Karl kept walking. "Why were you waiting there when they released me? How did that happen?"

"Long story. I wasn't sure you'd be let off," Karl said.

"How did you find out I was arrested?"

"Moru."

"Moru? How did Moru know?"

"No idea. He must have seen you outside the jail. He found me in town. By then I was wondering where you had got to. He was super excited. He was practically screaming, doing these crazy pantomimes that made no sense until he showed me the jail. Moru saved your skin. What did you do, anyway?"

"I bumped into Manjo when I was walking around. I punched him in the face."

"Good God. You slugged Manjo?"

"Yeah. Some people saw me do it."

Karl walked ahead of me as he talked. "Even though you were locked up, I figured the police still might show up at the temple. Don't worry. I went back and got rid of the weed. Then I went out again for a couple of hours. It was dark after I got back when the police arrived."

"The police came?"

"They didn't treat me roughly, never checked my passport or searched my things. They saw you weren't there, but they weren't sure what to do with me. When they worked out that you were in jail, I asked them to bring me. Toward morning, they let me stand in that open space where we just met."

I tried to take all of this in. "But why did they let me out?"

"I played the one trump card we had."

"You went to see Swee'Pea?"

"Yes. I had to move fast."

"And she used her influence with her uncle-what's-his-name?"

"Nelson. She promised to help."

"How did you find her?"

"Pure luck. Plus I had her note."

"She got me out of jail all right. But what strings are attached?"

"We're helping her get out of the country."

"How will we do that?" I asked.

"We'll find out." Karl laughed. "We're all in this together now."

"Where is she now?"

"Waiting at the temple, I hope."

"How'd she get me out?"

"Go ahead, ask her. She called Uncle Nelson while I was there. She sweet-talked him. Laid it on thick, played *femme fatale*, coaxed him, romanced him, made him think he'd get what he craved if he let her American friend out of jail."

"Uncle Lieutenant Colonel Nelson thinks she'll jump into his arms?"

Karl nodded. "She's quite an actress. He fell for it."

"No kidding."

"When he finds out she's gone he'll be mad as hell. His thugs could show up at the temple at any moment. Right now he's probably got checkpoints on every road out of Fort Portal with orders to detain her. And us."

When we got to the temple, Swee'Pea was waiting for us, all ready to go. The yellow dress was gone. She wore jeans and a sweatshirt. She was excited to see us. She waited for me to shower, pack up, pay the Ismailis. Promising to talk later, she started off due west out of town. We followed behind. All she had with her was a small bundle tied in a piece of cloth, which she carried on her head.

23. MOUNTAINS OF THE MOON
(KARL)

We set out from Fort Portal before noon on April 3. Swee'Pea led the way. We were starting a long, evasive, high-altitude backwoods detour to outrun Uncle Nelson and his henchmen. The point was to take us off the grid for a couple of weeks and spare us at least a hundred kilometers of exposure on the road south to Kasese. But that still left hundreds more kilometers to Kabale. And even if we made it to Kabale, how would we cross the Rwanda border?

I was peeved at Jake, that blockhead, for getting himself arrested, which forced Swee'Pea to break cover with Nelson. Now Swee'Pea was hotfooting it out of the country with us.

"You'd think Nelson would not be quite so naïve," she deadpanned.

We were playing with fire. Probably we were already dead meat. If Uncle Nelson's soldiers found us, they might kill us on the spot. Then they'd deliver Swee'Pea to Nelson, intact, as it were. I had been starting to agree with Jake that we should help her. Now, we were duty bound; we'd be babysitting Swee'Pea for at least the next fifteen days. Or maybe she'd be babysitting us.

Before we left Fort Portal, Swee'Pea pulled me aside. "Karl, I'm so grateful to you both for coming with me. I will never forget this. I owe you so much."

"You really should thank Jake," I said, and left it at that.

The truth was we probably needed Swee'Pea as much as she needed us. She was slight, graceful, yet defiant, just a college kid, this small young woman in revolt against the Ugandan military. We admired her toughness. But we were plenty scared.

First stop was a backroads store to buy provisions for our tramp in the Ruwenzori highlands: Rice, beans, bread, salt, canned milk, tea, sugar, instant coffee, cheese, oatmeal, matches, cups, bowls, spoons, soap, spaghetti, cook pot, lantern, kerosene, clothesline, candles, chocolate.

Leaving the store, Swee'Pea said, "Do you have a tent? We'll be far from villages. There may be hyenas. I'm sure it will rain."

"We have a tent," Jake said, "though it may be a little cramped for three."

"I don't take up much space."

"What about a sleeping bag?" I asked.

"One thing I don't have." Swee'Pea went back into the store and bought a soft cotton blanket for forty shillings.

Outside again, we headed west, following the track for an hour or two until it became a trail. Then the way veered firmly south, steeply uphill. Mist was descending from the mountain. Before long we were sopping wet. We got out our hooded sweatshirts. We lent Swee'Pea a long-sleeved plaid shirt and a watch cap.

After thirty minutes of laborious hiking up the steep trail I called out, "Where are we going, Swee'Pea?"

She stopped and looked back. "Swee'Pea? Who is that?"

"Swee'Pea, that's the nickname we gave you. Like a sweet pea. Sounds like your name, Swepani." I didn't mention Popeye.

She repeated it once or twice.

"You don't mind?"

"No, I think I like it." She nodded. "We're going to a village called Karangora. I know a Twa guy there, Njobo. You'd call him a pygmy. He'll guide us if we can find him. I went hiking in these hills with my girlfriend two or three years ago. That's how I met Njobo. Don't worry, he'll ask for a pittance. We gave Njobo's family first-aid supplies. And an old rusty knife."

After hours of walking, asking farmers for directions, we got to Karangora. The area was highly cultivated hill country. Forests covered the slopes above us. Whenever the mists parted, we could see bamboo thickets higher up. We were gaining elevation, approaching the shoulders of the snow-capped Ruwenzori range, Ptolemy's Mountains of the Moon, the mythic source of the Nile. But the Ruwenzori peaks were in the clouds thirty miles away to the southwest. We were high above the Fort Portal-Kasese road, which in the coming days appeared as an indistinct thread below us, though we were sure it was being intensively watched by Nelson's men. We faced a two-week walk to strike the road south of Kasese, Swee'Pea told us.

Finally, outside the village, Swee'Pea asked a small boy to find Njobo. We waited on the path, buying potatoes and cauliflowers from passing farmers, while trying to stay warm. It was a lot colder here than Fort Portal. Njobo arrived within five minutes, a friendly, sturdy guy who came up to my chest. He was about half-a-foot shorter than Swee'Pea and not nearly as dark. They palavered in Swahili, happy to see each other. Swahili was the one good thing Nelson had taught her, the army's command language, the closest thing to a national language in Uganda. Njobo immediately agreed to guide us. He asked us to wait. When he came back, he proudly took a shiny polished knife out of his raffia-palm bag to show Swee'Pea. It was the old, rusty one she had given him years before.

With Njobo in the lead, we climbed and climbed two hours more on ever-fainter paths. It was almost dark when we stopped at a large tree. Jake seemed to hit it off with Njobo, even though they could not communicate even one word, but they were always laughing and horsing around. Jake and Njobo put up the tent, arranging our tarp outside the tent like a vestibule. We found plenty of damp wood and soon we had a good fire. Our canteens were full after crossing streams all day. Dinner was rice, potatoes, and greens. Njobo cut a palm heart for dessert. We sat on logs watching the flames.

Swee'Pea wrapped herself in her blanket. "What do you think about our cannibal president?" Her face shone brightly from the fire.

"He doesn't seem so bad up here," I said.

"How did the coup happen?" Jake asked. "Was Obote so terrible?"

"Amin thought so," I chuckled. In the flickering light I could see Swee'Pea's skeptical look.

"Obote was used to being in charge and seeing his orders followed," she said rapidly. "But with regard to Amin, he didn't think things through. In the end it proves this: The president must not leave the country after telling the army commander that he may be fired and investigated when the president gets back." She gave me a long look to make sure I understood.

I was embarrassed by how little I actually knew about Uganda. Swee'Pea picked up on this right away. She rightly assumed we needed remedial instruction on Ugandan politics. Especially me, the so-called Africa expert from Oxford.

"How are the Baganda doing under Amin?" I asked.

"Not good," said Swee'Pea. "Baganda are on the bottom, with the other tribes Amin doesn't like, especially Obote's Langi tribe. At least he's not killing us like he's killing the Langi. The West Nile people are on top, Amin's Kakwa tribe, plus the Lugbara, and Amin's Nubian killers from Sudan. We Baganda may be a big tribe, but we're less than a fifth of the population. Even under Obote we didn't count for much against everybody else."

"That's the biggest tribe in Uganda, isn't it? The Baganda?" I asked. "Right in the middle of the country?"

"We thought we were special." Swee'Pea sighed. "We were foolish, we Baganda. The British treated us like a nuisance, but we made ourselves their pets, thinking we would increase our greatness, our prosperity, our fame. We were so rich, we thought, so numerous, so intelligent, so indispensable, the country could not survive without us. The truth was, we were isolated. Everyone hated us. We wanted the plum jobs in government or the professions or business. We let the people from the north take the guns. Soldiering was too low a job for us Baganda."

"But your Uncle Nelson is an officer in the army."

"That's true, Jake." Swee'Pea considered this. "Nelson, how do you say that? He was the black sheep of the family. An obvious failure. That's why he joined the army." She poked the fire with a stick. "Nelson is a capable killer. A politically astute monster."

I was admiring Swee'Pea's dumbed-down analysis for us muzungus, and her poise and self-confidence. And her beauty. She was under five feet, a head shorter than me and then some.

"Still," I said, "shouldn't the Baganda be Uganda's natural leaders? I mean, you had every advantage."

Swee'Pea laughed. "Many Baganda would agree with you. But we Baganda were far too narrow-minded," she lamented. "We insisted on our king, we reveled in our king, we gloried in our king, the Kabaka. We were reactionaries, wallowing in the past. Over one hundred years ago the Kabaka, King Mutesa, hobnobbed with Speke, the first English explorer to reach Uganda. We thought we were important. We resented the British, who had to tolerate us. But we didn't see how much the British protected us, or how much the other tribes resented us. What could the Kabaka do for us, after all? The Kabaka only wanted to continue being the Kabaka. We should have been the natural leaders of Uganda. Instead, we got trampled. We're a sad story of political incompetence." She threw her stick into the fire.

I persisted. "But why all this killing, Swee'Pea?"

She groaned, as though it were so much old news. She grabbed another stick. "Well, the British created Uganda, stuck us all together in one country with borders that they drew. But Ugandans don't trust each other. Politics here is tribal, and so your tribal identity is also your political loyalty. Every tribe fears the tribe next door. Hates it. Envies it. That didn't much matter when the British ran things. But now it matters. Unfortunately, our president is the most paranoid and ruthless man in the country. General Amin is killing his enemies by the thousands. Do you want money and power? Kill someone on Amin's enemies list. That's how Uncle Nelson rose in the ranks. For Amin, anyone close to Obote is an enemy, anyone who was in Obote's government, a friend or associate, or a kinsman, no matter how distant, anyone who belonged to Obote's clan or tribe. Even members of tribes friendly with Obote's Langi tribe, like the Acholi, are marked for killing. And that is a lot of people. Your tribe may be your death sentence, especially if you're a soldier."

"But why all the tortures?" I pressed.

"Because they can, Karl." The firelight glinted in her eyes. "Because they can do it, and who's to punish them? They are drunk with power. No one can touch them. Amin's the only one they must please."

Jake insisted on sleeping under the tarp with Njobo, leaving his tent to me and Swee'Pea. The tent would be cramped with three, he said. This was awkward. By the time I got into the tent, Swee'Pea was asleep, all the way over on one side. She looked small, wrapped in her blanket. I arranged my sleeping bag with my head in the corner opposite from her head. By morning, somehow, all that was undone. It was a cold night. We woke curled up together in the middle of the tent.

After breakfast Swee'Pea and Njobo held a powwow, a good fifteen-minute back-and-forth to decide the route for the day. Swee'Pea wasn't just along for the ride, like Jake and me. She was running the operation, aggressively questioning Njobo, pointing precisely to various spots on a scrap of map she had brought, arguing about the route, which villages to bypass and which to give a wide berth, where to cross streams and where to camp. She clearly knew the geography and its pitfalls. She wrapped her head with military precision in a bit of gay cloth. She was a wily guerrilla leader, outwitting the enemy, shrewdly leading her tiny, unarmed band through insecure terrain.

We covered maybe ten miles a day. Njobo took us in and out of the forest higher and higher on the mountain, a steep route that crossed the ribs of the massif, skirting deep ravines and forbidding ridges. It was rainy season; the streams were almost impassable.

On the second night at dusk we looked out on an unbroken sea of clouds. It grew dark and a frothy mass of stars spread above us. Cutting bamboo for poles, Jake and Njobo made a proper self-standing tent with our tarp some distance off. At bedtime Swee'Pea and I were left alone in Jake's tent again. After the night before, we felt less inhibited. Something had changed, but we acted like nothing had. We didn't speak. That night, haltingly, by degrees I felt the edges of Swee'Pea's body, her hips, her shoulders, her arms, smelled the scent of her hair; her hands explored my hair, my chest, and my arms. We kept our clothes on, of course. The night was cold and there was frost when we woke up.

It had drizzled overnight, then froze, and the frozen path quickly turned to mud after the sun came up. Mud covered us all up to our knees. It was a slog, but Swee'Pea suffered from her flimsy shoes, barely better than sneakers. So far we had been lucky with the weather, but our luck would not last. Sure enough, it began drizzling again and around noon the rain forced us under the tarp, but we were soaked. We called a rest day. We needed it. Legs were sore and lungs ached from the altitude. Njobo led us to a clearing at the edge of the forest, full of long grass, and old, rotting trees. I set up the tent on a thick bed of moss. Soon we had a big fire going. Everyone was dead tired. Eventually, we made dinner.

That night Swee'Pea and I made love for the first time. Jake and Njobo were under the tarp tent on the other side of the clearing, leaving Swee'Pea alone with me sitting on some big rocks in the cold wind. The grass and moss everywhere around us were drenched and starting to freeze.

Swee'Pea put her head on my lap, looked up at me, put her arms around my neck. Her eyes glittered under the dark sky. She dazzled me. I had not been with a woman since Helen came to Oxford.

"Let's make love," she said.

"What about you getting pregnant?" I said immediately.

Swee'Pea didn't answer, drawing my lips down to hers. I felt her hot body pressing me, her tongue hot in my mouth. My mind raced. I resisted, saying we hardly knew each other, and weren't we going to split up soon? But I was losing the battle. The rain started again. What should I say about Helen's pregnancy? We kept kissing until we could no longer ignore it. Or was it the rain? The rain came down in buckets. We dove into the tent.

"My period should be any day now," she whispered. "It's safe."

That night was as dark as any I can remember. She looked beautiful to me, her delicious neck, her round breasts, her soft rump, even though it was hard to see her in the darkness. Her waist was very small. She had no hair on her body except below. We did not sleep much. Between blanket and sleeping bag ontop of the thick moss we made love while rain thundered on the tent fly. Somehow the tent held and we stayed dry.

Next morning Jake was smirking as he handed me two cups of steaming tea. "What a storm," was all he said. Njobo was grinning, almost chuckling. *Yes*, I thought to myself, *it's all so obvious*.

"If you want to take the tent tonight," I told Jake. "It's yours."

"Wouldn't dream of it."

Though far above the road, we sometimes could make it out below us, we even saw vehicles. This life for the four of us continued day in and day out, marching uphill, marching downhill. Our legs were getting stronger by the day. We lost track of time, hiking through canyons, across evergreen parkland and weird, giant vegetation that grew at these altitudes, camping, making dinner, telling stories.

Swee'Pea and I were delirious with discovery.

"Karl," Swee'Pea whispered one night, "I love when you're inside me."

"I love being inside you."

She kissed me. "I love when you move that way."

"You mean, like this?"

"Yes." She panted, breathing in sharply. "Yes, yes." She pulled me close. After a long while Swee'Pea whispered, "Should we marry?"

I didn't know how to answer. "I hope so." It was enough. I imagined she was smiling. But it seemed reckless. Wasn't it clear we'd have to split up when we left the mountain? Or when we got to Rwanda? I started ignoring *What then?* questions.

"You will be my pretend husband." She kissed me.

To my shock that morning Swee'Pea declared she would carry my pack. Ignoring my complaints, she insisted it was her duty, what a good wife would do. I protested, reminding her we were not really married. That made no difference to her; she wouldn't hear of it. Our guerrilla commander and political instructor was now my pretend wife. It took getting used to.

The weather turned sunny. The quiet on the mountain was overwhelming, the bamboo waving soundlessly in the cool air. I never would have noticed the silence without Swee'Pea's soft singing behind me. Her lithe form marching under the orange load, one attractive arm raised to steady it. Her eyes lowered demurely when she noticed my gaze, a blushing smile spreading subtly among her features. She wouldn't let me near my pack to carry it. That wouldn't seem right. I stopped thinking about how my life made no sense. Swee'Pea's life didn't make any more sense than mine.

Game started to appear, small antelopes, duikers, bushbuck, pangolins, aardvarks, many kinds of birds. One afternoon we came across an abandoned coffee plantation. Piles of derelict, rusted equipment surrounded the main house. We stopped to explore. Probably built in the late '40s or '50s, after the Second World War. This plantation must have been a small gem. It was so far from any villages we wondered how it could have been built at all, yet it had been so thoroughly looted practically nothing remained. We found one spot inside where no water came in, where the roof was still watertight in what had been the kitchen, though the windows were missing. In back was a grassy area on a knoll where we all sat in the chilly twilight trying to catch glimpses of volcanoes far to the south on the Rwanda-Zaïre border. It was here that the planter's family must have had their picnics. I gathered firewood, helped Njobo prepare dinner until Swee'Pea noticed. She affectionately pushed me away, taking my place next to Njobo.

"You are my pretend husband," she repeated that night. "I love my pretend husband."

"You're too real for pretending."

AT DAYBREAK, WE LEFT the coffee plantation. Jake and I had not spoken much on the mountain, but he had been dropping hints about wanting to split. Now he spelled it out, announcing at our lunch break that he was going off by himself once we hit the road. He could travel rapidly alone but insisted that Swee'Pea and I also would move faster and be better off without him. A threesome would attract attention. I wondered about that. He was right, as far as that went, but imagining that somehow Swee'Pea and I would not attract attention was a joke. As long as we were in Uganda, we'd be in someone's crosshairs. I didn't blame Jake at all. He was right. Things had changed fast since Swee'Pea and I became lovers. In fact, she was my new partner. Jake said he'd meet up with us in Kigali. From there we'd all go on together with Howard and Beatrice to Bujumbura, then down to Nyanza Lac to see Bertrand. We were way behind schedule, anyway. Though I had lost track of the calendar, I guessed it was around April 15, the day we were supposed to meet Howard and Beatrice in Kigali.

That night Swee'Pea told me we'd strike the road soon and that Njobo, his job done, was planning to leave in the morning. Njobo had described the path that would lead us to a point in the road beyond Kasese, adding to take care of wild animals because we were getting close to Queen Elizabeth National Park. When we woke up that morning and got dressed, he was gone.

"I told him to take anything he liked," Jake told us. "After looking through what was left, he asked for the matches, the sugar, and the salt."

"Did you pay him?" Swee'Pea asked.

"I tried. He refused to take money."

It took the three of us half a day to get down to the road, working through bush humming with insects until, astonished, we were standing on asphalt. We backed off fast, jumped into the thicket. Then we divvied up the camping gear or junked it. Jake wanted to give us the tent. I wouldn't hear of it. Swee'Pea agreed. We gave it back to him with many thanks, but we kept the tarp. We stayed in that spot for hours, ate what was left of the food, watched the nearly silent road. We were already miles beyond Kasese from what Njobo said.

It began to rain and quickly became a deluge. Jake chose that moment to leave us.

"Remember, under the Primus sign in Kigali," he waved. "We're already a day late."

The rain came down harder.

"We'll be there," I called after him, "unless we get shot."

"See you in—" the torrent muffled his words and swallowed him up.

When it cleared, I heard a car. It sounded like a diesel. It took a long time coming. I flagged it down, a tan Land Rover pickup. The driver was friendly, told us to hop in the back. He was going straight through to Kabale. We squeezed into the bed with three passengers and a load of plantains under a close-fitting tarp. Kabale was still many hours away to the south, about three hundred kilometers.

Luckily, there were no checkpoints. But it didn't matter. Within hours, Uncle Nelson's soldiers caught up with us. We were parked by the side of the road. The driver was up front eating his lunch. He'd buttoned up the canvas tightly after the other passengers had left, as we squatted amid heaped plantain bunches. A pale green Mercedes sedan drove up. I watched through a small crack in the tarp as two soldiers got out, erect and menacing. They walked right up to the bed of the pickup, their guns glinting. The driver hopped out. He starting acting, that's all I can call it. It was a noisy, stylized, distracting, ingratiating act, followed by loud threats from the soldiers, soothing murmurs from the driver, followed by sharp laughter. We didn't breathe. Hands all over the tarp, one homicidal eye squinting to see inside. A fly had settled on my arm, spun around, buzzing, crawling to my elbow, wading in my sweat. I didn't twitch, didn't slap it. *This fly might outlive me*, I thought. An arm thrust under the tarp, the driver grabbing a plantain to show it off.

The voices grew fainter, indistinct. We heard urgent footsteps, doors slamming, an engine starting, wheels spinning on gravel as the Mercedes pulled away.

The driver got in the cab and started driving. Swee'Pea and I looked at each other with disbelief as we jounced around with the plantains, held onto each other for what seemed like hours. Over the road noise Swee'Pea explained what had happened. The soldiers had asked the driver what he was carrying. Plantains, he told them; he had been parked for a few hours waiting for cargo, he said, which had just arrived. They said they were looking for two muzungus and a Ugandan girl. They gave descriptions. He said he'd seen three muzungus maybe an hour back, but no Ugandan girl. He led them straight to the other side of the road under a tree to show them where the muzungus had been standing. He told them they might fit the description. He said a white Nissan pickup stopped for them. It was heading north. One soldier asked him to confirm the pickup was heading north—not south. The driver repeated what he said. The other soldier remembered passing a white Nissan pickup heading north about twenty kilometers up the road. They rushed to the car, speeding off toward Kasese.

I still can't figure out why that driver wanted to help us. He liked us, or maybe he didn't like the Ugandan army. After three or four more hours over a rough road, he stopped just outside Kabale, as we had requested. We thanked him many times, offered him money. He just shook his head and smiled.

"You two have fun."

I shook his hand. "We were dying when those soldiers appeared."

He laughed. "You just have to know how to talk to them."

To ATTRACT LESS ATTENTION we walked into town after sunset. We found a hotel right away. *Mountains of the Moon Hotel*, the sign said. It was a small place off the main street, just four or five rooms, all of them empty as it turned out. The proprietor and his wife looked us over doubtfully. Frowning, they said they had no vacancy. But once Swee'Pea told them we were just married, on our honeymoon, everything changed. They shook my hand, slapped me on the back, hugged us. They were beaming. They pumped us about the wedding. Swee'Pea told them all they wanted to know, in detail: The exorbitant bride price, how it went on for seven days and seven nights with hundreds of guests, the small herd of goats that were slaughtered, the fifty – make that seventy, cases of beer that were drunk. It sounded like quite a bash.

They gave us their best room, showered us with plates of fruit, loaves of bread, cakes, a sofa, a chair, another chair, extra blankets, a table, even a small heater for the cold.

Swee'Pea and I held hands after they left, embraced, kissed, made love, made love again, lay together for hours, napping. It was our first chance to really look at each other up close with the lights on. For the first time I told Swee'Pea about my life: Dropping out of Balliol College, my fitful, sporadic writing for Harold, Howard, and Beatrice, Lamu, America, protesting the Vietnam war. Swee'Pea explained she urgently had to get to Tanzania before her money ran out. One of her relatives was there. I said my money was running low, too. That was one of those *What then?* questions I had vowed to ignore. I never mentioned Helen to her.

Swee'Pea wanted to become a doctor. She had spent three semesters before the coup studying medicine in Israel until she was called back. That explained her English ability. She asked about my plans.

"Undecided."

"Aren't you going back to Oxford? You'll be happy there. You could teach. Write books."

"What would I write about?"

"About Uganda. About Africa."

"I know next to nothing about Africa."

Swee'Pea laughed. "You know me."

WE DECIDED TO STAY put for a few days. But I refused to let Swee'Pea go out by herself. What if she went out and didn't come back? I thought we shouldn't leave the hotel at all, but Swee'Pea predicted we'd have no more trouble from soldiers. She doubted the army was much concerned about this part of Uganda or the Rwanda border.

"Amin is not going to be attacked from Rwanda," she declared. "He's worried about Tanzania. Amin and Nyerere are not exactly friends."

Kabale is a mountain town over six thousand feet high in the far south of Uganda in the Kigezi district, about fifty kilometers from Rwanda. Often cold and misty, it got hot when the sun came out. Big low clouds constantly rolled in. It was apt to rain at any moment. The streets were gluey mud. Bamboo forests covered the western hills. People were friendly. Nothing was going on, which was perfect. Still, nothing attracted attention faster than Swee'Pea and I walking around town together. Swee'Pea didn't reach my shoulder, didn't weigh a hundred pounds. Plus the Black-White thing. People definitely looked at us. There were no soldiers.

We found a tiny branch library staffed by a short, wiry, energetic man named John. He had a great selection of Western literature—Dickens, Coleridge, Wordsworth, Trollope, Fitzgerald, Tolstoy, Faulkner,

Dostoyevsky, Henry James—but no readers, not surprising since he was so choosy about his borrowers. He was delighted we wanted to read but we had to work hard to convince him to lend us books.

"How do I know you will return my books?"

"We will," I said. "We promise."

"But how do I know? Where are you from?"

"I'm from Kampala," Swee'Pea said. "Makerere University."

John turned to me.

"I'm from Cincinnati by way of London."

Swee'Pea corrected me. "He's a graduate student at Oxford."

That did it. We picked out a few books. Too few. John pressed more books on us. What about Thackeray? What about Hemingway? George Eliot? Blake? We each brought a pile of books back to the hotel. The hotel owners were surprised.

"You'll be busy," they laughed. "Do you really have time for reading?"

They had a point. There were sardines and bread for lunch, tea of course, lettuce and tomatoes from the market, and cucumbers, and tiny bananas, about as long as your finger.

"What will we do with so many books?" I said, when we finished eating. We put the books away.

Swee'Pea got really close. "You could start reading now." She was standing on her toes, kissing my neck. "If you wanted to," she laughed. Then she pulled my head down and kissed me again. "You could start with Thackeray." She hugged me, looking me in the eye with a roguish smile. "Or you could try William Blake." We kissed some more. We did not get much reading done. Eventually it was evening, and we had to get out of bed to find dinner. I waited for Swee'Pea to get ready. When she finished dressing, we found a small restaurant. We were the only customers.

"What were you studying at Oxford," she asked, "before you came to Africa?"

"Honestly, I wasn't at Oxford more than a few weeks," I said. I was reading about Rwanda, about why people kill each other, how murder gets mixed up in politics. This political killing is spreading through Africa. They call it revolution, but it always comes down to killing."

Swee'Pea was thoughtful. "Doesn't killing help politicians gain power and their followers to get rich?" she asked, arching her eyebrows. "Kill your enemies, steal their goods. That's how it works here. Political slogans propel the politicians. But people do the killing because they will profit."

"True. But does political change have to involve murder?"

"Not if everyone agrees on the rules. But how often does that happen? It's easier to motivate people to act if there is an enemy they can hate."

"So, this gets personal fast. For example," I said, "why would I kill your family? Just theoretically speaking, of course. We've been neighbors for years, say. It's hard to believe that we've hated each other all that time."

"Fear," she said immediately. "You would kill us if you thought we might kill you. Maybe we had our eyes on your cows. Why does your family have more cows than my family, anyway?" She narrowed her eyes. "It's unfair! How do you explain that?"

"We're better than you, don't you see? Because we have more cows."

"Not if we kill you and steal them."

"Maybe you're the one who should be studying at Oxford."

She smiled. "Don't be silly. You're good at this, Karl. This is your field."

I wondered if she was right, or if I even had a field.

"Swee'Pea, you seem like a natural."

"You're wrong. I only know what everyone knows. I really have no time for politics. I want to study medicine."

It was hard for us to leave Kabale. In the first place, we had all those books to read. But really, we could not leave each other alone. We stayed a week. It rained constantly. We just loved the place. When the time finally came, we went to find John at the library. Returning his books was a matter of honor. He was happy to see us.

"Did you read all the books?"

"Every one. Cover to cover," I said.

The proprietors gave us a big discount when we checked out. Another wedding present. They even found us a car going to the border post at Kisoro. The problem for Swee'Pea and me was not getting to Kisoro so much as deciding what to do after that. But first we had to cross the border. We walked up to the customs hut, handed our passports to a tall, light-skinned official with a longish nose. He looked at my passport, flipped through the pages, stopped at the *No Facilities* stamp. Then he quickly leafed to a blank page, stamped it, handed it back to me. *April 22, 1972.* For Swee'Pea, he went to consult with another official, taking her passport and leaving us standing nervously at the hut. After several minutes he returned asking to see Swee'Pea's Uganda ID card. She fished it from her bag. For two breathless seconds he looked it over, then handed the documents back to Swee'Pea, pointing out she didn't need a passport to travel to Rwanda. Her ID card would do. He smiled, said good day. She and I squeezed hands, practically skipping to the car park to find a ride to Ruhengeri in Rwanda.

"He was Tutsi," Swee'Pea said.

"Who was?"

"The customs guy. His family probably fled Rwanda in the '60s. Many Tutsis live in this part of Uganda."

WE SAT IN THE back of a small pickup. A narrow road was cut into the side of a wooded gorge with big trees on a high slope to our right and a steep drop-off on our left into the Rift Valley. The sun shone brightly through the haze. There before us were the volcanoes, the ones we were straining to see from Ruwenzori. They lined up one after another, smallest cone in front, each one taller than the next, four of them arrayed on a fault line. The huge bulk of Karisimbi in back stuck through the clouds, with another giant, Mikeno, off to the right. Rwanda was announcing itself dramatically.

MAP 4 – FORT PORTAL TO RWANDA AND ZAIRE

24. BLOOD ON THE KNIFE
(KARL)

"It's over here." Swee'Pea pointed to the street corner.

There it was in the distance, a huge Primus sign over a bar. *La Reine des Bieres.* The Queen of Beers. It was 5:45 on the evening of April 23, eight days late for the rendezvous. We had no idea if our friends were in Kigali. *On their way? Left without us? Already in Burundi?*

"Karl, I'm tired." Swee'Pea's large eyes looked at me with her absolutely frank expression.

"Let's go once around the block, then come back. If they don't show up by six or so we'll find a hotel, check the post office in the morning." We kept walking.

Rwanda was not a great place for tourists. Deeply rural yet densely populated, the country had a claustrophobic, walled-in feel to it. Traveling the roads amid dozens of close-packed hills hundreds of feet high, each with villages perched on top, isolated you from country life. Snaking around the hills, crossing shady streams, passing the odd rural storefront, the roads were almost deserted. Kigali, the capital, was tiny, just fifteen thousand souls with little pavement. At least I spoke a little French, which helped, but Rwandans were on their own peculiar wavelength.

The country astonished me. It was almost exactly what my readings with Harold had prepared me for. Unlike Ethiopia or Uganda or Kenya, Rwanda was not diverse. Rwanda was the opposite of diverse. Hutus, the overwhelming majority, were plainly in charge. Newspapers conveyed a triumphalist ideology, praising Rwanda's majority-rule republic, making clear that defending it meant suppressing the Tutsis and keeping Tutsi exiles out. Tutsis, the former lords, were now second-class citizens, if they were really citizens at all. What I saw in the newspapers implied they weren't human, but *inyenzi*. Cockroaches.

Swee'Pea and I had crashed back to earth after our Kabale idyll. At least Uncle Nelson's soldiers couldn't reach us here. Yet, our future was doubtful, precarious. We didn't speak of it. I still had no idea what to tell Swee'Pea about Helen. By now Swee'Pea and I were certainly a couple, if not definitely headed toward marriage. I didn't see how I could leave her. I didn't want to leave her. In Ruhengeri I took her clothes shopping because she had almost nothing to wear. That was the first time I ever bought clothes for a woman. It made her happy. Still, my money would last only a few more months.

Usually Swee'Pea was easy-going, humorous. She liked to tease me with "Is that what Oxford thinks?" when she wasn't sure she agreed with me. She also could be calculating, truculent, formidable when defending her point of view, as I had learned in Fort Portal. In Rwanda Swee'Pea was a stranger. She had no family, little money, and no profession. She felt uncomfortable; she was the one complaining about claustrophobia, but for some reason Hutus took her as one of their own. Yet when people stopped her on the street to speak to her, they were surprised when she could not understand Kinyarwanda or even French. She was short and dark, true. But was she really a dead ringer for a Hutu? I couldn't see it.

Swee'Pea took my arm, pointing at the café. "There they are. Your friends."

Beatrice and Karl sat outside under an umbrella. Beatrice was fanning Howard with a menu. She looked at Swee'Pea curiously. "Well, who is this?"

"Beatrice, this is Swee'Pea," I said. "Swee'Pea, this is Beatrice."

"Sveepy? Oh, this will give me trouble! Sveepy, I think we will be great friends." Beatrice immediately took Swee'Pea's hand, laughing.

Then she took Swee'Pea's other hand.

"Sveepy, I've been in Africa for months and I still can't get used to the heat."

Swee'Pea smiled as Beatrice mangled her name. "I've been here all my life. You never get used to it. I'm so glad to meet you, Beatrice." They hugged each other a long moment.

Howard leaned forward smiling. "Hey mate! Listen, have you seen Jake? What happened in Uganda?"

We walked back to their hotel, Beatrice and Swee'Pea arm-in-arm. Beatrice looked tall beside Swee'Pea. We took an adjoining room. Up in their room Beatrice said, "I suppose you and Jake went back to Nairobi, too? No? Then why have we been waiting a week? And where is Jake, by the way?"

"Jake took off by himself," I said. "Said he would meet us here."

"He's lost, then? Going back to Nairobi cost us a week," Beatrice continued. "As it was, we arrived on April 16."

"Did you like Uganda?"

Beatrice made a face. "Rwanda is better. At least no one's getting killed here."

"Not at the moment," Howard mused.

Beatrice gave him a long look. "We both speak good French, so that makes it easier. Not that we've made any friends." Beatrice pulled her chair closer. "How did you two meet, anyway?"

Swee'Pea and I laughed. "It had something to do with Uncle Nelson," I said.

Both Howard and Beatrice gave puzzled looks. While leaving a few things out, I told them about our adventures, starting with Lonnie, our visa problem, Jake's dustup in Fort Portal, Swee'Pea's intervention with her Uncle Nelson, trekking over the Ruwenzori escarpment, almost getting caught by soldiers on the Kabale road, and the Mountains of the Moon hotel.

"It seems you could have been killed several times on that trip," Howard said.

"You were brave to leave Uganda on your own without family or friends to go to," Beatrice said. "Where will you live? How can you support yourself? And I still don't understand how you met Karl."

Swee'Pea's eyes caught mine. "Leaving Uganda may seem foolhardy to you. But leaving seemed less dangerous than staying. I felt desperate." She took my hand in both of hers. "Now you mention it, I don't actually know what I will do. I can't stay here. I don't speak French. I can't go back to Uganda. Probably I will go to Tanzania. That's where many Ugandans are going now. I think my mother's brother, Martin, is in Tanzania with his family. I don't know him well but perhaps he can help me."

"We're planning to go to Tanzania after Burundi." Howard turned to me. "I got a note from Bertrand two days ago. He's waiting for us in Nyanza Lac."

"How's he doing?"

"It's hard to tell. Burundi is passing through a strange moment."

"Many African countries are," I said.

Beatrice stood. "Come, Sveepy. Let's talk, shall we?" Swee'Pea led her out the door to our room, turning to wave and smile at me.

I could see Howard had a million questions, just like Beatrice.

"You and Swee'Pea look fairly serious. Is it serious?"

"Possibly. Complicated, though."

"You'll have time to think it through." He paused a moment. "What about Helen?"

"What about Helen?"

"No need to get upset."

"Swee'Pea doesn't know about Helen yet." Howard looked surprised. "You know, Howard, I really like Swee'Pea. But this wasn't planned out."

"When is Helen giving birth?"

"Soon."

"I'm not trying to torture you."

"No kidding? Helen wrote me in Addis."

"Really?"

"I guess I never mentioned it. Plainly, she hasn't forgotten me entirely. Did I tell you about Ernestine, her former lover? No? I can't figure out what Helen wants."

"I see." Howard furrowed his brows. "It seems you've got two women now. Good luck making up your mind," he laughed.

"Thanks."

"What about Oxford?"

"Something else I don't know. Every passing day it's harder to see how Oxford could possibly fit in with my life. If I'm with Helen, then it's back to Ohio. If I'm with Swee'Pea, it's Tanzania where we'll probably starve to death." We sat silently for a moment. "I have no ticket home."

"That's a problem. I at least have a ticket."

"What about you and Beatrice?"

"We have fun," Howard smiled. "She's really brilliant, you know."

"A bit moody?"

"She's always searching for the truth. Decisive. Though she often changes her mind. She's relentlessly critical. But quick to defend her friends. We fight. We make up. It seems to work here in Africa, I mean, the two of us. Back in Europe? One of us would have to move. Would she move to Paris? Would we both move to England? I can't see myself in Germany speaking German. What would my parents think? My dad was in the British army in North Africa. My mom lived through the Blitz. They'd croak if they heard me speaking German with my German girlfriend."

"Beatrice wants to de-Nazify Germany, right? She can't very well do that from London or Paris."

"We'll have to work it out."

"Lamu seems so far away now."

"Lamu was peaceful," Howard agreed. "Uganda was horrifying. Beatrice was right. Many dreadful things going on there. They got so busy killing each other they forgot to tell the tourists not to bother."

"What about Rwanda? Or Burundi?"

"You've studied Rwanda, haven't you? Then you know Rwanda and Burundi are bookends, mirror images, with their differences strangely amplified by history. Same size, both about one hundred miles square. Traditional kingdoms. Populations about four million each, with Hutus outnumbering Tutsis four-to-one. But Tutsis still control Burundi, unlike so-called democratic Rwanda, where Hutus have massively outvoted Tutsis."

"And chopped a lot of them to bits. If you ask me, Africa's real Jacobins, or Bolsheviks, are the Hutu radicals here in Rwanda," I said. "The Tutsis are getting it in the neck."

Howard exhaled slowly. "Around here there's always blood on the knife. Blood flows quickly, like opening a spigot. Maybe there's still some hope for Burundi. Burundi society was more fluid, more inclusive. They never had a rigid caste system like Rwanda, or a Tutsi monarchy."

"How can Burundi be immune? What happens in Rwanda affects Burundi. And vice versa."

"You're right. When Tutsis get killed in Rwanda, Tutsis in Burundi see what might happen to them if Hutus were in charge. Events in Rwanda take their toll in Burundi. Tutsi refugees in Burundi burn for revenge against Hutus. Who can blame them?" Howard lifted a thermos the hotel staff had brought. "Coffee?" Coffee was the rule in Francophone Rwanda.

"What's this about Burundi's deposed king?" I asked. "The Mwami? There was a picture of him shaking hands with Amin in the Ugandan newspapers. I forget his name. Isn't he back in Burundi?"

"Strangely, he is. His given name was Charles Ndizeye until he became King Ntare V. Or Charles Ntare, as he now calls himself. He arrived in Burundi from Uganda after six years in exile on March 30."

"March 30? That's the day they looted the Israeli embassy in Kampala."

"Charles," Howard continued, "the former Mwami, was arrested the moment he stepped off his Ugandan helicopter. Very mysterious. Lots of conspiracy theories. Loose talk about white mercenaries."

"He's a Tutsi, isn't he?"

"Charles Ntare? No. He's a Burundi royal. Not a Tutsi."

I watched a gecko skitter on the wall. Freeze. Skitter a foot more.

~

As we were getting ready for bed that evening, Swee'Pea took my arm. "Karl, I have to talk to you." Something serious. She made me sit.

"Karl," she said, her eyes opening wide, looking straight at mine. "Karl, I think I'm pregnant."

I did not know what to say. I felt tissue thin, like a leaf. My mouth opened three times, but no words came out.

"Karl, I know you're going to think I tricked you. I told you it was safe for us to make love because my period was due soon. That was true. I don't know what happened." She sat down next to me. "Karl, you must understand. I would not have chosen this moment to get pregnant, alone in a foreign country, without a husband or even my family." She began to cry.

After a moment I held her close. "You're not alone, Swee'Pea, though it's true we're not married. But are you sure? It hasn't been very long."

"Yes, I am sure," she sniffled. "I've been feeling nauseous. My period was late. I didn't tell you, but in Ruhengeri I went to see a doctor. He examined me. He said I was pregnant."

"How did you do that? You don't speak French."

"It wasn't easy," she giggled through her tears, wiping her eyes. "It wasn't easy at all. Do you remember? I left you in the cafe after we went shopping? Just before we left for Kigali?"

I remembered sitting there and wondering where she had gone. And also wondering what had become of her period.

"All right, Swee'Pea. There's something I need to tell you that I haven't mentioned before."

That serious look again. "You're already married?"

"No. My former girlfriend Helen is about to have a baby. Unless she had it already. We haven't communicated much. She says I'm the father."

"Helen and I are pregnant at the same time? How did you manage that?"

I sat thinking for a moment. "Well, Swee'Pea, what should we do?"

"No, no. It's what you want to do. What do you want to do, Karl? I think you need to decide."

∾

Next morning in a café I banged a glass with my spoon.

"I have an announcement."

Beatrice smiled broadly. "What fun! What kind of announcement?"

Swee'Pea looked at me.

"We're going to have a baby."

"Just like that? A baby? This is a surprise," Howard said. "Didn't you two just meet?"

Beatrice was beaming. "A baby? A baby? Do you mean to get married?"

"Marriage? It is a possibility," Swee'Pea said. "Maybe not this week."

"We don't have any firm plans right now, except the baby," I said. "There are a few details to work out, like where we'll live, money, higher education, careers."

"Trifles," Beatrice shrugged.

"Trivialities," Howard agreed. "Lord, I ask myself those same questions every day. Sometimes more often."

"We're excited," Swee'Pea said. "We're really excited."

"You're both very brave," Beatrice said.

"You think so?" Was this courage, I wondered, or more insanity? All our good cheer was bravado, though Swee'Pea and I tried not to show it. At least Howard and Beatrice played along.

"This calls for celebrating," Howard said.

"Yes," Beatrice said. "We must celebrate."

"Maybe we should wait until we get to Bertrand's house," I said.

"That's fine," Swee'Pea said.

"We'll have a big party," Beatrice beamed.

"You can invite all the relatives," Howard smiled. That got a big laugh.

"To Sveepy and Karl," Beatrice said, holding up her café au lait.

"Hear, hear. To Swee'Pea and Karl." Howard held up his cup.

"May they have many babies."

"How many?" Swee'Pea looked first at Beatrice, then at me.

"Five? Six?" I smiled.

"That's a lot!" she laughed as she hit my arm. Within an hour we found a truck going to Burundi.

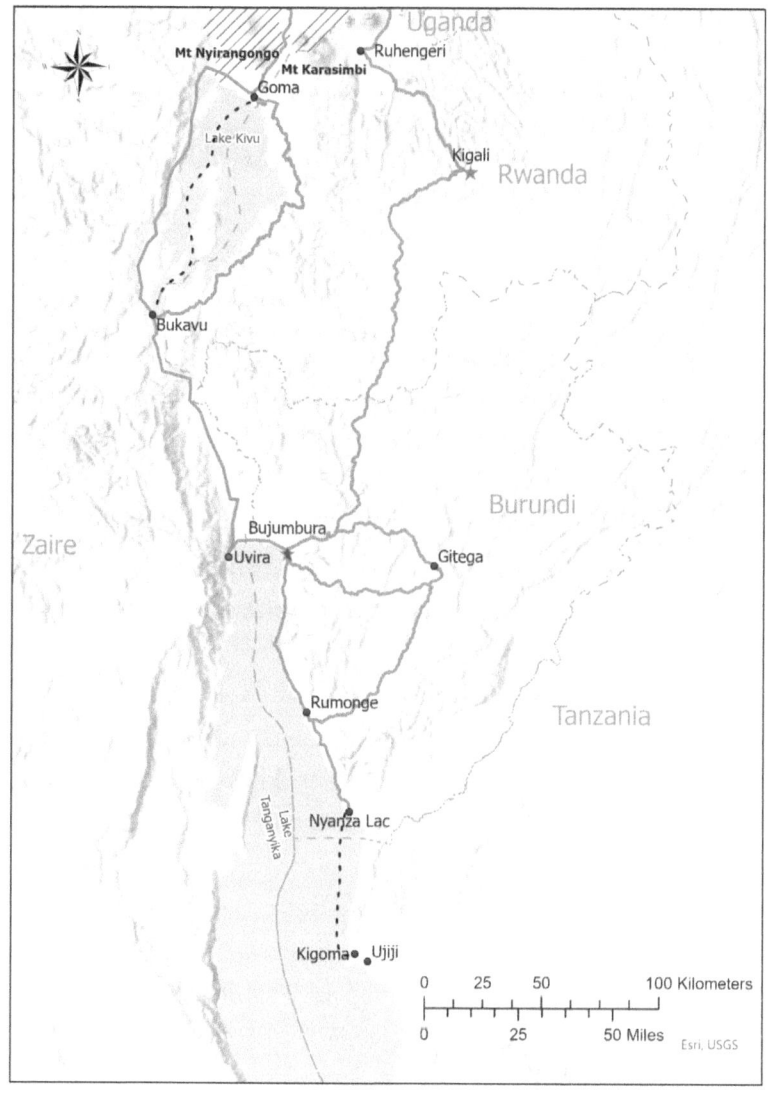

MAP 5 – JAKE AND KARL'S ROUTE TO BURUNDI AND TANZANIA

25. END OF THE ROAD
(KARL)

Another day, another exhausting ride in the back of a tiny Japanese pickup, the four of us crammed in with eight others, a flock of chickens with their legs tied together, plus piles of baggage. We'd been on the road all day since early morning in Kigali. A bad road followed the shoreline south from Bujumbura along Lake Tanganyika. To our left the Burundi hills rose into the clouds. In the west, to our right, above the choppy blue lake water lightning slashed dark mountain ridges in the Congo, now renamed Zaïre. Here at least the sun was shining. We reached Nyanza Lac, Bertrand's lakeside town, just before dusk. It was the end of the line in Burundi. In a few days we hoped to cross into Tanzania, another ten klicks on, maybe have a look at the chimpanzees at Gombe. Serengeti beckoned, then Arusha, Kilimanjaro. After that, who knew?

Swee'Pea felt nauseous all day. She didn't complain, but I often saw her pretty face contort. She'd lean modestly over the side of the jouncing truck bed to vomit, wiping her mouth discreetly with a small handkerchief, then sitting erect again. It wasn't the best way to travel for someone in her condition. I was fine, as were Howard and Beatrice, soaking up the sunshine. The two of them had reconciled again after a blowup in Bujumbura. They had a pattern—a blow up, followed by new fondness.

We kept passing refugee camps huddled by the lakeshore, Congolese who came across Lake Tanganyika in '65, supposedly fleeing the bloodthirsty Simba rebels.[24] Locally they were known as Mulélists after Pierre Mulélé,[25] the Congolese Maoist.

With the sunlight in my eyes and the jarring, uneven road, I fell into a reverie. I recalled meeting my tutor, Harold Higgins, one day in his office last fall at Oxford.

"You see, ideology can create blind spots," Harold had remarked. "The Congo refugees were Simba supporters. They moved across the lake to Burundi not so much to escape the Simbas, whom they rather liked, but to flee Tshombe's[26] white mercenaries, who were shooting up the eastern Congo and squashing the Simbas. But those Congolese refugees, like the Simbas and the Rwanda Hutus," Harold continued, "like all the African hard Left, they hated Tutsis. Saw them as strutting aristocrats who deserved the guillotine."

"Wait, I'm confused," I had objected. "Didn't a left-wing Tutsi government in Burundi help arm the Simbas? Why would they do that if they hated Tutsis?"

"That's correct. This is where things start to get jumbled." Harold winked. "The Tutsis saw the Simbas as allies against the detested Belgians."

"Of course! The Belgians provoked a Tutsi bloodbath in Rwanda, didn't they?"

"Several," Harold nodded. "And there's the blind spot. Their loathing of Belgians, who were still very influential, blinded the Burundi Tutsis to rashly import this fifth column, these pro-Simba refugees, because they hated Belgians. But somehow forgetting they also hated Tutsis."

Harold liked leaning back in his chair while he pontificated, his hands folded behind his head. "In November '65 General Mobutu swept in and Tshombe, the great Simba tormentor, was forced into

---

24   "Simba" is Swahili for "Lion."
25   Pron: Mu-LAY-lay
26   Pron: CHOM-bay. Moïse Tshombe, President of the secessionist Katanga Republic 1960-1963, Prime Minister of the Democratic Republic of the Congo 1964-1965.

exile. But the Simba refugees in Burundi were cautious, waiting to see what Mobutu would do. Before long, Mobutu had his own mercenaries in the eastern Congo. And in '68 Mobutu finally lured Pierre Mulélé, the Simba Maoist leader, back from exile with many promises and assurances, and then quickly had him tortured to death in the most sadistic way imaginable." Harold paused to open his eyes wide. "His limbs were sawed off and his eyes gouged out while he was still alive. After Mulélé's arrest and execution, the refugees knew they had to stay put. They were embittered, and they plotted, and their hatreds festered in their camps by Lake Tanganyika in Tutsi-ruled Burundi."

With that nugget from Harold rolling around in my head, the camionette jolted to a stop. We were stiff from the ride. We got down, hauled out our back packs, brushed ourselves off, and headed to rest under a corrugated tin roof held up by two barkless tree branches. Howard asked us to wait while he went to find Bertrand, leaving me with Beatrice and Swee'Pea.

"How are you feeling?" I touched Swee'Pea's soft arm above the elbow. She smiled at me.

"Oh, you know."

"Beatrice?"

"A bit grimy," Beatrice sighed. "And hungry."

"I'm sure we both could use a bath," Swee'Pea laughed.

The street was active. School kids walked home in their uniforms. The open market down the street was buzzing. A truck or two rumbled through swirls of dust. Swee'Pea was happily chatting in Swahili with a woman shopper. Many people spoke Swahili in this part of Burundi, like they did across the lake in Zaïre. Just then, Howard appeared with a tall young man.

"This is Georges. Lucky, I bumped into him. He's a senior prof at Bertrand's school."

We fell in line following Georges, who led us south through town paralleling the beach, then turned left at a road that mounted a steep hill.

Swee'Pea and I lagged behind. From out of nowhere, a slightly built young man walked straight up to Swee'Pea. They huddled, jabbering in Swahili until Swee'Pea gave him a strange look. He instantly froze, backed off, then hurried away, his eyes wide with panic, like he had swallowed a plum that was caught in his throat.

"Who was that?"

"I honestly don't know," Swee'Pea said, watching his retreating form. "He thought I was someone he knew."

"What did he want?"

Swee'Pea hesitated, looking up at me. "He said the strangest thing."

"What was it?"

"He said, 'Why aren't you in the forest with the others?'"

"In the forest?"

Swee'Pea shook her head. "I really don't know what he meant by that."

I couldn't make heads or tails of it, either. Howard was up the hill, waving. I waved back and we continued trudging along. Howard, Beatrice, and Georges turned right, finally halting in a shady grove at a bungalow with a wide veranda. Bertrand was standing on the porch and smiling, his arms folded. A hefty man dressed in khaki shorts with a large beard, short hair, he looked like a Jesuit.

"*Bienvenue. Comment vous allez?*" He leaped down the stairs, and with a servant collected our gear. It was spacious inside with plenty of empty rooms for us to spread out. Bertrand was a *stagiaire*, a volunteer teacher at a Catholic school. He apparently lived alone. Like Howard, Bertrand was a keen student of African affairs. Books were piled everywhere.

We greeted Alphonse, the amiable cook, then Etienne, the houseboy, who had helped lug in our stuff. Beatrice and Howard spoke fluent French, so they did most of the talking until Bertrand noticed that Swee'Pea and I were struggling. Then he switched firmly to English, which he spoke well.

At first there wasn't much to say with all of us unpacking, cleaning up, unwinding after a hard day, flopping for a few moments of calm. Howard came around collecting money for food. It was my turn to pay. I gave him twenty dollars in Burundi francs for the four of us. Before sunset Etienne dashed out with an empty basket. He reappeared after dark. Around eight o'clock we sat at a bountiful table. We were starved. Alphonse brought out plate after plate. A feast.

Then I ruined it. "So, what's going on in this part of the world?"

Bertrand sighed, rubbing his head before launching a conversation that continued past midnight. But first he wanted to talk about his students, who fascinated him. "They're so energetic, so hardworking, so intelligent. Imagine, they all have mastered French. It's completely unlike Kirundi, their mother tongue."

Pulling his chair forward, Bertrand looked around the table, finally settling his eyes on Swee'Pea.

"Howard tells me you're from Uganda? It's a place where you better be careful what you say, at least I have the impression."

"I think I would agree with that," she laughed. "What about Burundi? We're all so curious."

"What's going on here?" Bertrand shook his head. "My sadness that Burundi has failed to avoid bloodshed. It's all because of this Tutsi-Hutu thing."

"It's not so unique, is it? Tribalism?" Beatrice asked. "It's all over Africa."

"Maybe violence is not unique," Bertrand began slowly, "but Hutus and Tutsis are not tribes. Or even ethnic groups. Or castes, like in Rwanda."

"No?" Beatrice looked doubtful.

"Everything changed after independence. Today you can talk about Hutu and Tutsi politics. But in the past people in Burundi never identified as Hutu or Tutsi. There was no Hutu point of view, no Tutsi point of view. Now many Hutus see themselves as a vast underclass."

"Well, aren't they?" Beatrice countered.

"That's what the Belgians told them. But no."

"Bertrand's right," I butted in. "Hutu and Tutsi were status markers, partly based on owning cattle. Everyone here is cow crazy. But society was fluid. Hutus became Tutsis and vice versa. Intermarriage was common."

"Ah, the professor!" Beatrice goaded me.

"Ha ha. But Beatrice, Hutus held important posts at court, even governorships. There was no political rivalry. The Burundi monarchy was respected, and neutral. And Burundi and Rwanda really are unique."

"Unique? Really?" Again, Beatrice was skeptical.

"Isolated, traditional kingdoms, quite old," I continued. "They had pervasive, unifying cultures and languages."

"Yes, I know they're kingdoms, or were," Beatrice said.

"In Rwanda," Howard said, "the king always was a Tutsi. But the Burundi kings belonged to a separate courtier class, neither Tutsi nor Hutu. The *Mwami,* as the kings in both countries were called, survived independence in Burundi. The old Mwami had been on the throne for fifty years when he fled for his life in '65."

"Wait, I heard that the Mwami just returned to Burundi," Swee'Pea said. "By helicopter. From Uganda."

"Yes," Bertrand said, "it's true. That's the old king's youngest son, Charles Ntare. He's only twenty-four. He arrived a few weeks ago, on March 30. By helicopter. Compliments of Idi Amin."

"This gets a bit convoluted, doesn't it?" Beatrice folded her arms, leaned back in her chair.

"Charles was in exile for six years," Bertrand said. "He became the Mwami in '65 when his father fled, and then he was deposed the next year, in '66, when he was out of the country. Suddenly he's back, with no warning or explanation." Bertrand looked at Swee'Pea. "He claims he just wants to be an ordinary citizen. Says he isn't king anymore. Some people think Amin kidnapped him."

"That isn't hard to believe."

"Maybe he was just homesick," Howard said.

Bertrand frowned. "I can tell you the Mwami's return has completely upended the conversation here. It so happens that for the past year the president and his ruling party have been searching for royalist plots under every rock. And then the ex-king himself steps off a helicopter! Now they suspect that Charles, who is guarded night and day, who cannot leave his confinement, or use a telephone, or meet anyone, is somehow organizing an invasion of foreign mercenaries. They're going nuts with their conspiracy theories, I tell you. We're on a knife's edge. It's like the whole country is holding its breath, waiting for something to happen."

Bertrand took a long drink of beer, wiped his mouth. "Please don't think the old Burundi was a paradise. Poverty was rampant. It was profoundly unequal. None of that mattered. What really destabilized Burundi, and Rwanda, were democracy and majority rule. That's right. Universal truths for us Westerners. They're poison here."

"That's because politics becomes all one thing or all the other, isn't it?" Swee'Pea said. "I mean, the parties create political identities, and the politicians sell them."

"Things fell apart in '65," Howard said. "Am I right?"

"The killing began after that first election," I nodded.

Bertrand put his palms on the table. "That's correct. In '65, the old Mwami, Charles's father, finally called an election. He'd put it off as long as he could. Hutu expectations were through the roof since they are the great majority. Not surprisingly, Hutu politicians won the most seats in parliament. But trying to maintain equilibrium, the king declined to appoint a Hutu prime minister, naming a courtier instead."

"English elections can be exciting, but normally no one gets killed," Howard laughed.

"Naturally, many Hutus were furious," Bertrand continued. "Then they gambled, and lost. Hutu army officers revolted, shot the prime minister, attacked the palace. The old king fled the country, never to return. With him went the monarchy's last shreds of legitimacy, the faith that the Crown, the country's central institution, was above politics." Bertrand folded his hands. "The army fractured. Repression was fierce. The Tutsi-dominated army shot scores of Hutu soldiers and Hutu politicians."

"Either way," Howard said, "a bloodbath was unavoidable."

"It seems to me," Beatrice said, "those Hutu rebels lost more than their lives. Because of what they did no Hutu can be given a position of trust."

"Quite so. The government won't hire Hutus now to do anything."

"How did the rest of the country react in '65?" Swee'Pea asked.

"Hutus revered the Mwami. Plus, they believed he was the only force blocking a Tutsi power grab. Suspecting Tutsis had forced him out, they began killing Tutsis in the countryside, torching their homes. In revenge, the army killed Hutus. They massacred five thousand before they were done."

Alphonse laid out plates of fruit and cakes. We had all fallen silent. Everyone was staring ahead, as if in a trance, listening to the insects throbbing outside in the vast African night. Swee'Pea was fading. Beatrice was playing with a bottle cap.

"Bertrand, all I hear on the government radio is nonstop revolutionary jargon," Howard said.

"Marxism is in fashion everywhere," Beatrice scoffed. "Everyone is a Marxist these days."

Bertrand smiled. "President Micombero fancies himself a revolutionary, on a par with Danton or Robespierre, and you can see why. He started out on the bottom, as the son of provincial cow herders. Then he became the army's first African officer, crushed the Hutu uprising of '65, deposed Charles, established a republic and abolished the monarchy. So you see . . ."

"But I think Micombero has every reason to fear revolution," Howard said. "He may spout Marxist rhetoric and claim Burundi is a revolutionary state, but his Marxist slogans won't work. They'll come back to bite him. His military regime has no mass legitimacy. Did he forget he's trying to preserve Tutsi minority rule? He's actually the opposite of a revolutionary."

"He might have started out as a peasant or proletarian," Beatrice laughed, "but this isn't revolutionary France. It's really gone to their heads."

"Imagine, president of a country at age twenty-six." I winked at Swee'Pea. "That's not much older than me."

Swee'Pea rolled her eyes. "Does Micombero really know what he's doing?" she asked.

"Not entirely," Bertrand said. "He's walking a tightrope, thinks he's rooting out counterrevolutionary plots."

"Sounds like Micombero was at the right place at the right time, like Idi Amin," Swee'Pea said. "Amin was the army's ranking Ugandan at independence."

Howard leaned in to whisper something but Bertrand shook his head. "No, I'm not worried about what my staff might overhear. Believe me, they've heard far worse. And in French. Besides, I'm sure the authorities don't pay much attention to what happens down by the lake here in Nyanza Lac. We're about as far from the capital as you can get." He pushed his chair back. "Let me find another Primus."

Bertrand came back from the kitchen with two large bottles. "We're lucky to have electricity, or else no cold beer." He smiled, filling glasses all around.

Then Swee'Pea said, "When I was a little girl in Uganda we saw pictures of Tutsi refugees streaming in from Rwanda, thousands of them. I remember my parents telling me that thousands of Tutsis were being killed in Rwanda, their bodies thrown into rivers for crocodiles to eat."

"When did this killing in Rwanda start?" Beatrice asked.

"While the Belgians and the Catholics were preaching majority rule and Hutu emancipation," I piped up, "anti-Tutsi pogroms kept breaking out. In '62 at independence, the pogroms became an official reign of terror. Tutsis were assaulted on the street, taunted to go back to Ethiopia, or Egypt, as if they were foreigners."

"Karl, I had no idea you knew so much about Rwanda," Swee'Pea smiled at me sleepily.

"'Overthrow the Tutsi oppressors.' What a perfect revolutionary slogan!" Beatrice sneered, throwing her bottle cap onto the table. "What it really means is physically eliminating thousands of people. The Rwandan government openly calls them cockroaches."

"Let's say," Howard began calmly, turning to Beatrice, "you're a Hutu. You have a Tutsi neighbor. Say you're in debt to him. Or maybe he once did something or said something you didn't like. The politicians are screaming to get the Tutsi boot off Hutu necks. Anyone can throw a match on a thatch roof and watch it burn like a torch. You look around and see other people killing their Tutsi neighbors. Now what was once unthinkable is not so unthinkable anymore. If your neighbor dies, you can steal his cattle. Rape his daughters and his wife. Your debt vanishes. You get your revenge. Life opens up. You may even take his house, his barns, his fields, his farm implements. There's no penalty, no sanction, no punishment for killing Tutsis. You can kill as many as you like. That's what it was like in Rwanda a few years back."

"Howard's right," I said. "Late in '63 things really got bad in Rwanda. Tutsi killings began in earnest. The British philosopher Bertrand Russell compared them to Nazis murdering Jews. Except the Hutus were even more systematic, more ruthless. More brutal. They used pangas." I made chopping motions with one of the knives on the table. "They boasted of being the master race. More than four hundred thousand Tutsis fled for their lives."

"It was tremendous." Bertrand paused a moment. "That's a tenth of the population. Can you imagine how this tidal wave of terrorized, destitute Tutsi refugees from Rwanda affected Burundi politics?" he asked, looking around. "No one in Burundi, Hutu or Tutsi, could ever say anything positive about Hutus after that."

"To me," Beatrice said, "this sounds exactly like what we Germans did in Europe. The evil starts at the top. Political leaders spreading racial hatred as a path to power. Once your Jewish neighbors disappear or are deported, everything changes forever, doesn't it? You can take their property, move into their apartment. Everyone is complicit up to their necks. There's no going back. It constantly accelerates. And it's contagious. I think Burundi is infected."

Stroking his beard, Bertrand said, "Burundi's political institutions go back centuries. They're much older than many European countries. But we're not in a good place right now. Suspicion, mistrust, hatred are rampant. The government is making things worse."

"How so?" Swee'Pea asked.

"Well, the government is incompetent. It's corrupt. It discriminates against Hutus."

"In that case the Kigali newspapers are right," Beatrice said. "They claim Hutus can't get jobs in Burundi."

"That's true, I'm afraid. The Tutsi government wants people they can trust. They often hire family members. Loyalty is more important than ability. Even Tutsi high school dropouts with connections are getting big jobs. Hutus resent this, of course. Especially educated Hutus."

"Here's the problem as I see it," Howard said. "Tutsis hold practically every government job, right? They control the army. They've completely shut out the Hutus. What option do Hutus have besides armed rebellion?"

"It's a self-fulfilling prophecy, this talk of Hutu insurrection," I said. "Tutsis are afraid. But the more they oppress Hutus, the more Hutus want revenge. If you asked me, I'd say Micombero is sitting on a volcano."

"*C'est vrai.*" Bertrand swirled beer around his glass. "Hutu extremists are in power in Rwanda. Tutsi extremists are running Burundi. For Tutsis, Rwanda is their biggest nightmare. But if I were a Hutu here, Rwanda might be my temptation."

Beatrice glanced up sharply. "You're saying Burundi could go the way of Rwanda, aren't you?"

"But in which direction?" Swee'Pea asked. "Who will die?"

"*Eh bién*," Bertrand sighed. "Obviously, the government's greatest fear is a Hutu uprising. But who would lead it? Practically all the Hutu soldiers and politicians are dead or in jail."

"Unless!" Beatrice grinned. "Unless Hutu insurgents are quietly burrowing underground, like the Old Mole."[27]

"Maybe." Bertrand stretched his neck, looking at the ceiling. "I think just now Micombero is more worried about Tutsis who want to bring back the monarchy."

Etienne called to Bertrand. "*Excusez moi*. Apparently, I have a visitor." The screen door slammed as Bertrand walked outside onto the dark veranda. We could hear a hiss of quick utterances peppered with notes of surprise and separated by long pauses until Bertrand returned, lost in thought.

"Interesting. That was Georges, by the way. One of the Tutsi profs. It seems we have some unexplained absences among the junior Hutu profs at school."

"What do you mean?" Beatrice said.

"A bunch of them haven't shown up for days. They've vanished. No one really knows where they are," Bertrand said.

"How strange!" Howard said. "No one knows where they are?"

"Oh," Swee'Pea said, "that reminds me, Bertrand. Something odd happened on the way here. A young man rushed up to me and said something I didn't understand."

"What did he say?" Howard asked.

Swee'Pea looked around at everyone looking at her. "Apparently, he thought I was someone he knew. In Swahili he asked me, 'Why aren't you in the forest with the others?' Then, realizing his mistake, he ran away."

"The forest?" Beatrice sat up. "The forest? That's where my radical German friends would go to make bombs. The forest is good for two

---

27 *We recognize our old friend, our old mole, who knows so well how to work underground, suddenly to appear: the revolution.* Karl Marx

things," she declared, "witchcraft and insurrection. It sounds to me like they're sharpening their knives in the woods."

Everyone was quiet. What a damned cauldron we'd walked into! At least we'd only be here a week, at most. With those somber thoughts in our heads we turned in for the night, though Howard lingered to talk with Bertrand. Swee'Pea and I headed to our room. We hadn't had a moment to ourselves all day. Someone knocked on the door. Howard was pacing in the corridor.

"What's up, Howard?"

"It's actually worse than we thought. Bertrand told me every young Hutu schoolteacher down to primary has been missing since last week. Georges claims they're all in Tanzania."

"But that's— What could it mean? They're plotting something?"

"Or they know something's going to happen in Nyanza Lac. Beatrice is bouncing off the walls. She says we have to get out. Leave Burundi. Tomorrow."

"What?"

"Bertrand thinks it'll all become clear by the weekend. There's some big official meeting on the twenty-ninth. Saturday night."

"What day is this? Tuesday?"

"It's Tuesday, April 25." Howard looked at his watch. "About one in the morning."

President Idi Amin of Uganda (right) shakes hands with former King Ntare V of Burundi in Kampala, Uganda, March 30, 1972. Charles Ntare, the twenty-four-year-old former *Mwami* (king), was arrested in Burundi shortly after their meeting on charges of leading white mercenaries in the invasion of his country. (AP Photo)

26. MAY DAY
(JAKE)

Not sticking with Karl and Swee'Pea had consequences. First of all, I never got to Rwanda. After I left them in that downpour a French guy stopped who was not going to Rwanda, but to Zaïre, via the border crossing at Ishasha River. He took the right fork off the Kabale road after only a few miles. It was still raining like hell when we reached the fork. I didn't want to get out in the rain, so I decided to continue with him to Zaïre. Later, I sent a postcard from Goma to Kigali *poste restante* to tell Karl I'd meet them in Burundi at Bertrand's place in Nyanza Lac. They never got it.

Jean, the driver, a movie producer, was filming something in Zaïre. His English was so-so. We drove through Queen Elizabeth National Park around the southern end of Lake Edouard. When the rain stopped, the fog cleared. There was wildlife in great numbers everywhere on the plains—elephant, giraffe, zebra, wildebeest, buffalo, antelope. It was dreamy, unearthly. Neolithic.

We crossed into Zaïre's Kivu province. I held my breath at Ugandan passport control, but they ignored the *No Facilities* mark and stamped me out. Jean left me in Rutshuru. Basically a truck stop at a crossroads, Rutshuru is not for honeymooners. The place made me feel like a marked man, where everyone turned to size me up whenever I entered a room. The bars in Rutshuru were filled with hungry women. I won't say they were unattractive, but mostly they were persistent. After several aggressive encounters, and dreading having to overnight there, I remembered my tent. So I walked out into the dark. Maybe it was a bit risky with me stumbling around trying to find a clear patch of ground off the road that was not in the middle of someone's shamba.[28] Finally I located what I thought was a pretty good spot near the road but out of town. I was tired. My sleeping bag was still dry, somehow, after all that rain. I slept well, though I heard something snuffling outside the tent near my head before dawn.

A loud humming noise awakened me. I looked out. Bees. The air was full of them. The tent was covered with bees. I jumped out nimbly as I could, zipping the tent flap behind me. Bees were swarming everywhere. I remembered our pastor back home in Nebraska quoting Psalms. *"My enemies surrounded me like bees, but they were extinguished like fiery thorns."* Bees shot left and right, landed on me, crawled all over me. Lucky they were more interested in the tent. I had camped next to a tree with a giant beehive dangling from a branch about eight feet above the ground. A seething mass covered the blue rain fly. I was afraid I'd have to abandon the tent. I walked across the road to wait them out, hoping the bees might fly off. It took several hours but they started to thin out. Most of them swarmed back to the hive. It was tricky shooing the bees away, tricky to take the tent down, pack everything up, hike out with them flying all around divebombing me. I got stung a few times. Rubbing the welts on my arms and my neck, I flagged down a truck going to Goma.

Goma was a fine place to spend a week. Its mile-high elevation brought hot dry days and cold nights with occasional downpours. Beautiful cauliflower, broccoli, and all kinds of Western vegetables abounded, I guess because of the cool climate and fertile soil. I missed Karl, and Swee'Pea. I liked Swee'Pea fine, but she had stolen my partner. Though I bumped into a few travelers like me in Zaïre, I was pretty isolated. I couldn't speak French and the Zaïrois spoke no English.

But some Europeans I met did speak English. In the '60s the

---

28 Cultivated plot.

Simbas drove out all the Whites, I heard. Now White people were back running everything—shops, businesses, restaurants, hotels, gas stations, churches, hospitals, the airport. Hell, Greek Cypriots were driving the trucks. It was like independence never happened. The place was like South Africa, without Apartheid or White police. I figured Mobutu was getting a big cut of the action.

Then there was this volcano. Less than ten miles from Goma back up the road toward Rutshuru a volcano called Nyiragongo was erupting like Mount Doom. I never saw Nyiragongo from the road coming down from Rutshuru, I was too close to it. But in Goma it filled half the horizon. By day, it shot an endless column of noiseless billowing white smoke and ash straight into the stratosphere. By night, lightning bolts illuminated that huge cloud, silhouetting the dark cone, while red sparks flashed from the crater. No one in Goma paid it the slightest mind, like it was the most normal, most harmless, and most boring thing. Nothing they could do about it, of course. The ash was clearly falling somewhere else.

But I was fascinated. Next day I caught a ride out of town and got off at the trail marker. It was a tough slog up to tree line, over eleven thousand feet, then a scramble up the scree to the summit. The wind was frigid. My fingers were too frozen to zip open my pack. The crater was a mile wide at least. In the center was a pool of seething red lava with fountains of molten rock exploding at intervals hundreds of feet into the air. Some fool had actually pitched a tent directly below me on the crater floor.

To the south of Goma is Lake Kivu. And on another day, I climbed the hills above the deserted shoreline. The lake is fifty miles long and you couldn't see the other end. The lake water was fairly pure, swimmable, but stinking of volcanic sulfur. I wondered if lava from Nyiragongo someday might pour into Lake Kivu and boil off the water. It seemed like the whole landscape was getting ready to blow.

From Goma I took the ferry to Bukavu, a pleasant town on the southern end of the lake, where I spent some days trying out restaurants. I hitched down to Uvira on Lake Tanganyika, where I overnighted. Uvira was hot; it's half a mile lower in altitude than Bukavu or Goma. Bujumbura was clearly visible at the head of the lake. After an hour of walking and sweating I reached the Burundi border. Scowling at me, the customs guy stamped me in for one month. The stamp read *28 AVRIL 1972.*

Bujumbura was on edge, like the whole city was having a nervous breakdown. It was surreal. The place was tense, suspicious, watchful. Everyone was unfriendly, sinister, depressed. I don't think I saw a single smile that day. Shopkeepers, waiters, people in the street gave me weird looks, watched me when I passed. Not out of curiosity, like in Ethiopia, but out of suspicion. I found a cheap hotel, telling myself I'd leave town the next day.

It was Friday night. I went out to have a drink. As I sat at the bar two men at a table across the room whispered to each other, their eyes on me. After ten minutes of this, up walked a lanky guy, who'd been sitting by himself.

"Please follow me," he said curtly in English, like it was an order. I walked with him out of the bar. He turned when we got to the street.

"Can I drive you anywhere?"

"I'm in a hotel around the corner. What's the matter?"

He took a step toward me and lowered his voice. "Those guys in the bar?" I nodded. "They were talking about killing you. They think you are CIA."

"CIA? Not me. Who are they?"

"Shh. Shh. Military intelligence." He drew closer, whispering. "They hang out at this bar. We hear rumors every day of a mercenary invasion."

"Me? A mercenary?"

"You look more like a hitchhiker to me than CIA," he agreed, quickly looking over my shoulder at the bar.

"Why do you want to help me?" I asked.

"Those guys," he jutted his thumb sharply over my shoulder back toward the bar, "they're nuts. They believe their own propaganda. Now the Mwami is here, everyone is nervous."

"Wait a minute. Who's the Mwami?"

"The former king. Charles Ntare." I looked at him blankly. He continued, sounding irritated. "In 1966 when Charles was away, the military took over and ended the monarchy. Charles stayed in exile. One month ago, out of the blue, he's back. No one knows why."

Still made no sense. "Where is this Mwami now?"

"He's under house arrest in Gitega."

"What's all this got to do with me?"

The man shook his head, as if signaling it had nothing to do with me.

"So let me get this straight," I continued. "Military intelligence thinks I'm part of a mercenary army to reinstate the Mwami, who is currently under arrest?"

"I know this makes no sense to a foreigner."

"Is that why everyone is acting so strangely?"

He put his hands in his pockets, slowly nodding his head. "There's a legend, or a superstition, that the coming of a new Mwami could signal a Hutu rebellion." I was gaping at him. The man looked to the side, digging his hands deeper into his pockets. "This has happened before in our history," he insisted. "Many Hutus believe the Mwami is on their side. Please go back to your hotel now. It's dangerous for you to be on the street."

I got to my room, but before I fell asleep I heard a click. Someone had locked the door to my room from the hallway. I was locked in. I pounded on the door. Nothing. Then I went back to bed. I was probably safer locked in my room anyway. Around seven in the morning, I heard the lock click open.

It was Saturday morning, April 29. Monday was May Day, a national holiday. It was the start of a rare three-day weekend, someone told me. I had thought to spend the holiday in Bujumbura, but not now. I wanted out. I took a bus to Rumonge,[29] a big town a few hours south on Lake Tanganyika.

That afternoon the air in Rumonge was electric; I sensed it right away. Something was happening but I didn't know what. Crowded streets, perhaps normal for a Saturday, bunches of high school-age boys milled around, talking among themselves, truck traffic driving both ways through town, soldiers manning a roadblock by a new building. One student, speaking English, told me several ministers were expected that evening for a big government meeting. I figured I'd go on to Nyanza Lac Sunday to find Bertrand. Perhaps Karl, Swee'Pea, Howard, and Beatrice were already there. They probably were wondering what happened to me.

I walked to the edge of town through a brief shower, found a place to put my tent near a large tree and the beach on a small, abandoned field near the road. I waited until almost dark to pitch the tent. No one bothered me. I was bored. I had eaten something in town. There was nothing to do. It got too dark to read. I went to sleep.

Some sharp noises woke me up. It sounded like shooting. Like a machine gun. My watch said 7:30. I listened. I opened the tent flap. People were running both ways along the road. The shooting continued. I heard screaming, shouting. Or was it chanting? In a flash I knew I had to hide. But where? I crawled out of the tent. On the other side of the tree was a tiny shed. Turned out it was a corn rick. The door was flimsy. I forced it and secured it from inside. I lay down, burrowing deeply into the ears of corn. I could still see the road and the tent well enough through the corn and the cracks in the wall. It was 8:15.

The shooting continued all night. I wondered if this was the Hutu rebellion that guy in Bujumbura had told me about. I dared not move a muscle. I couldn't sleep. Then I saw them, a group of young men approaching through the dawn mist. They had machetes. They went straight to my tent, which was maybe a hundred yards from the rick,

---

29   pron. Ru-MOAN-gay

looked inside, looked around, then left. At that point, I knew I would have to abandon the rick. The tent would attract others. But before I could move, another group advanced from the road toward the tent. They slashed it with their machetes. They then approached the corn rick, surrounding it, peering inside. I kept still as I could, hoping the cobs covered my feet and legs. Someone cut down the door. At that moment, there was a sharp whistle, like you might hear at a basketball game. On the road I could make out a long double file of men holding machetes jogging slowly toward town. By my corn rick they were arguing. Then they left.

I slowly raised myself from the heap. The door was lying on the ground outside. Making sure no one was watching, I sprinted to the tree. I climbed as high as I could, at least a hundred feet off the ground. I looked and looked. Something was wrong. The road was littered with bodies. From the tree I could see trucks full of young men passing in both directions. Groups of people passed on foot waving machetes, shouting *"Bahutu Oye! Bahutu Oye!"* They were cheering for the Hutu, that much was plain. And they shouted *"Mayi Mulélé!"* but I could not understand it. And they hissed *"Batutsi zi!"* I guessed that meant Down with the Tutsi.

So far I was safe in the tree. No one could see me from the road. I had no food, but that was okay. I had to pee from time to time, but I found a way to do that. Late in the afternoon I was asking myself how long I'd be stuck up the tree when I saw a child looking up at me near the trunk. I didn't move but he kept looking at me. Then he disappeared. I didn't know what to do. *Get down fast,* my mind told me, but I had run out of hiding places. While I was thinking it over a group of four young men approached the tree. They did not look friendly. They wore red headbands. One had a pot on his head, painted red. They shouted in some language for me to get down. They had machetes, but I was a hundred feet above the ground, so I ignored them. We had a standoff until someone turned up with a rifle.

I climbed down. I shook so badly descending I almost fell off the tree. They stood waiting. Some were tattooed, some dressed in black. They were not happy with me. I expected them to kill me. But they didn't. They pointed their blades at me, shouted, made me empty my pockets, took my cash and travelers checks. I had to put it all on the ground before they would touch it. They were pretty hopped up. Their eyes were bloodshot. They questioned me in a few languages, but that went nowhere. I confessed to being an American tourist, but that made no difference. Gesturing with their pangas, they indicated I was to walk in front of them. There were three of them now. We began walking back to Rumonge, passing scores of dead bodies on the road, all of them with deep machete cuts. Flies swarmed everywhere. Hutu death squads were killing every Tutsi they could find.

After five minutes of walking my captors noticed something in the bush. Two of them dashed off the road, flushed out a woman. She stood. They took a few steps back, careful not to touch her. Then they prodded her with machetes until they were back on the road. *"Batutsi zi!"* one of them screeched. While I stood there, they taunted her, waving their pangas, screaming at her. Slowly, frantically, she removed her clothes. She stood naked, crying and sobbing. She was about seven, eight months pregnant. They pushed her down with the flat side of a panga. She kneeled, wailing, sobbing, bowing to them, throwing up her arms. One guy, shorter than the rest, swiped at an arm as she flung it up, cutting off a hand. She held up her severed wrist and looked at the blood spurting from it, amazed, as if she were in a trance. Another man in a red watch cap walked up. With a savage downward flick of his panga he sliced open her big belly. The fetus popped out, rabbit-sized, onto the road. They attacked it like it was a snake, hacking it to a red mash, while the woman screamed uncontrollably. The short one lunged forward. With an overhand smash he lopped off her other hand, then sliced off part of her foot. He whirled and made a savage cut to her shoulder. That was the sign for all of them to chop her and cut her until she was ripped to pieces, until there wasn't much proof that this bloody mound of bone and flesh ever had been a human being. The intact umbilical cord still attached what was left of the mother to the fetus, a grimy red splotch in the dust.

I prepared to die. I whispered the Lord's Prayer. I pictured my mother and father back in Nebraska. My sisters. Our farm. *Our Pastor taught us the Avenger of bloodshed does not forget the cry of the downtrodden.* But these ghouls ignored me. They wiped their machetes clean on the dead woman's clothes. Then we resumed our march into Rumonge. I couldn't believe I was still alive.

We entered a shop, stepping over a dead woman on the floor and pools of her thickening blood still seeping from a deep gash in the neck. Flies were intense. In the back several muzungus were sitting on the floor, guarded by a rebel. They were killing every Tutsi on sight but not muzungus. No, they were under orders, I had guessed. A man behind the counter in a crocheted white skullcap, I assumed a Pakistani, was selling merchandise to customers, just like it was an average day. One of my captors spoke to him in Swahili. It wasn't Kirundi. I'd been hearing Swahili in Goma and across the Lake in Zaïre. I jumped when the Pakistani spoke to me in clear English.

"They want to know your profession."

"I'm a, uh—" I was stumped for a moment. "Tell them mechanical engineer."

He translated this. There was a lot of talking.

The Pakistani then said, "They want to know, can you repair a truck?"

"I can try. Do they have tools?"

More talking. We left the shop. It was night now, Sunday night, April 30. We walked into a building near the main street and entered a deserted apartment where they locked me in a bathroom with a grilled window. My brain whirled. Too strung out to sleep, I stared at the ceiling and the walls all night. The lights worked.

I dozed off toward dawn. It was Monday. May Day. Someone yanked open the door. I found a cup of coffee on the floor, which I quickly drank. Two young men with machetes, one tall, one short, signaled me to follow. They led me down side streets to a field and a big dump truck. They produced a toolbox and made clear I was to go at it. They threw the keys to the truck on the ground in front of me and waved their pangas around. They gradually got bored watching me and sat under a tree in the shade. Lucky, they had no idea what I was doing.

I checked the electricals. The battery and the electricals were good, but the truck wouldn't start. Fuel was the problem. Right away I discovered the fuel filter was clogged. The fuel gauge was busted, and so I stuck a long stick down into the tank to check the fuel level. The tank was near empty. I told them they needed diesel, *mazout*, a word I had learned in Zaïre. The tall one went off to find some. That slowed things down. I pretended to work on the truck, took off the valve cover, put it back on, took it off again. The day grew hot and as I sweated, tsetse flies stung me right through my sopping shirt. Big, tough flies, I whacked them, hard, when they landed on me, but they just flew off and came right back at me. Two hours later the tall one returned with a heavy tin full of fuel. I checked it was diesel and carefully poured it into the tank. No surprise, the truck still wouldn't start. I reckoned nothing was wrong with the truck but the fuel filter, which I could easily bypass. But I was playing for time, trying to run down the clock on the rebellion. I hoped it was running out of steam. Or else maybe they'd already overrun the entire country with pogroms spreading everywhere. I wished I could hear what was on the radio. Ah, it would be in French anyway, or some other language I couldn't understand. Where was the Burundi army?

Damned if I'd give them a working truck no matter how badly they wanted it. But my two pals with the machetes were getting impatient as the day wore on. I kept fiddling with the engine and swatting flies. They gave up on me around four o'clock, placed the tools in the passenger side, made me put the truck keys on the ground again, and marched me back to the flat. Then they locked me in the bathroom again. I remembered I had not eaten in two days.

At dusk I heard a distant buzz. It got louder. It was a helicopter. I looked out the window. A helicopter flew by spraying the main street with machinegun fire. The helicopter made several passes. I heard screaming and shouting. I supposed it was the Burundi air force. Locked in a bathroom I had the best seat in the house. I got some sleep that night. By dawn I wondered what was going on. It was quiet, like everyone had cleared out. I figured I maybe could open the old-style, keyhole-type door lock with a bent nail, so I went to work extracting a nail from the baseboards. It took me about an hour. I bent the nail this way, that way. In another hour I got the door open. Immediately I ran for the truck. They had left the tools. I removed the fuel filter, then joined the fuel lines, hot-wired the ignition. The truck started. I had like five gallons of fuel. Tanzania was about sixty kilometers down the road. That was plenty.

I drove off. Except for the bodies on the roads and in the fields, Rumonge was deserted. When they saw the helicopter, I was thinking, the rebels knew the jig was up and ran to ground. I drove and drove, cruised along, avoiding bodies and debris. *The Lord is my light and my salvation. Whom shall I fear?* Rebels jumped out of the way at the few roadblocks that were still manned; sometimes they shot at me but the truck easily pushed obstacles aside or rolled over them. I never slowed down. Once a giant log on the road forced me off through a meadow, but I kept going.

As I approached Nyanza Lac, I wondered about Karl and Swee'Pea and Howard and Beatrice. I hoped they weren't in Burundi. *Did they ever get to meet Bertrand?* A rifleman stepped into the middle of the road from behind a flimsy roadblock, drawing a bead on me. I admired his nerve. The truck was going about fifty miles an hour, gaining on him every second, but he calmly stood and pulled off two rounds. But not before I ducked my head. The windshield shattered. The truck burst through the roadblock. I sat upright and saw his rifle still pointing at me when the truck hit him. Maybe he wanted to die. Through a side mirror I saw his body on the road. He died easier than a tsetse fly. A little like Pudge.

∼

The way ahead was now clear, but I feared I wouldn't get through the crowd rushing to the border. A helicopter bobbed into view in the side mirror. It dove down to the treetops and strafed the road. The truck bed clanged as .50 caliber slugs hit it. All ages raced forward, old people, women, children, youngsters, and many young men. They were Hutus, mostly, I had guessed. They had ditched the machetes. The helicopter made another pass, guns roaring. I blasted the horn. People rippled out of the way, dotting the road with the dead and dying.

The human torrent surged toward Tanzania, pursued by the Burundi air force. I had to slow down. People scrambled onto the bed and pulled open the passenger door, jumping into the cab. I could barely turn the wheel because of the crush in the front seat. I finally stopped the truck, jumped out, but the panicked crowds pushed me forward. Dust rose into the air churned by hundreds of unshod feet. The crowd started to thin and slow down. I walked another half mile. There were soldiers on the road with rifles. They spoke to me in English. I was in Tanzania.

27. SERGEANT MASINDA
(JAKE)

Jubilant though I was after crossing the border, I was not out of the soup. Not by a long shot. In Tanzania I was a bright speck of white foam in a black sea. Barking at me in English, the border guards stripped me naked, found my passport in my underpants, and led me behind a building to a group of Whites they had collected, Belgians mostly, sitting on the ground under guard. I was the youngest, the only English speaker.

A heavyset sergeant appeared. He picked me out of the group, led me off to a separate, small building. His name was Masinda. He said he was holding me on suspicion of being a mercenary. Apparently, the Burundi government was broadcasting this particular fantasy night and day, about Charles Ntare's mercenary army, I found out later. The Tanzanians believed it, too, or wanted to. It's easy to blame your troubles on the imperialist foreigners. On people of a different race. Well, there'd been all those White mercenaries just across Lake Tanganyika in the Congo not so many years ago, never mind they'd gone in on orders from the Congolese government to restore order. I'll always remember the industrious Sergeant Masinda. He interrogated me for days. I assumed I would be shot.

Masinda was disciplined, patient, and relentless. Plus, he had stamina. He kept at it, all alone, day-in, day-out, making me repeat my story at least two hundred times, pouncing on the slightest slip or variation, until I was practically gaga. Why had I entered Burundi? Who did I meet there? How many mercenaries did I know? What did

I do in the States? Who had recruited me? What weapons had I used? How many people had I killed? What had I done in Uganda? Where had I trained? Who was paying me? Why had I gone to Rumonge? Where did I get my tent? He demanded the names and nationalities of my non-existent comrades and superior officers from this Never-Never military organization.

Many of Masinda's questions were hard to answer. For instance, how could someone claiming to be a tourist, with no connections in Burundi, who could not even speak the languages, have acquired a truck? What I had done in Uganda also was not easy to explain. Letting slip something about our long trek across Ruwenzori was a mistake. To Masinda it sounded like infiltration, or cover for a suspicious training mission. I thought it was best not to mention Swee'Pea. Or jail. Or the British Embassy. Or Lonnie. Or Pudge. Soldiers searched me, searched me again, spread-eagled me on the sand for hours, beat me with rifle butts. If I had lost my passport in Burundi, I'm sure they would have shot me on the spot. My precious passport posed its own problems. The *No Facilities* stamp proved to Masinda that I had entered Uganda illegally, possibly by stealth. By stealth? I pointed out that the Ugandan authorities were well aware of my irregular visa status. Hence the stamp. Plus they had stamped me out. That stumped him.

The Tanzanians locked me in an outhouse. It was a smelly, thatched affair, a big step down from my high-end accommodations in Rumonge. Sometimes they brought me a little cooked rice and water. *One day at a time,* I kept telling myself. After maybe two weeks of constant interrogations and beatings, a young military intelligence officer came up from Kigoma. I feared he would convene a military tribunal, sentence me, and put me before a firing squad. But that was not it. He was trim, shorter than me or Masinda, good-looking with a mustache, calm, decisive. Lieutenant Murombe and I quickly became friends. For lack of a better word, he saved me.

∼

From the start I could see there was bad blood between the veteran Sergeant Masinda and the upstart Lieutenant Murombe. Masinda was sure I was guilty as hell. But there was pressure to release me from higher up, or so I gathered, possibly because a dead American would pose problems in Dar es Salaam. And orders were orders, thank God!

By the time Lieutenant Murombe reached me it might have been blindingly obvious that the bedlam in Burundi was not due to invading White mercenaries. After Murombe arranged my release, we took the boat together to Kigoma where I got cleaned up at an army camp. Murombe had a doctor look me over, gave me some clothing and shoes and an old army rucksack, bought me breakfast, handed me a hundred shillings, apologized for how I had been treated, and sent me on my way.

"You're a brave man," he said, shaking my hand.

I stood alone on the street where Murombe left me. I had no idea where I was.

28. BY THE LAKE
(KARL)

The sun was setting over the mountains in Zaïre. The lake shimmering gold. We were in Ujiji, down the beach from Kigoma, Tanzania, the sixth African country I'd seen since leaving England.

Beatrice squinted, pointing at a figure on the beach trudging slowly toward us. "Who's that? Looks like a white man."

"That's Jake!" I said, jumping up.

When he saw me running, he dropped his pack. I hugged him so hard we both nearly fell over.

"Jake. You're alive!"

"So are you!" We embraced, laughing. He looked beat.

"Jake, we were afraid you didn't make it. We were afraid they killed you."

He laughed. "Sorry I missed you in Kigali. Is everyone here?"

"Everyone. We all want to see you. Come, come." I picked up his pack. It weighed nothing. "What happened to all your stuff?"

"It's a long story. The Tanzanian military gave me this pack. I guess they felt bad for me. I lost the tent and everything else."

Howard ran up, excitedly. "Jake, Jake, you are a man of surprises."

"Life can be surprising."

"Another grand entrance. Remember how you arrived in Lamu during that wedding procession? How are you, old man?" Howard slapped him on the back.

Jake winced. "All right, except for this." He pulled up his shirt to show us a badly bruised, slightly bleeding wound above the hip where the bandage was coming off. "The Tanzanians let me go yesterday. I was locked up. They beat me up a little. They thought I was a mercenary."

Howard looked at the injury. "It could be infected. We'll get you to a doctor."

"Jake, let's look at you." Beatrice kissed him on both cheeks. "My God, you've lost weight. You need to eat."

Swee'Pea was next. "Jake, is that you?" She took both his hands in hers and started to cry. "I am so happy to see you."

I spread out my sleeping bag for a picnic on the beach. Swee'Pea ran back to get our food—a little rice, some fish stew, a few bananas. We sat spellbound listening to Jake describe what he saw and did since we parted in Uganda. Jake confirmed that Hutu murder squads in Rumonge had begun killing Tutsis after dark on Saturday, April 29. The story about Jake's May 2 escape from Burundi left us speechless. I didn't understand how he survived.

We found a doctor to patch him up, then found a restaurant. The five of us sat around a table together again for the first time since Mombasa.

"You know," Howard said, "Ujiji is where Stanley met Livingstone."

"What?" Beatrice said. "Who?"

"Henry Morton Stanley? The American journalist?"

Beatrice shook her head.

"Hired by *The New York Herald* to find David Livingstone, a missionary Scotsman who'd been missing for years."

"That was a hundred years ago, wasn't it?" I asked.

"Almost exactly. At the end of 1871, six months after leaving Zanzibar," Howard continued. "Stanley arrived at that ridge above town." Howard waved vaguely behind him. "And found Livingstone. And became famous. And set off the scramble for Africa."

Jake looked up briefly from his second plate of chicken. "I never heard of Stanley or Livingstone."

That Monday evening at Bertrand's house in Nyanza Lac, what now seemed ages ago, we all had a sinking feeling in our stomachs when we learned that practically every young Hutu schoolteacher in town had decamped for Tanzania or simply disappeared. And that strange young man who had blabbed some seriously secret information to Swee'Pea . . . These were clear signals. And hadn't Bertrand assured us that practically every option was closed for Burundi Hutus except rebellion? After working on Howard all that night and into the next day, Beatrice had urged us all to leave. Immediately. She was calm but implacable; young Hutu schoolteachers must have known something was coming and wanted no part of it. Or maybe they were preparing to join in. We spent two days trying to convince Bertrand, but he waved off our arguments, accusing us of overreacting, of panicking.

"I don't expect the Apocalypse," he kept repeating.

Glum, he stood alone on the veranda when we cleared out early on Thursday morning, April 27. We were skipping town and abandoning him. We got to Kigoma by ferry later that evening, two nights before the uprising, as it turned out. We weren't sure about anything, of course, and when news of the rebellion hit we were in shock like everyone else.

By May 2, the Hutu rebels already had killed hundreds of people, most of them Tutsis. But the rebels had bungled badly, and the army regained its nerve. On the night of the insurrection rebels failed to capture the national radio station in Bujumbura, while their clumsy attacks on military bases put the army on high alert. The Hutu countryside knew nothing of the revolt.

News of massacre and counter-massacre trickled slowly out of Burundi, while panicked Hutus and Tutsis flooded into northwestern Tanzania. Within days there were thousands of them in and around Kigoma. We were worried sick about Bertrand in Nyanza Lac. In fact, no one saw Bertrand again. Howard told me Bertrand almost certainly perished on the evening of April 29, at the big municipal meeting he had been so keen to attend. That night's meeting and others like it throughout Burundi, we learned, had been traps sprung by rebel collaborators to wipe out local Tutsi officials as the insurrection was unloosed. Howard later went to France with Beatrice to console Bertrand's family. We had been the last friends to see him alive.

Shellshocked Europeans in the streets of Kigoma told me their desperate stories while I struggled with my poor French. That evening, while writing a dispatch for Harold, Swee'Pea said, "Karl, do you realize you're in a unique position to record history? I wonder why you aren't taking advantage of it?"

"Sure, Swee'Pea. Isn't that what I'm doing?"

"If you ask me, you're missing the story."

This ticked me off. "What do you mean? I'm interviewing everyone I can find."

She shook her head. "Karl, this isn't a story about how a few Europeans got the fright of their lives. Most of them escaped without harm. The rebels were not even trying to kill them."

I was slow to understand what she was getting at.

"This is a major event, Karl," she went on. "It's world news. You're right at its doorstep. You've got to do more than repeat second-hand information and rumors from a few muzungus. Maybe some of the Catholic Church people have an inkling but most Europeans don't have the slightest idea what's going on. You need to talk to the Africans. They're the ones who suffered through this. They actually know something."

"How will I do that?"

"I'll help you. Some refugees speak French, some speak Swahili. You've got to jump on this, Karl. It's a big opportunity. And there's no one else who can do it besides you."

Swee'Pea was right. She might have added that Kigoma was about as accessible for international news reporters as Tibet.

Next morning, and day after day, Swee'Pea and I went to interview Hutus and Tutsis in the teeming camps that grew up overnight. I'd ask the questions, or sometimes she asked the questions. She translated both ways. At night we tried to make sense of our notes. It was tricky. Many of our sources had something to hide. For example, lots of rebels had fled for their lives to Tanzania, but they had astounding insights, when we could get them to open up. There was also a sprinkling of Burundi army deserters who could give up-close accounts of the massacres being perpetrated by the Burundi army. Howard and Beatrice soon joined us. We recruited several trilingual French-Kirundi-Swahili speakers who interpreted and reported for us. Money was tight. They needed every cent we could pay them. Everyone wanted the truth to come out.

At one point, after we recorded a particularly grisly murder, Swee'Pea put her arms around me and hugged me tight. She was shaking and sobbing. "Karl, you know the army would have killed me if we stayed in Burundi?" I squeezed her back. "God bless Beatrice," I said. I thanked God we got out when we did.

Swee'Pea somehow scrounged an old typewriter. From scores of interviews, we pieced together the story of the aborted revolution and the ferocious murders that followed.

The insurrection's intellectual authors were disaffected Hutu students, who, being Hutus, had no career prospects in Burundi. They had spent the years after the failed revolt in '65 shuttling quietly between Burundi and Tanzania, surreptitiously gathering recruits, money, and arms, not to mention secretly trucking thousands of machetes, or *pangas*, into Burundi, while training foot soldiers in the forest. The rebels hired Swahili-speaking Congolese, former Simba rebels from Tanzania and from the refugee camps along the lake, to oversee ritual scarification and tattooing and teach them magic spells. To turn bullets into water, for instance. Rebel planning in the lakeside towns of southern Burundi was meticulous. But the campaign itself was poorly thought out. The sleeping Hutu giant the rebels needed to enrage did not live in the towns. As events unfolded, the rural Hutu masses were hostile or indifferent to these citified killers. At first, they even helped the army hunt them down.

Hutu savagery in southern Burundi, which Jake saw firsthand, was like nothing compared with what came next. When the army rolled into Rumonge and Nyanza Lac, they didn't bother picking up rebel suspects. They simply shot every Hutu in sight, tens of thousands of them. And they likely would have shot Swee'Pea, too. This bloody spasm swiftly became planned butchery. When nerves steadied after the initial panic, the Tutsi government ordered the army to eliminate all educated Hutus, even those with a smattering of grade school. Their cold logic—exterminating them now would buy twenty years of peace. Each day refugees brought sickening news of mass executions in Burundi. At night, we learned, the bodies were being dumped in deep trenches near Bujumbura's international airport.

Before summer ended the Burundi army had shot more than one hundred thousand people. The killings continued into 1973. They averaged a thousand killings a day for months.

I wrote to my parents from Kigoma in early May telling them where I was. It was a short letter. I left out anything that might worry them, which meant I left out almost everything. My mother wrote back immediately, enclosing a letter from Helen. I opened it with trepidation.

> *May 27, 1972*
> *Dear Karl,*
> *Your mother was kind enough to contact me with your new address. I know you must be wondering about the birth. The baby was born on May 5. It was a fairly easy delivery. I've been breast feeding, changing diapers, learning to be a mom. It's a beautiful baby boy, by the way, strong like his father. And what a loud voice. He eats a lot! And he's making me sore, he sucks so hard. I have something to tell you, Karl. It's a feeling I had*

the first time I saw the baby. It's just, when I first looked at him, it's so overwhelming, Karl, to hold a baby that's your own. But that's not what I mean. Something was different about the baby from what I expected. I mean something about the way he looked. No, there's nothing wrong with how the baby looks. Like I said, he's beautiful. Karl, I spent nine months dreaming about you and me and the baby and about us being together as a family, but I now realize the baby isn't yours. That was a big shock. I was sure you were the father but you are not the father, Karl. I miscalculated. If I'm being honest, I miscalculated a lot. I should not have been seeing another man when I was still with you. Then I somehow got pregnant when I didn't mean to. And I got pregnant with someone else. You remember things were getting rocky with us last summer? And you made it clear that you were going away? And I cried in bed on the last night we were together? I was beside myself because you were leaving. I traveled to England after I got pregnant just to see you again. To see if you wanted me. I hoped you wanted me. I was sure it was your baby. I was so sure. But the baby isn't yours, Karl. He looks exactly like his father. Exactly. The father's name is Mark Guthrie. I don't think you know him. We saw each other once or twice the month before you went to Europe. Of course, I never told you. This pregnancy wasn't supposed to happen, but I guess things got a little out of control.

Last week I told Mark that he's a father. He was so happy about it. This is confusing for me. I thought you were the one I was in love with. I cried and I cried for you. But I am in love with Mark and we will be married soon.

Please write to me Karl. Scream at me, blame me, criticize me all you want. It's OK, I deserve it. I miss you, believe it or not. Even though things have changed, I miss you a lot. I would love to hear from you, even if it's one line to say that you got this letter. I have no idea what you are up to (and neither do your parents

by the way). And I never got that picture of you riding a camel.
   Fondly, Helen

I felt drained after reading Helen's letter. Howard and Beatrice screamed with laughter when I told them. Swee'Pea was shocked when I told her, though I can't say she looked disappointed.

"You know what this means?" Swee'Pea said when we were alone.

"No, what?" I had no idea.

"It means, Karl, that I will now consider marrying you. If you want to ask me, that is. Before I was not so sure I wanted to marry you."

"Why not?"

"I don't like polygamy. To me it sounded like you were going to have two wives. I didn't think I could go for that."

"So," I said, holding her by the waist, "you want to get married?"

"I might consider it." Swee'Pea smiled, looking straight into my eyes. "I might. If you ask me. But you haven't asked me yet, Karl."

"Right. I haven't asked you." I took a deep breath. "Swee'Pea, I have nothing to offer you. No money. No position. No prospects. We have a roof over our heads for the moment. I don't know how long that will last. But if you marry me, I promise I'll be a good husband."

She looked at me doubtfully. "You'll work hard?"

"I'll work hard."

"And you'll love our family?"

"I will."

"So?"

"Swee'Pea, will you marry me?"

Swee'Pea gave me that deep look again. She threw her arms around my neck. "Of course I'll marry you, Karl. Don't be so silly, Karl. Of course I'll marry you." And she kissed me.

A whirlpool of preoccupations had descended on me—reporting the Burundi killings, worries about Bertrand, money, now the wedding. But I took an afternoon off to unleash some real brain power—my friend Beatrice—on what the hell had happened between me and Helen. I made Beatrice read Helen's two letters after I explained our history together, our phone conversations, her visit to Oxford.

"Like, why did Helen leave Oxford the day after she came to see me?"

Beatrice looked skeptical. "At this point, Karl, who cares? Helen is out of the picture. Isn't that what counts?"

"Listen, Beatrice, Helen's pregnancy completely changed my life. Since last October she's practically all I thought about. But I just can't understand her."

"I see. All right, I'll give it a try." Beatrice scanned the letters again. "Look, it's clear Helen was never completely honest with you, Karl," Beatrice said, waving the letters. "She leaves too much out. If she wanted you to understand, she might have started with something like, I don't know, 'Karl, I realize from my actions and my words you never guessed what was really going on.'"

"That's completely right."

"Here's what I think. Helen didn't mean to get pregnant. Supposedly she was on the pill, and the pill is close to one-hundred-percent effective. But who knows? She may have stopped taking it. Or maybe it was an accident. But the main thing is she couldn't be completely sure who the father was, even though she keeps insisting she was sure it was you."

"But what about Ernestine? Where does she fit in?"

"Something to do with the intensity of the Women's Movement. Over the months she and Ernestine were thrown together, they developed a secret closeness. You were never around to see it."

"I don't see Helen as a lesbian."

"Maybe not, though people are complicated. Ernestine definitely was a wild card, though it does seem they were attracted to each other. But let's be clear. The possibility of being with Ernestine offered Helen an unexpected way out of her predicament. Ernestine was sort of an emergency exit, an insurance policy. In the end Helen decided to take it."

"How do you mean?"

"Karl, if Helen was with Ernestine, another woman, who the father was wouldn't matter."

"Ah!"

"Unfortunately, the Ernestine thing didn't work out. Probably it was never going to work out."

"But why did Helen come to Oxford?"

"Oh, Karl." Beatrice held her face in her hands, gazing at me with patience and affection like I was some naïve youth. "I believe she really did love you. Plus, she was desperate. And she was hoping you would accept her unconditionally, no questions asked. Then she could stay with you and take her chances. And if it turned out months later the baby was not yours, by then you two would be so attached to each other that maybe it wouldn't really matter. At that point you'd probably be married."

"Hmm. Helen got very irritated when I wanted to talk about us."

"Exactly. You never questioned your paternity. But you questioned the relationship. That was a red flag for Helen. You weren't ready to sweep the past under the rug and take her unconditionally. And time was short. She made a snap decision and headed back to gamble with Ernestine."

"Why did she call me when she moved to Michigan?"

Beatrice shrugged. "She didn't want to give you up completely. She made you repeat your offer for her to stay with you, right? Maybe things with Ernestine weren't rosy. Maybe she was weighing going back with you at some point, though she wasn't going to tell you or Ernestine that. But then you took yourself out of the picture by heading to Africa, of all things." Beatrice smiled. "I'm glad you did. I never would have met you if you had stayed in England."

∼

IN OUR SEAT-OF-THE-PANTS JOURNALISM collective, we pooled resources and emotion. Beatrice and Swee'Pea were the political analysts. Howard was the editor. For some reason they insisted that I do all the writing and take all the bylines. We stayed up late in our shack by Lake Tanganyika night after night, arguing every angle. From the hundreds of individual interviews we assembled, I published several detailed articles in the British and American press, but only after a long delay. That was the price of being an unknown writer, who was promoting accounts of a puzzling conflict from an obscure part of the globe, while waiting for mailed replies from newspaper editors that took months to arrive. Telephone calls were prohibitively expensive and out of the question. Plus, the Tanzanian authorities harassed us for not having journalism visas. My only regret was that instead of focusing the world's attention on the Burundi genocide, my lack of contacts, experience, and resources delayed publication of the articles until November. By then two hundred thousand people had lost their lives, and the world had mostly lost interest.

I also concentrated on writing a long essay, which I sent to Harold in Oxford, "Politics and Murder in Central Africa," which we changed to "The Politics of Murder in Central Africa." I couldn't deny that the deaths of thousands of people were improving my prospects. I knew what my father would say.

29. MAYI MULÉLÉ
(JAKE)

I always wondered why the Hutu rebels didn't kill me right off when I climbed down from the tree, or after I had watched them slaughter that poor pregnant woman. Plenty of Europeans, Belgians mostly, were taken hostage and survived their rampage. The rebels just wanted to kill Tutsis as fast as possible, and especially loved killing pregnant Tutsi women and their children. Nits make lice.

I had seen a race war, all right. It just wasn't the race war Pudge lusted for. First of all, it was Black-on-Black. No Whites were involved, and Pudge wouldn't have seen a dime's worth of difference between Tutsi and Hutu. He'd be licking his chops at the idea of Blacks killing other Blacks. It was too good to be true. He'd have settled back to watch the fun, grinning broadly, while cracking open another beer.

The Burundi killings were no war; this was mass murder. I mean, trained killers slaughtered unarmed civilians who had no idea they were being hunted. It's not like two rival armies duking it out. I listened to Howard and Karl's highfalutin' mumbo-jumbo analyzing the Hutu-Tutsi divide as "ethno-racial constructs" or "politicized social identities." Take your pick. But race? It's not some bright biological line. Race hatred may be nonsense, but it infects human minds and tempts politicians, and in Burundi conditions were perfect. The place was boiling with hatred, and people were scared. Funny that I had to go through all that and see it up close and almost get killed to finally understand that race is a man-made notion, a dependable illusion, a mad fear all of us constantly carry around in our brains just waiting for some damned switch to flip. I admit it's powerful. I had seen racial hatred unleash immense emotional and political power. The Hutu death squads exploded with energy. I had seen it. Hatred made them demons, almost superhuman. The German Nazis grew their extreme hatred of Jews; they cultivated and nurtured it. They dispossessed and eliminated the Jews, intensifying and perfecting their hatred. Then they unleashed that fiendish fury and attacked the world. And they almost won. Pudge had been hankering for a redo. You can kill it, but it won't die.

Karl and Swee'Pea explained a ton of things about Burundi that had baffled me. Like the men with the whistles. They were death-squad leaders. Dressed in nothing but feathers and palm leaves, each of them stood last in a double line of several hundred machete-armed, cannabis-drugged killers. They all smoked bangi[30] as a sacrament, while the squad leaders silently propelled them on a half-trot into unsuspecting villages. The whistles controlled the attacks. A long blast brought the column to a halt. A short, sharp blast unleashed a frenzy of killing. Victims were cut to pieces, above all Tutsis, but Hutus who refused to join in the slaughter were fair game. They also killed any killers who were slow to kill.

To prepare the troops for battle, sorcerers recruited from former Congolese Simba rebels among the lakeside refugees cut incisions on the killers' bodies and taught them mystic oaths to turn bullets into water. That's why they kept shouting *"Mayi Mulélé! Mayi Mulélé!,"* which means 'Mulélé water.' They were boasting that bullets were harmless to them, sweet revenge for Pierre Mulélé's torture and dismemberment. But touching an uninitiated person nullified their fantastic invulnerability to bullets, or so the sorcerers claimed. No surprise that my Rumonge captors, before taking anything from me or giving anything to me, like my money or the keys to the truck, made me lay them down on the ground first.

---

30   ganja, marijuana

There was plenty of scope in Burundi for a well-placed Tutsi seething with hatreds to make a name for himself. Take Albert Shibura who became Burundi's mastermind Hutu exterminator, a man who could have given Pudge plenty of tips on how to run a race war. Karl told me all about this engineer of the Hutu Holocaust. A highly placed Burundi government minister with deep connections to the police and the army, Shibura somehow survived the April 29 bloodbath at the municipal meeting he himself had convened in Rumonge, that fatal Saturday night of the insurrection, while I huddled in my tent down the road. Shooting his way to his car, somehow evading roadblocks and Hutu death squads, Shibura drove like a banshee to Gitega, the old royal capital, with one thought—to execute Charles Ntare before he could escape to rally the Hutu masses, as legend predicted, and launch his phantom armies. Some say he personally shot the young Mwami dead in his cell. Of course, Pudge himself would have seen this Black killer as just another—that hateful word—and wondered what the fuss was about; just one Black killing another. What Pudge didn't get was that racists don't need white skins.

A good thing that Pudge was too lazy, too narrow-minded, too prejudiced, too plumb unschooled to be able to admire a man like Burundi's "exterminator-in-chief" and his henchmen, those genuine "ethnic entrepreneurs," as Howard called them, that special breed of genocidal Tutsi or Hutu fanatics. Adolf Eichmann understudies, if they even knew it. Trouble is, once the killing starts, no one can predict where it will stop. Or who exactly will die.

Clearly, President Micombero had taken his eye off the ball. First, he was distracted by imaginary royalist plots, then unnerved by the Mwami's surprise return. The actual Hutu conspirators organized their insurrection right under Micombero's nose.

The timing was perfect; no one saw the revolt coming. But those miscreants didn't think it through. Sure, they terrorized Tutsis, stampeded them, created a panic, but they only killed a couple of thousand at most. Mass Hutu uprisings and killings of Tutsis in the countryside as they had hoped for just didn't happen. Rural Burundi had no idea what was happening by the lake. But the rebels and their bloody three-day rampage brought on an anti-Hutu extermination campaign by the Burundi army, which was far worse. Hundreds of thousands of Hutus died, we later found out.

Howard's hunch why the rebels didn't kill me and the other muzungus was that the fledgling Burundi Hutu Republic wanted to avoid complications with the global powers.

That day I was released in Kigoma, lucky to be alive and feeling beat more than brave and with no idea where I was going, I marched south along the beach and blundered into Karl, Beatrice, Howard, and Swee'Pea. Things started looking up right away. They were like my second family, especially Karl and Swee'Pea. They were overjoyed to see me. I was crying and laughing, though laughter hurt my bruised ribs. They made me tell them again and again my stories about the uprising and my time in jail. I explained it all to Karl in detail for his newspaper articles. It was a squeeze fitting five of us around a derelict table in that woebegone shack by the beach, but I loved it. I didn't want to leave. I built a lean-to outside with our old tarp, found a scrap of mosquito net, and just lay around for days, eating and sleeping. I even gained a few pounds.

In particular, I had long chats with Beatrice. She was curious about my experiences on the oil rig. She was the first person I told how I had killed Pudge, though I begged her not to repeat it. She pumped me about racism in America. She liked my stories about the poker games on the oil derrick. She would have done the same that day on the rig, she said, seeing how it was him or me. She insisted I shouldn't feel guilty for killing Pudge, as I hadn't intended to kill him, but she agreed the law wouldn't necessarily see it that way. Cutting and running didn't make me look innocent. We talked about forgiveness. If you want someone to forgive you, you must confess and apologize. But forgiveness is something only victims can grant. And when had White supremacists or Nazis ever asked for forgiveness? Especially dead ones.

Pudge's hatreds had done him in; I finally saw that. Personally, I was fed up. I couldn't stand thinking about Pudge anymore, not after Burundi, watching those machete-swinging murderers and wondering when they'd kill me. Not after Tanzania, when they might have taken me out and shot me at any moment. I wanted to get out of Africa. No surprise there. But I was not going back to the States. I was sad I could not get news about my sisters or my uncle or tell them where I was, or what had become of me since I left Louisiana, or even send them money. After what I had seen and survived, just maybe I was a bit less afraid about the police catching me than I once was. But I couldn't figure out my next move.

By mid-June, after I spent weeks recovering from my five-day holiday in Burundi and fifteen days, all expenses paid, with the Tanzanian army, it was screamingly obvious that our combined finances would not hold. I was dead broke, and my four friends soon would be. When I had recovered enough to travel, Karl and Howard staked me two hundred dollars to reclaim my stolen travelers checks in Nairobi. They said they might scrape by until September or October, but then what? They waved off my promises to pay them back, but I made up my mind to do it. Those lost travelers checks came close to five thousand dollars.

AFTER A FEW DAYS in a bus, I arrived in Nairobi one evening during a blinding rainstorm. I had to run under an awning until the rain stopped. It was my third time in the city. The hustlers and the scams were old hat. I retreated to a small hotel. I avoided people. When I wasn't taking care of business, I stayed in my room reading and writing in my journal. I went down to Mombasa for a few days to look around the docks. Luckily, Karl wrote me in Nairobi at *poste restante* after they moved to Arusha, or I never would have found them again.

30. HAROLD HIGGINS
(KARL)

Jake was transformed after a fortnight with us in Tanzania, though he refused to visit the refugee camps. He seemed calmer. He had lost the black cloud following him. For the first time since I knew him, he seemed totally happy. He'd lost his jumpiness and volatility. You'd think being held prisoner several times in less than a month might make him tense. But he was the opposite—steady, meditative, serious. He was more self-confident, sure he could succeed at whatever he chose to do. He became vocal, even militant on politics. He was scathing on the Hutu rebels and the Tanzania army, not to mention Idi Amin. He and Beatrice became fast friends. He was curious about Berlin; she wanted to hear about Louisiana. Then he left for Nairobi. We weren't sure when we'd see him again.

June stretched into July, the dry season in Tanzania. Howard and Beatrice wavered about returning to Europe. Unlike me, they had plane tickets; like me, they were almost broke.

In mid-August, the four of us took a long bus ride to Arusha, near Kilimanjaro. It's wealthier than Kigoma with better weather. We found a cheap house for the four of us, a tiny place with two small rooms and an outside kitchen and privy. For me and Swee'Pea it was paradise. A few days after we got there, while we still were working on piles of notes from Kigoma, a local Danish development team hired me to compile reports and code the results. They had a massive backlog, so there was plenty of work. They soon hired Howard, as well. We even brought work home for Swee'Pea and Beatrice, which they did together at night. It didn't pay much, but our earnings covered rent and food and gave us a small surplus.

"You should write to Harold," Howard said when we arrived in Arusha.

"I wrote him from Ujiji. I've been writing him all along."

"Really?"

"Amazing how the prospect of starvation concentrates the mind. Oxford is looking better and better. And Swee'Pea is keen to go back to medical school."

"So, you're headed back to Oxford?"

"Not so fast. I'm not a student anymore. Even if I'm accepted back, I've no idea how we'll buy plane tickets or keep body and soul together in Oxford. The remnant of my bank account may cover one semester of tuition."

"Beatrice wants to try Oxford. I suppose I may have to give up the Sorbonne."

"*Dommage.* Maybe the four of us could room together?"

"My boy, that will soon be a noisy five," Howard pointed out. "But we could be neighbors."

Harold's reply to my letter from Ujiji was the last thing Beatrice picked up from the post office the day we left Kigoma. In the rush to leave she had packed it with other papers, and it remained unopened for days until she finally found it again and handed it to me. I howled reading it. Harold had liked what I had sent him, immensely.

> *July 20, 1972*
> *My dear Karl,*
> *To say I was surprised to receive your long essay would be the year's biggest understatement. I was floored by the wealth of firsthand observations you recorded of the genocidal events in Burundi of late April and May 1972, which are still ongoing. With some minor*

editing I had your essay typeset and circulated to the Balliol faculty. It was published (forgive me, without your permission) and serialized in the University newspaper. (I enclose their cheque for £200.) Since then I have not stopped receiving insistent demands from the press for more articles and vociferous queries about the identity and whereabouts of "the missing Oxford student," while the clamour of praise for the student's brilliance is deafening.

I am glad you described your conditions in Tanzania. I am trying to arrange for you and your family to return to Oxford for the fall semester. Your undeniable fame here has opened up a number of excellent scholarship opportunities. I mean to say that I doubt you will have to pay, or at any rate, pay much, for tuition or for room and board, probably for several years. Nor will there be any trouble getting you accepted into a PhD program in history or politics. The only questions I have are whether you want to do it, and whether you are able to return to England at this moment.

Please respond quickly because I have many irons in the fire. I must know soon which iron to strike with.

Yours sincerely,
Harold

That night, with everyone huddled around the table drinking beer, reading and rereading Harold's letter, in midst of our celebration there was a knock at the door.

Jake stood there smiling. "I realized I never really said goodbye."

Beatrice hugged him. "Come in, come in, leave the bugs outside."

In comes Jake, completely unexpected, and joined us at the table, still smiling. Jake held up a bottle of beer to ask for silence. Then he looked at me. "In Nairobi I got all my travelers checks back, so I came back to repay you and Howard. But, you know, to quote Hans, now I have too much money and not enough to spend it on, so I'm giving you and Swee'Pea some cash." He waved a large yellow envelope. "I think you can use it."

"But Jake—" I spluttered.

He held up his palm like a traffic cop.

"No, hear me out," I said. "I already owe you so much. Your firsthand accounts of what you saw in Burundi were the main reason my articles succeeded. I was already paid for some of them. My reporting would not have been possible without you."

Jake shook his head impatiently. "You've got a baby on the way, a new wife. You're far from home. You're basically broke." He pushed the envelope toward me. "Think of this as a student loan."

Jake was right. We needed money. The envelope contained twenty-three hundred dollars, plus a few thousand Tanzanian shillings. We shared a big chunk of it with Howard and Beatrice. Jake was moving on. He was done with Africa. He wanted to work again, see the world, live his life.

On the night before he left, Jake gave a speech. Or maybe it was a sermon. He was fiery.

"I've seen hatred in Louisiana. I've seen it in Uganda, in Burundi. We humans are cursed with it." He put his elbows on the table, his head in his hands. He sighed deeply. "It's common. Hatred is common. Common as drugs, delusions, disease. It's a shortcut to power and greatness.

"Our pastor liked to tell us what Micah, the prophet, said. 'Shame on those who lie in bed planning evil and wicked deeds, then rise at daybreak to do them, knowing they have the power.'" He lay his arms flat on the table, palms up. "What power is greater than killing people without limit or fear of sanction?" Jake's eyes gleamed by the light of our kerosene lamp. "Murder becomes normal, fashionable. Don't say 'It can't happen here.' It's already happened, wherever you are. It can happen again. Like Beatrice explained, the politicians start it, they profit from it. They tell us, 'Those people must be eliminated. They are not even people. We must kill them now.' Jake lowered his voice. "Murder begets murder. Once the killing starts, it's hard to stop."

Jake left the next day, but not before he confessed what had been on his mind for the past year. He confessed to what happened on the oil rig off the coast of Louisiana, how Pudge had died, and that onboard the *Scylla* he had learned that the American authorities and a man named Hink were looking for him. He felt guilty for killing Pudge. He was still on the run.

"Jake, it was an accident. The guy was trying to kill you," Howard said.

"This wasn't your fault, Jake," Swee'Pea said. "You should not feel guilty."

"You've got to stop carrying it around everywhere with you," Beatrice said. "This Pudge was a maniac who would've been happy to see you dead."

"It's not that easy. It's not that easy for me," Jake said.

"I know you feel like you can't go home with this thing hanging over your head," I said. "But it can't be resolved until you do."

And then he was gone. We got postcards later from Singapore, Jakarta, and Yokohama.

SWEE'PEA AND I DECIDED it made no sense to head back to Oxford with her about to give birth, then have to find housing, adapt to Europe and a new climate, face British racial attitudes and uncertain finances, while I enrolled in a demanding graduate program. Better to have the baby in Africa, then head for England next May or June. We decided to have the wedding in Arusha. In the meantime, the Danes told me they could employ us for another season. I wrote to Harold thanking him effusively for his great news and begging him to allow me to return the following academic year. To my relief, he wrote back to say that was entirely reasonable. He assured me that would work out even better because he would have more time to make arrangements.

Uncle Martin did not get to Arusha in time for the wedding. Swee'Pea's father, on the other hand, did. He arrived the day before the ceremony in mid-October. A warm, gregarious man, he was full of praise and encouragement for us but full of vitriol for Idi Amin. He gave us ten thousand shillings as a wedding present. Six or seven months pregnant, Swee'Pea was radiant around her dad. She was even more radiant at the wedding. We invited all the Danes. They even gave us a week off. Howard was best man; Beatrice was bridesmaid. We were married on a warm day within sight of Mount Meru and Mount Kilimanjaro. Beatrice and Howard volunteered to do the cooking.

We spent our honeymoon on the other side of the wall from them making love constantly. When we rested Swee'Pea would lay on her side with her back to me and my hand cupped over her breast. This energetic spooning had a name. We called it "Choo-Choo." Swee'Pea's big belly and full breasts were a constant turn-on. We could not get enough of each other.

We learned from Swee'Pea's dad that her evil Uncle Nelson was dead. It so happened that Nelson was escorting an unlucky prisoner to the killing cells of Kampala's notorious Makindye Prison when the detainee grabbed a semi-automatic rifle from an unwary guard. He emptied the magazine on Uncle Nelson and ten other guards before he was shot down.

Swee'Pea and I were making a new beginning, so far removed from what I thought was possible or even likely one year ago. I was amazed. After the honeymoon I made a list of what I learned in my travels.

First, my father was right to be careful about trust. Trust is like investing. You can invest wisely or foolishly. Sometimes it pans out, sometimes not. But watch out for wishful thinking and hubris, which twist human emotions, including your own. Be true to others. Above all, be true to yourself. And trust yourself, or you'll never improve or succeed. The best investments are love and friendship, for their dividends are endless. As for love, there is no guarantee. It can be false or fleeting. But if it is true hold onto it. Never let it go.

Hard work, humility, discipline, patience—the Pietist

virtues—are powerful. But finish what you start. Do what you say you'll do. Cherish love and hope, mercy, and justice. And don't forget exuberance, optimism, or laughter. The point of life is to enjoy life.

31. TWO IF BY SEA
(JAKE)

I needed a plan. I didn't have one.

I was amazed by Karl's change in fortune. In the blink of an eye he had a family and a career. He was a soon-to-be husband, father, journalist, academic. I hoped he and Swee'Pea wouldn't suffer in Britain or America because of the racial thing. I could see they loved each other. Race didn't matter to them, or to Howard and Beatrice. Or me. But I knew it still mattered to a lot of people.

Nairobi is much closer to Arusha than Kigoma. I managed to get back to Arusha and find the gang in one day. My friends were shocked by the money I gave them. I figured before long I'd find another job, while I could see that those four intellectuals would be lucky just to scrape by. Besides my sisters, I really had no one else in the world anymore but them. They had saved my life at Ujiji.

I wanted to stay on with them in Arusha, but I knew I had to go. I was a bachelor, and I didn't fit in. I had to find my own path, like in Uganda when I left Karl and Swee'Pea on the Kasese road in a downpour. I loved them all and I hated to say goodbye. But it was hardest to say goodbye to Karl, who was like a brother.

I got on the bus and spent weeks in Mombasa looking for work on a ship, but no luck. I kept at it, hoping for a break. I was down in the dumps, feeling friendless like I hadn't felt since my days in Chicago and New York.

One sweaty day in a Pakistani restaurant, baffled by which curry to choose, the hot or the very hot, a young woman walked up to my table. Her brown hair was pulled back in a ponytail. She had a slim, feminine face. She was tall. She probably had half a head on me. Saying her name was Bridget, she asked if she could sit with me. I said sure. She told me she liked this restaurant but had not been back for some time. She wanted to try it again. I pulled out a chair for her.

Bridget smiled. She begged my pardon for being so forward and assured me she was not in the habit of introducing herself to strange men, but I looked "interesting," and maybe a little out of place. That's why she spoke to me. I was glad to have her company. This time I didn't head for the exits like I used to when a woman got too close for comfort. I guess I was open to something new.

Bridget was perky and older than me by a few years. We talked about this or that, about the hot Mombasa weather, about the Pakistani food, also hot, about Kenya being a little boring. I could tell she was Swedish from her accent. But when I mentioned the only other Swede I knew, Sven Torvalson, she gasped.

"Oh, you know Sven? How is that?"

I told her of our meeting in Mombasa last winter, how he hired me, the voyage of the *Scylla*, the letter Sven had given me that was now lost to the Burundi rebels.

"But I know Sven, too. We work for the same company."

"You work on a ship?"

"Yes, I do. I'm a purser. The name of the ship is *Flamboyant* out of Göteborg. It's docked in the harbor at the moment."

My thoughts were whirling. "You don-don't suppose," I stuttered. "Uh, do you think the captain might need an assistant engineer?"

Bridget looked at me with new interest. "Let's go see the captain."

That's how it began with Bridget and the *Flamboyant*, which was set to cruise to Iran, India, Singapore, Hong Kong, and Southeast Asia. Luck was going my way. As it happened, the captain was happy to hire me. The ship was sleek, well run, and the pay was better than on the *Scylla*, once I became a regular employee.

Under the circumstances, Bridget and I quickly had to decide a few things. Was this something real? Maybe we'd go to Sweden. Honestly, I didn't like the idea of getting back on a ship after that close call on the *Scylla*. But Bridget made me feel comfortable in my skin, in a way I had never felt since my parents died. I just stopped worrying. We were soon on our honeymoon voyage, me and my Viking bride, contemplating a shipboard wedding.

I told Bridget about my family, about my hometown in flat Nebraska, about Karl and Swee'Pea. I told her about Louisiana, and I told her about Pudge and how he died. I told her about Karl and Helen, about Howard and Beatrice, about Ethiopia, about Turiye and Lorraine, about my sisters and my parents, about Lamu, what happened in Uganda in Fort Portal and on Ruwenzori, about how I saw people in Burundi die, about how the Tanzanian army captured me and wanted to shoot me. I told her how I really felt about everything. And how I felt about her. I told her everything. We stood by the railing, looking out to sea. Softness was slowly oozing into my life. I started saving up to hire a good lawyer.

32. JOURNEY'S END
(BEATRICE)

I still don't know how she did it, but Bridget Holmstrom managed to find Howard and me in an Oxford pub one dismal December afternoon at the end of 1973. I had an awful premonition when I saw this tall, brown-haired woman with a grave expression striding toward us, then hearing her Swedish accent and her name. I knew Jake was dead.

"Oof." She sat down heavily, almost fell off the chair, looking like she hadn't slept in weeks. Howard squeezed Bridget's hand and assured her she was among friends. We'd been out of Africa six months at that point, since June 1973. We both were studying law at Oxford and had just finished exams. We got her tea and a bite to eat, and for a long moment she was silent, breathless, staring at the food. She closed her eyes as though recalling in detail every last thing she didn't want to remember. She was determined, disciplined, tough like steel. But it was no good, and she cried and she cried before she took a deep breath and told her story.

"It happened in Chile last spring," she began, staring straight ahead. "We were in Valparaiso. We'd been all over the Pacific by then."

It was dawning on me that we'd heard nothing from Jake for almost a year. We hadn't seen him since August 1972, before Swee'Pea and Karl's wedding.

"Jake sent us postcards," Howard said.

"Postcards. That's right," Bridget continued in a kind of trance.

"He showed me the postcards. Jake and I married last winter. There was a lot on his mind." She looked at us. "He kept talking about 'Justice, justice. And mercy,' he'd say. 'And we should walk humbly with God.' He sometimes sounded like a preacher."

"That's Jake," I said, looking at Howard.

Bridget nodded. "He wanted to get off the ship. He wanted us to get off in the worst way and go back to Sweden. To do what I don't know. He'd been a farmer, he said. Farm in Sweden? My career was on ships. We kept talking about it. He spoke of his trouble in Louisiana, how he'd killed a man, though the way he told it, it was hardly his fault. And there was a scare on board the *Scylla*."

Her voice had fallen to a whisper. I recalled in Ujiji Jake had let slip something about his panic on board the *Scylla*, but then he clammed up and wouldn't say more. We leaned closer and tried to ignore the din in the room.

"The ship stopped in Valparaiso to take on cargo." She went on. "A few sailors boarded, and when Jake saw one of them, a gaunt man with scraggly hair, he told me right then he had to flee, to get off the ship. I didn't understand this properly. Why did we need to leave? And where could we go? We both had jobs on the *Flamboyant* and we knew no one in Chile."

She sighed deeply, pushed her plate to the side, covered her mouth lightly with her fingers, her eyes resting somewhere on the ceiling. "We were needed on the *Flamboyant*. I had to make excuses, but we got off the ship, down the gangplank and into the bars near the port where we spent a day and a half whispering about what to do. The *Flamboyant* was leaving the next evening. Maybe we'd find a different ship, Jake said, or maybe we could fly to Sweden. Jake was afraid. He said he was trying to protect me from those men. But I still didn't understand. If those men were dangerous, couldn't we just tell the captain?"

Bridget paused, folding her arms across her chest.

"It was on the afternoon before the *Flamboyant* sailed and it finally sailed without us. We came out of a bar and onto the sidewalk at a roundabout. Traffic was passing swiftly. Three men standing on the other side of the street saw Jake and me, the gaunt gringo and two others. They were pointing at us.

"He's got a gun," Jake said.

The man with the gun, the gringo, started shooting.

"Shooting? At you? From across the street?" Howard gasped.

"Yes, he was shooting at us through breaks in the traffic. People on the sidewalk fled. It was just us and them. Jake told me to get down, and as soon as I did a bullet hit me in the side. Jake could see I was bleeding. We looked up and saw that one of the men had started to cross the street toward us. He had something in his hand. Jake told me to stay put. He gave a shout and ran into the street. Jake pulled out a knife. He wrestled with the man in the street and stabbed him in the arm. The cars swirled around them, horns blowing. It was crazy. Crazy! The man held his bloody arm and stumbled back the way he came. I also crossed the street to follow Jake, but it was hard. I was bleeding, and in pain, and there were so many cars. And then the man Jake had stabbed grabbed me and held me from behind. I screamed and shouted and bit his hand, and as he let me go, I watched Jake stab the gringo in the arm and the chest. But the third man punched him hard, and they overpowered him."

"Didn't they have a gun?" I asked.

"Out of bullets, I guess."

Bridget cupped her face with her hands and kept speaking with her eyes closed. "There was a police van stuck at the turn. I waved at it frantically. The officers got out fast with their automatics. They could see what was happening, but there was no time. The men had dragged Jake into an alley, and they were beating him with an iron bar and kicking him after he fell, kicking his body with their bloody boots. The police fired warning shots. They flung the three of them against a wall and marched them away in manacles."

"Oh my God. Oh my God." I couldn't hold back the tears.

"Bridget," Howard said, "was Jake dead? Was he dead, Bridget?"

"Yes." Bridget sat up. "Jake was dead. There was blood everywhere, bloody footprints, the bloody iron bar. His head and face just a bloody pulp."

"Oh, not that handsome face," I said.

"Yes," Bridget said. "The police covered Jake with a sheet. They found a black pistol on the ground and took it away for evidence, along with the iron bar. Then an ambulance came, and I rode to the hospital with Jake's body."

"And you were shot!"

"I was full of blood." Bridget ran her fingers through her hair. "The wound in my side hurt a lot but it turned out to be minor. Elvin Baxter, that was the gringo's name."

"Elvin Baxter," I repeated.

"Bridget," Howard said, "do you know who this Baxter was or why he wanted to kill Jake?"

"I never heard his name before," Bridget said. "The police later told me Baxter was wanted in the States for extortion and aggravated assault, and that he would be extradited after trial. The two others, Peruvians, were tried quickly and deported."

Bridget, Howard, and I guessed this Baxter was linked somehow to that awful Pudge.

"What happened with Baxter?" I asked.

"So, Baxter nearly died." Bridget shifted in her seat, took a sip of water. "Jake had almost killed him. Baxter spent weeks recovering in a hospital under armed guard. I was in daily talks with lawyers and prosecutors while waiting to testify at Baxter's trial. Jake's body was at the morgue the whole time. I had nightmares night after night. I was so sad."

"We had no idea," Howard said, shaking his head.

Bridget nodded again. "In early August Baxter was transferred from the hospital to prison. A few days later he escaped. On the morning of the trial."

"No!" I said.

"The Chilean guards went after him. And he died running. Hit by a truck." She sighed. "A messy end to a messy life, I suppose."

"But it was neat," I said.

"It was neat," Bridget agreed. "A woman had come out from the American embassy in Santiago for the trial. We became friends. She was very useful to me in deciding what to do next. I was done with my life on ships. I could not bear to think of working on a ship ever again. And I kept asking myself how this could happen. And how could they have known that Jake was in Valparaiso on the *Flamboyant*? It tormented me. It didn't seem right to return by myself to Scandinavia and abandon Jake in Chile. I'd heard so much about his sisters. So I decided to bring Jake back to them. We left Chile the first week in September."

"You brought his body to the American Midwest?" Howard asked.

"That's a long way," I said.

"Uh-huh. I had their address and Jake's uncle Paul. It was hard to arrange. The embassy helped me figure it out. But I paid for everything."

"You got out just before the coup in Chile," I said.[31]

"Luckily," Bridget sighed. "Missed it by a week. To Minnesota I went. They're teenagers now, Emily and Margaret. They and Paul, they all were so kind to me. It was good for me to be with Jake's family. We grieved together. I finally had people I could talk to. Jake had written them when we were married."

"The four of you buried Jake?" I asked.

"We were the only mourners. They didn't want me to leave. I stayed and stayed. Now I'm on my way home. But," she looked at me, "I wanted to stop in England to find Jake's friends." Bridget smiled slightly. "Jake never stopped talking about you."

"And you're going back to Sweden?" I asked.

---

31 On September 11, 1973 the Chilean military under General Augusto Pinochet overthrew the government of President Salvador Allende.

"Yes, yes, of course. At last. My family has no idea what became of me. And neither do I. Honestly, I have no plans." Elbows on the table, she banged her forehead on her fists. "Jake was the bravest man I've ever known. He was so kind to me. He wanted to be kind and merciful. But not to his enemies. He was clear about this. Not when they wanted to kill him and his family. Never."

SINCE THE MOMENT HE appeared on Lamu, I was drawn to Jake. He was resilient, optimistic, Jake was, despite what he'd been through, and he was a reliable friend, when he wasn't feeling hunted. His many talents surprised us all. No matter what, he always landed on his feet. Maybe that was why he didn't mind taking risks. Though I could not see why he would ever consider setting foot on any ship after what happened on board the *Scylla* with Hink, that name I finally remembered. Well, his sweetheart was a mariner and that explains a lot. And he wanted to leave Africa in a hurry. And they had been talking about going back to Sweden. But I guessed his panic on board the *Scylla* must have been about Hink, this Baxter, who was clearly after him.

Jake was a crusader against the darkness, against the racist fringe. He was fearless, someone you were glad was on your side, like John Brown. I had my orderly lawyer's mind, I told myself, and my cool deliberation. I was quietly preparing myself to take down those Nazi bastards in my own country using the pitiless vise of the law. But Jake was hot, impulsive. He'd glimpsed the truth, and it gripped him a little too strongly. And he'd been alone. And he brooded. He was on a mission, even if he did not grasp it. He was like a hermit in a cave—until he met Bridget.

We told Swee'Pea and Karl the bad news over the phone and they hurried to meet us and Bridget. They brought their baby girl with them, asleep and swaddled in the stroller against the cold. Swee'Pea had given birth in Tanzania around the first of the year 1973, almost twelve months earlier. We'd all arrived in Oxford late last spring thanks to Jake's blessed money. Karl and Harold Higgins helped Howard and me enroll in time for the fall term; Swee'Pea was starting medical school in January in only a few weeks. Howard and I both thought the baby looked a lot like Karl.

Swee'Pea was all tears in her huge winter overcoat, praising Jake for his bravery, for being a hero. She hugged Bridget. Karl was silent at first, but he was plainly shocked.

"I figured I might never see Jake again," Karl finally blurted. "It's terrible that he died in this way. That day he found us on the beach at Ujiji, I thought he was indestructible. Like he'd risen from the dead. He was my brother, the brother I never had."

"He said the same about you," Bridget nodded.

Howard and I brought Bridget home with us. We had this ridiculous freezing flat, just three chairs, a table, a hotplate, and a bed. But we admired her so, and we could not do enough for her. She slept with me, the two of us in the bed and Howard on the floor. Howard told her that Jake had taught us all about character and courage, friendship, and generosity. The four of us—no, the five—were with Bridget practically all day, every day, at every meal for over a week. We had no money, next to none, but we would not let her pay a penny for anything.

The day came when Bridget had to leave. She gave us her phone number and address in Sweden, and we gave her ours. Swore we'd keep in touch. We took Bridget to the station. We hugged her one. She hugged us all. She got on the London train. She all waved.

Acknowledgments

It is hardly possible to praise everyone who contributed in some way to the writing, editing, production, and marketing of this novel, which was years in the making, yet many individuals leap to mind. First of all, my mother, to whom this book is dedicated, nagged me constantly to write "something about Africa." Some people need to be nagged. David Horowitz, my old traveling buddy, supplied insights which found their way into the manuscript. At various points I pestered every friend and relation I could corner for feedback on the manuscript. Special thanks go to Raymond VanOver, Gershom Sacks, Hugh Gerechter, Ellen Sisco, Eric Solsten, Andrea Wasserman, Julie Gray, Jake Harper, Stephen Peng, Johanna Brusa, John Hollosy, and Jonny Meister. I also would like to thank Amaryah Orenstein for suggesting how to organize and refine the early drafts. I extend my profound appreciation to Steven Douglas, who designed the clear, detailed, historically accurate maps, and also to Rochelle Sacks, who produced brilliant photos for my author's website richardsacks.com. Mimi Brian and Alina Zyszkowski contributed selflessly, skillfully, and enthusiastically by helping me brainstorm marketing strategy and draft marketing materials. My sincere respect and admiration goes to the outstanding scholars, René Lemarchand, Jean-Pierre Chrétien, Jean François Dupaquier, and David Martin, whose superb research and analysis are reflected in the text, though any factual or other errors are completely mine. Finally, and most of all, I wish to thank my brilliant and perceptive wife, Aida Sobol Sacks, who without murmur or complaint plowed through each new draft and commented honestly on what was working and what was not.

www.ingramcontent.com/pod-product-compliance
Lightning Source LLC
LaVergne TN
LVHW041747060526
838201LV00046B/933